Marilyn L Rice

BORN IN 1951 at Chilwell, Nottingham, Marilyn L Rice was educated at Lady Manners Grammar School in Bakewell. She studied at Crewe College of Education and at the University of Keele, where she was awarded a B.Ed Degree in 1973. She began her teaching career at Atherstone Grammar School, then became Head of R.E. at Comprehensive Schools in Sandwell.

Since she began writing in the 1980s she has studied Leisure and Tourism at the University of Birmingham and has worked in the travel industry.

4ᵗʰ July 2002.

To Sid.

Time is a precious gift.
Make the most of every moment.

Best wishes.

Marilyn Rice

This book is dedicated to my father,
CHARLES WILLIAM RICE
1921-1993

He was a loving, caring man who gave me encouragement, support and guidance
in all of my endeavours. I have so much to thank him for.

Published by Marilyn L Rice
West Bromwich, West Midlands. B70 7PA

All incidents and characters in this novel are fictitious. Any similarity between Irene
Stephenson and any other characters, to any person living or dead is pure coincidence.
However, the historical events as recorded in Charlotte's diary are factual.
The author is indebted to various publishers for allowing her to use their publications for
reference purposes. A complete list can be found in the acknowledgement section after
the 'Epilogue'.

ISBN 0-9539451-0-3

Printed and bound in Great Britain by The Basingstoke Press 75 Ltd.

A copy of this book is held at the British Library.

Time & Tide
Marilyn L Rice

Marilyn L Rice

The Prologue
Whistbury, 1st January, 2000

CHAMPAGNE CORKS were popping. 'Happy Birthday! Happy Birthday! Fifty today. Congratulations. Many happy returns.' Irene felt all of her fifty years but managed to smile her thanks. She looked around at the people cheering in the room; they had been celebrating since yesterday, because this was no ordinary birthday. It was 1st January, 2000: yesterday had been the last day of the old century. Out with the old, in with the new!

The twentieth century had been associated with inventions, speed and change. Looking round the room there was only one obvious sign that the last century had ever existed and that was the television in the corner. The rest of the room seemed to be in a time warp with the Victorian era, the decor was green: green wallpaper, green carpet, green curtains, green three-piece suite, green ornaments, green vases. They all blended in, with the aspidistra taking pride of place on the table in the front window, just as it would have done in the Victorian parlour. Grandma just loved green!

Irene continued gazing round the room. The picture rail that Grandma had refused to have taken down separated the wallpaper from the ceiling by about eighteen inches. It was heavily adorned with family pictures: over the fireplace were grandma and grandpa; on the other walls were pictures of grandma's brothers and sisters and above the piano, opposite the fireplace, Irene could see photographs of herself and her parents. Even the green carpet was not a fitted one but older and threadbare with nicely polished floorboards round the edge of the room. Heating came from a coal fire; Grandma did not find carrying buckets of coal easy at the age of ninety-one but she would not have a modern gas or electric fire, that would have been cheating! She said that the reason she had lived so long was because she had worked hard and if she went on doing this she felt she could live to be a hundred!

Irene looked over at her grandmother seated in the corner between the television and the table. She looked well and was obviously delighted to see a new century, even if her preference was for the Victorian days.

7

She was wearing black, as she had done for every party since 1960 when Grandpa died. She was still in mourning and made sure everyone knew it: almost forty years of widowhood and thirty-four of marriage prior to that. Irene marvelled: many marriages do not last even four years today. How times have changed!

Grandma could remember parties held there on New Year's Eve ever since 1939. Despite the Blitz, blackout, rationing and uncertainty that the war had brought, Grandpa had given a party. He had been too old to join up and so had vowed to give both troops and civilians as much fun and entertainment as was possible. The New Year's Eve party had become a tradition. This one had brought in not just a new year but a new century. Grandpa would have been delighted.

Seated at the piano was Charlotte, Irene's mother. She had been playing through the evening as she usually did. She and her mother were the only two people in the room who could remember that first party. Charlotte had been just twelve years old then, but she could remember it clearly. The piece she was allowed to play was always her first and last piece at any party: 'Danny Boy'.

Someone gave Irene a glass of champagne. She raised it as people sang 'Happy Birthday' to her mother's accompaniment. Her father, Wills, was standing by the piano at her mother's side. She looked up at him. If there was one man she had relied on all her life, it was her father. He was her idol. He had never let her down. He had helped her through good times and bad, always supporting her. He was always there for a shoulder to cry on, someone to come home to when everything else had failed. He looked at her now, his little girl, fifty years old.

As 'Happy Birthday' came to an end someone started singing 'Twenty-one today,' to which Irene replied, 'I wish, I wish!' and laughed as she remembered her twenty-first birthday and many of the others in her life. Then her gaze went to the leaded lights in the windows which her grandfather had had put in. Outside she could see the first white, feathery flakes drifting down.

'It's snowing,' she shouted, 'just like it did fifty years ago. What a start to the new millennium!'

Everyone's gaze turned to the window and the atmosphere in the room was euphoric. They were like children seeing snow for the first time.

As the excitement of the toast died down, Irene managed to leave the room without being noticed. She glanced into the dining room where the remains of a buffet lay and then went upstairs and into the back bedroom. She looked around: very little up here seemed to have changed in fifty years either. There was a double bed, a different one but still in the same place. The carpet had beautifully polished floorboards round it. The wardrobe and dressing table were the same furniture her mother had had since childhood.

They made it to last in those days!

Irene walked over to her favourite place, the rocking chair by the window; she sat in it and started to sway gently to and fro. So this was where it all began...

Chapter 1
Whistbury, 1st January, 1950

'IT'S A GIRL. Congratulations! You've got a beautiful daughter,' said the midwife.

Charlotte was relieved; after the agony of the birth she did not really care what she had produced. She was just glad the ordeal was over. The midwife tied and cut the cord and placed the baby in Charlotte's arms. Looking on and smiling was Charlotte's mother, Elizabeth. She was a proud grandmother, probably even prouder than her daughter.

Downstairs there was a party. It was just after midnight, 1st January, 1950. It had been a special New Year's Eve after the war-torn years of the forties. The second half of the century had begun, a new decade and one of hope for the future. There was rebuilding, not only of destroyed homes but of lives as well. A National Health Service and Education system had been introduced by the new Labour Government. Winston Churchill, whose skilful leadership had led Britain to victory in 1945, had lost power in the first election after the war; his leadership had been ignored, a swing to Labour made Clement Attlee the new prime minister. Everything was going to be great. King George VI and Queen Elizabeth had been a tower of strength to the country, refusing to leave for a safer haven. Even the young princesses had stayed at Windsor. Some courtiers had suggested that they should go to Canada until after the war but the Queen had been adamant: she would stay with the King, he would never leave Britain and the princesses would stay with them. Now in peacetime the King would lead the country forward again.

Charlotte had been feeling uncomfortable all day but the labour had not started until the late afternoon. This meant that she had spent the evening upstairs with only the midwife for company. Her husband, friends, neighbours and relations had been sent downstairs to enjoy the party and were banned from seeing her until the birth was over. She did think it was inconsiderate of her baby to choose that night of all nights to come into the world. Missing the party was a big disappointment to her.

John, Charlotte's father, was playing the piano. The guests were singing, they were relaxed and happy. All evening they had been eating, drinking, smoking and generally celebrating. The men were saving their cigars for the great news – would it be a girl or a boy? Above all there was a new air of optimism in the house.

William Stephenson had been asked many times if he wanted a boy or a girl. He had said that he did not mind, but secretly he wanted a boy. Wills, as the family knew him, had been orphaned at seventeen with only an elder brother for comfort. He missed his father and planned to share with his son the things he had enjoyed with his father: cricket, football, hunting and farming: he would move and live on a farm again so that his son could grow up with animals around him, just as he had. A daughter would not be interested in cricket or football; She would not want to support Nottingham Forest. It had to be a son!

Upstairs Charlotte was holding her daughter. Elizabeth shed a tear of joy; she was a grandmother and she intended doting on her granddaughter. Elizabeth agreed with the midwife; the new arrival was a beautiful baby.

Charlotte could not see any beauty in her newborn child. In fact, she thought she was ugly. The more she looked at her daughter the less maternal she felt. She had been told, with some excitement, that the time of birth had been 12.08 am on 1st January, 1950, but she could not begin to understand why it seemed so important to everyone. She was just glad that it was all over. Never again, she told herself, never again, but outwardly she made herself appear happy to be a mother.

The midwife had cleaned up and was making Charlotte freshen herself to look presentable for her husband. This was the last thing Charlotte wanted. After all her hard work all she felt like doing was sleeping. The midwife was insistent; she must brush her hair, put make-up on, sit up and smile. The price she was paying for being born a woman had never seemed so great. Men had it easy by comparison!

The midwife told Elizabeth that it was time for the father to see his daughter. Elizabeth went downstairs into the front room, smiling she looked at Wills and said, 'It's a girl. You've got a daughter and she's fine, they're both fine,'

Everyone in the room was jubilant. The birth on such an auspicious morning was the icing on the cake.

Then Elizabeth went over to her husband, kissed him on the cheek, 'Congratulations, Grandpa!'

John was delighted, he had a granddaughter; he was going to enjoy spoiling her.

Wills however was stunned and disappointed. He felt cheated. God had let him down again. He had been brought up to be a good Christian, his parents had taught him to say his prayers and thank God for everything. This God had repaid him by taking his parents from him, and now God had given him a daughter instead of a son. God was cruel. He heard Elizabeth say that he could go upstairs and see her.

'In a minute,' he replied, finishing his drink. He forced a smile as he went through the door, but his tears were of disappointment, not joy. He sauntered up the stairs, went into the back bedroom and walked round the bed to his wife's side. Then he saw his daughter's little face. It was a poignant second and one that he would never forget. The disappointment vanished, and in an instant he became a very proud father. Being a father was the most important thing in his life. She really was beautiful and the best thing that had ever happened to him. Now he had a reason for living, a new purpose in life. She was dependent on him; he needed to work to support her and give her the best start in life. One day he would be a grandfather and he would remember this moment. He thought he could see his mother's features in her face, her green eyes, chubby little nose and cute mouth.

He kissed his wife on the cheek and took hold of his daughter. There was not a happier man on the planet at that moment. Turning towards Charlotte he said, 'Well done, darling. Thank you. She's the best ever New Year's present.'

Charlotte looked up at him. 'Yes, she was worth all the morning sickness, swollen ankles, queuing for bananas and feeling fat.' Secretly, she knew none of this was true but it was important to please her husband, to say and do the right thing. She knew that she was going to lose her freedom; her life could never be the same again – this infant was going to demand her constant attention, and for that reason she already loathed her new offspring. Charlotte was a jealous person – she was jealous of her cousins and jealous of anyone who took the limelight away from her, and this new arrival was certainly going to do that.

As Wills gently rocked his daughter, his mind was firmly in the future: his daughter was a child of the fifties, a new generation, she would want for nothing. Charlotte looked up; she realised that he had been cradling her for several minutes.

'You'll soon tire of that,' she said.

'Never. I won't. Not ever.'

'What about changing nappies?'

'Any time.'

'Who's going to get up when she cries in the night?'

'Yes. I'll do all I can. There's only one thing I'll definitely leave you to do.'

Charlotte could not believe her ears. Looking after babies was the woman's job. Was he really going to help her? Did he know what he was letting himself in for?

'What's that?'

'Feeding her, of course!'

This was something that Charlotte had given little thought to. Suddenly, she was gripped with horror at the thoughts of this creature sucking at her nipples for nourishment. How cruel of Mother Nature to inflict such a thing on women.

'What shall we call her?' Wills broke into her thoughts.

They had discussed this already, and both had come up with several names. Wills had decided on boys' names and Charlotte on girls'. So it seemed as if she would get her own way on this.

'Irene,' she stated positively. 'I think it means "peace" in Greek. It'll remind us of those famous words, "There will be peace in our time". Let's hope there will be peace in the future for her.'

Wills thought for a moment. This was deep thinking for him and he was not a profound man.

'Fine,' he replied, 'but let's have a second name – Joy. I want her to have a lot of joy and happiness in her life.'

'Irene Joy, yes, I like the sound of that; it's got a nice ring to it.'

There was a knock and John popped his head round the bedroom door.

'Come in, Dad,' said Charlotte, 'and take a look at Irene Joy.'

John, followed closely by Elizabeth, walked round to look at his granddaughter. Wills handed her carefully to John. Irene was oblivious of all the fuss. She slept through it all, as babies do, unconcerned about hope for a peaceful future.

'Irene Joy, that's nice,' said John. Although neither he nor Elizabeth were really concerned about the name. They were just delighted to have a healthy grandchild.

'Great! Then that's what it's going to be, Irene Joy Stephenson,' Wills replied.

The midwife, a silent observer, smiled and looked out of the window; she had witnessed this scene so often before. 'It's beginning to snow. I'd better be going now. Everything seems to be all right.'

Just the mention of the word 'snow' brought a renewed fervour into the room. They all repeated the word as if they had never heard it before. New year, new decade, new life and snow. Things from now on could only get better!

Chapter 2
Silkington 1950

THE EARLY DAYS of the fifties drifted slowly by. Charlotte and Wills returned to their own home, a cottage at Silkington, a small village in Nottinghamshire.

Wills went out to work daily; he was employed by Graham Williams to do contract work on farms in the area. Charlotte stayed at home with the baby; there was no other option as this was expected of her.

Wills had a new lease of life: he had not been this happy since his own childhood. He loved returning home in the evenings to see his little girl. She seemed to develop more each day and as she grew, so did his pride. He watched her crawl and take her first steps, but sadly he was still out at work when she uttered her first words. Such was the fate of fatherhood.

Charlotte, on the other hand, found motherhood boring. She resented her loss of freedom since Irene's birth. She had never developed a maternal instinct and wondered why other women thought babies were a joy and a blessing. Wisely, she kept these thoughts to herself. She was unable to spend money on herself any more. In fact, she had very little money of her own. She was now dependent on her husband for spending money and resented this fact.

Before her marriage, money had not been a problem. She had had a job ever since leaving school at fourteen and had been allowed to keep what she earned. It was little enough, but it gave her independence. John Hamilton was well known for his generosity and caring nature. He had continued to give his daughter free board and lodging until the day she married.

The only hardship she had ever experienced was that of war. Even then there was a thrill and some excitement. The philosophy was to live for the moment as it might be your last and her father had given several parties. She had never in all her twenty-two years been as poor, or as bored, as she was now. Others might envy her for her marital state and motherhood, but even had she been aware of this it would have provided little consolation. She felt alone and isolated: they lived in a small village with no real community life, or at least not one where she could be the centre of attention.

Her only pleasure seemed to be when they went to have Sunday lunch with her parents. She looked forward to the few hours they spent in Whistbury each week. They were her only joy and escape from drudgery and reality. Sadly, time went slowly waiting for the weekend to come round and then it went so quickly.

After what seemed to Charlotte like an eternity, 1950 came to an end. They spent both Christmas and New Year with her parents and celebrated Irene's first birthday there. Then, all too soon, the fun was over and it was back to her routine of boredom and drudgery.

Wills had kept his word, so that when he was not working he was only too happy to look after Irene. Charlotte knew that she should be grateful that her husband was such a good and devoted father, but his enthusiasm only served to make her feel even more inadequate. Her resentment and boredom continued to grow.

Left alone through the long days of 1951, Charlotte's misery and self-pity were her only companions. She longed for the day when Irene would start school. At least then she would have some freedom during the daytime. She could find a part-time job during school hours and have an income of her own again. Providing she took Irene to catch the school bus in the morning and was home in the afternoon when she returned, work was an acceptable option. That possibility was the only glimmer of hope Charlotte could see on the horizon.

October, 1951 brought a general election to Britain. This resulted in a change of Government. The Conservatives were voted back into power and Winston Churchill was prime minister again. Charlotte knew very little about politics, but she had every confidence in Mr Churchill. Her father was a bank manager; he had always been a strong Conservative and she, believing politics to be a part only of the male role in life, had followed in her father's footsteps.

Christmas and New Year came and went. Irene's second birthday was celebrated in grand style with a party and wonderful presents. Elizabeth and John enjoyed doting on their granddaughter. Charlotte was delighted to spend the festive season with her parents: it was cheaper and much more fun than staying at home. On 2nd January, 1952, she resigned herself to another year of discontent as they returned to their own home. Life continued and the bleak winter days crept slowly by; she longed for the warmth of spring and summer.

Sadly, before the spring arrived, the nation was in mourning; the King had died in his sleep at Sandringham. On 5th February he had enjoyed an end-of-season shoot and had retired as usual in the evening. The valet found the King dead the following day when he took him his early morning tea.

At the end of January, only a week before his death, he had been photographed by the Press at London Airport waving Princess Elizabeth off on a foreign tour. The King had looked pale and drawn. The Princess and the Duke of Edinburgh were undertaking a marathon royal tour of East Africa, Australia and New Zealand instead of the King as it was thought that he was not strong enough to endure such a long foreign tour. However, it was to be cut short, going no further than Kenya.

The exact time of the new monarch's ascent to the throne is unknown. The Princess Elizabeth had spent the evening watching wild animals from an observation post known as 'Treetops', set in a giant fig tree. She will probably be the only monarch to ascend to the throne whilst in a tree thirty-five feet above the ground. Little did she realise that night that it was to be her last of relative freedom. The sheltered family life that the King had allowed her to enjoy as a wife and mother to her two small children was over. When the news of his death reached her, she knew that from that moment on she must always put duty first. She could remember, all too well, the Abdication of 1936 and how it had changed their lives. Her father had taught her about the privilege of sovereignty and the responsibility which went with it. She had declared her dedication to duty in her twenty-first birthday message to the Commonwealth. Like King George VI she must accept the role allotted to her. The New Elizabethan Age would begin with her Coronation in 1953.

The first seeds of change were being sown...

Chapter 3
Coronation Day, 2nd June, 1953

IRENE WAS three and a half in June, 1953. She enjoyed the Sunday jaunts to see Grandma and Grandpa, who lived in 'the big house', a detached property in Almond Blossom Avenue. She had seen the pink blossom on the trees earlier in the year and thought how nice it must be to live in such a pretty avenue. There were only five houses on Grandpa's side of the road and he lived in the middle one, No. 5; opposite were two small cottages and a church, Christ Church Whistbury.

Sometimes, if they went early to Grandpa's they would go to a service there; on other Sundays they went to their own village church. Irene had realised that Sunday was a special day of the week; it was a day when Daddy did not go to work. It was a family day, but it was an important day when you went to a special building and worshipped God. This God lived in Heaven and He had made her; she did not really understand this, but it seemed important to thank Him for her existence. In the evenings she would kneel by her bed, put her hands together and say her prayers. She would thank God for that day and ask Him to bless each member of her family. Then there was the final prayer for her soul; this was a mystery to her because she could not see how anything could escape out of her body when she died, but grown-up people understood all about this.

One day she would be a grown-up person and then she would understand everything; she would be able to do what she wanted. No one told adults when to go to bed or to be quiet; they did as they pleased. Being a little girl was hard, but being a grown-up looked like fun!

She knew that 2nd June was going to be an important day because the Queen was going to Westminster Abbey to be crowned. There was something called a 'television', which you could have in your home, and watch the whole event without going to London. Grandpa was buying a television and they were all going to watch the Coronation on it. It cost a lot of money, more than £80; Irene could not imagine what £80 looked like but Grandpa always seemed to have a lot of money.

On that day Daddy was not going to work and they were going to Grandpa's early in the morning. On the last Sunday in May, Irene was more excited than usual when they went to see her grandparents. She knew that she would not have to wait a whole week before their next visit. The more the grown-ups talked about the event, the more it excited her.

So, on the Tuesday morning, dressed in their Sunday best, she and her parents set out on their journey to Whistbury. The car was a small black Ford model with room for four people. Irene knew that she always sat in the back seat behind Mummy and that Daddy always drove. They chugged along at about twenty-five miles an hour; the car would not go any faster. Whistbury was only ten miles from Silkington and the journey via the city centre usually took about thirty minutes. There was little to impress Irene on the way; the scenery was unchanging, just trees and fields until they reached the city, and then boring houses which all looked alike. Occasionally, they would see another car on the country roads but there were never many. In Nottingham, there were usually people about and a few vehicles but very little to interest a three year old.

Irene was excited when they turned into the avenue; she could not wait to see Grandpa again. They parked on the road; she leapt out of the car and ran up the garden path. Grandpa had a large garden at the back of the house and at the front he had a lawn bordered by flowers. On the other side of the path were bushes dividing the garden from the drive which led to the garage. Beyond the garage and back garden there was a small stream; Irene thought that the fairies lived there. It was a well-maintained garden, because Grandpa employed someone to keep it nice and tidy, and it was much, much larger than the garden they had at home.

Inside the house they were all mesmerised by the 'box' in the alcove between the fireplace and bay window in the front room. It was switched on and there was a test card on it; Irene had never seen anything like it before, it was a large box, with a glass screen at the front, sitting neatly on a table.

Grandpa explained that it was a 'Decca D17' table model and had cost 83 guineas. This made Charlotte jealous: she wanted one but knew that they could not afford it; she would have to be content with her radio. But Charlotte was never content; she always wanted what other people had. Grandpa continued to explain that the aerial outside on the chimney picked up signals transmitted from the British Broadcasting Corporation and it relayed the signals down to the television by means of a cable. He showed them how the aerial was connected to the back of the set; they could see that it went through part of the window frame and then up on to the roof. Irene rushed out to look at the roof; she saw, attached to the chimney, a funny looking thing which she thought was made of wire. So this was an aerial!

When she went back inside Grandpa was explaining that one of the knobs beneath the screen turned the set on and off and another one controlled the sound. Irene thought it was a 'magic box'. Wills was intrigued by the modern technology: he thought the television was an invention which had great possibilities in the future. Perhaps every home would have one, one day. Charlotte just smiled.

Grandpa picked up the newspaper and told them that the television was a symbol of the new Elizabethan Age. When the Queen was crowned in the Abbey that day, people would be watching the event in two and a half million homes. This had never happened before; it was going to be a historic moment. Two and a half million homes! Irene was absolutely flabbergasted! All those homes had one of these magic boxes. Not only was it being transmitted in Britain, but people across the Channel, in France and Germany, would also be able to watch this royal event on their own magic boxes.

The neighbours from No. 7, Mr and Mrs Maycock arrived. John had invited them for the day because they did not have a set. The other people in the avenue either had sets or were going to relatives, apart from the occupants of No. 1; they were going to London, to the Mall, just as they had done when King George had been crowned in 1936. They said there was nothing like being in London to experience the true atmosphere of the occasion; people who had television sets in their homes would miss a lot of the live atmosphere.

According to the programme, the broadcast was scheduled to start outside Buckingham Palace at 10.15. By this time, everyone was seated with their eyes clearly focused on the set in the corner of the room. The television showed just how crowded the Mall was. They tried to look for their neighbours, the Ellingtons, but it was like looking for a needle in a haystack; when the camera zoomed in on the crowds, it was just a sea of faces, they soon realised that they were going to be unable to find their friends.

At 10.26 am the Queen's Coach emerged, with the Queen and the Duke of Edinburgh and an impressive sovereign's escort of cavalry. There were coaches and lots of people in splendid uniforms; Irene thought it was like fairyland. The Queen had a beautiful dress on and she was smiling as she waved to the people. This had never been seen in homes before and even though it was only in black and white it was very effective.

The Queen was not due to arrive at the Abbey until 11 o'clock and so Elizabeth was rushing in and out providing tea and biscuits. She was always the perfect hostess, as was expected of her in her role as a bank manager's wife. Unlike her daughter, Elizabeth had always been content to be at her husband's side; she wanted no more from life than to be a good wife and mother. However, on this occasion, her efforts were not fully appreciated, as they were all far too interested in what was happening on the television. They were spellbound!

The service seemed to go on forever. Irene was not sure what it was all about; but it was obviously an important moment in history. She could not understand what the adults were saying as they looked at various people, the dresses and Westminster Abbey; they had never seen inside the Abbey before. It seemed strange that, for the first time, people in their own homes had a better view than those in the Abbey or those who had gone to London for the occasion. It was as if the world had gone mad: everything was topsy-turvy.

It all led up to the great moment when the Queen was crowned. Four-year-old Prince Charles was looking away at the vital moment and missed seeing the Archbishop place St Edward's Crown on his mother's head. After this came the moment of enthronement when the Queen, assisted by the Archbishop of Canterbury, the bishops and other peers of the kingdom, moved to her throne. In her left hand she carried the rod with the dove, the symbol of the Holy Spirit, and in her right hand the sceptre with the cross, signifying her regal authority.

All of this could be seen clearly on the television. Once seated, she carried out her first duty of accepting homage from her princes and peers. The first person to pay homage was the Duke of Edinburgh, who declared his allegiance to her and then kissed her gently on the cheek. He was followed by other members of the Royal Family and then the peers and peeresses, all adorned in glorious robes. As an extra bonus, the music throughout the whole pageantry echoed not only in Westminster Abbey but in so many homes as well. The service ended at 1.50 pm and there was a pause in the broadcasting.

This gave time for conversation, reflection and for Elizabeth to bring in sandwiches and more drink. There was no point in switching the set off: the audience were just as happy looking at the test-card.

They found time to read the newspapers during the brief interlude; these told of another momentous British achievement. On 29th May, Edmund Hillary and the Sherpa Tenzing Norgay had reached the summit of Everest: the highest mountain in the world had at last been conquered. Hillary was a New Zealander and Norgay a Nepali, but these were minor details; they were members of a British expedition. It was certainly a day for the British to be proud; two crowning glories gave the nation reason for post-war optimism. Change was in the air; the euphoria and excitement were apparent everywhere. Nobody seemed to know what was happening but there was new hope for the future. The war was well and truly over and times had to move forward. They could never go back; they must advance yet there was no fear of the unknown.

At 2.15 pm the broadcast resumed; the Queen was leaving the Abbey; she came out to step into the Golden Coach after her crowning. A camera looked down to show the sceptre and orb in her hands and the royal robes of State around her. When she was safely in her carriage the journey back to the palace began. It was the long way home after an already long day but such was the price of duty. All along the route the crowds, undeterred by the rain, stood cheering at their newly crowned monarch and chanting 'God save the Queen!' She, from her fairy-tale golden coach, waved cheerfully to them.

The traditional balcony appearance was made and it was noticed that Her Majesty had given Prince Charles his first medal, The Coronation Medal. She appeared on the balcony to hear chantings of 'We want the Queen. We want the Queen. Long live the Queen!' Prince Philip, Prince Charles, Princess Anne and other members of the Royal Family joined her. The crowds, by this time, were drenched but even the dismal British weather did not dampen their enthusiasm. The only thing that managed to quieten them was the fly past of 168 jets in formation; they roared across the sky. By now, it was 5.45 pm. Irene and her family were still watching the magic box. They thought that they had had a much better time than people in London, and a better and drier view!

The television coverage continued well into the evening. Later that night, there was a firework display on the River Thames but Irene was not allowed to watch it; it was far too late for a three year old. Wills and Charlotte decided at 6.30 pm. that it was time to go home; Irene was so tired after such an exciting day that she was asleep when they reached Silkington.

The crowned queen made her first broadcast to the nation that evening. It was transmitted on both radio and television and introduced by Sir Winston Churchill. Charlotte and Wills listened to the Queen thanking her people for their prayers and support on her great day. She pledged herself to the people and stated, 'Throughout all my life and with all my heart I shall strive to be worthy of your trust. In this resolve I have my husband to support me. He shares all my ideals and my affection for you... Therefore I am sure that this, my Coronation, is not the symbol of power and a splendour that are gone, but a declaration of our hopes for the future and for the years I may, by God's grace and mercy, be given to reign and serve you as your Queen.'

It had been a long and exciting day; Irene did not mind missing the evening's entertainment. A queen had been crowned, she had seen it with her own eyes on a magic box; the grown-ups had called it a television and she had heard that the highest mountain in the world had been climbed.

The new Elizabethan Age had well and truly begun; the unchanging lifestyle of Britain was due to be shaken up. Soon the bad old days of the Depression and a war-torn Britain would be remembered fondly as 'the good old days': they would be like the Southern States of America before the Civil War, days that were 'gone with the wind', lost forever in the deep archives of history.

Things were beginning to change...

Chapter 4
Silkington, 1953

AFTER THE GREAT EVENTS of 1953, Charlotte counted the days until Irene was old enough to go to school: there were 575 until 1st January, 1955 and term would start a few days after that. She consoled herself: she had come through more than that, the worst was behind her. It was summer and warm so the coal bill was less; she only made a fire when they needed water for a bath on Friday nights. Wills was able to do overtime and although he stayed at work longer, that meant more money; she could afford to visit the hairdresser's and pamper herself. Life did not seem so bad until she remembered the television set; all she had was a radio. Her daily excitement of 'Woman's Hour' suddenly seemed very mundane. Listening to 'Mrs Dale's Diary' and 'The Archers' was definitely second best. The daily life of Ambridge was boring after a coronation!

Irene remained blissfully ignorant of her mother's predicament. She knew that it was summer, one of the four seasons and the warmest; autumn and the long cold winter would follow it. Spring would eventually come and there would be pretty blossom on the trees, leaves would sprout forth again and flowers would brighten the days. She liked the spring flowers: snowdrops, primroses and daffodils; she had enjoyed the walks earlier in the year when they had picked lots of wild primroses.

The church was the focal point of the small rural community where she lived. Irene was intrigued by the large weather-worn stones which were on either side of the small path leading to the porch. The writing on them was barely legible but it was clear that some of them had been there for more than 150 years. The large wooden door would creak when opened, but once inside there was a strange air of stillness. There were only twelve pews, six on each side of the nave, and if all the village came to a service they were crammed like sardines in a tin. The front pew was reserved for the squire and his family, an age-old tradition. At the back was the font and belfry but the prettiest part, for Irene, was the beautiful stained-glass window portraying Jesus on the Cross and the angels surrounding him; she could sit and look at that for hours. There was no electricity and no organ; Mrs Bacon, who ran the village post office, was the pianist and all the services were held in either the morning or afternoon. There was no Evensong, not even in summer when the nights were lighter. The church was opposite the Hall where the village squire, Stephen Patterson and his family, lived. Like so many small churches, it had been originally built for the family at the Hall, and only later became the centre of the village community.

Mrs Bacon ran the post office from the front room of her home, Oak Tree Cottage, or No. 10 Elsbridge Lane. Outside the cottage were the red telephone kiosk and post box; but Irene liked the big oak tree in the garden best of all, it just seemed to grow and grow. The post office, church and a small village store served the community of about fifty houses and the Hall. The majority of the villagers were born and bred Silkington people. Wills and Charlotte moved there when they married; not having lived there for the dozen years or so it took to be accepted, they were 'newcomers'. Wills liked the village people and was happy to talk with them in the lane, or at social gatherings like bonfire night, whist drives, beetle drives and parties, but Charlotte did not fit in to the village cycle of life. She was a town girl and preferred dancing or the pictures in Nottingham to any form of village activity. The locals tried hard to make her feel welcome, as village communities do. Sometimes, life could be more lonely and isolated in a town full of people than in a small village with only a few occupants. For Charlotte, it was the reverse; she was her own worst enemy but unable to see it.

Home, for the family, was the middle cottage in a row of three, No. 4 Elsbridge Lane. Irene knew the occupants of Nos. 2 and 6, but the other villagers were people she saw only on Sunday at Church or, in passing, on the lane; she did not know their names. The village was a mile's walk from the main road and it had only two lanes, Elsbridge Lane and a smaller one, both leading to fields.

There were few children in the village; Irene knew no one of her own age. Sometimes, she felt quite lost amongst the adult company; they would discuss things that she did not understand and then, when they talked to her, they seemed to use a different language. She was aware of the great divide between her small world and the one in which her parents lived.

The cottages were owned by Graham Williams, who lived in another village. Irene knew that her father worked for him, while she stayed at home with her mother. This cottage was smaller than the house Grandpa lived in; it did not have a front garden or garage and the front door opened straight on to the lane. Daddy parked his car on the grass on the other side of Elsbridge Lane by the hedge; beyond the massive privet were fields. Few people in the village had cars, and most days Daddy's car was the only one she saw. When he returned in the evenings she would rush out to greet him; he would pick her up and call her his 'little angel'. They would walk inside together and she would watch him eat his meal before her bedtime. After she had said her prayers and crawled into bed, he would read her a story. This was her favourite time of the day.

The cottages were very basic; two rooms upstairs and two rooms downstairs. The stairs were opposite the front door and in the room considered to be the main parlour which was only used on special occasions. There was a door through to the back room which served as a kitchen, bathroom, dining room and living room. Upstairs were two bedrooms. Irene's overlooked the back; the back yard had a small area of garden at the bottom which Wills used for growing vegetables. The rest of it was paved, and had three small brick buildings: one for the toilet, which was an Elsan, better described as a large bucket with a seat, which was emptied weekly by the Council, a shed, and a coal-house. Wills kept his garden tools in the shed; it was also home to the bath tub which came into the kitchen once a week. Friday night was bath night! The tub was placed in front of the fire and filled with bowls of hot water. This was the night when Charlotte remembered her blissful pre-marital days with her parents; they had a proper bathroom and inside toilet. She had not realised the full extent of country life in a small cottage. At least they had running water and electricity, which was more than some of the older cottages had, but Charlotte did not find this comforting.

When she looked round the small cottage and surveyed their possessions, she felt an even greater discontent; her parents seemed to have so much by comparison. In Charlotte's living room there was a table, four dining chairs, two easy chairs, her radio, a cooker, sink unit and the kitchen range, which was a fire with a side oven and back boiler to heat the water. In the front room they had a beautiful three-piece suite and sideboard; both were wedding presents. There was a cupboard under the stairs which served as a pantry. The bedrooms only had the basic items of beds and wardrobes plus Charlotte's dressing table.

Charlotte knew having a car was an extravagance they could not really afford; Wills could have cycled to work like most people in the village did or walk to the main Nottingham Road and catch the bus. However, she could not bear the thought of not having a car. Except for the war years her father had always owned one and she hoped that one day she would get a provisional licence and learn to drive. She had suggested it but the response had been laughter; her mother did not drive: driving – and understanding mechanics – was a male domain. Good women were housewives who were content to be driven by their husbands in the evenings and at weekends.

Their neighbours were older than Wills and Charlotte and were real country folk. The couple at No.2 were Fred and Betty Thompson; he was in his fifties, she in her forties. Fred had been born in a house near the church and Betty had come from the next village. Fred worked with Wills for Graham Williams as did the other neighbour, John. He and his wife Joan were both in their late thirties and Silkington born and bred. For these people there was nowhere on this earth as idyllic as Silkington. Charlotte privately questioned their sanity; how could anyone be content in a place which had absolutely nothing to offer but a wilderness of trees, fields and flowers?

Betty was content to stay at home each day and always seemed to find plenty to occupy her time, knitting, embroidery, painting, making jam or chutney and reading were just some of the many things that interested her. She had taken Charlotte and Irene with her when she went picking flowers and berries, and had tried to show Charlotte just how interesting country life could be. It was Betty who Charlotte reluctantly thanked for showing her how to make jam, but she still had no interest in country ways.

Joan, her other neighbour, worked during the day but was home when her two teenage daughters returned from school. Despite their efforts at friendliness, Charlotte still felt an outsider; these were not her type of people. Who were Charlotte's type of people? She did not encourage neighbourliness but then complained that they did not invite her into their homes. She made sure that her daughter was seen to be well mannered and Irene was taught to say 'Good morning, Mrs Thompson' or whatever was appropriate. The villagers soon decided that Charlotte should be classified as a snob; but they adored Irene who, with her dark curly hair, green eyes and smile, could capture any heart.

Irene soon realised that there was a routine to their lives. During the week they ate at certain times and listened to radio programmes at set times. At weekends things were different, Daddy finished work at lunchtime on Saturday. She looked forward to Saturday afternoon when they went into Nottingham to do the shopping and on Sunday she would see Grandpa. This was her life's pattern until she started school.

Sometimes, on a Saturday, they would visit relatives before returning home. There were several aunts and uncles on Mummy's side of the family; but her favourite uncle was her father's elder brother, Uncle Jim. He had invested his share of their inheritance in a tobacco and confectionery business. Irene loved the aroma in the shop, a mixture of tobacco, and chocolate, which Uncle Jim always gave her a bar of before she went home. Uncle Jim was married to Aunt Julia; they had a son, Martin. She liked her cousin; he was four years her senior and already at school. He would tell her about it and she listened eagerly, longing for the day when she was old enough to start there.

The other relative they visited frequently was mother's cousin, Mavis. She had married Gerald in 1952; Irene had to call them 'aunt' and 'uncle', even though they were really her cousins. Charlotte was jealous of Mavis, because she thought her cousin had a better lifestyle. Mavis and Gerald lived in a semi-detached, spacious property which they would eventually own outright after the last mortgage payment. In their childhood days they had played together and been as close as sisters, but their friendship drifted in adolescence after Mavis went to the grammar school. It was at that early stage in her life that Charlotte first experienced disappointment and jealousy; she felt that she had let both herself and her beloved father down by not passing the eleven plus for the grammar school. Mavis met Gerald whilst at school and it seemed that she was blessed with happiness and success. Little did Charlotte realise that Mavis envied both the relationship she had with her father and the lavish lifestyle she led with her parents. Mavis's parents were more thrifty; parties, holidays and extensive wardrobes were extravagant and unnecessary. However, it was Mavis who gave Charlotte the idea that was going to make her life more exciting. One Saturday afternoon, when they arrived, Mavis was writing copiously in an exercise book. Charlotte quipped, 'Is that a novel you're writing?'

'No. A diary.'

'A diary?'

'Yes. I'm keeping a record of our family life, historical and social events. Something to hand on to our children so they will know about the past.'

'Are you pregnant, then?'

'No.' She sighed, she desperately wanted a baby. There was a pause before Charlotte said, 'What sort of events have you written about?'

'Well, the Coronation, naturally and last year there was the testing of the 'H' bomb in Russia and the end of the Korean War. Then on 12th September, John F. Kennedy married Jacqueline Bouvier in Rhode Island, America. I've included a press cutting about that.'

'Can I see?'

'Certainly.' Mavis handed the book to her.

The idea of keeping such a diary was beginning to appeal to Charlotte. She read the press cutting and some of the other events of 1953. John Christie was hanged on 15th July for the Rillington Place murders; she shivered as she was reminded of his heinous crimes. In cricket, England won the Ashes back from Australia for the first time in twenty years. She remembered Wills being excited about the event, which was meaningless to her, but obviously an important part of sporting history. She looked up at Mavis. 'And this year?'

Mavis turned over a few pages until she came to 1954

It began with daily accounts of their life and weather reports before mention of the end of food rationing, the Billy Graham Crusades in London and New York and a lengthy account of the Queen's Commonwealth tour. Roger Bannister created a world record by running the mile in less than four minutes.

'Where do you get all your information from?'

'Newspapers and the radio. Where else?'

Charlotte's mind was made up. She had a new hobby which she hoped would make her boring life more interesting. On Sunday, she collected a notebook from John's Supply and at the end of the year, she was able to recall such events as the eclipse of the sun on 30th June and her great war hero Sir Winston Churchill's eightieth birthday on 30th November. Abroad, Gamel Abdel Nasser was the new prime minister of Egypt and there was the awful earthquake in Algeria and subsequent political unrest. She smiled when she read about the end of the French war in Indo-China and Lester Piggot becoming the youngest jockey, at eighteen, to win the Derby on Never Say Die. Oxford won the hundredth boat race; she was not sure why she had included that but Germany winning the football World Cup and the maiden flight of the Boeing 707 were more important events.

She had also noted a change of behaviour amongst the youth of the fifties; they were discontented and not prepared to accept the way of life dictated to them by their elders and the Government. A new group, called Teddy Boys, had established themselves and were beginning to rebel in ways which she and her peer group would neither have dared or even thought of doing. She put her pen down and congratulated herself on her last statement:

'The dormant volcano of the country's youth is beginning to erupt.'

Chapter 5
Whistbury and Silkington, 1955

ON MONDAY 3RD January, 1955, Irene started school. New Year's Eve and her birthday had been celebrated, as usual, with Grandma and Grandpa. Although she was in her bed in the smaller of the two front bedrooms, Irene was well aware of what was happening; she would drift off to sleep only to be woken by the singing downstairs. She knew she was going to be five before morning. The church bells began to ring; the clock chimed twelve slow strokes and she heard cheering from downstairs. Now she was five!

Life was fantastic! She had waited so long for this moment; she was a Big Girl and old enough to go to school, like her cousin Martin. She was wide awake and saw no reason why she should not join in the party; after all, it was HER birthday. She climbed out of bed, put on her dressing gown and then, clutching her teddy bear, went downstairs. There seemed to be grown-ups everywhere; they had glasses in their hands and were shouting, 'Happy New Year!' and kissing each other. She looked for Daddy; he was kissing Mummy; even Mummy appeared to be happy. Irene had noticed that Mummy always seemed angry these days and spent a lot of time shouting at Daddy. She could not understand why, but Mummy also seemed to be getting fatter; this was a mystery which only grown-ups understood.

She went over to her father who lifted her up, 'Well, well, and what are you doing out of bed, then?'

Irene was speechless; everyone was looking at her. Perhaps coming downstairs was not such a good idea after all; and where were her presents? Charlotte scolded her and told her that she should still be asleep. Sleep? How could anyone sleep with bells ringing and a party going on?

Wills was clearly displeased with his wife's attitude and, much to Irene's relief, said that he would take her back to bed. He made her say 'night-night' to everyone, and carried her upstairs and carefully tucked her – and teddy – into bed. Going downstairs into the adult world had turned her excitement into misery and sadness, but she was soon asleep.

Later that morning, when the debris had been cleared away and all that remained of the traditional party were memories and hangovers, all the attention was focused on Irene and her misdemeanour seemed to have been forgotten.

There were lots of presents and cards with '5' on them; her best present always came from Daddy; this year it was a large teddy bear, almost as big as she was. He told her how proud he was of his 'little angel' and on Monday she was going to school. He gave her explicit instructions about behaviour; she was to be very good, quiet, listen and do as she was told. Of course she would; Irene would do anything for Daddy. Grandma had baked her a big birthday cake with five candles on it; she blew them all out in one go and received a round of applause and 2/6d from Grandpa. Her eyes nearly popped out of her head; 2/6d was a small fortune to a little girl. She was very happy when she said her prayers that night and remembered to thank God for all her presents. That tired her out and she slept well.

The festivities were over for another year and on the Sunday, after Church and lunch, they returned to their humble country cottage. Charlotte, who had been longing for 1955 for so long, thinking it would bring her freedom, was depressed because she was pregnant again. She had told Wills that she really did not want another child and had prayed for a miscarriage; many, including Mavis, considered her to be blessed. In Charlotte's view they were insane. Even Wills could not understand why she did not want another child; surely, every woman wanted children? What was wrong with his wife? However, he was a tolerant man and thought that she would change after the birth; he was still blissfully ignorant about her lack of maternalism and the way she had really felt about Irene's infancy. Charlotte, like most women of her era, knew little about sex; it was a taboo subject. She had just done her duty, 'lain back and thought of England': this was the only advice Elizabeth had given her. It must be her husband's fault that she was pregnant and he did not understand. He was a man!

Charlotte sighed as she prepared her daughter for school on that special Monday. Well, at least, it was special for Irene; dressed in her new clothes, brown skirt, jumper and coat and clutching her small teddy.

She set off with her mother to catch the school bus. She would have liked to have taken her big teddy bear but Daddy said he was too big to carry to school; he would be happier sitting in the front room waiting for her to return. They walked past the post office and up to the junction where the smaller lane, which was more of a cart track, led off Elsbridge Lane. There was a handful of adults with six other children waiting for the bus, standing on a well-trodden grass verge by the side of the lane. The small blue bus (the only one to come into the village) would chug down the lane and carefully reverse round into the cart track; those who lived in the cottages along it insisted that it was really a lane, but that was debatable.

All the children were older than Irene; two of them were her neighbours who attended the secondary school, so there were only four children going to the primary school. Charlotte handed her daughter over to Mrs Green, a teacher at the school. When the bus arrived and the driver had made the usual manoeuvre, Irene got on first with Mrs Green and sat on the front seat next to her. She noticed how the other children were given a farewell kiss from their mothers; Charlotte seldom caressed her daughter and saw no reason for such an affectionate display.

Undeterred by her mother's lack of affection, she looked out of the window as they passed the church with its beautiful window, the imposing Hall opposite and the red brick cottages lying behind neatly-cut privet hedges before they reached the main road. They travelled for about a mile and a half before turning off for the next village, Elsbridge. Irene wondered why she lived in Elsbridge Lane, if she had to go all this way round to reach it. It did not occur to her that in former pre-transport years the way to Elsbridge from Silkington would have been by the footpaths across those fields! There were two other stops on the way and more youngsters boarded but they were all older than Irene. Soon she saw Elsbridge County Primary School, another red brick building with large windows which gave ample light but were deliberately high up to prevent children from looking out and being distracted from their lessons.

On the opposite side of the road there were a couple of three-storey houses but of greater interest to Irene was the shop situated between them which sold sweets. Mrs Green took her through the gate in the iron railings which surrounded the school and the headmaster's house. They walked across a small yard to a red door at the side of the building; this led into a cloakroom. Mrs Green showed her where to put her coat and beret; there was a clothes peg with her name already above it which made her feel important and welcome. Then she was taken into a large room which they called a 'hall' but it was totally different from the large building they called Silkington Hall where she had been to fetes. All the children assembled here and the headmaster came in and they sang 'All things bright and beautiful'.

There were prayers and a reading from the Bible before they were welcomed back to school for the new term. The pupils were then dismissed and everyone seemed to know where to go.

A room divider had been set up to change the hall into two smaller classrooms; desks and chairs were placed in rows and each child took his or her place. Irene was introduced to a Miss Smith, a small elderly lady with grey hair neatly piled on her head in a bun; she wore all black: black shoes, black skirt, black jumper, black cardigan, and the coat on the back of her chair was also black. She was the infants' teacher and told Irene where to sit; Irene remembered what Wills had told her about being good and politely said, 'Yes, Miss Smith,' and 'Thank you' when she was given paper and pencil; she was keen and eager to learn everything. Miss Smith wrote the letters of the alphabet for her and told her to copy them; she already knew the alphabet and could read some special children's books with help. However, she practised writing the letters and then she wrote some of the words she knew; she thought Miss Smith was pleased.

At 10.30 they were told it was 'playtime'; Miss Smith asked Hillary Edison to look after Irene. Hillary was six months older than Irene and lived in Silkington; she was one of the four who had got on the bus and Irene had also seen her at Church. Hillary collected two milk bottles and gave her one and a straw. Apparently, they had a third of a pint of milk every morning. Then she had to put her coat on and go outside for fresh air and to the lavatory; this was what 'playtime' meant and it was a mid-morning daily ritual. The milk was nice but going out in the cold seemed like madness! However, she put her coat on, went out of the back door and found another playground. On the far side of the playground was the toilet block and beyond that was the school playing field and a large sand-pit; in the freezing cold it was not appealing, but in the summer it would be a different story.

After the break, they returned to their desks and had another lesson before lunchtime. At noon, the hall changed its appearance yet again and became the dining room. The meals came in a van and were served from a large table placed between the two stoves which provided heating. These were like two furnaces, fed frequently by coke from a scuttle to keep the room warm; a fire-guard surrounded them to prevent the children from getting too close. In January, the children would swarm round like bees round a honey-pot at any opportunity. The meal and the stoves provided relaxation and satisfied the needs of hunger and warmth before the afternoon session. The afternoon followed the morning format until the school day ended. Outside it was dull and dreary; as Irene waited for the bus with Mrs Green, she thought about her first day of school; she had not learnt a lot but there would be more tomorrow.

Back in Silkington, Charlotte was being dutiful and waited for her daughter to return. Irene climbed down the bus steps and ran to her mother; they walked hand in hand down the lane together. She told her mother about her day, but the real excitement was when Wills came home to his 'little angel'; he listened to her account of her day and then tucked her up in bed.

The next morning, Irene woke up earlier than usual and was eager to have her breakfast and go to school; a whole new world had opened up for her and she wanted to enjoy it. Her second day proved to be more interesting than the first. She liked Miss Smith, who was still wearing all black, and she made more friends, although Hillary was her 'special' friend. There was another classroom at the far end of the hall where the headmaster, Mr Sanderson, taught the eldest children. Altogether, there were about sixty children in the three classes; many lived in Elsbridge, the largest village in the area, but the others were brought in daily on two buses from the smaller surrounding villages.

Irene now had a new routine in her life. Each weekday morning she went to school, but the weekends were just as before, with Sunday being the really important day. When she arrived at school she left her outdoor clothing in the cloakroom and then went into the hall where Miss Smith took the register. After that, Mr Sanderson brought his class into the hall and they would all sit on the floor for morning assembly. At 9.20 they split up into three classes, in which they were taught for most of the time; singing, dancing and PT seemed to be the only other occasions when they were taught as an entire group. Irene liked her new way of life and particularly looked forward to telling her father all about it in the evening.

Charlotte, on the other hand, disliked her days of sitting at home alone and feeling fat. Although she was able to occupy herself writing in her diary which was a 'retreat from reality', she was dreading the birth of her second child. Some women had told her that it was easier with the second one, something she chose to disbelieve; she managed to convince herself that in fact it was going to be far more painful.

Wills, however, was delighted with the way his life was now turning out. He had a job he liked; even if he earned £100 a week instead of £4.10s. he would still not be able to satisfy his wife's craving for money; consequently her moans did not worry him. His cottage was adequate and nice to come home to in the evenings; he had a gorgeous daughter and a second child on the way. He would like a son but either way he would have a job, home, wife and two children soon. What more could a man want from life?

Early in February, Irene found that there was to be another change in her life; she was to have either a brother or a sister. For that to happen, they were all going to spend some time with Grandma and Grandpa. A week or two with Grandpa was definitely a bonus, but having to miss school was a disappointment; she liked seeing Hillary and the other children every day. It was like a breath of fresh air away from the adult world.

However, it is the grown-ups who decide. When Wills came home from work that Saturday in mid-February, the car was loaded up and they prepared to move their whole lives over to John and Elizabeth's. It was going to be hard for Wills, as he would have to do the ten-mile journey to and from work each day. As usual, he had allowed his wife to have her own way; she did not want the baby in her own home or in hospital, but delivered by the local midwife at her mother's.

Irene climbed into her usual place in the back and they set off. From the conversation, Irene thought that her brother or sister would be arriving at Grandpa's in the middle of the week. She wondered just how it was coming: the postman delivered the mail through the letterbox. Should she watch carefully in the mornings? Why was there so much fuss over this delivery? Had there been this much fuss when she came? Where had she come from? She had a birthday, 1st January. She had arrived on that day but from where? These questions suddenly occurred to her but it did not seem the right time to ask Daddy.

They arrived at Whistbury in the middle of the afternoon and Irene rushed straight in to see Grandpa. She noticed that there was a lot of fuss made around her mother; it must be because she was so much fatter these days and found it difficult to move about. There was talk about Wednesday, but Monday was Valentine's Day; it would be nice if it came on Monday. Irene's curiosity was heightened by the odd bits of conversation she picked up; when would it arrive?

The weekend passed by with a lot of tension. Wills left for work on the Monday morning. He kissed his wife goodbye, not knowing that when he returned in the evening he would be the father of a son; his dearest wish was about to be fulfilled.

Charlotte was fine at 6.30 am when Wills left. She struggled to get up and joined her parents and Irene for breakfast, although she was not really hungry and her back was aching. John was concerned about his daughter but knew he had to go to work: banks do not run themselves. By mid-morning her waters had broken and Elizabeth helped her back to bed.

Elizabeth was alone with a daughter in labour and a granddaughter to look after.

Irene could hear her mother screaming out in pain at intervals and was frightened.

Elizabeth told her to stay in the front room, play with her toys and everything would be all right. She thought she had better do as she was told, but wished Daddy was there; he always made everything all right. She heard her grandmother make a telephone call and then another woman arrived.

Upstairs, the drama continued until the afternoon when the midwife uttered those immortal words, 'It's a boy!'

Charlotte was exhausted. It had not been any easier the second time and she said, as she had done five years earlier; never again! This time, though, she had the deja vu feeling as she watched the midwife cut the cord and place her son in her arms. Elizabeth was ecstatic: she now had a grandson!

While the midwife finished clearing up, Elizabeth went downstairs to tell Irene she had a brother. Her eyes lit up, but why had she not seen him arrive? How had they managed to sneak him in? She was still mystified.

Elizabeth called John with the glad tidings and knew there would be a celebration at the bank. It was unfortunate that the last person to hear the news was Wills. He walked in the door later that evening to see his in-laws waiting for him with a bottle of champagne. Irene rushed to him, as she usually did, shouting, 'Daddy, Daddy, I've got a little brother!'

He could hardly believe it; his family was complete. His wish had been granted, a son and a daughter, he was so lucky; he must thank God for his good fortune. He went upstairs to his wife, and Irene followed. For the first time the whole family were together: Charlotte, Wills, Irene and baby James.

Wills was the proudest man in the universe; he was holding his son with his daughter by his side. Charlotte was smiling, but inside she was experiencing a private hell. She had another five years of torture ahead. She did not have maternal feelings and nobody understood how she felt.

At the end of the week they returned to their home and their new family life began. Irene adored her brother and was eager to help look after him; she would watch over him in his cot, and fetch and carry things for him. All he seemed to do was eat, cry and sleep. Had she been like that once? He had to be fed, bathed and changed regularly and sometimes he would wake them up in the night, but she did not mind any of this. She noticed that her father tended to do more when he was home than her mother did. But Daddy still had plenty of time for her: she was still his 'little angel'. She had also noticed that there was another difference between boys and girls; other than the fact that boys wore trousers and girls wore skirts. He had a little something extra which she did not possess. This had heightened her curiosity about the differences between the sexes but her questions did not receive direct answers. She assumed that she would find out all the answers when she was a grown-up.

When the summer holidays arrived, Irene had been going to school for seven months and was making good progress despite all those disturbed nights. She could read, write and add up well for her age and most important for her was Daddy's pleasure at her progress. She and Hillary were still close friends; they sat together in school, played together and told each other their secrets. Irene particularly enjoyed talking about James. Hillary was an only child and she liked hearing about his development; it was as if they were sharing him.

For Wills and Irene those first months of 1955 were blissful; they were both unaware of Charlotte's private hell. In her spare moments, Charlotte escaped into her own fantasy world and wrote in her journal.

'May: there's a general election. The Conservatives have been re-elected and Britain now has a new prime minister, Anthony Eden...

Bill Haley is a household name as "the father of rock 'n' roll"; he's an American singer and guitarist and the first to bring this style of music and dance to the masses. He's recorded "Rock around the Clock" in the film, "The Blackboard Jungle"; this new revolutionary music has led to rioting in cinemas with people dancing in the aisles...

The rebellious American actor, James Dean, has been killed in a car accident. He was idolised by today's young people and a cult figure for their rebellion. His second film "Rebel Without a Cause" has been released; it's a study of juvenile delinquency amongst the middle classes...

Internationally, the Cold War between the United States and the Soviet Union continues, as does the nuclear arms race.

A new race has started: who will be the first into space?

Ruth Ellis, found guilty of murdering David Blakely, is hanged at Holloway Prison. This execution is hastening the campaign in Britain for an end to the death penalty; the campaigners claim that capital punishment is barbaric, inhumane and outdated...

It is clear that our main roads are going to be congested in the future as more cars are being manufactured and more families are wanting one. The first motorway plans are being made; there are to be two lanes and a "hard shoulder" for emergency use only. The idea of such roads, without traffic lights or islands, is for people to drive more quickly to their destination, without stopping or being held up...

Good news for those lucky people with a television set; from this month, September, in some areas there's going to be a choice of two stations. Commercial television is beginning!'

Charlotte sighed as she wrote that comment: she longed for a television set. The summer holidays were over, the new term had begun; there was an autumnal feeling in the air as the trees shed their leaves and the nights drew in.

James was seven months old and to Irene he seemed to be growing rapidly. Wills watched his son growing and thought of the fun they would have at football matches and playing cricket together. His 'little angel' was also growing up quickly; soon she would be a young woman but she would always be 'Daddy's girl'.

For Charlotte the private hell was becoming unbearable. Each morning she would feed her family, see her husband go to work and then take Irene to the school bus; the other mothers would 'coo' over James in his pram. She would then spend her day with nappies, washing and endless household chores. If she went out she had to take James with her; in the afternoon, she would return to the junction to collect Irene.

There was no escape from motherhood: she hated her son and wished he had never been born. The weekends, once more, were her salvation; she had been through all of this before; she was on a merry-go-round and there was no getting off. John was the only one to feel that his daughter was not the happy mother she should be. His solution was money: he thought if she had some money of her own she would have some financial freedom. He was, unknown to Wills, already giving his daughter 10 shillings a week and had been since Irene was born.

He gave her £5 to buy herself something which made her even more depressed; she had to do something to get sympathy and attention.

One October evening, Irene looked for her mother and James at the junction; they were not there and there was no sign of them coming up the lane; all the other mothers were waiting. She had never walked down the lane on her own before: Where was her mother? She began to cry. Hillary's mother picked her up and tried comforting her, but it was in vain.

Ann Edison decided to take Irene home. She walked down the lane with a tearful Irene holding one hand and her daughter holding the other. She knocked on the door but there was no reply; hearing the radio blaring on inside, she assumed that Charlotte was in; she knocked again and shouted.

Betty Thompson was reading in her front room and heard the commotion outside. Looking out of her window she saw Ann and the children: something must be wrong. She went outside to see what she could do; both women knocked, then hammered on the door and shouted while Irene continued sobbing. They tried the door and found it unlocked; they entered and rushed through to the back room. Charlotte was in the chair, motionless, apparently sleeping and James was safely asleep in his cot. On the table was an empty tablet bottle and a glass with some water in it. Irene rushed to try and wake her mother but it was impossible. She sobbed and sobbed, her little world had crumbled.

Charlotte was still breathing. Neither of the women knew anything about first aid but James appeared to have been fed and changed recently. Betty went to the phone box and called for the ambulance while Ann picked up the cot and took James and the girls into the front room. She tried comforting Irene but nothing could stop her sobs. Was her mummy dead? Why?

Betty returned; the ambulance was coming from Nottingham and would take about thirty minutes. Both women stayed, Betty kept going into the kitchen to look at Charlotte. They were relieved that she was still alive when the ambulance arrived; it had been a long half hour for both of them. The men asked for details and for Charlotte's husband.

'When will Daddy be home?' one of them asked Irene. She shook her head; she did not know; sometimes, it was five o'clock, sometimes later. She heard the grown-ups talking and making arrangements. Betty was not sure when Wills would be home either; she had the same problem with Fred, sometimes they worked overtime at short notice. She left a note for her husband and agreed to go in the ambulance with Charlotte whilst Ann stayed with the children. Bill, her husband, was not coming home until later in the evening.

Irene watched her unconscious mother carried out by the ambulance men who, having very little knowledge of medicine, did not know whether she would live or die. There was a stomach pump at the hospital, ready and waiting, but that was still half an hour's drive away.

The ambulance set off and Irene waved it goodbye. Where was God when you needed him? She said her prayers each evening and always asked him to bless Mummy. Why had this happened? Had she not been a good girl? Was God punishing her? Where was Daddy? How long would he be? What was he going to say? Would he blame her? These thoughts were whizzing round her head: nothing could console her.

Eventually, much to Ann's relief, they heard the car coming down the lane: Wills was home. Ann explained the situation; he was clearly devastated. How could she do that to him and her children? It was thoughtless and selfish; she had her role to play and he had his. He worked hard, sometimes long hours, to provide for them when he would rather spend time with his children; but being a man he was not blessed with that opportunity. She had everything and yet it was not enough.

Wills decided that the best thing would be to take his children to Elizabeth for a few days. He had to go to the hospital and also bring Betty back; Fred would be working for another hour. He went to the phone box and called his mother-in-law; John was home and they arranged to meet at the hospital. Wills thanked Ann for all that she had done and a very relieved Ann took her daughter home. She privately questioned Charlotte's sanity and her sympathy was not for Charlotte but for Wills. Having a wife who behaved in such a way was an embarrassment and a burden.

Meanwhile, Wills collected some things together for the children, loaded the car and set off for the hospital. John and Elizabeth were already there and Charlotte's stomach had been washed out. She had clearly waited until the afternoon to act out her plan; if she had taken the tablets in the morning it would have been fatal. It was thought that it was done deliberately to attract attention away from her children towards herself and should, therefore, be ignored. She had not really intended to kill herself or she would have taken more tablets and earlier in the day. She was not a real suicide risk and should be given the minimum amount of attention to discourage such stupidity in the future. She was sleeping when Wills arrived.

John and Elizabeth both sympathised with Wills. When they saw him with their grandchildren they, too, questioned their daughter's sanity. What damage had she done to Irene? What was she putting her daughter through, coming home to find her mother in such a state? Then, like most parents, they wondered where they had gone wrong. Was it their fault that their daughter had done this awful thing? The neighbours had become involved. What were they thinking? What was Betty thinking of them as a family?

Wills looked in and saw his wife sleeping; there was nothing to do but wait. Fred would be home by now and he must take Betty back. It was painful kissing his daughter goodbye and telling her to be good; Mummy was going to be all right.

They went their separate ways. Later, when Wills arrived home to an empty house, he sat down and wept. Why? Why? Oh Why? There was no answer.

Wills carried on working; Charlotte recovered, came home and they were reunited as a family unit. Her little plan had failed; she had not been given the kind of sympathy and attention she wanted. Even her own father was disappointed with her. She was back to her routine of boredom and drudgery for another four years. Her actions had made her less popular than before and soon she realised that, instead of being better off, she had made her own situation worse. Now people did not see her as the good wife and mother; she was a silly failure.

As far as Irene was concerned, her world had crumbled. She had experienced her first disaster in life; things could never be the same again. She could not rely on her mother any more and she would never forgive her for abandoning them.

That year came to an end and, as usual, they spent Christmas and New Year with Elizabeth and John. The traditional party went ahead; Irene was in her bed listening to the singing and cheering downstairs when the church clock chimed twelve slow strokes. Another year was over; this year she had a brother and she was six!

The hands of time were marching on.

Chapter 6
Silkington, 1956

THE HOLIDAY was over; 1956 had begun. Irene started her second year of school life; she was still in the infants' class with Miss Smith but she had learned a lot since last year and was proud to be able to tell Daddy that she was top of the class in spelling and sums. She was also intrigued by the fact that Miss Smith was still wearing black clothing every day. She knew that widows wore black as a sign of mourning for their deceased husbands, but Miss Smith was a spinster! She could never ask such a personal question because it would be considered impolite: it was an unanswerable puzzle which she and her friends pondered over in the playground.

Hillary and Irene were still the best of friends. They sat together, worked together, played together, shared secrets and were inseparable. It had been noted that not only were they always together but they even looked alike and could easily be mistaken for sisters. They both had black curly hair, green eyes, similar features and were the same height. They liked the same things and both adored James. Such comments made Hillary's mother feel uncomfortable but she would laugh and say that in time she was sure they would be different.

For Charlotte the dreaded routine of being a housewife and mother had started again. Each morning she would go and meet the other mothers and join in their conversation while waiting for the school bus. No mention was ever made of her suicide attempt although they all must have thought about it privately. Irene would also wonder if her mother would be there in the afternoon: she knew that she could never rely on that again.

Charlotte's imprisonment, as she saw it, continued throughout the weekdays of a bleak and dismal January in a sleepy village where nothing seemed to have changed in centuries: the weekends were a release.

Wills had realised in the early days of their marriage that giving his wife a house-keeping allowance was the same as throwing it down the drain; she had no idea of the value of money. Considering that she was the daughter of a bank manager this had come as rather a shock. He had resolved it by doing the weekly shopping himself. That way they had enough for their needs and some left over, which he banked for a rainy day. He still had most of his inheritance invested and if Charlotte knew how much money they really had she would have had the spending spree of a lifetime. Wisely, Wills kept their financial matters to himself. John continued giving his daughter pocket money which she frittered away, usually on things for herself: new clothes, make-up, jewellery and chocolate. Wills would notice when Charlotte had something new and guessed that his father-in-law was still giving her pocket money. It made her happy, and that was all that mattered.

So, weekends were an exciting time for the whole family. After finishing work at midday on Saturday Wills would drive into Nottingham. He would take Charlotte, Irene and James to relations whilst he did the shopping and then if Forest were playing at home he would go along and support them.

The main family talking point throughout January was James's first birthday; he would be one on Tuesday, 14th February, Valentine's Day. It was decided that the celebrations should begin at the weekend; they would visit Jim and Julia at their shop on the Saturday afternoon and then go straight to Whistbury and spend Saturday night there. There would be a family party on the Sunday. Elizabeth would bake a cake and prepare a special birthday tea as well as Sunday lunch, which would relieve Charlotte of an extra catering problem, so she was delighted with the idea. James was oblivious of all the excitement but Irene was thrilled; it was going to be like 1st January all over again and she had been told that she could help open his presents.

Irene could hardly wait for that special weekend; it seemed as if it would never come. When the calendar turned to February, she was counting the days up to Saturday, 11th; it was like waiting for Christmas! After what seemed like an eternity, that important Saturday arrived at last.

They loaded the car and set off for Nottingham. Irene was really excited because she was going to see Uncle Jim and Grandpa on the same day. Cousin Martin was standing on the pavement, outside the shop, waiting for them. She always thought that the shop looked impressive, sandwiched between a greengrocer's and a chemist's, on a busy street in the city centre. Jim had bought that shop when it had been a haberdasher's and changed it to sweets and tobacco. He reckoned that the position between two shops which sold essential goods would make it into a goldmine for him; he had been right. It had a large window on each side of the door with displays in them, and a large sign above the windows and door advertising:

'Stephenson's
Tobacco & Confectionery'

There were huge blinds which were pulled down to shield the window displays on sunny days and prevent the chocolate from melting; however, most of the displays were cardboard! Young Martin was eager to show her the display in the right-hand window, which he had put together that morning; he would be ten in March and Jim had decided that it was time he started earning his pocket money. Irene was impressed, particularly, with the big heart advertising Valentine's Day. There were only two more days to buy chocolates for your valentine and Martin had made a superb display using large dummy chocolate boxes. Jim knew that on Monday he would sell more large boxes of chocolates than at any other time of the year: it would even exceed the demand on Christmas Eve. He was a shrewd businessman and prepared for Monday's onslaught with his stockroom full of expensive, top quality chocolates knowing that most men leave it until the last minute to buy them. He was also aware of his nephew's first birthday; there was a special chocolate heart put aside for James, with his name on it. It was a pity James would be unable to recognise his name; a child's first birthday is clearly more exciting for the parents and relations than it is for them: Irene had no recollection of her first birthday.

After admiring Martin's efforts they went inside and Uncle Jim kissed his niece affectionately before giving her the customary bar of chocolate; Irene and her cousin then went to his room to play cards and dominoes. The adults spent the afternoon in idle conversation and cooing over James; Julia thought he seemed a little fretful but Charlotte could see no reason for concern over her son's health. Jim usually left the shop to his assistants when his family came but there were too many customers for that and so he kept popping downstairs into the shop. His business venture had been so successful that he had another reason to celebrate: he had bought a second shop in another street, close to Nottingham Castle. His strategy was that people would call in for sweets, ice cream and cigarettes either on the way to the castle or after leaving it; his customers would not only be local people but visitors as well. Jim was certainly good at business; he would be employing more staff, and he saw it as the beginning of his empire. He told Wills that he should be doing something constructive with his inheritance instead of leaving it in the bank.

Wills was delighted at his brother's success and congratulated him. He remembered the time he had spent with Jim and Julia, after his National Service days, working in the shop before he was married. He was much happier working out in the open air; there was no way he was going to stand behind a shop counter again. He was also aware of his brother's health problems; he had failed his medical on the grounds that he had a heart murmur. He felt that Jim should be taking life easy but he seemed to thrive on work. Did he really have a serious health problem or had it been blown out of proportion to escape call up? Only Jim knew the answer to that one.

After tea they went to John and Elizabeth's; the front room was adorned with paper chains to give it a party atmosphere. The only person not in a partying mood was James but the adults did not let this spoil their enjoyment. James was put to bed in the evening and Irene kissed him on his cheek before going to bed herself. She knew that the grown-ups would be downstairs drinking and watching the television until late in the evening. Tomorrow, however, would be a great day with presents and a cake. She would go to sleep and then tomorrow would come more quickly.

It was still dark when she was woken by a lot of noise. James had something called a temperature; Grandma was concerned because he had a rash, but it was neither measles nor chickenpox; she had not seen anything like it before. The doctor arrived and then she heard Wills and Charlotte take James to the car: they were going to the hospital. She got out of bed but Grandma told her not to worry, James was ill but he was going to be looked after in hospital. Mummy had been in hospital last year and she had been made better; that thought comforted Irene as she went back to bed.

The next morning Mummy and Daddy were back but there was no party: the presents remained unopened and she was to remain with Grandpa until the evening. Wills and Charlotte spent most of the day at the hospital; they returned with grave faces and the news that their son had meningitis. Irene did not know what this was, but soon he would be better and their domestic bliss would continue. They returned to their own home and the next morning Wills went to work and Irene went to school as usual. Hillary was a comforting friend but her mind was not on her work. Why was she not allowed to visit her brother?

That evening she was taken to Hillary's home and told to stay there, with the Edisons, until they returned from the hospital. They were late back and their gaunt faces showed there was no change in his condition; Ann and Bill looked concerned. Irene and Hillary could not understand why he was not getting better if he was in a hospital. However, they were tired and did not ask questions. Wills and Charlotte took Irene home and prepared themselves for the next day, James' first birthday.

That wet Tuesday morning was one they would never forget. Wills had left for work as usual, but Mrs Bacon, still in her dressing-gown, came rushing out of her cottage and flagged him down. Few people had telephones in the village and the post office was always used as an emergency number. The hospital had called: James was dead; he had died at 6.45 am. Wills was stunned; one year ago he had been drinking champagne and celebrating the birth of his son. Now he was to mourn his death. Why? Life was unfair; he had never had the opportunity to play football with him. He would never have any of those father and son conversations; neither would he see his son grow to manhood. At that precise second all his dreams were shattered; the words were still going round in his head. Dead! Dead! No! It could not be true. He looked at Mrs Bacon's face and understood the anguish she was feeling as she uttered the words, 'I'm so sorry. Is there anything I can do?'

Wills thanked her as he fought back the tears; men do not cry.

Charlotte was collecting the milk bottles from the front doorstep when she saw Wills; her heart missed a beat. He did not notice Irene, coming down the stairs, as he shouted, in a shaky voice, to his wife, 'He's dead!'

Those were the words Irene heard; she would never see her baby brother again. On Saturday evening she had kissed him goodnight as usual and remembered him in her prayers but she had not realised that she would never see him again. She burst into tears; Wills picked her up but could find no words of comfort. Charlotte had mixed feelings of guilt and relief; she had her freedom now but what would people think?

Routine and normality were always the order of the day in rural life and Irene was sent to school as usual. After she had left, the arrangements were made but she was not told about them; that week and weekend were just the same as any other, and on the Monday Irene again went to school.

She did not see the tiny coffin outside the church, nor the pretty flowers surrounding it. She did not see it carried into the little church and placed at the front by the altar, with the angels in the window looking down. She was not with her parents and grandparents in the squire's front pew; she did not see her relatives and neighbours shedding tears, neither did she hear the church bell toll. She did not see the mourning and sadness as they said their 'goodbyes', nor hear the vicar's words about her brother; she did not participate in the singing or the prayers. She did not see that tiny coffin placed in the prepared grave behind the church because when she came home from school, it was all over. She was never allowed to say 'goodbye'.

Spring came that year after the long hard winter; but for Irene, it did not bring the usual warmth and joy. In those winter months she had learned that life was cruel and nothing could be taken for granted. She had lost her brother and she could no longer trust or rely on her mother.

Silkington, like other sleepy villages, continued living a rustic lifestyle, recognising events in the outside world only when they had an affect on them. Most of the historical and social events Charlotte recorded in her diary had no effect on village communities. As 1956 drew to a close, she looked back at her year's work; there were isolated comments about the family but *'James is dead'* and *'the funeral'*, were the only references to the loss of her son.

'The Duke of Edinburgh announces an award scheme for enterprising young people. Premium Bonds are introduced, a new government scheme where investors rely on a number selecting machine called ERNIE to select their bond number and make them rich. There's a new transatlantic telephone service. The Olympic Games are in Melbourne, Australia. A new air speed record of 1132mph has been made by a fighter plane.

In America, President Eisenhower is elected for a second term of office. In Montgomery, Alabama, a bus boycott by the black community has begun, a black woman started it all by sitting in the section of the bus allocated to whites and steadfastly refusing to move. A young Baptist minister, Martin Luther King is becoming well-known as a civil rights leader; impressed by the non-violent approach shown by the Indian, Mahatma Gandhi, he has started such protests with the aim of breaking down the barrier between white and black communities. By a non-violent boycotting of the buses and inconveniencing themselves, the black community hope to change the rules so that black people are allowed to sit anywhere on the buses, and even next to white people.

In South Africa, there's also discrimination against the black population known as 'Apartheid', which means the separation of people based on the colour of their skin; this 'Apartheid' was formally established in 1948 and laws have been passed to enforce it.

Whilst the civil rights movement is growing in the United States, the white minority in power in South Africa are remaining steadfast in keeping the black

South Africans under strict control. All Africans over the age of sixteen must carry a passbook issued by the Native Affairs Department; white employers, policemen and civil servants can ask to see this document at any time and failure to produce it may result in arrest, fine or imprisonment. Both black South Africans and black Americans know that they are going to have to fight for freedom.

At home, in Britain, our 'volcano of youth' is erupting. The 'Teddy Boys' have made their presence felt and now another youth group labelled 'Angry Young Men' are voicing their opinions through writing. John Osborne and his contemporary writers, Kingsley Amis, John Braine and Alan Sillitoe are presenting the post-war youth as it is, lost in an old, traditional and archaic society. They want change and they are the only ones who can instigate a change; the 'youth volcano' will continue to erupt until the authorities become the hardened molten rock.'

Charlotte congratulated herself on her use of language and the comparison of the youth with a volcano; she had always liked writing and found vocabulary and syntax fascinating. Writing this journal was the best thing she had done in a long time, even if Mavis had thought of it first!

'Prince Rainier of Monaco marries the actress Grace Kelly. Arthur Miller marries the actress and sex symbol Marilyn Monroe.

Elvis Presley has his first hit records, "Heartbreak Hotel", "Hound Dog" and "Love Me Tender".

Films on release this year are "The Seventh Seal", "High Society" and "The Ten Commandments".

She sighed, as she read the last entries, and closed the journal; her visits to the pictures had been sadly curtailed since her marriage.

Irene's routine continued through the remaining years of the decade; in school she progressed from the infants' class to Mrs Green's junior class and finally to Mr Sanderson and the top juniors.

The main school year began in September and as the days crawled towards Christmas the weather grew colder and the nights longer. On 11th November at 11.00 am, regardless of the weather, Mr Sanderson would assemble the entire school on the playground and remind them of those who had given their lives in the two world wars for the freedom of others; they stood in silence for two minutes and then the Head would say a prayer. This was followed by words from Binyon's poem, 'For The Fallen':

'They shall grow not old, as we that are left grow old:
Age shall not weary them, nor the years condemn.
At the going down of the sun and in the morning
We will remember them.'

The school always replied with the words, 'We will remember them'.

In December there was the end of term Nativity play and they made calendars and Christmas cards. The spring term was one with little interruption until Easter; the holiday came to coincide with the religious festival remembering the Crucifixion and Resurrection of Christ. With the exception of August, school holidays were designed specifically for worship at significant times in the Christian calendar. The next school holiday was Whitsuntide to celebrate Christ's ascension to Heaven; they were told that holidays had originally been Holy Days. As good Christians in a Christian country, people were given time off from their work to worship God, just like on Sundays.

After the Whitsun holiday in May, there were three main events which signified the end of the school year: sports day, prize giving and the annual trip to the seaside. The seaside trip was the highlight of the whole year and all the children looked forward to this special treat; it would be either Skegness or Cleethorpes. Some of the mothers came and every child took sandwiches and a bucket and spade; spending a whole day, or about five hours after the slow travelling, on a beach building sandcastles and paddling in the sea; this was every child's idea of Heaven.

An annual event in Nottingham which they always visited as a family treat in October was Goose Fair. Irene would save her September pocket money; she loved the dodgem cars, the roundabout, and picking straws or tickets to win a prize. The origin of the fair, over six hundred years ago, for the selling of geese seemed to have been forgotten. Wills would throw coconuts or shoot at the rifle range to win her a teddy bear; one year she actually won a goldfish all by herself.

On 2nd May,1959, every Nottingham Forest football supporter was jubilant: Forest were playing in the FA Cup Final against Luton at Wembley. They won 2-1; it was a weekend Nottingham would never forget. The crowds thronged the streets as the team paraded through the city on an open-top bus proudly displaying the cup. Wills took Irene into the city to see the spectacle; it was something they would both remember for the rest of their lives.

There was one other night in the year that Irene enjoyed and that was 5th November when the villagers went to a bonfire in the field behind the Hall. A massive mound of wood, cardboard, paper, old furniture and bits and pieces materialised; the aim seemed to be to create a larger bonfire than the previous year. The beginning of the mound was usually a fortnight before the Big Night and everyone in the village would make their contribution. A large fireworks display was put on by the Patterson family, who also provided the guy for the top of the mound; tradition dictated that the fire was lit by the squire at 6.30, after he had placed the guy on the top. There would be tremendous excitement as he climbed a ladder to add the final touch before setting it alight and then the colourful fireworks display started; no one seemed to notice the cold. Clad in winter woollies with warm gloves, scarves and hats they would stand mesmerised by the spectacle. After the main display people would let off their own fireworks; toffee apples and parkin, made by the mothers, were handed out.

All too soon, the excitement would come to an end and all that was left were the dying embers. A mound which had taken so long to build was reduced to ashes in little more than a couple of hours; it was all over until the following year when there would be the excitement of building an even higher mound.

The Stephenson family life carried on after James's death but for Irene and Wills life could never be the same again. Charlotte, on the other hand, felt that life was getting better; she had a part-time job with Stephen Patterson, an author who employed her during school hours to type his manuscripts. Sometimes she would carry the typewriter home and do extra hours whilst Wills was working. Weekends were still spent with members of the family and attending a church service either at Silkington or Whistbury.

Irene and Hillary remained the best of friends until a routine weekend visit to Nottingham in the autumn of 1958. They went to see Jim, whose second shop was thriving and who was thinking about buying a third shop in Derby. When they arrived Julia was leaving with two suitcases and they could hear raised voices coming from the flat. They went upstairs and were surprised to see Ann and Hillary.

During an argument between Ann and her husband, the truth regarding Hillary had slipped out: she was in fact Jim's daughter. Ann had first met Jim in 1947 when she worked in a bank in Nottingham; Martin was a baby and Jim had felt neglected by Julia. They had had an affair; when Ann realised that she was pregnant she had married to avoid the shame of being an unmarried mother and led her husband to believe that Hillary was a premature baby. She thought living in Silkington was the perfect answer to her predicament; it was unfortunate that Wills also lived there.

Ann had never been into the shop in Nottingham and had not met Wills before she came to the village. When the two girls became bosom friends she was horrified; it was even worse when comments were being made about their similarities. She had tried hard to keep the truth to herself, but the truth has a habit of coming into the foreground when it's least expected. Bill had grown suspicious and, on finding out the truth, had thrown them out.

The adults seemed to be in a state of shock but for Irene, Hillary and Martin it was an even greater blow. It explained why Irene and Hillary were so alike; they were cousins. To Irene, it seemed that the adults made the rules up as they went along; her friend was now her cousin; she had lost her brother eighteen months ago but her cousin Martin had now gained a sister.

After all the confusion it was decided that Ann and Hillary should have the flat above the second shop; Hillary was to move to a school in Nottingham leaving Irene to spend the rest of her time at Elsbridge school as a loner. When they visited Uncle Jim she was never to mention Aunt Julia and she was never to call Mrs Edison 'aunt'. Families were certainly complicated!

As the Stephenson's static family life continued throughout the decade, society was undergoing changes, which were to affect their lifestyle and which Charlotte wrote about.

1957

'January: Sir Anthony Eden resigns as prime minister because of ill health. He's succeeded by Harold MacMillan...

March: The treaty of Rome is signed in an attempt to cement relations in Europe...

October: THE SPACE AGE HAS ARRIVED! The Russians have launched Sputnik 1 into Space; it's the first time anyone has attempted to place a satellite in orbit round the Earth. The first "flying saucer" has travelled round the Earth at 17,000 mph. The Victorians would never have dreamed of such an event but now the race between Russia and America to put a man on the moon has begun...

In South Africa and America the black communities continue their struggle for equality with whites. Martin Luther King has impressed people with his successful bus boycott and has founded the Southern Christian Leadership Council (SCLC) as the focus of his civil rights movement...

In the United States in Arkansas, nine black students attempted to enrol at the all-white Little Rock Central High School; initially, they were barred on the orders of the State Governor. They suffered humiliation, and were the cause of community riots from the militant whites who objected to integration, as they persisted in their attempt to receive an education. Eventually, they were escorted into the school on the instruction of President Eisenhower; their perseverance has paid dividends and paved the way for many other black students...

The "volcano of British youth" is still erupting; the young have found an outlet for their pent-up frustration in the form of music and dance. Revolutionary singers have come on the scene bringing a breath of fresh air to music: Cliff Richard, Marty Wilde, Adam Faith and Billy Fury have all made their debut. The Angry Young Men are still writing; John Braine's "Room at the Top" has been published...

1958

January: The Common Market comes into force: France, West Germany, The Netherlands, Italy, Belgium and Luxembourg have set up a 'common market' with the aim of sharing economic growth.

February: MUNICH AIR DISASTER. The Manchester United soccer team were flying home from Belgrade after a match when the plane crashed, killing seven of them; Matt Busby, their manager has survived.

The British H-bomb has been tested on Christmas Island; people are concerned about nuclear weapons. No one can forget those killed in Hiroshima, Japan in 1945 when the atom bomb obliterated the entire city; as countries invest in nuclear arms there is considerable panic over the prospect of a nuclear war. The concern has led to the launch of the CND Movement by those Campaigning for Nuclear Disarmament. In April they set out on a peaceful demonstration march from Trafalgar Square to Aldermaston, the atomic research establishment in Berkshire; it was the first "Ban the Bomb" march and took four days to reach its destination...

The Fifties summarised: Things are changing; materialism is becoming more significant than spiritualism. The Billy Graham crusades continue, but as people become wealthier it's easier to turn away from God. There's a new element creeping into society, the idea of "keeping up with the Joneses". It's important to have a car, refrigerator and television and it's necessary to work in order to be able to afford labour-saving devices like electric vacuum cleaners and washing machines. What was once a luxury item is quickly becoming a necessity. Harold MacMillan is using the famous American slogan, "Some of our people have never had it so good"; he's adding the question, "Is it too good to last?" Only time will tell whether we're being lured into a false sense of optimism or not.

The State has taken over many of the family roles by creating a welfare system;

the extended family is breaking down. As the family units become smaller, greed and self-interest are gradually replacing the community spirit so prevalent in previous decades and throughout the war years. Socially, things are changing too: class barriers are breaking down. The tradition of the young debutantes being presented to the Queen ended in 1958; even "High Society" is aware of the changing times.

Changes can be seen in the fields of fashion and architecture. Clothes are being made to be simple and short lived as opposed to being good and durable. Coco Chanel's suit, originally designed for the twenties, is popular; Dior's last collection, in 1957, introduced the waistless "sack", popular for its ease and convenience. In footwear, the stiletto heel has been introduced and liked for its feminine look and the way it complements outfits. In architecture the same idea of convenience, rather than durability, is the order of the day; simple "blocks" have started to appear as opposed to the ornate Victorian designs. Britain's following America: the tower blocks which are already high in the skies of Manhattan will probably be over here in the sixties.

The television's increasing in popularity but is not posing a threat to films and cinema. Recently made films are: "The King and I", "Around The World in Eighty Days", "Ben Hur", "Gigi" and "Room at the Top".

In the field of science, radio telescopes at Jodrell Bank in Cheshire and Cambridge are now completed; in technology, stereo recording has begun. Russia has launched Luniks, which have photographed the far side of the moon. There's a new air speed record of 1520 mph made by a USAF pilot; the hovercraft has made its maiden voyage across the English Channel and the first section of the M1 motorway (London to Leeds) is open.

Britain has had another general election and the Conservatives were re-elected with an overall majority of one hundred seats. Mr MacMillan continues as prime minister; he's restored Britain's faith in the government after the Suez Crisis of 1956 when president Nasser of Egypt had blockaded the canal with ships in an attempt to take control of it from the Franco-British consortium.

As the fifties come to a close the decade is seen as one which has initiated change. There's a new monarch on the throne. It has been an era of fear over nuclear arms, an era which saw the Suez crisis and the beginning of the Space race; an era when youth has spoken out; an era when the black population has begun to fight for equality; an era with great advances in technology and science; an era of new music; an era which brought the "Affluent Society".

The seeds of change are growing...'

Chapter 7
Silkington–Fordingham 1960

THE CHURCH BELLS were ringing: the clock chimed twelve strokes. There was the traditional party downstairs, but the cheering seemed greater this year because they were saying 'goodbye' to a decade; farewell to the fifties and hello to the sixties!

Irene waited eight minutes and smiled; now she was ten and had reached double figures like her cousins. She reflected on the changes in her life during the fifties: starting school, James, her cousins, the family, two of her great uncles had died. However, she still had a lot of relatives, and in a few hours' time, she would be opening presents from them.

Eventually, she fell asleep; later that morning, there was the usual clearing up and the celebrating of her birthday. They were spending the weekend at Whistbury and returning on Sunday night ready for Wills to start work in the New Year.

Irene expected their family life to continue in sleepy Silkington as it had done all through the fifties. She was in for a surprise: life was going to change drastically. Wills remembered his vow when Irene was born: he wanted to live on a farm again.

Early in February, they went for a long drive into Derbyshire. Although they were adjacent Midland counties Irene was amazed at the difference in the scenery. Instead of red brick houses and privet hedges all she could see were stone cottages and stone walls. Was it really another county in England or was it another country?

They went to a large Hall, twice the size of Silkington Hall, in Fordingham, a village much larger than Silkington. It had a main road but several other roads as well; proper roads which led to other places and did not resemble cart tracks. Wills was interviewed by Lord Fordingham for the post of estate manager on his five hundred acre estate.

Wills and Charlotte went into the Hall while Irene stayed in the car. The prospect of living in such a place excited her; but Fordingham was a long way from Whistbury: Would they still see Grandpa every weekend?

Time & Tide

When they arrived back home Wills and Charlotte had a serious discussion; she was told not to mention their visit to anyone, especially Grandpa and Grandma. Adults continued to puzzle her: What was all the mystery? Either they were moving or they were staying. If they were moving her grandparents would know anyway and if they were staying, why did their little excursion have to be a secret?

Nevertheless, when they visited Whistbury on Sunday she remembered what she had been told and kept quiet about their trip into what had seemed like a foreign land. She kept looking at Grandpa, who seemed to be getting old quickly; he would be sixty on 1st April. She knew that Grandma was planning a surprise party and that was something she had to keep quiet about as well. Irene was beginning to wonder if all adults ever did was keep secrets from each other: What was the point of that?

She did not have to keep the secret of their visit to Fordingham for long. On Saturday, 20th February, Wills told her that they would be moving on Monday week. Just think – 29th February, the day that only comes once every four years!

That Saturday afternoon they went to see Mavis and Gerald and, also, Jim to tell them the news. At Uncle Jim's Irene had another surprise; Aunt Julia had returned from her self-imposed exile. Martin greeted Irene with the delightful news; he had really missed his mother and found it difficult to accept Ann Edison as a substitute.

Martin was thirteen, almost fourteen; he had passed the eleven plus examination and now went to the grammar school. Each time she saw him he would tell her of his new lifestyle there; she had realised that if she passed this test when she was eleven a whole new range of subjects would be available to her. The prospect of learning Latin and French thrilled her; then there were sciences, she would belong to a 'house' and there would be competitions between the 'houses'. Martin played rugby and cricket but she would learn to play hockey and tennis. These exciting thoughts kept whizzing round in her head; she knew she must work hard and pass this eleven plus examination.

However, on that Saturday, they had more important things to discuss, rather than school. His reunion with his mother had overwhelmed him; he had not expected her to return having received only birthday and Christmas cards with money in them since her departure eighteen months ago. They did not know that she had been staying with a distant cousin in the West Country and earning a living as a barmaid. She said that her reason for returning was that she missed her family and had decided to forgive Jim for his 'slight indiscretion'!

The adults wondered if her return had anything to do with Jim's continued success. He had at last found a third shop in Derby and Ann was originally going to look after the Nottingham shops while he moved on to Derby. Julia's return meant a change of plan however: she and Jim were to stay in Nottingham while Ann and Hillary moved to Derby. Ann was not overjoyed at the thought of moving again; neither was Hillary because she was settled at school and did not want to find herself as the 'new girl' yet again. However, as the children knew only too well, they did not have a say in these changes. Such decisions were made by grown-ups who should know what to do for the best. The children often wondered whether the decisions they made were based on good judgement or insanity.

On that Saturday afternoon, when it was clear that all of their lives were to change and they had no control over the changes which were to affect them, Hillary joined Irene and Martin in his room. Would they see each other as often? Irene was to be in a village near Buxton in the Peak District, Martin would remain in Nottingham, whilst Hillary was in Derby. The three places were miles apart; they had been thrown together as family and now they were being separated. They had, in their short lives, learned that life was upsetting, even at times cruel: this was just another episode which confirmed that fact.

They rejoined the adults when Wills and Charlotte were about to leave. For the first time Irene noticed the similarities in the appearance of all three women: fair hair, a light brown but not blonde, they all permed their hair to give it waves and curls, and all had a left side parting; their facial features were similar although their eye colours differed; they all wore make-up and a prominent red lipstick and their statures were similar, about five feet in height, considerably shorter than Jim and Wills. The Stephenson family were much taller, almost six feet and the children seemed to favour their fathers more than their mothers in looks and height. They were all growing quickly; Martin was already five feet-nine inches tall and had earned himself the name of 'lanky' all through school.

The family returned to Silkington and prepared for Sunday. They were going to tell John and Elizabeth that they were moving to Derbyshire. Their new home would be about one and a half hour's drive from Whistbury, so they would only be visiting once a month in the future.

Charlotte knew that her father would be disappointed, but at least she was happy to support her husband in his choice of employment and they were going to live in a pretty little village; John and Elizabeth would be able to come and stay with them.

For Charlotte, there was one further problem; she had never cooked a Sunday roast in her life!

Although it was too early for the pretty blossom, Almond Blossom Avenue looked more attractive than usual that Sunday. As expected the news was not greeted with enthusiasm and Sunday dinner was a quiet affair. That was to be the last of the weekly visits which had taken place almost without a break since their marriage in 1948; leaving that afternoon was very emotional. They promised to come in the middle of March and unbeknownst to John they would be coming in the evening of 1st April for his surprise party.

That last week of February was one which Irene would never forget. She did not have a lot of things of her own but she packed them all very carefully into boxes, only keeping with her the one big teddy bear which Daddy had given her on her fifth birthday. She had found it very comforting, particularly after James's death. Saying 'goodbye' to her classmates was easy; she had not had a close friend since Hillary had gone to Nottingham. There was one thing she seemed destined never to discover, one of life's mysteries forever: Why did Miss Smith always wear black? A strong element of sadness in leaving Silkington lay in what they were leaving behind: a part of them was to remain in Silkington forever. James was to lie in a grave in the little church cemetery: nothing could change that. The last 'goodbyes' were said on the Sunday to neighbours and village friends who all wished Wills every success and happiness – and meant it. When they spoke to Charlotte, it was out of politeness; they did not think that she would make any more effort to accept rural life in Derbyshire than she had with them.

That was the first Sunday that Charlotte attempted a Sunday dinner, a very basic egg and chips, far from the traditional roast. Her excuse was that she did not have the time because they were too busy preparing for the next day; she promised to cook them a proper roast dinner in their new home next Sunday.

On the Monday morning, with a last lingering look at what had been their home since they married, Wills locked the door of the empty cottage and took the keys to Graham Williams. He and Irene travelled in the car whilst Charlotte went in the removal van.

They reached Fordingham in the early afternoon. Irene could not believe the size of their new home, the estate manager's cottage. The men were taking their possessions in through the back door from the van parked in a massive courtyard; a yard big enough to house all three of the cottages and backyards in Elsbridge

Lane. On one side of this yard was the back of the Hall; a large brick building with four floors including the cellars and original servants' quarters which were located in what was known as the 'basement'. The doors to the 'basement' area led off from the courtyard; Irene looked up and saw the massive chimneys towering over the battlements. The cottage was situated at the side of the Hall, and what lay beyond the courtyard was more than Irene could ever have imagined.

She walked up the three steps to the back door and found herself in the kitchen, which was twice the size of their previous one, but it had a similar kitchen range with a fireplace and oven. She continued exploring, across the room two doors were open; one was a proper walk-in pantry and the other led into a hall. At the far end was the estate office, but in between that and the kitchen were the lounge and staircase. Opposite the stairs was the front door which led outside to a patio area and some steps leading down to their private lawn and garden. She walked first into the lounge where their three-piece-suite had already been placed and then into the office, already furnished with a desk, shelves, chairs and a telephone! There was another door leading outside; she noticed that the office door could be locked. From this room her father was going to be running the estate; she would see more of him now and that had to be better!

She ventured upstairs to where Charlotte was organising things. On seeing her daughter, Charlotte called her to come and look at her room; she went into the first door on her right and was amazed at its size. Her small carpet and basic furniture seemed lost in it; the window looked out on to the garden, as all the bedroom windows did. Next to her room was a slightly smaller bedroom, which would remain unfurnished for the time being, and at the far end of the corridor was a bathroom. It had a proper bath, toilet and washbasin: No more Friday nights bringing the bathtub into the kitchen! At the other end of the corridor, beyond the stairs and over the office, was the largest bedroom; the furniture looked lost in there as well. Irene thought she was dreaming and pinched herself – but it was true. This was her new address:

Orchard Cottage,
Fordingham Hall,
Fordingham,
Nr. Buxton,
Derbyshire.

Some cottage! It had an office, three bedrooms, a hall, staircase, a proper bathroom and their own nice garden. She unpacked her few possessions and put them away.

Wills spent the afternoon in his new office, acquainting himself with the files and map of the estate. Tomorrow, he would call his workforce in individually, and try to establish a good working relationship with each of them. Wills was a fair man but he would not tolerate any kind of slacking on the job. If a job was worth doing, it was worth doing well; his father had taught him that and he always put every effort into everything he did.

Charlotte was organising the home and that did not take long; the carpets and furniture were soon in place, even though they looked out of place in such large rooms. She was happy at last. She liked this larger cottage; it had a proper bathroom and for the first time since Irene's birth, Charlotte was content to be a housewife and mother. She was not the Lady of the Manor (that was Lady Fordingham who lived next door), but she was already planning a new look for their new home. She had saved some money from her typing job. What she hadn't let on to Wills was that in the early years of the fifties she had taught herself to be more careful with money. In fact, the whole decade of the fifties had been a learning experience for Charlotte! By teatime they were all hungry and she cooked their first meal in their new home; for the second time in two days they enjoyed egg and chips. After all the excitement they slept well, and the next morning they ate breakfast together round the table in the kitchen. Afterwards, Wills went to work in his office just along the corridor, but any ideas that Irene had of interrupting him were soon squashed when she found that the door was locked on the inside. That morning he interviewed each of his staff, starting with the head gardener who lived in the smaller cottage on the estate.

Alan Stanton was a gardener by profession but his present post was also deputy estate manager. So, in his five years of working for Lord Fordingham, he had become familiar with farming life and was capable of organising the farm labourers in the estate manager's absence. In fact, he had been in command for ten days since Wills' predecessor had left.

Wills was pleased to see Alan standing outside his office door at 9.30 am as instructed; he liked people to be punctual.

They first discussed the 'market gardens', where vegetables and fruit were grown both for sale to the public and for the family and estate staff; this was one of the perks of the job: vegetables would be free from now on. Then they discussed each of the five greenhouses, and then the flower gardens, maze, lawns, orangery, three orchards and conservatory. The greenhouses contained plants for sale to the public at regular intervals throughout the year and also for planting out in borders. The orchards produced apples, pears and plums for them and for sale. All sales had to be recorded by the head gardener and certified by the estate manager; Lord Fordingham would ask for all the estate books twice a year and Wills knew that there was no room for mistakes. The money which he banked in the Gardens Account had to tally with the accounts in the head gardener's ledger.

After discussing the management of the gardens they moved on to where Wills' heart really was, the farm. He had a close affinity with nature; it was something inbred in him, inherited from his father and grandfather. Farming had been their love, life and livelihood; Wills was a chip off the old block! There were cattle, sheep and horses, land to be harvested and woods to be looked after. They went through the stock book and movement records for the animals and sorted out their work programmes, establishing when extra staff were required and where they came from. Open days and harvesting were the main occasions when extra hands were needed and the young people from the village could be relied on to assist.

After their conversation Wills looked across his desk at this plant-loving man; born in 1925 in the village and educated at the village school, he spent four years working as a locksmith in Buxton before being called up. After the war he had decided to find a job doing what he really liked, and found a gardening job at another Hall in a nearby village. He was promoted to assistant gardener and then moved to his present post in 1955. His wife, Mary, worked part-time in one of the village shops and their son, Daniel was ten and attended the local school. Wills liked this man and was sure that they would work well together; he liked his sense of humour and love of nature. Alan was about five foot six inches tall and clean-shaven, his blond hair was parted on the right, he had blue eyes and a protruding nose which overshadowed his small mouth and gleaming teeth. He was also rather plump which Wills assumed was due to living off the fat of the land.

After their discourse Wills met the two garden assistants and four farm labourers; these seven people were his responsibility. Two of the farmers lived on the estate with their wives in the stable flats and the other four came in daily. The gardening staff, Mark Adams and Billy Foster, were the youngest: both seventeen, they had come to work on the estate after leaving school; they lived in the village and were the best of friends. Wills decided their appearance and attitude were good. Alan had spoken highly of them, he had known them since they were born and Wills felt sure he would be satisfied with them. They were happy to continue helping out on the farm side of the estate and had a convivial nature; they were typical, easygoing, rural lads.

He moved on to his farm staff. Two who lived on the estate took it in turns to do the morning feeds, but there were no milking herds, which Wills thought was a blessing. John Bateman lived in one of the stable flats and Luke Morton in the other. Both of their wives worked daily in the Hall. These two men were 'on duty' on alternate weeks during the evenings for emergencies alongside either Wills or Alan. Such duties were a part of their conditions of service and for which they received free accommodation, rates, coal and electricity; their pay was almost like pocket money. The men accepted the fact that at certain times the hours were long and the job demanding with no overtime, but their love of animals and perks of living in such a beautiful place meant that they were happy to accept such conditions.

His last two employees were strictly nine-to-five people; it was a fair day's work for a fair day's pay. Fred and Bobby, local bachelors in their early twenties, saw the work as a job and not a vocation; they received vegetables and fruit like the rest of the staff but at harvest times they were paid overtime.

After interviewing his staff, Wills took a tour round the estate. Whilst he was thus occupied Charlotte was unpacking the few remaining boxes, laying the stair carpet and putting up curtains; Irene followed her around like a shadow. The stair carpet covered the stairs but not the hall and landing; their four carpets were placed in the kitchen, lounge and two bedrooms but they did not possess any spare for the third bedroom or bathroom. Neither did she have curtains for those rooms; the curtains which she had already put up were too small for the windows and so they did not close properly. It was fortunate that spring and summer were on the way and not autumn and winter! She knew that Lord Fordingham paid for wallpaper and paint, but not labour. Suddenly, the idea of spending her time decorating seemed quite appealing; when this was done she could buy curtains and carpets to match and there was the third bedroom to furnish. She thought about the £65 she had saved; it could be her contribution and that should please Wills.

That evening was the end of a perfect day in the Stephenson home; Wills turned out to be totally responsive to Charlotte's idea of redecoration. 'Good idea. I'll ask for the pattern books. Which room first?'

'The lounge.'

'Mmm. You really think so? You haven't wallpapered before. Mary and Alan have done their cottage. We can ask them for some tips and advice.' He paused. 'Let's start with our room. We can practise on rooms that people aren't going to see first.'

'You're probably right.' Charlotte really wanted to do the lounge first because she hated the large floral print. However, she could not fault her husband's logic. Then much to her surprise he said,

'The car's getting old. It may not get us to Nottingham now the journey's further. I think I'll trade it in for a newer one and perhaps a television and a fridge as well.'

Neither Irene nor Charlotte could believe their ears. Charlotte did not know about her husband's extra effort at saving money, or that some investments he had made on his father-in-law's advice had yielded some good dividends.

Irene had noticed that they had a telephone but was disappointed to hear that it was for work purposes only, but they could receive incoming calls. That had put paid to her idea of phoning Grandpa!

That first week was one of discovery and excitement for Irene. On the Wednesday, Charlotte decided it was time to investigate the village; she and Irene began the walk round the rough-surfaced and very stony lane which led from the courtyard, through the orchard, to the staff drive (the preferred name for the tradesmen's entrance!). Eventually, they reached the end of this equally stony track, flanked by trees; hidden beyond those trees were green pastures, which were named the upper and lower paddocks, and farm buildings. On the Buxton Road they turned left and walked past a field and six detached stone properties, all standing in their own grounds, before reaching the 'T' junction. They turned right onto the main road and went past a proper post office, a grocery shop, butchers, newsagents, two public houses, many cottages and some larger houses before reaching the church. Next to the church was the school – another grey stone building with high windows and, like Elsbridge School, Victorian in style.

Charlotte took her through the girls' cloakroom area, into the main school building. Mr Blake, a youngish looking man of about thirty, was seated at his desk at the front of a classroom next to the familiar stove, surrounded by a guard. Charlotte thought he seemed too young to be a headmaster, but then this was a small rural school. He wore dark-rimmed glasses and his hair was black, slowly going grey. When he stood up to greet them she could see that he was of slim build and over six feet in height, taller than her husband. He was towering over them and smiled politely as he introduced himself; he already knew who they were. Every newcomer is known about before they arrive in village communities, and he had been expecting her to come and register Irene some time that week.

One boy in that room had seen Irene before: Daniel Stanton. He had seen her at the bedroom window looking down at their garden on Monday, but she had not noticed him walking up the lane on his way back to school. Now that she was closer to him he could see her attractive green eyes, her happy, smiling face and her black, natural curly hair. Soon the boys would be swarming round her; he wanted to be the first, and the last; she was going to be his childhood sweetheart.

Irene knew of Danny's existence but had no idea what he looked like. She was occupied telling Mr Blake about her achievements in her previous school and oblivious of what was happening in the classroom. It was decided that she would begin on the following Monday.

They left the school and sauntered round the village; it was so much larger than Silkington. Behind the church and school and beyond the main road, they found a recreation ground with swings, a seesaw and a roundabout. There was also a cricket pitch, and the Village Institute where they held all kinds of community activities. It seemed as if the village had grown between the church and the Hall. On the other side of the main road, behind the properties, the River Dove was flowing slowly through the village.

This pretty village could trace its history back to Anglo-Saxon days; it had been named 'Fordingham' because the only way into what was originally only a small community was over a ford. The River Dove flowed in a semi-circular fashion round the village, isolating it from the rest of civilisation and protecting it from invasion in bygone days. 'Ham' was the old English word for village; hence the name, 'Fordingham'. Lord Fordingham could trace his ancestry to medieval days when the lord was the 'Lord of the Manor'. The land between the church and the Hall had originally belonged to the Fordingham Estate, but had been sold off piece by piece as the village developed.

There was only one place left to explore after the village, and that was the estate; Wills took his family on a stroll round the gardens and some of the fields. Their cottage was surrounded by the estate orchards; hence its name, Orchard Cottage.

Wills led them to the staff drive where they could see the paddocks and farm buildings; an area already familiar to Irene. Then they went in the opposite direction and came to another courtyard; the top courtyard where there were stables and two flats. Half of the stable block had been converted for garaging the family cars; but in the remaining stable area were three beautiful horses; one was chestnut brown and the other two dapple grey. They were ridden by Lady Fordingham, and by her children when they were home from boarding school; it was Bobby's job to look after them and keep them groomed. Going through the courtyard led them round to the front of the Hall and main drive, an 'out of bounds' area to staff unless working there. Wills made it very clear to Irene that she must never venture beyond that point; she could see that the front entrance was impressive with gardens and trees and that the drive was approached from the main road. Irene worked out that if she turned left at the 'T' junction in the village, instead of right she would eventually come to that entrance and at least be able to look up it at the flowers and trees, even if she was not allowed to actually walk up it. On the other side of the Hall beyond the front entrance, Wills told them that there were gardens, a maze and a massive lawn leading down to the River Dove. Sadly, it was an 'out of bounds' area! She could only imagine what it was like.

Wills took them back through the courtyard, down the lane past their garden and beyond the orchards; the lane eventually led to the fields and woods. Before they reached the fields there were five greenhouses with hundreds of plants which would be sold to the public, the 'market gardens', and the gardener's cottage. This smaller cottage had only a lounge, kitchen, two bedrooms and a bathroom.

After seeing what they were allowed to see, Wills took them through some of the fields and one of the woods.

Irene found the whole place overwhelming; there were more sheep and cows than she had ever seen and she was a country girl! She was also a lucky girl to be living on a lord's country estate.

That weekend it seemed strange not seeing any relatives and she missed Grandpa; the previous weekend's missed visit did not affect her so much because she was preoccupied with moving. Now, she was settled and had seen the village and estate; the only real excitement of the weekend was Charlotte's first attempt at cooking roast lamb. They were surprised to find that their Sunday roast was at least edible; it was enjoyed with potatoes and vegetables grown on the estate.

After dinner they spent ages looking through the wallpaper samples, although they were only decorating the one room, they were planning for all of them. Mary Stanton had promised to help Charlotte start stripping their bedroom paper on

Monday afternoon, after her shift at the shop. Wills then suggested the most sensible thing would be to move into the third bedroom. If only they had thought about that on Monday! Once again they were moving furniture.

Monday morning came and Irene was up bright and early to walk to her new school; she had lived in Fordingham for a week but had not met any of the village children. She went into the schoolyard which was much smaller than her previous one, and there was neither a field nor a sandpit, which she found disappointing. She waited for the door to open; when it did, the headmaster emerged and rang a handbell. This was something new; she was used to a whistle being blown.

Mr Blake sat her at a front desk in the middle column of double desks. There were only eighteen children in the room, the entire number of years two, three and four junior children in the village. In the other room were the infants and first year juniors taught by Mrs Aster; Irene had made the school roll total thirty-four.

She was in the column with year three children; there were only six of them, including Daniel Stanton who was sitting two desks behind her. There were four pupils in year four who would be moving to secondary schools in Buxton in September and eight in year two, the largest year in the school.

The morning seemed to drag by; at break the two girls who sat behind her in class introduced themselves as Jane Benton and Katy Langton. Jane was a plump, round-faced girl with glasses and ginger hair, known affectionately by her peers as 'ginger nut'. Her family owned the grocery shop on the main road; it was her birthday on Friday and she was having a party on Saturday; she invited Irene, which Irene thought was a nice thing to do, it made her feel welcome. She was going to ask Charlotte if she could go and then she remembered, this weekend they were going to Nottingham on Saturday and returning Sunday. Sadly, she explained why she must refuse the invitation.

Katy was a tall, blonde, country lass and much quieter than Jane; she lived in a large house near the cricket ground. Her mother stayed at home and had coffee mornings; she was a pillar of village society. Her father was an accountant with offices in Buxton. Next year she was being sent away to boarding school; she would not be sitting the eleven plus or competing for a place at the Fordingham Grammar School.

Whilst the girls were engaged in conversation Daniel was watching from a distance. Mr Blake rang the bell at the end of break and they went inside for the second part of the morning. At lunchtime Jane and Katy walked with Irene until they reached their homes; she was walking alone for the last few yards along the Buxton Road when Daniel, who had been walking behind them, saw his opportunity. He shouted, 'Irene!'

Irene turned round, amazed that anyone should be shouting her name; she looked at him, there was something about him that made him special. She had vaguely noticed him in school and had seen him on the estate a couple of times. Now, she was really seeing him for the first time; his blond hair, blue eyes, and his gleaming teeth were smiling at her; in looks he certainly resembled his father.

'It's Daniel, isn't it?'

'Yes but most people call me Danny.'

'What do you want?'

'I'm walking up to the Hall as well. Why don't we walk together?'

They were only ten years old but both knew that there was a mutual attraction between them; she had had a 'relationship' with one boy, Martin and she had learned something about the differences in the sexes; having a boyfriend was different from having a girlfriend. She assumed that her feelings for all boys would be the same, but in that short walk she realised she was wrong. She felt something for Daniel and she certainly wanted to be his friend but this was so different from her feelings for her cousin: feelings were certainly strange. What was happening to her?

There was little time for conversation on that first short walk home; Charlotte had lunch ready and Wills asked his daughter about her morning. She told him about Jane and Katy and her start in Arithmetic and English. It was so nice to come home in the middle of the day and have a proper meal with Mummy and Daddy. Charlotte was preoccupied with the thoughts of paper stripping; she had seen Mary come home in time to prepare dinner. When the men were back at work and the children at school they were going to make a start! Irene found her mind wandering to Daniel all through lunch; she did not know why this boy should occupy her thoughts. Love was something she had heard about and read in books; it was the material that films were made of but the idea of it happening to her had never entered her head.

After the meal, it was time to return to school; Wills was back in his office and Irene said goodbye to her mother. Daniel was waiting for her on the lane; she found herself unusually tongue-tied. He seemed in command of the situation and told her a lot about a new type of country life. Life on a lord's estate certainly sounded different from life in a sleepy village; it was like a new world, a world of affluence which few people are privileged to experience. She had not met any of the

Time & Tide

Fordingham's but knew that she had to address them as 'Lord' and 'Lady' or 'Your Lordship' and 'Milady' and the children as 'Master' or 'Miss'. From Daniel she learned that Master Thomas was fourteen, Miss Lucille, twelve and the youngest, Miss Susan, ten; they would be coming home soon for the Easter holidays. Irene's relationship with Daniel was growing but it was difficult; he seemed so mature and she could not talk to him in the same way that she talked with Hillary, Jane or Katy.

That weekend Wills was 'off duty'; the Stephenson family went to Whistbury. The first weekend was an emotional reunion; they had not seen John and Elizabeth for three whole weeks. It was the longest period Charlotte had ever spent away from her parents and she had begun to realise how awful it must be to be orphaned. The time passed by quickly because there was so much to tell them. John was amazed to hear that Charlotte had started decorating a room; as a child she had always stayed well away from painting and decorating, it was too messy for her. Irene had started at a new school and had new friends but the best news came from John and Elizabeth; after almost eight years of marriage Mavis was pregnant, they were expecting their first child in September. There was to be another cousin!

When they left on Sunday afternoon they wished John a happy birthday for 1st April and said they would be back for Easter later in April. Irene knew they were telling lies when she had always been taught to tell the truth. Adults make the rules up as they go along and change them when it suits them. Is it any wonder children become confused?

The first of April was a great day, Wills was 'off duty'; John had been deliberately detained at the bank by a colleague and Elizabeth had spent the whole day preparing food and getting things ready, just as she had on New Year's Eve. When he opened the front door he found his family and friends all waiting for him, and he was greeted with a chorus of 'Happy Birthday'. Elizabeth wheeled the trolley out of the kitchen; it had a beautifully iced cake on it with *'Happy Birthday'* and *'60'* nicely piped on the top, and illuminated with candles. John attempted to blow them out; with Irene's help he managed it on the second attempt. A smiling John, now realising that he had been deliberately delayed, was going to enjoy the rest of the evening. He kissed his wife fondly on the cheek and uttered, 'Thank you, darling!'

He knew he was lucky to have such a supportive and caring wife; he then kissed his daughter and granddaughter as they gave him presents. Charlotte and Wills had bought him a new briefcase and Irene, with her own pocket money, had bought him a pair of cufflinks. He told Irene how much he liked them and then to her delight replaced the ones he was wearing with them.

The party went with a swing just as it had on New Year's Eve. There was plenty to drink, the decorations were up and Charlotte was at her usual place, the piano stool. This party was one that Irene was allowed to stay up for, well, at least until 10.00 pm She was then ushered to bed, but she could still hear her mother playing. As usual, she finished the evening with 'Danny Boy'; the song had a new meaning for her now because she had her own 'Danny Boy'.

On the Saturday afternoon they went into Nottingham and saw Uncle James and Aunt Julia well and truly reunited. The shops were doing well; there were still two weeks before Easter and Jim was optimistic about the takings from his Easter egg sales. Irene was able to spend some time with Martin; she found she could tell him all about her new home and school but she could not mention Daniel. This was strange, he had always been like a big brother to her and she had thought that she would always be able to tell him everything about her life. Martin still felt protective of his younger cousin but he, too, had secrets. There were things which he could not discuss with her; he was fourteen now and aware of the fact that he was on the threshold of manhood. They were both sadly leaving childhood behind them, for the emotional turmoil which life as an adult would inevitably bring them.

On the Sunday they enjoyed their family meal; the Sundays in Whistbury were going to be more precious now that there were fewer of them. It was soon time to go and the 'farewell' was quite emotional. John had given his daughter £5; he was still giving her pocket money despite their rise in living standards, but now it would be a monthly contribution instead of a weekly one. Likewise, Irene's pocket money increased to 10 shillings a month; both daughter and granddaughter were ecstatic. They waved a sad goodbye as they left the avenue and headed back to Derbyshire.

If only they had known what fate had in store for them. So often if we had had insight into the future we would have played our hand of cards differently, we would have chosen different words and actions.

On Good Friday, in the evening, just hours before they were due to return to Whistbury, the phone rang in the office. Charlotte answered it; she was surprised to hear her mother's voice and devastated to hear what she had to say.

'Oh Charlotte, your father's had a heart attack. He's de...de...dead.'

'Dead, No! No! He can't be.' Charlotte was getting hysterical, which only made Elizabeth's tears worse. There was a few seconds silence between the two women; they both had their private thoughts. Why hadn't their last words been, 'I love you'.

Did he know just how much they loved him? Had he died in pain? What had caused the attack?

Irene had followed her mother into the office and heard that awful word again, 'dead'. She wasn't sure who, but from her mother's reaction, she guessed it was her beloved Grandpa. Life had dealt yet another bitter blow. Charlotte turned to Irene, 'Go and find your father. He's somewhere in the gardens with Mr Stanton.'

Irene ran out of the cottage with tears streaming down her face. She went through the side orchard and looked across to the gardens; there was no sign of them. She turned and walked towards the greenhouses, Wills was in the middle one and saw his tearful daughter coming towards them. 'Daddy, Daddy,' she shouted and then remembered that she had been told never to shout in case there were guests of the Fordingham family in the vicinity. Shouting and dropping litter were totally forbidden. This thought made her cry all the more.

'What's the...?' He was unable to complete the question as Irene uttered through a veil of tears,

'Daddy, Daddy. Grandpa's dead.'

Wills recalled his own father's sudden death in 1944 and the heartache it caused. He, choking back his own tears, told her to go home and tell her mother that he was on his way.

Alan said that he would deputise if he wanted to leave right then. Wills thanked him and walked into what had been such a happy home for six weeks to find his wife and daughter in floods of tears. This time Charlotte knew what true grief was really like.

Wills asked what had happened and, through the tears, he gathered that John had been suffering from what he thought was indigestion for a couple of days. Then, suddenly, he got up from his chair to go into the kitchen and collapsed. Elizabeth heard him shout in pain and went to see what the problem was, but he had died instantly, the doctor said from a massive heart attack; there was nothing anyone could have done.

Wills drove his wife and daughter over to Whistbury. Mrs Maycock was in the lounge with Elizabeth; the whole avenue was shocked by the sudden death of a man they all respected. The pretty blossom on the trees seemed so out of place. Charlotte rushed over to her mother yet neither of them knew what to say.

Mrs Maycock broke the silence with, 'I'll make another pot of tea.' Edna Maycock remembered the Coronation Day that she and her husband had spent in that very room watching the television. They had accepted and enjoyed John's hospitality then, and only two weeks ago they had all been in that room celebrating the good man's birthday. He did not deserve to die: he was too young: he should have been allowed to enjoy retirement with his wife. Sadly, the cruel hand of fate had intervened. Edna went into the kitchen, taking Irene with her, thinking that the adults should be left alone.

Wills had been through this scenario before; he asked questions and decided what was to be done. John's body had already been taken for an autopsy to ascertain the reason for death. No one doubted the cause but John had been in good health and had not had the need of a medical practitioner in years. Under the law, the doctor was unable to provide the necessary death certificate because it was a 'sudden death'; it had to be reported to the coroner and then John's body would have to suffer the indignity of a post-mortem. This and the holiday period meant a delay in registering the death; it could not be done until next week. John had been a careful and thorough man all his life; his will and funeral arrangements had been left with his solicitor. It was late in the evening and there was little point in contacting him then.

Edna brought in the freshly-made pot of tea. Wills decided it was best to leave everything else until the morning; he thanked her and she left the grieving family. Irene was the only one who slept that night; Elizabeth lay awake clutching her husband's pillow and thinking about their wedding day, when they had vowed to stay together and love each other until death separated them. She was not prepared for it even if it was Good Friday, the day of Christ's Crucifixion; for her that was just a sad irony, the thought of going to church on Sunday and rejoicing at the Resurrection was just to much to bear; she wanted to cancel Easter but that was impossible.

Wills, in the next bedroom, was comforting his wife, who thought fathers were immortal, she could not envisage a future without him; he had been her idol and her 'cash box'. Was God punishing her for being a bad mother? Elizabeth had no reason to feel guilty but Charlotte was filled with guilt.

The next morning Wills phoned the solicitor at home; he was a friend of the family and fortunately not on holiday. He came immediately with the will, which included John's funeral wishes, and he assured Elizabeth that she was financially provided for. Charlotte had an inheritance of £1,000 and a sum of £500 was to be held in trust for Irene until she was twenty-one. Even money did not console Charlotte.

Time & Tide

The vicar arrived uttering his usual, well-rehearsed condolences; they decided that the service would be held on Friday, and it would be as John had planned. Wills continued to inform people; he was the bearer of bad tidings at a time when people were preparing for a celebration. When Edna offered to prepare the food for afterwards, a new lease of life seemed to come to Elizabeth; she had prepared so many meals and parties in her kitchen and no one else was going to take over; she was going to do the 'wake' and do her husband proud!

They had a sad Easter Sunday together; Wills returned to work on Monday to allow Alan some time away with his family; he left Charlotte and Irene with Elizabeth, but returned on Friday for the funeral. This time Irene was allowed to say her 'goodbye'. Easter, like Valentine's Day, would never be the same again.

By the time May Day had come, four months of the year had gone. In those four months Irene's life had changed beyond belief: she had a new home, new school, new friends in a new village, her Grandpa had died, she was experiencing new emotions, she was slowly growing up!

Throughout the following months, despite being shaken by John's death, they continued settling into their new home. Charlotte enjoyed decorating; she gave each room a new look. Irene chose the wallpaper for her own room: a cream background with small floral design because she felt it would make her room seem brighter. The third bedroom was given plain paper and then emulsioned in white. The landing, stairs, hall and lounge were also papered in a basic white and then emulsioned. The kitchen had a pale blue washable paper.

The furnishing of the third bedroom was a family shopping occasion. The final decision was a multi-coloured carpet and curtains, twin beds with a table between them and a unit consisting of a combined wardrobe and dressing table, modern furniture that would be completely practical. Finally, there was a bedside lamp and an alarm clock.

Wills decided to spoil his little girl and bought her a dressing table and desk; after all, she was growing up and needed more than a bed and wardrobe. He also bought the promised refrigerator and, before Christmas, he rented a television set, which they christened with the first episode of 'Coronation Street'.

Charlotte was happy to play her part in setting up their home; she bought the carpets and felt a certain amount of pride in being able to contribute from her own funds.

A new car was the final item on their shopping list; Charlotte decided that this was her ideal opportunity to learn to drive. A car had been launched in 1959 called the 'Mini': a compact, economical, box-like vehicle with a front-wheel drive engine. She had looked at both the standard and deluxe model but naturally favoured the deluxe at £537. She said that she would buy the new family car out of her inheritance money if Wills would teach her to drive. At first he was reluctant but eventually gave in to her insistent persuasion.

For Irene, every day in her new environment was a fresh experience. When she returned to school after Easter her friendship with Jane and Katy developed; they would spend their breaks together chatting in the playground, playing ball games or skipping. Sometimes, after school, they would go to the recreation ground and play on the swings; on other occasions they went to Jane's home and Mrs Benton would gave them crisps and lemonade while they listened to records and chatted. Jane's elder sister, Emma, attended the secondary modern school and she learned a lot about what happened to girls when they reached teenage years from her; she was only too keen to share her information with Irene and Katy.

Emma had reached puberty and the first stage of womanhood; she was old enough to have babies and had a boyfriend; Mrs Benton was always warning her not to 'go too far'. Unfortunately, that was the only information which Jane had: they were left wondering what 'going too far' meant. They had realised that babies came from the woman but how they got there was still a mystery. Irene recalled the time when she had first seen her brother; she remembered that her questions regarding the differences in the sexes had been craftily avoided by her parents.

On the farm her life was even more exciting. She watched lambs being born and bottle-fed two orphaned ones. Wills showed her how to pick up lambs by their front legs and carry them into the paddock; she loved to see these newly born creatures instinctively rise to their feet and make their first bleat. She got on well with all the estate staff and would often give a helping hand with the feeding or movement of animals from one pasture to another. That summer holiday was the happiest one she had ever had; she was outdoors most of the time and with her father. As the year progressed calves were born; pheasants were reared for the shoots and there was the harvest. After a year on the estate, Irene was glad she was a farmer's daughter; the land and outdoor life had so much more to offer than a street in the city.

Hillary and Martin both came and spent some time with them during that summer holiday; their lives had also changed but somehow they had adjusted. Grandma had taken all of her clothes, apart from her fur coat and black evening dress, to the church jumble sale; she had bought a completely new wardrobe, everything was black which reminded Irene of Miss Smith, her infant teacher from those almost forgotten days at Elsbridge School. Sadly, along with the clothes Grandma had lost her love and zest for life; a part of her had died with Grandpa. She continued with her household chores, just as she always had; she kept a nice house and garden so that her husband would continue to be pleased with her as his widow. She was still a bank manager's widow: appearances were still important, but she seldom smiled. The family made regular visits to Whistbury and sometimes Grandma came and stayed with them.

The village had an annual cycle of its own, but different from Silkington's; there was cricket in the summer and a harvest festival supper after all the farms in the area had gathered their crops in. Bonfire Night was an even bigger spectacle than the grand occasion it had been in Silkington. There were regular dances, fetes, jumble sales, coffee mornings, bingo sessions, whist and beetle drives in the Village Institute, organised by the WI or the church; Katy's mum seemed to have a hand in most of them.

The church had electricity, a proper organ instead of a piano and was much larger than Silkington Church, it was very much the focal point of the community. There was a rich blue carpet on the floor in the aisles and the nave going right up to the altar; there were stained-glass windows all round, but no angels over the altar looking down, just doves; there were choir stalls and a vestry (Irene did not even know what one of those was!). The Church of John the Baptist was very impressive but it did not have the strange stillness she associated with the little church in Silkington. Despite the change in the Stephenson's family circumstances they still went to church on Sundays and Irene also attended Sunday School: it would always remain a special day.

After the summer in their new home, the continual excitement of new experiences, the development of new relationships, the continuing attraction of Daniel and the birth of Nicholas to Mavis and Gerald in September, came the long, hard winter. Irene knew that winters were cold but this icy, freezing cold, which cut through the body like a knife and typical Derbyshire Peak District winter weather, was something she had not experienced before.

Charlotte spent her evenings with her notebook; she made sure she had a copious account of the changing times of 1960.

'BRITAIN

Britain agrees to fund a supersonic aeroplane capable of flying at 2000 mph; the estimated cost for each plane is £5 million...

March: a new £1 note is in circulation. Stirling Moss loses his driving licence for a year for dangerous driving...

June: plans to introduce colour television are shelved indefinitely; the first National Health Service hearing aids are introduced; at Coventry Cathedral, Epstein's last major work, "St Michael and the Devil" is unveiled...

July: Donald Campbell takes his new £1 million "Bluebird" car for its first test run...

August: beer's going up 1d a pint to 1/7d. (Wills is very displeased!)

September: "traffic wardens" and parking tickets are now in operation; Donald Campbell crashes "Bluebird" whilst driving at 350 mph, but he survives...

October: Britain's first nuclear submarine, HMS Dreadnought is launched; The Old Bailey jury rules that the novel, "Lady Chatterley's Lover", banned for thirty years, is not after all obscene; Penguin books had 200,000 copies ready for distribution at 3/6d each; it was on sale the day after the decision and was a sell-out on the same day!

31st December, the last National Service men receive their call-up cards; this marks the end of the scheme which started with conscription in World War II and means that the Forces will have to rely on voluntary recruitment in the future...

THE ROYAL FAMILY

There were two important Royal events this year. On 19th February, the Queen gave birth to a son, Prince Andrew Albert Christian Edward; he's the first child to be born to a reigning monarch since 1857, when Queen Victoria gave birth to Princess Beatrice. Later, in February, Buckingham Palace announced the engagement of Princess Margaret to Antony Armstrong-Jones; they were married on 6th May in Westminster Abbey and their honeymoon was a cruise in the Caribbean on the royal yacht, Britannia...

ABROAD (Summary – December)

There's the war in Vietnam; it seems to be going on and on... In Egypt, President Nasser has laid the foundation stone of the Aswan Dam... Many countries and islands have gained their independence: the French Colony of Togoland in Africa, British Somaliland, French Madagascar, the Belgian Congo, the French Congo, Chad, the Central African Republic and Nigeria...Cyprus became a Republic in

Time & Tide

August... During the Easter weekend there was an influx of refugees crossing the East German border to the West: in August the border between East and West Berlin was closed... In America, J F Kennedy won the Presidential elections in November...

The racial problems in America and South Africa continue... 21st March, a massacre in the black township of Sharpeville, South of Johannesburg; police fired on a crowd of between five and twenty thousand demonstrators killing sixty-nine black people. All black political organisations have been outlawed in Johannesburg; the ANC leader, Chief Luthuli set fire to his own passbook to start a passbook-burning campaign... 30th March, a state of emergency; the turmoil continued with further riots in Durban in April. Despite the blacks rioting for change and wanting an end to oppressive white rule, it continues; many of the white people are enjoying their decadent lifestyles unaware of the true situation of the native black people; for the white minority "apartheid" is an essential part of life. In America, a similar struggle continues... March, one-thousand black students stage a peaceful protest against segregation in Montgomery after Martin Luther King's successful bus boycott...

In Moscow, the fifty-three year old Leonid Brezhnev has succeeded Marshal Voroshilov as head of State in a Kremlin reshuffle...

THE SPACE RACE! In August, the USSR launched a spaceship carrying two dogs as a trial run for putting a man into space; it was a successful mission, the two dogs landing safely.

The first weather satellite, TIROS 1, was launched by the USA; it sent back pictures from a height of 450 miles showing cloud cover over the northeastern part of the States and part of Canada...

The Olympic Games were held in Rome...

Wolves beat Blackburn in the FA. Cup at Wembley...

In Zurich, a West German, Armin Hary, has created a new world record by running 100 metres in ten seconds... Another record has been made: the solo Atlantic sailor, Francis Chichester, sailed into New York in Gypsy Moth II, crossing from Plymouth in only forty days...

In the USA, the film, "Ben Hur" won a record ten Oscars. (Took Irene to see it at Buxton.) In June, Alfred Hitchcock's, "Psycho", was released...

On the television "Z Cars", a BBC police series has started.

The new decade has begun!'

* * * * * *

She put her pen down and thought about Christmas; it was going to be different this year. Wills had to be at work, which meant they would be unable to go to Whistbury until 30th December. Elizabeth would have to join them for the Christmas festivities instead: without her father it was going to be a sad occasion. Unlike Irene, she was not looking forward to Christmas; for the first time she would have to do all the catering.

Somehow she survived, through what she saw as an ordeal, the last days of December; on New Year's Eve, with some sadness, the customary party went ahead: the church clock chimed twelve. 1961 had arrived!

For Irene, the spring and summer followed the format of the previous year, but her life was to change again. This was her final year at junior school; she sat the eleven plus examination; along with Danny, they both passed and were given places at the Fordingham Grammar School. Their pleasure at passing was marred by the jealousy of their schoolmates; they found themselves snubbed by those they had thought were their friends; but they had each other. The eleven plus had thrown them together and cemented their relationship.

It was time for yet another change...

Chapter 8
Fordingham, August, 1961

FOR IRENE AND DANNY, the summer holiday was one of excitement and apprehension. They spent a lot of time together and when they were separated, due to circumstances beyond their control, they both counted the days until they could be together again.

They were separated for a whole week when Danny went to see his grandparents in Leeds. Mary's family were Yorkshire people and she liked to return to her native county to see them. Her true profession was nursing; she had met Alan after the war whilst she was living in Fordingham and working at the hospital in Buxton; she gave up her career when she married but her nursing training was invaluable whenever there were accidents on the estate. Irene marked off the seven days until his return on her calendar.

That summer brought a new experience for Irene. Charlotte had been happy learning to drive and spending her inheritance; now she decided that she would spend some of her money on a family holiday: holidays were the prerogative of the well-off. She could remember the annual seaside holidays from her childhood and felt that this was one of the things she had missed out on since marriage, but she was now in a financial position to rectify the situation. Consequently, the decision to spend a week in Torquay was her choice and not a family one; and it was she who decided that Elizabeth should join them.

So, the second week in August, only days after Danny had returned from Leeds, they were parted again. This time the Stephenson family were heading south and Charlotte was proudly driving her deluxe mini without the 'L' plates. She had passed her test in June and enjoyed the freedom of being able to go anywhere she chose when she wanted to. Wills expected her to grow tired of driving after the initial excitement was over but he was wrong. She loved it and, as long as she was happy behind the wheel, he was happy surveying the countryside.

Elizabeth expressed her disapproval of her daughter's newfound hobby: it was the man's place behind the wheel – she should be content just to sit in the passenger seat at her husband's side.

Irene thought that the holiday would lead her grandmother to come out of mourning and wear brighter clothes. She was mistaken. In the hotel, on the beach, shopping, travelling, whatever they did, wherever they went, she continued to wear her mournful black. Her mood was grim too, and cast a dark shadow over the whole holiday. This didn't help to assuage Irene's own misery as she counted the days to when she would see Danny again. Charlotte enjoyed it; Wills tolerated it; Elizabeth made sure everyone knew she was a widow. For Irene, it was a special treat to stay in a hotel and she liked the different scenery but she was glad when it was all over.

Back in Fordingham, Katy was getting ready for boarding school and Jane was preparing for a new life at the secondary modern school. The three girls who had become such good friends eighteen months before were planning to go their separate ways; the experiences of junior school and childhood they had shared were over. All the hours spent listening to music at Jane's home, all the time spent playing on the swings at the recreation ground, all the shared secrets, all the ball games, all the fun they had had with a skipping rope, all the girlish talk, had come to an end. Now they seemed to have little in common; they were at crossroads in their lives and all about to take a different path through life.

Tuesday, 5th September was the first day of the autumn term for all the children. Like them, Mary and Charlotte were aware of the fact that the day was drawing nearer and that their children needed uniforms for the grammar school. Charlotte drove them all to the shop in Buxton and they were kitted out with all that was on the lengthy list. Danny had his white shirts, grey trousers, burgundy jumper, school tie, cap, blazer, socks, outdoor and indoor shoes, mackintosh, gym kit, rugby kit and satchel. Irene had her white blouses, grey tunic, burgundy cardigan, tie, beret, blazer, socks, two pairs of shoes, mackintosh, gym kit, hockey kit and satchel. Mary and Charlotte had long white faces when they paid the bill! Fortunately, Elizabeth had given Charlotte £10 towards Irene's uniform and Mary's parents had given her some money for Danny's. However, both parents knew that this was only the beginning; in the summer they would need more things and, unlike those children going to the secondary modern schools who left at fifteen, grammar school pupils stayed in education at least until they were sixteen, or even eighteen. For the average parent sending a child to the grammar school meant making sacrifices in order to pay for the more expensive uniforms and other items. Mary and Alan were pleased to do this because they wanted Daniel to have every opportunity in life. Charlotte, however, resented it; she felt that the sooner her daughter began to earn a living the better. She had also noticed the strong father-daughter relationship that Wills had with Irene; it was like her own had been with John, Alas! she no longer had the comfort of her father and therefore resented the bond that was developing between them.

The uniforms were put away; all they had to do was wait for the big day. Irene had often seen Danny go up the lane and head in the direction of the stable flats. She thought that he must get on well with John and Luke, but why would he be going there when the men were working? She had seldom ventured into the barns and cowsheds preferring the gardens, fields and orchards.

On the Saturday afternoon, before term started, they were helping with the harvest when she decided to ask him why he spent so much time in the flats. He was surprised and said, 'The flats? I've only been in them a couple of times.'

'But you always seem to be going up there.'

He smiled and said, 'When we've finished the last load today, I'll show you where I go.'

By the time the last bales were stacked it was too late for them to go anywhere together. She looked at him; he whispered, 'Tomorrow!'

Tomorrow seemed to be a long time coming; in the morning there was church and then Sunday lunch; they had arranged to meet at 3.00 pm. She saw him walking up the lane towards the stables and went to meet him; he led her past the flats towards some large wooden doors that she had never really noticed before. Inside, in the dim light she could just see old hand ploughs and behind them pieces of equipment which, she assumed, were used before the arrival of the tractor and modern machinery, and should now be in a museum. Danny picked up the torch he had left just inside the door; by its light they went past the museum pieces towards a wooden staircase at the far end of the building. He took her up the stairs to his 'special place', the hayloft.

Originally, this building had been used for storing hay but since the new barns had been erected it had become redundant; Irene looked round in amazement.

'No one comes here,' he said.

She was speechless. From the torchlight she could see that he had furnished the area with some hay; there were books and stationery, a blanket and a couple of lemonade bottles. He went towards the large wooden doors, removed the bar from across them and opened one side to let the daylight in. 'Other people have tree houses. This is my "summer house" where I come to read. I want to be a doctor. I have to work hard and I enjoy the peace and quiet up here.'

'You mean no one knows you come here?'

'No one. You won't tell, will you?'

'How did you get the hay and blanket?'

'Just small amounts at a time. There can't be more than a bale. The blanket was over the implements downstairs. I washed it at the outdoor tap and brought it up.'

'Are you SURE Dad doesn't know?' emphasising the word 'sure'.

'Positive, neither does my father. This is a big estate, they see me leave the house with books but assume I'm going up to the fields, in the woods or the paddocks. Of course, I don't come in the winter, it's too cold! In another couple of weeks I'll clear it out but next spring I'll be back!'

He put his hand out towards her; she instinctively took hold of it. He was sharing his special place with her and they were holding hands. Now, it was her special place too; it was a secret that they shared.

He led her towards the open door; she looked out and could see how secluded it was. Sheltered on one side by the trees which flanked the front entrance to the Hall and on the other by farm buildings. Only someone working at the top end of the paddock and away from the farm buildings would notice the open door. As if reading her thoughts he said, 'I make sure no one's working in the paddock.'

They moved away from the door and sat down on the hay; there was an awkward silence between them; neither of them knew what to do or say next. They were aware of the mutual attraction between them but they were children playing an adult game and they were too young to know the rules.

Danny broke the silence by saying, 'You can come here if you like. I don't mind so long as you don't tell your father.'

'I'd like that. I won't tell Dad and I'll make sure no one sees me.'

He wanted to hold her hand again but didn't like to. Instead, he started talking about their new school. 'Are you looking forward to Tuesday?'

'Tuesday?'

'Yes. The new school. What do you think it's going to be like?'

'I don't know, but my cousin, Martin, you remember him? He's stayed with us a couple of times?'

'Yes.'

'Well, he likes it at his grammar school. He says the work is harder but more interesting. He plays rugby for the school team. He's made some new friends and forgotten the ones he had from junior school who ignored him. I keep thinking about what he's told me and then I don't feel as frightened.'

'I'm looking forward to it.'

'What! Really? Aren't you frightened?'

'No. I want to learn about physics and biology. I have to do well and get good 'O' levels, to go into the sixth form, take 'A' levels and then university.'

Yet again he had managed to amaze Irene and leave her speechless; this boy had a maturity beyond his years.

She had not thought beyond her first year; he wanted to be a doctor and knew that he needed good qualifications and a university degree. She had no idea what she wanted to do in adult life and had given no thought to anything beyond going to grammar school. The fact that the girls she thought were her friends had changed towards her since she had achieved her goal had given her second thoughts and added to her apprehension.

Danny was slightly apprehensive but that was not the impression he wanted Irene to have. He wanted her to see him as a strong individual and a boy she could rely on. She was going to be his girlfriend and he would protect her like the knights in shining armour of old. He looked at his watch and realised that it was almost time for tea. 'Come on! Time to go!'

He was being masculine and taking charge of the situation and she, in a trance-like state, obeyed him. He closed the door and shone the torch for her to see her way down the stairs; they both returned home, each having the other on their mind. Tuesday morning came; Irene put on her new uniform and went downstairs for breakfast. Wills was in the kitchen waiting for his little girl; it was six and a half years since he had watched her go to school for the first time. Now, as she walked into the room, he could see that she was growing into a young woman. She looked attractive in her grey gymslip and burgundy cardigan; the colours suited her dark features. After breakfast she put on her black shoes, grey mackintosh and burgundy beret with the Fordingham badge, with its 'FS' clearly showing, and picked up her new satchel and bag containing her house shoes. Wills was so proud of his little girl; he kissed her affectionately on the cheek and told her, as he so often did, to do her best.

She saw Danny on the staff drive and rushed to catch him up; they walked down

Time & Tide

to the 'T' junction together. Several boys and girls were waiting for the school buses but only three older boys were waiting for the Fordingham bus. They were standing a few yards away from the rest of them; the segregation was obvious; the majority waiting for the secondary modern school buses did not want to associate with the three boys wearing caps with 'FS' on them. The boys, who Irene vaguely recognised, told them to stand with them. They had had three or four years to get used to the fact that their being cleverer at school had made them social outcasts in the eyes of the others. Irene looked towards Jane but she turned away; she was with the older secondary modern crowd and had been told not to look at the snobby Fordingham children in their distinctive uniforms. The boys told her not to worry about them, they were only jealous and she would get used to that in time. The Fordingham school bus came first and the five of them boarded, leaving the bitter and jealous majority behind. Fordingham School was situated on the outskirts of Buxton; it had been founded in the early part of the nineteenth century by Lord Fordingham's great-great-great grandfather on land which had originally been part of his estate but was now owned by the Derbyshire Local Education Authority. They arrived at school at 8.45; everyone got off the bus and started walking in one of two directions. Irene was puzzled as she looked at the massive building beyond three entrances. One of the Fordingham village boys called out to someone named Christine, 'She's a first year. Can you take her in with you?'

Irene found herself being ushered in the direction of the girls' gate; Danny had gone in the opposite direction with the boys. She was taken down a driveway, past classrooms and into the girls' cloakroom. There were lists on the wall and she found she had been given peg no. 43. Christine, who was a fourth year girl, showed her where her peg was; here, she learned, was where she must put on her house shoes, leave her outdoor shoes in the rack provided and hang her coat and beret on the peg. Christine then directed her along another corridor towards the assembly hall. Outside the hall there were two elderly teachers wearing academic gowns; a woman was asking the girls for their names and then telling them which form they were in. Irene was in 1 Gamma (1G); she was sent into the hall where three teachers were waiting to collect the new children. Danny was already in the hall and standing with 1G: they were to be in the same form! He saw her join the girls of his form and was delighted.

They waited for the rest of the school to assemble; the staff then went up the steps to the stage and sat down on chairs provided. The headmaster was the last person

86

to enter; he, like most of his staff, was wearing academic dress. The staff had the luxury of chairs but the pupils were expected to stand throughout the assembly.

The headmaster, Mr Graves, announced a hymn number; everyone, except the first years turned to No. 228 in their hymn books; music could be heard from the organ at the side of the hall and the pupils sang 'Jerusalem The Golden'.

A reading from the Bible followed and then the headmaster said a prayer of blessing for the new term; there were one or two notices plus the welcoming of new staff. Most of this was meaningless to the new pupils but they stood and endured it

When it was all over, the staff left the hall first, then the sixth form followed by the fifth, fourth, thirds and seconds. The whole procedure was done with well-organised military precision; everyone knew when it was their turn to move and where to go. The poor first years who had been in the hall from the beginning were still standing when the hall had cleared; then their form teachers collected them and took them to their form rooms. They were seated in alphabetical order; this pleased both Irene and Danny because his surname preceded hers on the register. He was seated at the front of row five and she next to him at the top of row six; they looked at each other and smiled. Mrs Bennet, their form teacher, noticed the look and felt that she should keep an eye on their relationship.

The morning was spent in the form room where they received timetables, school information, books and the name of the 'house' they were assigned to. There were four houses, all named after past school governors (Fordingham, Richardson, Blaketon and Masefield); it seemed fitting to Irene and Danny that they should be in Fordingham House. Lord Fordingham was a governor, as his ancestors had been since the foundation of the school.

Looking at the age of some of the desks, they too, could have been there for 150 years. The original building was at the centre of the school and used as a sixth form block; the rest of the school had been built in stages until it was large enough to accommodate the present number of 600 pupils. There was a strong sense of history around the school in the form of pictures, wall plaques and information about former pupils and staff including those who had fought and lost their lives in both world wars. No one could doubt that it was a privilege to be entitled to walk along its hallowed corridors.

They were told about the numerous 'house' competitions in the arts, science and sport. Each year had three forms, Alpha, Beta and Gamma, taken from the Greek alphabet. The first-year forms were mixed but from year two they would be streamed: Alpha forms took Latin: Beta forms studied German as a second language after French: Gamma forms had extra Maths and English lessons on their timetable. On hearing this Danny knew that he wanted to take Latin, it was a prerequisite for entry to some universities; he told Irene and, naturally, she wanted to do the same. They both intended working hard to be given a place in the top stream next year.

They started lessons in the afternoon but most of them were timetabled for their form room; they only moved for sciences, gym, games, domestic science/woodwork, music and art. That afternoon they began with maths and English and Mrs Bennet was their English teacher. By the end of the day they felt that they knew this young woman, with short black hair and a beautiful smile, rather well. The final bell went and they were dismissed; it was time to change into their outdoor apparel and return home. There were several buses outside the school gates waiting to take these pupils to various parts of Derbyshire.

Irene left the building with the other girls through the girls' gate; the boys departed from the opposite end of the building. Danny caught sight of Irene and saw that their bus was parked nearer the girls' entrance than his; he walked up towards her and they boarded the bus together. They realised how lucky they were with only a ten-minute journey; many of the 600 pupils had a long bus ride ahead of them and would not reach home until after five o'clock.

In Fordingham they walked up the drive together but then went their own ways and did not see each other again that night. They both had exciting accounts of the day they started at secondary school to tell their parents. Wills was eager to hear about his daughter's first day at the senior school; she was not discouraged by her mother's lack of interest. Charlotte was showing her usual signs of jealousy; she had failed to obtain a place at a grammar school and was not enjoying hearing Irene describe this massive school and its organisation.

For the first week, every day was a new experience: new teachers, different ones for different subjects, new subjects and new friends. At breaks and lunchtimes boys and girls were separated, which meant that Irene and Danny were unable to spend time together and were forced to find new friends of the same gender from other villages. Although she was older than Irene, Christine was slowly becoming her friend.

Time passed and by the end of September it seemed as if they had been at the grammar school forever; life had changed yet again. They had become accustomed to the inverted snobbery and were unconcerned about being ignored by the secondary modern children. The harvest was over for another year; the Harvest

Festival and Supper were over; Danny and Irene had cleared out Danny's 'special place'. They were all prepared for the bleak days of winter that lay ahead of them.

Charlotte, too, was preparing for another winter; she had her thoughts and her diary to while away the long, dark, dreary days; she flicked through the pages.

1961

'BRITAIN

Dr Michael Ramsey is to be the hundredth Archbishop of Canterbury; Geoffrey Fisher has retired...

Edwin Bush is the first suspected criminal to be identified by means of an "Identikit" picture...

The latest sports car is the Jaguar E-type, capable of cruising at 100 mph; the solid top model costs £2,196... May: King Hussein of Jordan announces his engagement to Miss Toni Gardiner, a telephonist from Stratford-upon-Avon. (Lucky Miss G.)

The government has announced new universities at Canterbury, Colchester and Coventry... A new forty-three letter phonetic alphabet is to be taught to 1000 children as an experiment.

The PO has installed "pay-on-answer" phone boxes with pips when coins are needed and there's going to be a Post Office Tower in London...

10th August, Britain formally applied for membership of the EEC. There's talk of changing from "£/s/d" to decimal currency, with just pounds and pence.

There's a female Tory MP who has been given her first government job as a parliamentary secretary, a Mrs Margaret Thatcher...

It's the census year; the results show that the population has grown by two and a half million since 1951; the sharpest increase is in the south of England where more people are living in the suburbs and fewer in the towns. Some of the increase is due to an influx of immigrants...

ABROAD

THE SPACE RACE! In America, a chimpanzee ascended 150 miles above the Earth in an eighteen-minute flight to test the Mercury Space Capsule. Also in February, the United States fired the first "Minuteman" intercontinental ballistic missile. In the USSR an "Interplanetary Space Station" has been launched, aimed at Venus and the Russians have sent up a rocket containing a dog, which landed safely... APRIL, twenty-seven year old Major Yuri Gagarin is the FIRST MAN to

FLY in SPACE. In a four and a half ton Vostok spaceship he orbited the earth for 108 minutes and returned unharmed by his exploit. President Kennedy stated in Washington that America would put the first man on the moon. (It's so exciting!)

ISRAEL, Forty Biblical scrolls were found in a cave in Judaea; they tell of the isolated Essene Religious Sect, and it is possible that either John the Baptist or Christ spent some time with them before the start of their ministries. Also in Jerusalem, the trial is taking place of the former Nazi SS Officer, Adolf Eichmann. He's charged with fifteen counts of conspiring to cause death or persecution of millions of Jews; he's giving evidence but refusing to swear on a Bible...

The conflict continues in Algeria.

May: CUBA, Castro has proclaimed Cuba a socialist nation and abolished elections...

America's racial problems continue. After the bus boycotts there were successful "sit-ins"; then another non-violent attempt at desegregation: the "freedom rides", these mobilised the "sit-ins" by carrying bus loads of civil rights demonstrators into the prejudiced areas of the deep South; they suffered physical abuse and attacks but gained widespread support for the Civil Rights Movement.

31st May, South Africa became a republic and left the Commonwealth, but "apartheid" continues. Nelson Mandela, the ANC leader, eluded a police round up; the South African Police were carrying out mass arrests of black activists in an attempt to head off a nationwide general strike called by black leaders, detaining almost ten thousand black people...

July: East Germans are flooding into West Berlin; there's fear that the Communist regime is about to sever links between East and West and prevent emigration from the East to the more prosperous West. 13th August, East Germany closes the Berlin border by blocking it with barbed wire. 20th August, the BERLIN WALL erected...

The protests over NUCLEAR ARMS continues. April, thirty one people are arrested during an anti-nuclear protest outside the US Embassy in London. September, the USA and Britain call for a ban on nuclear tests in the atmosphere but Russia continues with its nuclear testing programme. 17th September, the biggest "ban the bomb" demonstration takes place in London and ends in violent clashes and the arrest of nearly 850 people. Amongst those arrested are the radical playwright, John Osborne and the actress, Vanessa Redgrave. At one point more than 15,000 protesters jammed Trafalgar Square on the day that the Russians exploded the twelfth bomb in a series of nuclear tests.'

The bleak Derbyshire winter came with a vengeance; the Stephenson family still found it hard to acclimatise to the extreme cold conditions that they associated with Siberia. The glorious summer months had wiped out their bitter memories of the previous year and they could not believe that it had been just as cold then.

Charlotte had only a few pounds left from her inheritance and savings. She was adamant that the car was hers and so Wills had told her that it was up to her to maintain it. She had not realised the total cost of running a vehicle; in her ignorance, she had assumed that after the buying it all they needed was petrol; she had not considered road tax, insurance and servicing. She concluded that she must find employment or sell her pride and joy. Luckily, the Fordingham Arms, one of the two village public houses, had a piano and wanted someone to play at weekends; this suited Charlotte and perhaps in time she would be able to play on other evenings; it gave her some employment and enabled her to run her car. Wills had use of the estate transport and did not really need another vehicle; it was one less expense for him.

Irene and Danny established themselves at their new school; they were careful not to hold hands in public or show any sign of affection for each other: such behaviour would have been unacceptable to both staff and the other pupils. Throughout the first three years they both made excellent progress working together, inspiring and helping each other. During the winter months they would do homework in one or other of their homes; they always stayed in the lounge – they were not allowed upstairs together; in the summer months their parents assumed they were in the gardens when, in actual fact, they were in their 'special place'.

As they approached adolescence they were told individually about the 'facts of life'. Well, at least Alan had a 'man to man' chat with his son. For Wills, such information should be passed on to a daughter by her mother; he assumed that Charlotte would do this. Charlotte's answer to the problem was to give her daughter a book about, 'Womanhood' and to pass on the same advice that Elizabeth had given to her which was, 'wait until you are married and then lie back and think of England'.

Fortunately, the school had taken on responsibility for educating the girls on the taboo subject of menstruation. They were given a letter to take home for parental signature; a lady was coming from a sanitary towel company to talk to them. When the day came for the talk the girls were taken from lessons to the hall; there was no mention of the topic in the classroom, but quite a few blushes. This talk and the book answered all Irene's questions; she now knew that soon she would have her first period and it would be the first stage of womanhood.

Both she and Danny were aware of their developing feelings for each other. They were pleased when the winter ended and spring arrived in 1962. They set up their hideaway and celebrated the arrival of spring with their first kiss; it was not passionate, they were only twelve years old but it was the kiss they would both remember.

For Irene, that summer was even better than the previous one; she and Danny were growing closer together and their hard work and determination had paid dividends; they were both going to be in 2A and study Latin. Throughout the summer holiday they were only divided when they each went to visit their relatives. Charlotte was not in a position to finance another holiday, so Torquay was out of the question. Hillary and Martin came to stay at different times; Irene enjoyed their visits but she did not realise that they were both very envious of all that she had.

Martin was sixteen and had taken his GCEs; he was going into the sixth form to study economics and help his father achieve his aim of owning a chain of shops. He had watched Irene grow up in his shadow but now she was different; she was no longer the little girl companion of his boyhood days but she was blossoming into a young woman and, as far as Martin could see, she had everything. She had the freedom of a country estate or most of it, a nice home, a faithful father who idolised her, and a mother. Although Julia had returned to Jim their marriage was not, and could never be, the same again; there was a cold distance and a lack of trust between them, but they were unaware that their son had noticed this.

Irene also had Danny, she was closer to him than she was to Martin, and this saddened him. Yes, Irene had everything; all he had was an over-ambitious and unfaithful father, the pungent smell of tobacco to come home to instead of the smell of fresh green fields, and a life of drudgery ahead of him in his father's empire. Martin was not a city boy, he was like his grandfather and Uncle Wills; he wanted a life on a farm but he was destined to be cooped up in his father's business. He could see no alternative to that; his cousin had everything he wanted, a country life and even a boyfriend!

Hillary felt the same way as her half-brother; she had been taken from a rural area to city life; her mother would always be the 'other woman' and through necessity was working hard behind a shop counter all day for her father's benefit. Although Jim was her natural father she still had cherished memories of her earlier years with her mother and Bill, whom she had assumed was her father. She had not seen him since their hasty departure in 1958 and she missed him. Hillary did not have a boyfriend and as she was a pupil at an all girls grammar school and her social life was non-existent she had little chance of finding one. From what Hillary could see her cousin had everything.

Neither of them realised how much Irene missed her brother or how often she thought about him left behind in Silkington. They did not know how deeply she felt the loss of her beloved grandfather; neither did they realise that the beauty and warmth of the summer would change drastically into a cold beast for the winter months. They did not suffer the bitter cold tucked away in the comparative warmth of the city; they did not know that Irene could not trust her mother and would have swapped the unaffectionate Charlotte for Julia or Ann's warmth and love any time. It is easy to assume that other people have a better lot in life, but it is seldom true.

Charlotte was as content as she ever was; her continuing jealousy meant that she and Irene were drifting further apart and as they drifted away from each other, Irene became even closer to her father. He was so proud of his little girl and was always telling her; he was delighted with her end of term school report; she was fourth in her class but had received top marks in English and French and she was going to be in the top stream next year. Danny had come top of the class and first in several subjects; Alan and Mary were ecstatic about his progress but Wills was satisfied and proud of Irene's achievements.

Both Wills and Alan had noticed the developing friendship between their children and welcomed it; the staff and even Lord and Lady Fordingham were pleased and felt that they were perfect for each other. They progressed through their second school year working even harder in order to keep their places at the top of the class; in the top stream the competition was greater than the previous year but they persevered. Danny showed exceptional skills in the sciences and appeared to have the required attributes to become a good doctor; he was caring and compassionate, thorough and dedicated in all he did. He was Irene's Adonis and she was his goddess Aphrodite, growing more beautiful every day; she was intelligent and talented as well – he idolised her.

Even Christmas and New Year had a routine on the estate; all the staff had some time off to visit families; Alan and his family always went to Leeds for Christmas. Wills held the fort and Elizabeth, still adorned in black, joined them and then they all went to Whistbury for the New Year. For Irene, visits to her grandmother's did not hold the same appeal; she would always go across to the cemetery, sit at her grandfather's grave and talk to him. Even, in the spring, pretty Almond Blossom Avenue did not look attractive any more, neither did the big house; in comparison with their present home it seemed quite small. However, each New Year's Eve Elizabeth put on a big party just as she used to; it seemed to give her a new lease of life but, sadly, when it was all over she would revert to her mournful ways.

The beginning of 1963 brought some of the worst weather for many years; the nation was experiencing heavy snowfalls, drifting and freezing conditions; the previous winters, even in the Peak District, had been mild by comparison. The Stephenson family thought that they would never become acclimatised to this awful weather. Day after day they struggled to keep warm and for Wills there was the greater problem of keeping the estate running and the livestock alive. It was the longest winter any of them could remember; they wondered if spring would ever come.

Irene's salvation, through what seemed to be a long night without any sign of dawn breaking, was Danny; every day they would struggle through the snow to the bus stop. Eventually, the bus would crawl into sight and, shivering, they would all board it; the bus would then at snail's pace make its way to school. Every day the school buses collected the pupils and deposited them at their seat of learning, but never on time. For a whole month the first two lessons were spent in the classroom; the timetable would commence after break. Even then, not all the buses had arrived; those fortunate enough to arrive before break would watch as those from further afield were still arriving at lunchtime. The latecomers would be summoned to leave early in the afternoon in order to get home before dark; the number of lessons they attended in a week could be counted on one hand but still they came. Life carried on as normal, the idea of not making the effort to get to school was unthinkable.

Danny kept telling Irene that the spring would come eventually, and they would see the daffodils again and enjoy spending time together in the hayloft; there were times when she found that hard to believe, but he was right. She was relieved at long last to see green fields again instead of white snow; Easter arrived bringing warmth and new life; the first lambs were born and she enjoyed feeding the orphans. The clocks were put forward; the days were longer and heavenly; nature had come to life again after a blanket of bleakness.

That summer the first mystery of womanhood was solved; she had her first period. It was special, she felt good about herself and grown up; she could not understand why some women referred to it as the 'curse'. Her mother frowned, her father smiled; he knew she was growing up and he dreaded losing her to a young man. The only person she could discuss it with was her friend, Christine. She was pleased to have met her on that first day; they had remained friends and Irene thought of her as an elder sister she could confide in. So many of the girls in her own year were jealous of her steady relationship with Danny.

In their third year and last year as juniors they began officially dating. On Friday evenings, as a reward for their hard work all week, they would go to the pictures in Buxton and watch a film together. Not only did they have their academic studies to concentrate on but they were also active participants in school activities; he played rugby; she was in the school hockey team; they belonged to the history society, drama club and debating society; they represented their house in inter-house competitions; they were young and seemed to have unlimited energy. Their school activities did not prevent them from helping out on the estate or with village activities, but Friday evenings and time spent innocently in the hayloft were special moments which they cherished.

In their 'special place' they would talk about their plans for the future; they would be taking different options in the fourth year but they would both take eight GCEs, and Grade 1 in each subject was their aim. Their 'O' level results would be their passport into the sixth form to study for 'A' levels. They would go to the same university even though they would be studying different subjects; she was not a scientist and had no intention of entering the medical profession. She would graduate and then take a one-year teacher training course. They would marry in Fordingham Church and spend the rest of their lives together as man and wife; they were in a cocoon of happiness and nothing was going to destroy that.

They continued in their blissful routine and rural life in Fordingham, but beyond the River Dove the seeds of change were growing; Charlotte continued recording it all.

1962
'BRITAIN
The year begins with post office workers on a "work to rule" campaign; there are delays in the postal deliveries and their campaign is aided by the severe cold spell. An outbreak of smallpox with many dying is causing alarm and leading to many being vaccinated. Dissatisfaction from industrial areas means that strikes are looming on the horizon for the spring. The unemployment figure at the end of January is 461,000 – it's the highest it's been since May, 1959.

Time & Tide

February: there's unprecedented traffic chaos in London caused by a one-day "unofficial" strike of workers on the underground...

May: the Queen attends the dedication service of the new Coventry Cathedral; built adjacent to the ruins of the old one, bombed during World War II, which have been left as a reminder of that war...

27th June, the Pilkington Report on television and radio is published; it attacks ITV but supports BBC; among its recommendations are that colour television should be available as soon as possible and another station be brought out by the BBC. (Not only more choice, but it will be in colour – Irene'll like that!)

24th September, the first woman County Court Judge, Mrs Elizabeth Lane QC, has been appointed and assigned to the Edmonton Circuit...

November: the Anglo-Japanese Trade Treaty has been signed, paving the way towards the extension of exports to Japan and Japanese imports to Britain...

December: a severe spell of heavy fog is covering most of Britain; the worst foggy spell for ten years; nearly 100 deaths in London alone have been attributed to the polluted atmosphere. After Christmas, blizzards, the worst since 1927.

1963

BRITAIN

There's a reduction in purchase tax from 45% to 25% on such items as radios, television sets, gramophone records, cosmetics and perfume and an increase in social service benefits.

January: Mr Hugh Gaitskell has died after a severe illness; he's to be succeeded by Harold Wilson as leader of the Labour Party... Mr Macmillan has addressed the Young Conservatives' conference in London and he's urged the youth of the party to work hard for victory in the next election; he wants to reconstruct Britain for the twenty-first century; his party is to lay the foundations for a happy and prosperous future.

March: Dr Beeching's report on British Railways is published; it advocates a complete re-organisation of the railway system, with many under-used rural services being cut and lines closed.

THE PROFUMO AFFAIR is dominating the papers. Christine Keeler, a friend of the society osteopath Dr Stephen Ward was introduced to Jack Profumo (the Minister for War) by Dr Ward. He also introduced her to Commander Ivanov, a former Naval Attaché at the Russian Embassy; both men had been visiting Christine at Stephen's

96

apartment. Profumo asked Christine to find an apartment of her own, but she refused to leave Stephen; the problems seem to have started when Stephen told her that their relationship was over because he could not afford the risk of a political scandal. In desperation, Christine talked to the Press and started the ball rolling; a woman sleeping with both a Russian spy and the Minister for War could lead to a breach of security... 22nd March, Profumo tells the House of Commons that he knows Miss Keeler but has not seen her since December, 1961, and there has never been any impropriety in the relationship... June, Profumo admits that he lied about his relationship with Christine: he's tendered his resignation...

8th August, an ambitious train robbery has taken place; over £2$\frac{1}{2}$million in bank notes has been stolen from the Scottish Post Office Express, which was ambushed near Cheddington Station after being halted by a fake signal... Twelve men have already been arrested and are to be tried at Aylesbury in Buckinghamshire... News of a proposed Channel link has been released; Britain and France have reached an agreement to construct a tunnel but no date for commencement has been given.

Negotiations are in progress on Britain joining the Common Market. There was a National Protest Meeting at the Albert Hall attended by 3000 people; it's clear that opinion is strongly divided over Britain joining. The prime minister says that a changed world has emerged since the war; this means a change of attitude and a reshaping in the framework of World Trade; Great Britain must be a close ally of the six founding members and share in Europe's expansion or else the political and economic strength of the six would be a harmful influence on Great Britain and Commonwealth.

October: Harold Macmillan is unable to lead the party conference; he's announced his retirement through ill health and the Queen has asked Lord Home to form a new Government. It's thought that the strain of the Common Market negotiations and the scandal of the "Profumo Affair" are the main factors which have led to this illness.

THE ROYAL FAMILY

April, 1963: Princess Alexandra marries Mr Angus Ogilvy at Westminster Abbey; the Archbishop of Canterbury officiated at the service which was watched by millions on television (including us!)

1964: Four Royal births: Prince Edward to the Queen, Lady Helen Windsor to the Duchess of Kent, Lady Sarah Armstrong-Jones to Princess Margaret and James Robert Bruce Ogilvy to Princess Alexandra.

Time & Tide

ABROAD

1962–1964

THE CUBAN CRISIS, October, 1962, the headlines suggest that the world is on the brink of a dreaded nuclear war; 15th October, President Kennedy learns that the Soviet Union is building a nuclear missile site on Cuba; Russian ships are approaching Cuba armed with more missiles; he's responding by blockading Cuba with forty warships. We wait with horror to see if the Russian Premier will back down... The missile-laden ships have turned back; Nuclear war has been avoided.

22nd January, 1963, the nuclear test ban negotiations reopen in Washington. Britain, USA and USSR are involved in the talks but little progress is made. July, negotiations take place in Moscow with delegations from Britain, USA and USSR; they all agree to a partial nuclear test ban treaty, this means that there will be no further nuclear tests in the atmosphere, under water or in outer space. This treaty is regarded as the first step towards world peace; it will come into force on 10th October when signed copies are exchanged simultaneously in Washington, London and Moscow.

THE SPACE RACE continues. Who will be the first to put a man on the moon? The first step is to land a rocket on the moon's surface. January, 1962, the USA launch a rocket from Cape Canaveral containing instruments for a moon landing, the launching goes smoothly but the capsule veers off course and passes the moon without landing on it... February, the USA's first manned flight takes place; Colonel Glenn encircles the earth three times in the Mercury space capsule, Friendship VII... May, another successful manned space flight is carried out... July, after several other attempts, the USA make a successful moon landing in Ranger 7, only ten miles off target... 1963, the Americans launch Faith 7, with astronaut Major Gordon Cooper on board, he completed twenty-two circuits of the earth before descending into the Pacific Ocean, in sight of the recovery aircraft carrier which was waiting for the landing; the mission was a complete success. In 1964, the States launches its communication satellite, Relay 2.

During the same period of time Russia has its own programme. May, 1963, USSR launches a rocket aimed at the moon; it's unsuccessful and passes the moon without landing on it... June 1963, they put their first woman cosmonaut into space; she travels approximately 1.25 million miles in under three days and completes forty-eight orbits round the world. In 1964, Russia launches two space stations, Electron 1 and Electron 2. 1964, the two super powers are closer to their aim of placing a man on the moon before 1970. Another challenge is beginning; they're launching space probes in the direction of Mars!

Jamaica, Uganda, Nyasaland and Malta have all achieved independent status. Northern Rhodesia has become the Independent Commonwealth Republic of Zambia and Southern Rhodesia is now known as just Rhodesia. Kenya is a single party state and the Federation of Malaysia has come into existence.

Canada: a general election has resulted in a Liberal Government, led by Mr. Lester Pearson... Pope John XXIII has died; he's succeeded by Cardinal Montini, the Archbishop of Milan who's to be known as Pope Paul VI. Italy celebrates the four hundredth anniversary of the birth of the pioneer scientist, Galileo Galilei... Adolf Eichmann, found guilty of war crimes in Jerusalem last year, has been hanged...MONTREAL, Elizabeth Taylor married Richard Burton; it's her FIFTH marriage! Mr Khrushchev joined President Nasser for the ceremonial opening of the second phase of the Aswan Dam project... A treaty of friendship and co-operation between Russia and East Germany has been signed in Moscow...The US Federal Trade Commission has ruled that from 1st January, 1965, all American cigarette packets must carry a government health warning... JAPAN has made a rapid recovery from the devastation of the war years. The Japanese are delighted with their newfound prosperity; they're the first country to produce transistor radios. Work's the order of the day and their continued efforts are paying good dividends; the industry is growing and a powerful economy is being established.

RACIAL PROBLEMS continue in SOUTH AFRICA and AMERICA. In South Africa, sentences of life imprisonment are passed on eight men found guilty of conspiracy against the Government, including Nelson Mandela... In America, the Governor in Mississippi has given effect to a Federal Court Order ending segregation at the university; the subsequent enrolment of a black student at the beginning of term in September, 1962 causes riots. Racial tension is on the increase; President Kennedy is trying to reduce it by introducing a law to prohibit racial discrimination and adding a clause which would make the segregation of different coloured people in schools in any State illegal; there are still riots and demonstrations in Alabama, Mississippi and other Southern cities; these problems in the South not only undermine Kennedy's authority but lessen his support from Southern electors... June, 1963, President Kennedy announces the details of his Civil Rights Bill... August: a tremendous civil rights demonstration is held in Washington; from the steps of the Lincoln Memorial, Martin Luther King addresses a crowd of over 100,000 people; he begins with "I have a dream..." and continues to speak of his hope for freedom and justice in the future for all races... September: the USA takes strong measures to enforce its policy of desegregation in the Southern States; the President takes command of the Alabama State troops and drafts units of Federal men into the troubled areas. As a result blacks are allowed to enrol in the State schools but white parents are withdrawing their children and riots are taking place in several towns... Sunday, 18th September, a time bomb explodes in a Birmingham, Alabama black church, killing four black girls. As a direct result of this a committee of black leaders led by Dr King appeals to the president for further help and he promises immediate assistance... 22nd November, 1963, a shocked world hears that President Kennedy has been assassinated in Dallas, Texas; his supposed assassin, Lee Harvey Oswald is arrested. Lyndon B Johnson is sworn in as the new president on the plane journey back to Washington. President Johnson pledges to maintain the ideals of John Kennedy; he wants to press forward the Civil Rights Bill and proposes reduction in taxes designed to restore buoyancy to American spending power. He's announced, as a memorial to President Kennedy, the renaming of Cape Canaveral to Cape Kennedy... Lee Harvey Oswald, President Kennedy's assassin, has been murdered by Jack Ruby... The US Senate pass the Civil Rights Bill on 20th June, 1964... November, President Johnson is elected in the presidential election as president in his own right... Dr Martin Luther King becomes recognised as the leading black voice in the States; his work has earned him respect from the world at large and honours are being bestowed on him culminating in the award of the 1964 Nobel Peace Prize.

SPORT

The Winter Olympics took place in Innsbruck, Austria and the eighteenth Olympic Games took place in Japan. Cassius Clay emerged as a heavyweight boxer. In 1964, at the final England v. Australia match at the Oval, F S Trueman took his three hundredth wicket, an unprecedented achievement!

1964

BRITAIN

The twelve men who robbed the Scottish Post office Express are all found guilty and given heavy prison sentences... A new £10 Bank of England note is issued, the first since 1943... It's the 400th anniversary of Shakespeare's birth... The 20th anniversary of the D-day landings are being celebrated by a reunion of representatives of the Allied forces on the sites of the Normandy landings... The Forth Road Bridge has been opened... The last issue of the Daily Herald is published; it's the Labour Party newspaper founded in 1912 and is to be replaced by The Sun... In the general election, the Labour Party are elected with a majority of five, and Harold Wilson replaces Alec Douglas Home as prime minister.

THE EARLY SIXTIES

Television, the luxury item of the fifties is slowly becoming a necessity in the sixties. On 23rd July, 1962, Britain presented its first formal transatlantic television programme with the help of the communication satellite, Telstar, a great scientific achievement. Popular programmes in 1962 are "Maigret", "Dr Kildare", "Sunday Night at the London Palladium", "Panorama", "The Billy Cotton Band Show", "This is Your Life". A new Sunday religious programme has come on the air, "Songs of Praise". The schools' programmes are going from strength to strength and Saturday afternoon's devotion to sport in the form of "Grandstand" is very popular. In 1963 two programmes make an impact: "Compact" and "That Was The Week That Was". Old films are immensely popular, as are musical shows like "Juke Box Jury" and "The Black and White Minstrel Show".

For children the BBC has introduced a new series about a time lord, "Dr. Who", who lives in the Tardis and travels through time and space. In April, 1964, the first live television pictures were transmitted to Europe, by means of Telstar II, over distances of up to 10,000 miles; another major event is the arrival in London and the south of the third channel, BBC2. All aspects of the media are developing at a rapid pace. In 1964, the hours of broadcasting on the radio are being extended in the early morning and late evening, from midnight until 2.00 am In April, 1964, a group of London businessmen put up money to float a 'pirate' radio ship, Radio Caroline, off the Essex coast, supported by advertising; it is to play "pop" music twenty-four hours a day. After forty-two years the BBC's monopoly on sound radio has been broken: commercial radio has arrived!

In the cinemas, some of the box office successes are "The Longest Day", "How The West Was Won", "West Side Story", "My Fair Lady" and "Mary Poppins". In addition, the Carry on... team, which include Sid James, Kenneth Williams and Terry Scott and other comedians, continues making films in the series which started in the late fifties. However, the film world mourns the loss of the actress, Marilyn Monroe, who's committed suicide: she is believed to have had an intimate relationship with President Kennedy.

Popular music is changing rapidly. Liverpool is making its mark on the world with the new "Mersey Sound". Brian Epstein's discovery, The Beatles, have arrived *and are taking the world by storm; 'Beatlemania' is everywhere, a new image has been born by the Fab Four – John, Paul, George and Ringo, who began their musical career in The Cavern Club in Liverpool; these young men are pop idols and the young are copying both their hairstyle and clothes. Another of Brian Epstein's discoveries is Liverpool's Cilla Black; some of the other groups are The Rolling Stones, Gerry and the Pacemakers, Freddie and the Dreamers and The Bachelors.*

The young are still attempting to make the authorities listen to them. The Teddy Boys of the fifties started the eruption of a dormant volcano and the youth of the early sixties are not going to allow it to cease until the volcano is extinct. The Mods and Rockers have emerged; the Mods neat in appearance, with short haircuts, crew-necked jumpers, anoraks and elastic-sided "Chelsea boots", they have motor-scooters, they like black soul singers and take pep pills. They are the complete opposite and sworn enemies of the Rockers, who have roaring "ton-up" motor cycles, leather jackets, jeans and greasy hair, and are the British equivalent of the American Hells Angels. Both groups are making their presence known by hooliganism and disturbances, particularly on Bank Holidays.

Amidst all that's happening, a new invention is slowly creeping into society, an outstanding example of electronic genius, the computer. It's capable of making calculations much more quickly than the human brain; the first compatible family of computers, the IBM System/360 has come onto the market. The computer is beginning to make an impression!

As 1964 comes to an end, I think the best comment of all has been made by Bob Dylan in his music: "The times they are a-changing..."'

🦋 Marilyn L Rice

Chapter 9
Fordingham, September, 1964

WHEN SEPTEMBER arrived, it was time for another change in Irene's life. She and Danny were no longer juniors, but seniors beginning their fourth year at the Fordingham Grammar School; this meant that they studied fewer subjects. Mathematics, Latin, French, English literature and language were compulsory for 4Alpha pupils; in addition, they opted for three subjects to study to 'O' level; his choices were physics, chemistry and biology but hers were geography, history and scripture knowledge. For Irene, there was a bonus to being one of the senior girls; she would be allowed to wear stockings instead of socks and a grey skirt as opposed to her tunic. The Senior Mistress would not allow skirts to be higher than three inches above the knee, which was annoying as long skirts were old fashioned and the new mini skirt was all the rage.

At least she was growing up, and by obeying the rules she was acting like a responsible adult. During the summer she, Danny and eight others had been confirmed by the Bishop of Derby; she was an adult in the eyes of the Church of England and had started taking Communion. Soon she would be sixteen and considered old enough for marriage.

Wills watched his daughter leave for her first day back at school. For a doting father she was growing up too quickly, but there was nothing he could do about the passing of time. His brother had been reminding him that he would soon be forty and that he should be thinking about investing in something for his retirement.

Jim had never forgotten the day, when he was fourteen and his father had taken him to the barn on the farm and said, 'Look, look as far as you can see.'

'Why?' he'd asked.

'Look!'

'I'm looking, Dad.'

'What do you see?'

'Fields, trees, hedges, cows, sheep. Why?'

Time & Tide

'Son, it's all mine. All that you can see, I own. This was my DREAM! When I was your age, I wanted to be a farmer; I set myself the goal of acquiring land; if I die tomorrow I'll have fulfilled my dreams. Look son, look and REMEMBER! Don't let the grass grow under your feet! Decide what you want in life and go for it.'

His father had known that the farm life was not for Jim, but that conversation had urged him on: his goal was the acquisition of an empire, an empire of good quality shops. He was concerned that his younger brother was stagnating; too content with the present to look to the future; he was right, Wills was content with his life and could not see any reason to think that far ahead, he did not have the same drive or motivation as his brother, but he had seen three stone cottages for sale on the main road: two near the Fordingham Arms and one opposite Ye Olde Tavern public houses. He was thinking about buying them and letting them out to tourists; property was always a good investment and tourism was on the increase.

Charlotte was not only an accomplished pianist playing at the pub in the evenings, but she was also a barmaid and happy with working as a 'fill-in' when required; it reminded her of her single days when her talents as barmaid and pianist had been utilised by the landlord of The Star public house in Whistbury. That was where Wills had first seen her, seated on the piano stool. She reminded him of his mother, who had been a talented singer and pianist; for him, it had been a case of 'love at first sight'. He would love her until the day he died.

But now it seemed as if they were drifting apart. They were both happy in their work but saw little of each other. Unlike Jim, he was not thinking so much about retirement as something which would keep him and Charlotte together, and also a family project before Irene flew the nest.

Wills chose his moment carefully; one evening in September when he and Charlotte were watching television, he mentioned the cottages and his idea. Further, if they bought at that time of the year they would have time to decorate and prepare them for the next tourist season.

Charlotte's response was one of amazement; she did not know that from his inheritance and subsequent investments he could afford to buy three cottages. She remembered how much she had enjoyed decorating and she would be the wife of a 'man of property'; the idea was very appealing. 'Sounds like a good idea,' she replied. 'What're they like inside?'

'Just a minute.' He got up and went into the office, returning with the details from the estate agents.

No. 34 was a detached property and the largest, opposite the pub with three bedrooms and some garden at the back. The other two, Nos. 14 and 20 were smaller and were at each end of a block of four cottages; much like their previous home at Silkington.

Charlotte quickly read the details; she was thinking how much fun it would be decorating and furnishing them. 'Let's go and see them.'

Wills smiled and called upstairs, 'Irene. Come down. We've got something to show you.'

Irene ran down the stairs and into the lounge; the television was still on but they were no longer watching it.

'Look at these,' Wills thrust the details of No. 34 into her hand.

'Are we moving?' she asked in horror. The prospects of leaving Orchard Cottage were daunting; she liked living on the Fordingham Estate, moving back into a small cottage with no fields, orchards or hayloft was unthinkable.

'No, but remember how much fun we had decorating and buying new furniture for here?'

'Yes, so?'

'So, how would you like the fun of helping to decorate and furnish Nos. 14, 20 and 34?'

Charlotte was silent. Irene was thinking about her homework and other commit-ments and wondering where she would find the time. Then it occurred to her that perhaps Danny could help: but why would they want to do it in the first place?

'Why?'

'Because your mother and I are thinking of buying them and letting them out to tourists.'

'Won't it mean a lot of work, advertising, maintaining, cleaning?'

Charlotte's expression changed to one of horror as the full extent of what she was letting herself in for suddenly dawned.

'Well, I s'pose it will at first, but when people know about them it'll be a piece of cake, m'duck!'

He had used that Nottinghamshire phrase, 'm'duck'. It was like a signal between them and she knew he wanted her support because her mother was having second thoughts.

'Daddy, darling, you have the most wonderful ideas. Let's go for it, m'duck!'

Time & Tide

She kissed him affectionately on the cheek; he smiled, and Charlotte noticed the rapport between them.

'I'll make the appointment with the agents, tomorrow'.

Irene went back upstairs. Charlotte knew that he would buy them and she would probably end up doing a lot of the work. Wills was happy; he was going to invest in something for the future and they would be working on the project together as a family.

That Saturday afternoon they viewed all three properties. On the Monday, all three had a 'SOLD' sign on them; by October half term Wills was a 'man of property'. Instead of being concerned about the bitter winter the Stephenson family were thinking about interior design and the next summer. They decided that trying to prepare all three properties for next Easter was an impossible task, so they would start with No. 14, one of the smaller ones and then continue with the others later; their aim was to have all three ready for occupation by August, 1965.

Wills was delighted with the way his family were united and embarking on the project. Charlotte spent most of her spare time at No. 14 wallpaper stripping; Mary often helped her in the afternoons. Wills and Irene occasionally managed a couple of hours in the evenings but at weekends when Wills was not working they were a happy family group with scrapers and hot water. The two smaller cottages needed bathrooms and kitchen units; these required specialist attention but before Christmas both properties had a reduced landing area and new small bathrooms. The project was put on hold during the Christmas and New Year celebrations. The January weather made painting an impossible task but work continued; the walls were papered and kitchen units and shelves were put in.

Another exciting part of the project was the furnishing; they calculated that they needed fourteen single beds, seven wardrobes and seven chests of drawers, mirrors, carpets, three dining tables, fourteen dining chairs and fourteen easy chairs, then there were all the cooking utensils and linen. They looked for sales of second-hand furniture and gradually bought all that they needed and stored them in No. 34.

No. 14 was finished by the beginning of March. As the Stephenson family admired their work and Wills thought about his depleted bank balance, some of the villagers congratulated them but others were opposed to local properties being used for tourists; they felt that the village would lose its rural character and become a glorified holiday camp.

Alan and Mary applauded the idea and were thinking of doing the same thing themselves; the Stantons joined Wills, Charlotte and Irene for a celebration 'fish and chip' supper at No. 14. They drank to the success of the venture, Wills privately wondered if he had made a mistake. He was relying on tourism becoming a growth industry for his success; if he failed he would have to sell the properties and after all the extra expenditure he would be selling at a loss.

Jim came to Fordingham at the end of March and reassured his brother that he was backing a winner. Jim's visits usually had a purpose; this time, it was not only to see the cottages but to tell Wills that he was investing in a fourth property. 'Don't let the grass grow under your feet! That's what I always say.'

Wills was aware of that fact, he had frequently heard Jim use the phrase, but he had no idea of the origin or why Jim seemed desperate to amass wealth. The new shop was at Matlock Bath; he was branching out and he, too, was aiming at the tourist market; this one was going to sell gifts, ornaments and souvenirs with 'Matlock Bath' printed on them, as well as tobacco and chocolates. Martin had left school after taking his 'A' levels and was going to stay in Nottingham while Jim moved to Matlock. As an added reassurance, Jim promised to advertise the cottages in all of his shop windows. It was through Jim's advertising that the first visitors stayed in No.14 at Easter; No. 20 was ready at the beginning of May and the third cottage was completed by August as they had planned.

Unfortunately, the weather was not good that summer. The two smaller cottages were let for a total of ten weeks and the third one remained empty. Wills had anticipated the problem of letting in winter and had hoped for 'six month' leases to people working in the area. He was lucky, a newly married couple were moving into the area to take up their first teaching posts at the secondary modern schools; they rented the detached cottage for a year.

Wills decided that things were going well for him; there was only one more thing that he wanted, another child; he kept hoping that Charlotte would announce her pregnancy and then his life would be complete. Charlotte was certainly not going to let that happen, she was enjoying herself far too much and had no intention of undergoing such suffering again. A new contraceptive pill had been available on the NHS since 1961; it was thought to be the most effective form of contraception and the easiest. Her great secret was that she was taking 'the pill'.

For Irene and Danny life was good; they lived on a pleasant country estate, enjoyed their school days and had each other. They were experiencing the sixties 'feel good' factor; their future looked bright and every day was full of sunshine.

Time & Tide

Friday, 27th May, 1966 was the last day of their fifth year in school. In the early afternoon Mr Graves assembled the fifth and upper sixth for the traditional final assembly; after the Whit Holiday they would return only to take examinations. The headmaster gave his annual pep talk and they sang 'Jerusalem', and then came the stony silence. The upper sixth had heard it all before; old grammar schools are steeped in tradition and traditions cannot be broken; the head boy knew he had to call for three cheers for the headmaster and then three cheers for Fordingham School. When this was over they were dismissed; pupils living locally left the school early but those living further afield, or who had not made arrangements to be collected, were obliged to remain until the school bus came.

Danny and Irene caught an earlier scheduled service bus to Fordingham and as they were walking up the drive, they both looked across the paddock.

'No one's working.' Irene said.

'We've got an extra hour,' he replied

'Shall we?' she asked

Together they both said, 'Yes!'

They ran towards the hayloft; this would be their last opportunity before Monday because Danny and his parents were going to Leeds for the Whit weekend. An extra hour to themselves was like manna from heaven; it was a gift from God, an opportunity they could not miss.

When they were safely in their haven, they threw their satchels down, took off their blazers, shoes and socks and sat in the hay. There was a bottle of lemonade and two cups in their hideaway; he picked up the bottle and filled both cups before handing one to her.

'Cheers!' they said together.

The sunlight shone through the open door; the birds were singing in the trees, and in the distance was the droning sound of the traffic on the road; they were oblivious of it all.

'I wish we weren't going away this weekend. It's a waste of two days for me.'

'The time'll fly by. We'll be back together before you know it and revising next week. Let's plan our final revision campaign.'

'We start with maths. So. Maths. Monday afternoon.' Danny said with his usual clear logical thinking and organisation.

'That's a good idea, then we can do literature on Tuesday, French on Wednesday, Latin Thursday. Friday's fun day then a quick maths review at the weekend.'

'Mmm. So, that's decided. What shall we do now?' he asked as he ran his fingers through the hay. He was looking lustfully at her; she was forbidden fruit but he longed for the day when he could explore the hidden territory beyond the school dress. He was sixteen, with a healthy sexual appetite and desired more than the permissible kissing and cuddling; he was legally old enough for marriage and sex, but society's rules and the Church's teaching told him that he must wait until they were married. With the future they were planning, he would have to wait another six years.

She looked at him and had a sudden desire to remove his tie. This was the 'swinging sixties' and the dawn of the permissive era; she knew that some of the girls at school had gone 'all the way'; they talked about the pain of the first time but also the relief. The first time was special and one that you always remember but the prevailing attitude was why wait until marriage? Virginity was fast becoming a cumbersome burden; once lost there was no turning back but at least she would know what it felt like to be a woman. She desperately wanted him to make love to her.

After removing his tie she smiled and then undid the top button on his shirt. 'Shall we?' she asked as she continued slowly moving down the buttons.

Had he misunderstood? If she was game so was he. He started undoing the buttons on her dress, as he got down to her waist he could see her bra and was eager to feel the young and tender breasts that lay beneath.

She removed his shirt, revealing his muscular chest, and he took off her dress leaving her in only bra and pants. He was aroused by the sight of her near naked body.

'Shall we?' she repeated.

'All the way?'

'The first time should be special. We're happy now. The sun's shining. We'll always remember this stolen hour.'

His conscience was telling him that it was wrong but his heart and sexual desire were telling him the opposite. He could not fault her logic; they were both legally of age and if she was willing why should they not go ahead?

He undid her bra, removed it and began caressing her breasts.

'All the way?'

'Yes, yes,' she whispered.

Impulsively, he removed his trousers and underpants. She saw his erect penis; she quickly removed her pants and took his penis in her hands guiding him towards her.

'You're Adam and I'm Eve,' she whispered, 'this is our Garden of Eden, our Paradise.'

In a careless and irresponsible moment, so out of character for Danny, but he was young and in love, he entered her. She lay back and as she felt him slowly move inside her she began panting with sheer delight. It felt good, she was ecstatic; it was a moment in time that she wanted to hold on to, a moment that should last forever.

As he lay on top of her, aware of her excitement, he felt a sense of relief. They were one now, a united couple, together forever; he withdrew slowly and lay beside her in the hay. Had they really done it? They looked at each other.

'Any regrets?'

'*Je ne regrette rien.*' Irene said, she was a woman; it had been special, spontaneous, natural and the right time.

'We seem to have got things out of order. You're supposed to go through a ceremony and take solemn vows first.'

'Does it matter?'

He thought for a minute and then said, 'You know what Mr Graves said this afternoon about not starting anything unless you're going to see it through.'

'With perseverance and determination,' she added trying to impersonate their head teacher.

Taking hold of her hands and in a serious tone he said, 'I'm going to see this through, Irene, I love you. Will you do me the honour of becoming my wife? Will you marry me?'

'Shall we elope to Gretna Green?' she replied humorously.

'No, I mean here and now.'

'What!' she exclaimed. 'Oh sure. I'll just nip and fetch the vicar. He can marry us here. Perhaps he'll take his clothes off, too, then we'll all be naked in the hay!'

'No, let's go through the ceremony ourselves, making our vows to each other.'

'We haven't got any rings.'

'Oh yes we have!'

He reached over to his satchel and took out a piece of string, ruler and a pair of scissors. He cut two pieces of string, each exactly six inches long. He put one piece round the third finger of her left hand and tied a reef knot so that it would remain secure; he then carefully removed it and told her to place the second piece of string round his finger.

Amazed at his knowledge of knots, and the fact that he seemed to be prepared for the occasion she said, 'You're so prepared, anyone would think you were a boy scout.'

'There used to be a pack of cubs in the village. It lasted for about a year. I learned a lot in that time.'

She had learned something else about him.

'Irene, will you marry me?'

'Yes, yes.'

He took her hand and said, 'I, Daniel Stanton, take thee Irene Joy Stephenson to be my wedded wife, to have and to hold from this day forward, for better for worse, for richer for poorer, in sickness and in health, to love and cherish until death us do part; thereto I give thee my troth.'

She replied, 'I, Irene Joy Stephenson, take thee Daniel Stanton to be my wedded husband, to have and to hold from this day forth, for better for worse, for richer for poorer, in sickness and in health, to love and cherish and to obey until death. Thereto I give thee my troth.'

He put the ring firmly on her finger, and she placed hers on his, then together they said, 'With this ring I thee wed, with my body I thee worship and with all my worldly goods I thee endow.'

Danny then said, 'I pronounce us man and wife. Let me kiss you, Mrs Stanton.'

They kissed and fell back into the hay laughing.

'We are truly married to each other until death,' he said, 'we've exchanged vows and given each other rings. So, how does it feel, Mrs Stanton?'

'Great, I love you, Mr Stanton. I wish we could stay here like this forever but I'll settle for going through school, university and life with you.'

'There's one thing that's going to separate us now, though.'

'What's that?' she asked.

'The time!' he replied. He was once again in command of the situation. 'It's five past four. We've only got ten minutes.'

Reluctantly, they dressed, had a long goodbye kiss and left the hayloft. Neither of them knew that they had been seen by someone in the orchard, someone who adored Irene; someone who, two years earlier, had seen them 'disappear' in the farm buildings, investigated and discovered their hideaway.

'See you Monday lunchtime,' he shouted after her.

She turned towards him, waved and smiled; it was going to be a long weekend.

Time & Tide

Later, in her bedroom, she switched her tranny on and tuned into Radio Caroline. The Seekers were singing 'I'll Never Find Another You'. 'How true, she thought to herself as she saw the Stanton's car go up the lane towards the drive. Danny was seated in the back, she waved and he waved back; she watched until the car was out of sight at 5.15 pm. There were sixty-seven hours until 12.15 pm on Monday; she did not know how she could survive without him for that amount of time, but she was a woman now and felt different. She fondled her ring and then carefully put it in her jewellery box to avoid any awkward questions.

She counted the hours, of what seemed to be the longest weekend of her life, in Fordingham; he counted them in Leeds. At last, the eagerly awaited morning came; Danny got in the back of the car and Alan started the engine; they were on their way home.

Irene was keeping a close eye on the time when she felt a cold shiver go down the back of her spine. 'Someone's walking over my grave,' she said to herself. It was 10.05 am, only another couple of hours to go. She was finding it difficult to concentrate; her mind was permanently wandering, wandering back to Friday afternoon in the hayloft.

Charlotte was working at the pub on that Bank Holiday Monday which meant that Irene was left to prepare the midday meal for herself and her father. He was working with John Bateman; the rest of the staff were on holiday. She began preparing a salad with cold meat and potatoes for their lunch; she was unable to keep looking out of the front windows to see if the Stantons were returning.

They were finishing their meal, when there was a knock at the back door. Before either of them could move, the door opened and Lord Fordingham entered the kitchen. They were surprised because Lord Fordingham had a great deal of respect for the privacy of the staff living on the estate; he always used the outside door into the estate office and had never come into the house without being invited.

He was of medium height and slim build with dark hair, moustache and thick-rimmed glasses. Whether he was walking round his estate, in the village or in Buxton he always had an air of dignity about him. He had the type of confidence which comes with money and a title; even when he was wearing clothes appropriate for working in the fields, he could never be mistaken for an employee; he still had a regal appearance as Lord of the Manor.

As Wills and Irene were about to stand up, in the usual respectful manner for their employer, he said, 'Please, don't get up.'

112

His voice was shaky and his solemn expression indicated that something was seriously wrong.

'I've got some sad news,' he continued, 'the Police have just been to see me. I'm afraid there's been an accident.'

Wills' first thought was Charlotte, he said, 'Not Charlotte, please no.' He had lost his parents and son, but he deeply loved his wife and could not bear the thought of losing her as well.

'No, William, not Charlotte but,' here he looked at Irene, 'the Stanton family. Just after ten this morning, their car went off the road and crashed into a tree.'

He paused and then said, 'They were all killed instantly. I'm so very sorry.'

There was a stony silence as if none of them really believed what he was saying. Irene uttered, 'No, no,' as tears started to fall down her cheeks.

Lord Fordingham continued, 'I'm sorry, Irene, I know you and Danny have been good friends since you came here.'

'Sir, it can't be true. It can't be...'

Her father interrupted her, 'Now, now, m'duck, calm down. His Lordship wouldn't tell us if it weren't true.'

She quickly gained her composure, fearing that she might give something away concerning the intimacy of their relationship or their hideaway, if she became hysterical.

'There was no other vehicle involved. They do not know what exactly happened. An eyewitness, who was walking her dog, said that the car was travelling at about thirty-five miles an hour along a straight road just outside Leeds, when it went out of control. It veered off the road, smashed a gate, went into a field and hit a tree. One possible theory is that Alan had a heart attack at the wheel. They managed to get them out of the car before it went up in flames but the actual impact had already killed them.' He paused before continuing with the more mundane matters of the smooth running of his estate. 'William, it may be some time before I can employ another head gardener. Master Thomas and I will help out in the meantime but I'm afraid it will mean longer periods of duty for you. When it's all been sorted out I'll give you extra holiday periods. Will you assemble the staff at 9.30 tomorrow in the estate office? I will address them all regarding this sad event and I will ensure that those who wish to go to the funeral do so, wherever it is held.'

'Yes, your Lordship,' was all Wills could utter. He had a lump in his throat as he recalled his first day at Fordingham and his meeting with Alan Stanton. He was only forty years old, an easygoing person with a heart of gold and a man who loved his work.

With the words, 'I'll leave you now,' Lord Fordingham made his exit.

Wills and Irene looked at each other; neither could speak, nor really believe it. While they were sitting in stony silence and disbelief, a distraught Charlotte came home. In rural communities such news travels at high speed. By 1.30 pm the whole village had heard of the accident; mourning and sadness had replaced the happy Bank Holiday atmosphere. Every villager had his or her own personal memory of the family; for some, it was the young Alan, for others, their marriage and family life together. For the Stephenson family, it was the friendship, help and support they had given them when they arrived.

Charlotte had never had a friend like Mary before; it seemed so unfair. How could it happen to such a nice family? The Stephenson family remembered the help Mary had given them with decorating their home, the further assistance with their new properties and the celebration meal at No. 14. Life on the estate would not be the same without them.

Irene went upstairs to her room; she opened her jewellery box and looked at the ring. Only three days ago they were so happy together; they were married and now she was a widow. Was it her fault? She had encouraged him; like Eve had tempted Adam in the Garden of Eden and the wages of sin was death. They had enjoyed one hour together; such stolen moments of bliss and now it was all over; all she had were memories and the hayloft. She went back downstairs.

'I'm going out for a walk,' she said to her parents, who were still in the kitchen.

Her walk took her straight to the hayloft, where she sat in the hay, and the tears flowed down her cheeks. She remembered the times they had spent together: the first day at junior school, he had called her name as she was walking home for lunch: the first time he had brought her to the hayloft and they held hands: their first kiss: in secondary school they had been inseparable. Only last Friday they had consummated their relationship and promised to spend the rest of their lives together.

Mr Graves had wished them a long and successful life. Danny had such great hopes, he would have made an excellent doctor and now his life was over; he would never achieve his true potential: it was such a waste of a life. If only she'd realised last Friday that it would be their last time together. If only...if only...

How often people use those words about what might have been, or will be in the future, usually the words are empty, shallow and meaningless.

All their plans for the future had been erased at that split second of impact. She was alone and began to realise why her grandmother had been so melancholy since her grandfather's death. Perhaps she should wear black for the rest of her days? But she was only sixteen; Danny had been also only sixteen; life was cruel, but then she already knew that.

The afternoon was slowly becoming early evening; she knew she would have to go home and display the stiff upper lip. She could not let her emotions get the better of her; Danny would want her to carry on with her life and get good grades in her examinations. She returned home; the Stephenson family ate their evening meal together, discussing their memories of the family who until then had lived next door. They each tried to occupy themselves during the evening; Irene returned to the planned revision campaign but her mind was still in the hayloft which she vowed to keep as a sanctuary and shrine.

The next morning the staff were duly assembled when Lord and Lady Fordingham entered the estate office. Lord Fordingham spoke of how highly he and her Ladyship thought of the Stanton family and how saddened they were by the tragedy. Mary's parents and sister would be arriving later to sort out the family's possessions and arrange the funeral, which would be on Friday afternoon, those who wished would be allowed to attend. Mark and Billy, the two young gardeners who had known Alan all of their lives, were fighting back the tears; they hero-worshipped Alan and saw him as a father figure. The assembled group were given their instructions for the day and then dismissed. It was hard but life on a farm must go on.

It was a difficult week which culminated in the funerals of the three victims at 3.00 pm on Friday 3rd June. Lord and Lady Fordingham and all the staff attended; Master Thomas remained behind with his sister, Lucille, to give the animals their afternoon feed.

The church was packed; as the service proceeded Irene remembered every minute of the hour they had spent together, exactly one week ago. The service began with the hymn 'Abide With Me', and then the vicar read one of the Psalms; this was followed by Lord Fordingham reading the lesson, taken from the New Testament: 1 Corinthians, Chapter 13, and all about love. It was very moving for all of the congregation; most people had tears in their eyes. The vicar spoke of the tragedy of a much loved family from their community, and the sad waste of a young life along with the lives of his parents. He emphasised that they were with God and had been taken together for a purpose which only God knew about; he told them that they should turn their sorrow into joy because their friends were now in a better place. That was cold comfort for Irene, who felt she had been left alone. After the address they sang 'The Lord is my Shepherd', and then there were the prayers for the 'dear departed', with the congregation joining in and saying the Lord's Prayer. Finally, they all sat and listened to the organist's rendering of the 'Londonderry Air', known as 'Danny Boy'.

There was not a dry eye left as they followed the coffins to the graveside for the final laying to rest and then it was all over.

Irene went to school on the Monday. Mr Graves spoke to her before the examination; he told her how sorry he was to hear of the tragedy, what a good person and pupil Danny had been and how much he had contributed to the school. There was to be a special memorial assembly for him at the end of term. She was aware of looks and comments from her peers and concern from the staff, but she appeared to have found a new strength which helped her through the exams they had both worked so hard for.

After the exams came the memorial service for which some of the fifth and upper sixth came back. Then there was the summer holiday which seemed longer than usual. The exam results were published; Danny's name was above hers on the list. Instead of the grades he had hoped for, there were just a lot of 'A's for absence. Her own grades were five '1's and three '2's; she had not managed to get all '1's, but such was life.

And life goes on...

Chapter 10
Fordingham, September, 1966

THERE WAS A SADNESS in the community; the villagers missed the Stanton family's smiling faces. Irene returned to school as a sixth form pupil, to study for 'A' levels in scripture knowledge, English and history; her sixth form peers expressed sympathy over Danny's untimely death. Somehow, the whole school seemed different; Danny was the individual who stood out in the crowd; his enthusiasm and zest for life left an irreplaceable gap in their class. She became a loner; it was just like the time she discovered that Hillary was her cousin. After Hillary left Elsbridge School she had felt totally alone, but this time the hurt was far greater.

There were changes on the estate. Billy Foster, upset by Alan's death, had resigned – his replacement was a school leaver from another village; Irene knew his name was Barry and that he came to work on a bike; she did not wish to know any more about him. Mark Adams, now a twenty-three year old man, of medium height, stocky build, with ginger hair and clean-shaven, was promoted to head gardener. He moved into the cottage with his pregnant wife, Jane; this was the Jane she had met on her first day at school, the plump, round-faced girl known as 'ginger nut', who had ignored her after she passed the eleven plus exam. For Irene, this was another example of how cruel life could be; not seeing Danny around the estate was one thing, but being replaced by pregnant Jane was an added insult. However, it was something she would have to learn to live with. Jane seemed to delight in pointing out, at every opportunity, that she was a married woman with a baby on the way while Irene was still a schoolgirl. Although, Irene would have liked Danny's child, she was content with continuing her education and had no real desire to settle down as a wife and mother.

This was something which Jane's lack of academic intellect prevented her from understanding; for her, it was a scoring points exercise which she thoroughly enjoyed. Her son was born on 14th February, 1967,and named Thomas Mark; his birth was the cause of much celebrating in the village, particularly by the new grandparents;

for the Stephenson family the event was welcomed with both joy and sadness as they, or at least Wills and Irene, remembered James left behind in Silkington Churchyard.

On 12th March, 1967, her cousin Martin celebrated his twenty-first birthday; Jim and Julia were delighted and hired a room at the local pub in Nottingham for a party. Wills, Charlotte, Irene and Hillary went, but Ann wisely stayed away. Hillary was a sixth form pupil studying for 'A' levels in Derby, but unlike Irene, she spent a lot of her time at parties and generally enjoying life. She had a boyfriend, Frank, who she had introduced to the family; life was good for her; it seemed as if the wheel of fortune had turned and she was the lucky one now. Her cousin had lost her boyfriend and was alone with a bleak future ahead.

The majority of the people present seemed to be Jim's friends and they were enjoying the occasion; the only person in the room who did not look happy was Martin. His father announced that he had a special present for him; he gave him an envelope which turned out to contain a photograph, deeds and keys to the next shop in the Stephenson empire; it was in Bakewell, the market town situated in the Peak District renowned for Bakewell puddings. The Matlock Bath shop had been a success and Jim expected his son to make a success of this one. Martin smiled and thanked his father but deep down he was unhappy; a shop was the last thing he wanted.

After the party in March the days seemed to pass quickly and the time that Irene was dreading arrived. They finished school on the Friday afternoon before the Whit Holiday; she went to the hayloft and with tears running down her cheeks she remembered their first and last time. She still had his 'ring' in her jewellery box; it was her most precious piece of jewellery. She would often take it, slip it on her finger and smile; it was getting dirty and frayed but she did not care; she would always treasure it.

The summer came; it was a special summer with the hippies declaring love and peace everywhere. Wills was doing well with his properties and made a further investment; he used the income from the properties to buy the two middle cottages, Nos. 16 and 18; now he owned the block of four and a detached property. Jim had five shops, including the one he had given to Martin, and Wills owned five cottages; the Stephenson empires were growing. To the onlooker, it seemed as if the brothers were in competition with each other, playing their own private 'Monopoly' game. Who would amass the most wealth? There was nothing further from the truth.

The distance between Charlotte and Irene was growing but neither of them worried about it. Jane was now seventeen and content with motherhood; Irene wondered if, in time, she would regret becoming a wife and mother at the young age of sixteen. Wherever Irene looked, she was greeted with happy, smiling people; even Elizabeth was looking happier than she had since John's death.

In September, Irene returned to school for her last year; she was made head girl, a great honour but without Danny it did not have any real meaning for her. It was time to make a decision about going to university; she looked at what each one had to offer. Christine had told her a lot about Durham; she picked up the prospectus for it but she was not enthralled; the idea of going to university without Danny seemed pointless, it would not be the same. So she decided on Buxton College of Education instead; she could train as a teacher and stay at home. Wills was delighted with her choice but Charlotte was disappointed, and tried unsuccessfully to persuade her to change her mind. Wills was so pleased that he promised to buy her a car for her eighteenth birthday if she passed her driving test before Christmas; she passed it in November.

The cold winter days had arrived and this year there was an added problem. Foot-and-mouth disease, the farmer's worst nightmare had become a reality, they were all aware of the disastrous consequences if even one cow showed any indication of the diseases; every single animal would be slaughtered. The thought of Christmas on the horizon was the only thing which seemed to generate any feeling of warmth. Bonfire Night was over; Remembrance Day had passed. She always remembered her days at Elsbridge Primary School on 11th November, when they observed two minutes silence outside regardless of the weather. That was one of the things that had disappeared in the sixties; they still remembered those who gave their lives for their peace and freedom but it was remembered on the Sunday nearest to the 11th November, a more convenient time than stopping everything at eleven in the morning on a weekday.

Christmas and New Year came; Elizabeth joined the Stephensons as usual. Although Mark and Jane remained at home for both Christmas and New Year and Mark did not really mind working during the Christmas period, Wills decided to keep the routine which he and Alan had used. This meant that on 23rd December, Wills called all the staff into his office, and gave them a miniature bottle of whisky and a cigar each before thanking them for all their work during the year. Then Lord Fordingham came into the office and made a short speech telling them how well they had all done and what a marvellous team he had working for him. He gave each man a Christmas card. Inside was a token of his appreciation: the junior staff usually got a 10 shilling note and those who had worked for a longer period of time £1. Wills and the head gardener received £5; for Mark this was an important rise.

Time & Tide

Lord Fordingham's compliments meant more to all of them this year, as the threat of the 'epidemic' was with them and so many other farms had been victims to the disease: so far, they had been lucky!

On Christmas Eve Charlotte collected Elizabeth while Irene decorated the tree and put all the presents underneath it. In the early evening they sat in the lounge with a large log fire burning in the grate. Later, they went to the Fordingham Arms where Charlotte played carols; Wills, standing by the piano with a glass of whisky in his hand, looked at his wife and daughter and felt so proud of both of them; they were so talented in their different ways. It was a wrench to leave the cosy pub for the final Christmas Eve event, the church service to welcome the birth of Christ.

When the service was over the village seemed to come to life as everyone wished everyone else a 'Merry Christmas'. Cards and presents were exchanged and then the village slept for a few hours before the celebrations started again.

Wills and John Bateman fed the animals in the morning and then the Stephenson family had a late breakfast before opening their presents. They ate Christmas lunch at 1.30 pm before watching the Queen give her Christmas speech on the television, the set remained on as they snoozed through the rest of the afternoon. Wills and John fed the animals before Christmas tea. The log fire burned continuously; the lingering aroma of Will's cigars with turkey was a significant reminder that it was Christmas.

Boxing Day came and all the excitement was over. Then on 30th December they all went to Whistbury. On New Year's Eve there was the party; Charlotte took her place at the piano. Irene thought back to all the years when she had been sent to bed and yet remained awake listening to the music and singing. She had always waited for the church clock to chime and then she knew she was a year older. There was the time when she was five and came downstairs; she would never forget that one! There was the first one after Grandpa died; that was a sad year. But this year she was going to be eighteen and old enough to drink alcohol when she went to the pub; if Wills had kept his promise she would also be the proud owner of a car.

The church clock chimed; the New Year had arrived! They waited the usual eight minutes and then started singing, 'Happy Birthday'. Wills opened the champagne; he remembered that poignant moment when he first saw his daughter: the moment that changed his life. Now, she was a young woman who would be going to college in September. After the champagne he gave her a small parcel; inside was a set of car keys and a photograph of a 1966 mini, which was back in Fordingham. She would not see it until later that day, but it did not matter; Daddy had kept his promise, as usual. The only miserable face in the room belonged to Charlotte; having invested in more property Wills had been unable to afford a new car but had found a good second-hand one. Charlotte realised that her daughter's car was a newer model than her own; she and Wills had argued about an extravagant present for her eighteenth birthday. Charlotte was determined to have a new car herself out of the income from the properties next year.

When they arrived home, her father took her to where the car was hidden; it was in the disused barn where old farm equipment was stored; nobody ever went there. Her heart missed a beat when she realised where he was taking her; inside the door was her shiny red mini all taxed and insured; she was just glad her father had not gone up the stairs and found the hayloft.

Irene completed her last two terms at school. That awful Friday arrived when they joined the fifth years for the headmaster's farewell speech. They assembled and the head addressed them; she could not believe it; she had heard that he used the same speech each year but expected some changes. However, it was the same piece of paper and looking very shabby. Danny did not get the long, happy or successful life. Would she do any better? The traditional pep talk, the three cheers and then the dismissal and, for Irene, a sad reminder.

She went home, returning only to take her exams; in August she collected her results, three grade 'A's; Wills was delighted. In September she took up her place at the Buxton College of Education and began her teacher training course.

Charlotte had amassed a record of their lives throughout the sixties; she had progressed from notebooks to files and had quite a collection. As the decade was coming to its close, she flipped through them, some items caused her to stop and remember.

'1965

January: blizzards are raging over most of England. The world news is dominated by Sir Winston Churchill's ill health. 24th January, he's died; our war hero has died; his body is to lie in state at Westminster Hall for three days. 30th January, the funeral's at St Paul's Cathedral; we watched it on the television. After the service he was taken to his final resting place, the churchyard at Bladon, a country village in Oxfordshire...

March: the sixty-seven year old Princess Royal, known as Princess Mary, the only daughter of King George V and Queen Mary has died...

April: the Greater London Council replaces the former London County Council... The price of inland and Commonwealth letter postage goes up from 3d to 4d...

June: The Beatles receive the MBE (Irene's delighted!) ...Ronald Biggs, sentenced for thirty years for his part in the Great Train Robbery has escaped from Wandsworth Prison with three other convicts...

July: Sir Alec Douglas Home resigns as leader of the Conservative Party; he's succeeded by Edward Heath... The Bank Holiday has changed from the first to the last Monday in August... The Mods and Rockers continue to make their presence known by behaving like hooligans at the coastal resorts on Bank Holidays...

September: Mrs. Justice Elizabeth Lane, the first woman County Court Judge in Britain appointed to Edmonton Circuit in London in September, 1962, is now the first woman High Court Judge...

November: the abolition of the Death Penalty Bill comes into force.

1966

March: Harold Wilson dissolves Parliament and there's a general election; this time Labour wins in a landslide victory with an overall majority of ninety-seven.

June: Sheila Scott, the British airwoman returns to Heathrow Airport after completing the world's longest flight in a single-engined plane. She's flown over 28,000 miles in thirty three days...

21st October, heavy rain has caused the collapse of a mountainous coal tip at Aberfan in South Wales. It's fallen on to a junior school and a row of houses; 116 children and 28 adults are dead; the nation's in mourning. The Queen and Prince Philip visit the site and a national disaster fund is set up.

November: The Prince of Wales celebrates his eighteenth birthday...The Aberfan disaster fund reaches £1million... Britain receives its first direct television transmission from Australia...

December: details are issued of the changes in the proposed decimal currency for Britain.

ABROAD

1965

America: Selma, Alabama, Dr Martin Luther King is one of 3000 blacks arrested; he was released on bail after advising his followers to halt their active protests; 14th, March, demonstration marches culminate when 10,000 coloured and white civil rights demonstrators march through the centre of New York. 15th March, President Johnson presents a new Civil Rights Bill to end all voting restrictions on blacks... August, he signs the Voting Rights Act to add 900,000 black voters to the electoral roll. Martin Luther King has won another victory for the black population adding voting rights to their equal rights on the buses and in education.

THE SPACE RACE continues in America and Russia. The United States launches Ranger 8 designed to send pictures back from the moon; it crash lands, after taking and televising 7,000 photographs of the moon's surface... 23rd March, the USA launches Gemini 3, their first two-man spacecraft; it completes three orbits of the Earth in under five hours and descends into the Western Atlantic... April, the first nuclear reactor is launched into orbit in space in a US satellite... June, the United States launches Gemini 4, during its third orbit Major Edward White steps out 150 miles above the Pacific and 'walks' in space for fifteen minutes; Gemini 4 holds the record for the longest US space flight and the world's longest two-man flight... December, Gemini 7 is launched from Cape Kennedy to rendezvous in space with Gemini 6; they travel together for $5\frac{1}{2}$ hours, separated by a distance of between three and ten feet at a speed of 17,000 mph. Gemini 6 returns to earth leaving Gemini 7 in orbit.

Russia sends a two-man spacecraft, Voskhod 2 into space and Lieutenant Colonel Alexei Leonov is the first man to 'swim' in space for ten minutes; this spacecraft lands off-course and under manual control, but safely, after completing eighteen orbits of the Earth in twenty-six hours... November, the Russians launch a spacecraft aimed at Venus.

The US Embassy in Saigon is blown up by Vietcong terrorists. There were general elections in Rhodesia which brought a sweeping victory for Ian Smith's Rhodesian Front Party; with a two third majority he's able to make constitutional changes... The Chinese explode an atomic bomb dropped from the air...The UK and France sign an agreement for a joint development of two new types of military aircraft... Gambia becomes an Independent Commonwealth State and Singapore leaves the Malaysian Federation to become an Independent State... General de Gaulle is re-elected as president of France for a further seven years... The Vietnam War continues, but there's a truce for Christmas.

1966, the Indian Prime Minister, Lal Bahadur Shastri, has died; his body is cremated on the banks of the Jumna River on 12th January; he is succeeded by Mrs Indira Gandhi... Australia changes to decimal currency; the Australian general election in March has given a clear majority to the right-wing People's Party for the first time since 1945... Malawi has become a Republic within the Commonwealth... Bechuanaland achieves independence... The Commonwealth Republic of Botswana and Basutoland become the monarchic Commonwealth State of Lesotho... Barbados, after 339 years of British rule, becomes the twenty sixth and smallest Commonwealth nation.

SPORT

1966

England hosts the Football World Cup... 30th July, the NATION'S CELEBRATING. WE'VE WON THE WORLD CUP! England's defeated Germany by four goals to two, a superb team effort by their manager, Alf Ramsey. Captain Bobby Moore and Geoff Hurst scored a hat trick, three of the four goals. (I'm no football fan, but even I feel proud of our country's achievement; Wills and the men are ecstatic!)

THE MID-SIXTIES!

"A time of adventure and discovery".

There's a scheme to convert British telephone numbers to an all-figure system and the post office has begun distributing postal codes. Satellite systems are developing. Europe has a new idea for road transport, a common network of main European highways named as 'E' roads. Despite tragic air disasters, the aviation companies are still designing newer, larger and faster aeroplanes. Speed is becoming an important factor in daily life; the railways are also designing faster trains, changing tracks to accommodate them and moving to electronic signalling.

Education is seen as THE key to the future and is changing. Rote learning and formality are outdated; the new idea is to learn by doing and enjoying work in an informal and friendly environment. A new form of "comprehensive" education is gaining in popularity; advocates feel that children who fail the eleven plus exam are penalised for the rest of their lives, but comprehensive schools mean equal opportunity for all. (I'm all for that!)

The cinema continues to show films and attract audiences despite competition from television programmes like "The Saint".

Spy films are successful, particularly those featuring the men from UNCLE which began as a television programme.

"Batman and Robin", "Dr Zhivago", "Born Free" and "The Sound of Music" have all been box office hits.

Mary Quant is the great name in fashion; her ideas have made London and Carnaby Street, the centre of the fashion industry; she's launched the ultra-short mini-skirt and become a lead for other designers to follow.

Fashion, music, the media, Labour Government, and high-rise living. Life's good, regardless of the world's problems, the war in Vietnam, the starving, the homeless illustrated so well in the documentary "Cathy Come Home", the sick and the dying; in Britain there's a feel good factor; it's the "swinging sixties"; life's euphoric! One long party and no one can imagine it ever ending!

1967

The youth volcano is now extinct; the new youth group are known as the hippies; a term which began in America and describes the youth cult whose slogan is "Make love not war", a protest against the war in Vietnam. These young people are identified by their way-out, off-beat style of clothing adorned with baubles, bangles and beads; they wear their hair long, often decorated with flowers and they talk about flower power, peace and love; they are associated with smoking pot and taking LSD and they advocate freedom, peace and community living. Here, they have given birth to the "permissive era" and the "baby boom" associated with the change in attitude and lifestyle of the sixties. After the Teddy Boys and Angry Young Men of the fifties, the young see themselves as now in a position to make the world a better place for future generations; the revolution has taken place.

BRITAIN

Donald Campbell has been killed on Coniston Water, in the Lake District, whilst attempting to break his own water speed record... Jo Grimmond resigns as leader of the Liberal Party; his successor is Jeremy Thorpe... Plans have been announced for the new town of Milton Keynes in Buckinghamshire.

March: the 61,000-ton oil tanker, Torrey Canyon has run aground on the Seven Stones Reef between Lands End and the Scilly Isles causing 100,000 tons of crude oil to spill into the water off the Cornish coast... Sandie Shaw has won the Eurovision contest for Britain with Puppet on a String...

May: Francis Chichester arrives back at Plymouth after taking seven and a half months to complete the 28,500 mile voyage single-handed around the world; he's a record-breaker, the first man to sail alone around the world...

August: Brian Epstein, the man who discovered The Beatles at The Cavern Club is found dead in his home... The "pirate" radio stations, which have been playing non-stop pop music since 1964, are signing off; only Radio Caroline remains...

September: the BBC begins a new radio programme to replace the outlawed pirate radio stations, Radio 1; the Light, Third and Home Services have been replaced by Radios 2, 3, and 4.

October: Clement Attlee has died; he will be remembered for the post-war welfare reforms... the Queen Mary liner leaves Southampton to become a floating hotel, in America.

FOOT AND MOUTH disease is spreading rapidly across the British countryside; thousands of animals have been slaughtered. There's disinfectant by the front entrance; we have to thoroughly disinfect our shoes before we come on to the estate and everyone is using the front entrance; the staff drive is closed. We are all terrified of the dreaded disease affecting our livestock. Wills is in a permanent bad mood; he seems to have a personal relationship with each animal; if they have to be slaughtered he'll be devastated; government compensation will not console him. We all pray that we will be spared.

Abortion has been legalised – with guidelines. I suppose it will stop "back street" abortions and make termination safer.

ABROAD

In America, Cassius Clay has announced that he wants to be known as Muhammad Ali after his conversion to Islam...

27th January, three astronauts are killed in a launch pad fire at Cape Kennedy; they were undergoing a simulated launch for the first Apollo mission scheduled for February when an electrical spark caused a fire and they could not escape from the burning capsule...

Biafra's claimed independence from Nigeria...

June: the "six-day" war in Israel, against the Arabs has resulted in victory for Israel but not total peace; Israel has taken back the Gaza Strip from Egypt, the Biblical towns of Bethlehem, Jericho and Hebron from Judah and most of the West Bank but more importantly for the Jews, the recapture of The Wailing Wall from Jordanian control enables them to pray at this holy site for the first time since 1949...

General de Gaulle is visiting Canada and rallying support for the Quebec separatists who want to break away from the rest of Canada, stating, "Long live free Quebec"... Russia celebrates the fiftieth anniversary of its Revolution... Dr Christiaan Barnard carries out the first heart transplant operation on a human being in Cape Town, South Africa... The Australian prime minister, Harold Holt, drowned in the sea; he's replaced by his deputy, John McEwan... The Concorde supersonic airliner has been seen for the first time at Toulouse, in France.

TELEVISION is presenting the long running drama "The Forsyte Saga".

The Independent Channel has launched "News at Ten" in an attempt to rival the BBC's "Nine 0'Clock News"...

July: "Batman and Robin" have arrived on television screens around the world; BBC2 has begun broadcasting in colour... September, twelve-million British television viewers watched "Coronation Street's" Elsie marry her wartime American lover, Steve Tanner (including us!).

FILMS

"Georgy Girl" and "Alfie" made in Britain have won Hollywood awards. Other memorable films are "Bonnie and Clyde", "The Graduate", "Camelot", "The Dirty Dozen", "Thoroughly Modern Millie" and "Barefoot in the Park".

In the theatre Tom Stoppard has made his début with his "Rosencrantz And Guildenstern Are Dead" at the National Theatre in London after its run at the Edinburgh Festival. The musical "Hair" has opened at the Public Theatre in New York's East Village.

POP SCENE

The Monkees originally designed for an American television series have taken the UK and American charts by storm with their record, "I'm a Believer". When the group came to Britain they were greeted by thousands of screaming teenagers.

Monkeemania has hit Britain just as Beatlemania did. This summer of 1967 has become known as the "Summer of Love", the young people are listening to Procol Harum's " A Whiter Shade of Pale" and Scott McKenzie's " San Francisco (Be Sure To Wear Some Flowers In Your Hair)".

Other groups and singers in the charts are The Seekers, The Beatles, The Supremes, Cliff Richard, Tom Jones, Engelbert Humperdinck, Vince Hill and Jimi Hendrix.

1968

BRITAIN

Free school milk for secondary school children is abolished... Decimalisation begins with the introduction of 5p and 10p coins... Enoch Powell has delivered his "Rivers Of Blood" speech regarding the influx of immigrants in Britain, he sees the devastating effect of allowing their continued entry on the Welfare State...The first liver, heart and lung transplants have taken place in Britain; sadly, the receiver of the lung transplant, a fifteen year old male only lived for twelve days; but transplant operations are in their infancy...In literature, the Booker prize has been launched... Margaret Thatcher has been appointed Shadow Transport Minister in the Government.

ABROAD

Mauritius declares independence... Yuri Gagarin, the first man to venture into space, has died... Pierre Trudeau succeeds Lester Pearson as Canada's prime minister... Jackie Kennedy marries Aristotle Onassis... In America, the Republican, Richard Nixon wins the presidential election.

SPORT

The Winter Olympics are being held in Grenoble, France and the Olympic Games in Mexico City. In football, Manchester United win the European Cup making Britain the winner for two successive years following Glasgow's 1967 success.

OBITUARIES

Two tragic deaths this year were the assassinations in America of Robert Kennedy, the younger brother of President John Kennedy, and the civil rights leader Martin Luther King. The world was shocked to hear of these untimely deaths and mourned with the families. Bobby Kennedy was shot in a Los Angeles hotel whilst he was campaigning for the forthcoming election. Martin Luther King, remembered for his non-violent approach in protest marches, his bus boycotting and famous "I have a dream..." speech was killed at a motel in Memphis, Tennessee.

1969

BRITAIN

January, the Ford Motor Company has launched the motor car and 1600 of their female workers have won the right to equal pay with their male colleagues...The ex-test cricketer, the Revd David Sheppard has been appointed Bishop of Woolwich... Paul McCartney has married Linda Eastman... April: Sikh busmen in Wolverhampton have won a two-year battle to be allowed to wear turbans at work, in accordance with their religious beliefs... The QE II liner makes its maiden voyage and Britain's Concorde its maiden twenty-one minute flight, one month after the French Concorde...

Manchester City beat Leicester City (1–0) in the FA Cup final...

There's high-grade crude oil in the North Sea.

A seven-sided fifty new pence coin is in circulation... Rupert Murdoch has bought The Sun newspaper...

The Divorce Reform Bill has been passed making the total breakdown of marriage sole grounds for divorce... Edward Heath has appointed Margaret Thatcher as the Shadow Education Spokesman; the government has authorised twelve new local radio stations.

Prince Charles has been invested as Prince of Wales at Caernarvon Castle.

ABROAD

Newly weds John and Yoko Lennon spend their honeymoon in bed in the presidential suite of the Hilton Hotel, Amsterdam; it's a "bed-in" for peace and the message they wish to convey is "Make love not war".

Rome, St Christopher and thirty other saints have been dropped from the Liturgical Calendar... Monaco, Graham Hill has won the Grand Prix for a record fifth time... France, President de Gaulle resigns and is succeeded by Monsieur George Pompidou...

Los Angeles, Sirhan Sirhan is on trial for Bobby Kennedy's murder; his request for execution has been denied; he claims that he does not remember killing him...

Memphis, James Earl Ray has pleaded guilty to the murder of Martin Luther King and has been jailed for ninety-nine years...

August, THE pop festival at WOODSTOCK! A Pop Festival for the hippies.

THE SPACE RACE

NASA has selected Neil Armstrong and Edwin "Buzz" Aldrin for the first moon landing. In May, Apollo 10 was launched with three astronauts on board as a rehearsal. It orbited the moon and dipped to within 9.4 miles of the moon's surface before returning to land safely in the Pacific. 21st JULY, AMERICA makes history, and wins the Space Race by successfully putting a man on the moon. 723 million people in 47 countries around the globe were watching their television screens when the "Apollo 11" spacecraft landed on the moon. Neil Armstrong walked out of the capsule and stepped on to the moon's surface stating, "That's one small step for a man, one giant leap for mankind."

So the decade has come to an end. The decade which has seen transplant surgery, Concorde, the widespread use of the computer heralding the technological age; changes in fashion, changes in housing, changes in education and a different kind of music. The decade that has introduced the hippies and the decade when the youth of its day was heard. The decade when moves were made to obliterate racism, when

Time & Tide

Martin Luther King shared his dream of freedom with the world. The decade which ended with a moon walk. The "Swinging Sixties", the time when the seeds of change have grown quickly; they are now ripe and ready for the harvest; a harvest, to be reaped in the seventies. The sixties are over; they will be remembered as the decade that changed the world.'

Chapter 11
Fordingham, January, 1970

THE DAY OF Irene's birthday arrived, as it had done annually since 1950: Irene was now twenty. This year there was a difference; the age of majority had been reduced, by the Government, from twenty-one to eighteen. She, like all the other young people between eighteen and twenty-one, suddenly received complete adult status. Her peer group throughout childhood and adolescence had dreamed of that magic age of twenty-one, when tradition maintained that they would receive the 'key to the door'; they had looked forward to the great celebration and had expected to feel different. She could remember how she had longed to be a grown-up because adults had so much more freedom and fun; now that time had arrived, earlier than expected and without ceremony. Wills told her she could still have her celebration party at twenty-one, but it would not be the same.

When the New Year celebrations were over the Stephenson family returned to their home as usual. Unlike the beginning of the sixties, there was no change in Irene's way of life.

She was in her second year at college, but it was not much different from going to school. Each day she drove into Buxton, but now drove further as the college was on the other side of town. She attended lectures just like the lessons in school; the only difference was that she received assignments and the marks counted towards her final grades, as opposed to homework essays which were not part of her 'A' level grades. She, also, received a grant from the Local Education Authority which was to pay for her board and lodging as well as books and personal needs. Wills allowed her to keep all of it; not having to pay rent meant that she was extremely affluent for a student; he was just pleased that his daughter had decided to live at home.

In her first year she had found that she had more in common with the mature students who were also day students, as opposed to resident ones. Her own age group, who lived in the halls of residence, seemed extremely immature to her. They were more concerned with enjoying life, with going to the pub, with dancing and with partying. They were away from home for the first time and behaved as if they had been let off a leash.

There were six halls: three for men: three for women. Each had a warden and strict rules regarding visitors going into rooms. Breaking the rules seemed to be part of the fun; the men could boast to their friends about how they had managed to keep a girl in their room overnight and how good their sexual exploits had been; the girls, likewise, could tell their friends how they had succeeded in keeping a male in their room all night without getting caught by the warden. All of this seemed very childish to Irene.

She was studying English literature, history and education along with supporting studies; the latter was simply a crash course in all subjects of the curriculum qualifying teachers to teach them at a basic level. After all, the general principles of teaching are the same in all subjects; the main attributes required are the abilities to plan lessons, organise the teaching material, communicate and establish a rapport with those being taught, as well as gaining their respect through good discipline. Those attributes were tested on teaching practice when the aspiring teachers of tomorrow were placed in schools for a period of time during each year of the course.

Irene's first practice had been during her first term and at the junior school in Fordingham. Mr Blake was still the headmaster; she had enjoyed being there and found the teaching easy. However, life in a small rural junior school is very different from a large secondary one as she was about to find out.

Her second practice was in a secondary modern school near Matlock. From experience she knew that travelling anywhere in Derbyshire in January was an ordeal in itself. When she arrived home after her first day she was exhausted but still had to prepare her material for the next day. She wondered how teachers survived a whole term in school; they must have the stamina of a hundred athletes. Teaching entailed going into classrooms daily and communicating with large numbers of young, captive, but not always willing audiences; she thought that people who took on that task for a living must be saints.

As the practice continued she found that she established a good rapport with the children, and knew that there was job satisfaction in helping these youngsters and playing a part in their development. She listened to comments in the staff room, from staff who had taught there for over twenty years; they discussed ex-pupils and what they were doing with their lives: some of the present children were second or even third generation pupils. The older staff talked of the days when they had taught their parents; it became clear to Irene that for these veteran teachers, they had was a true vocation and that was something which, in time, she wanted to share with them.

At the end of the practice, she was sorry to have to say 'goodbye' to many of the children; she wanted to continue being a part of their life; returning to college routine seemed mundane after such an illuminating experience.

She completed her three-year training course and was awarded her Certificate in Education. Her cousin, Hillary received a BA degree from Sheffield University but had no career interest in mind; she had spent most of her time enjoying life and saw no reason to spoil her fun by settling down to work; she was happy accepting money from Jim in exchange for the odd hour spent in one of his shops. She had a string of boyfriends; when tired of one, she would carelessly cast him aside like a piece of litter thrown into the rubbish bin; she seemed void of any real emotion. She and Irene were like chalk and cheese; Irene wondered how they could have been such good friends in their early childhood days. Why were they so different now?

Both Stephenson empires were doing well. Wills had been able to have long term leasing on the large cottage; it was never empty, as soon as one lot of tenants left another party moved in; this meant continuous income and very little hassle. The four smaller cottages had only been let through the tourist season and usually on a weekly basis. Each weekend Charlotte and Irene spent Saturday morning cleaning and preparing them for the next guests. Wills had traded in Charlotte's car for a new one; consequently, his bank balance had not recovered since his outlay on the first properties. They were a family with property and two cars; for Charlotte that was very important; it gave her a social status above many of the other wives in the village.

Irene's twenty-first birthday was not the grand occasion she had imagined it would be. Despite Wills' promise that she would have a big party, Charlotte could see no reason to have a second party after the traditional New Year's Eve one. Irene did not have friends that she wanted to invite, so the event ended in a compromise. Jim, Julia, Martin, Ann and Hillary all went to Whistbury on New Year's Eve.

Irene returned to college to start her one-year B Ed degree course in early October, 1971; it was to be a year of intense study in English and education. She, along with only twenty students from her year, had reached the high standard required in the certificate course and passed the university entrance exams in order to be offered a place on the degree course. Wills had been delighted; he would be happy if she had spent the rest of her life at college. Like most doting fathers he found it hard to come to terms with the fact that his little girl was now an adult.

In the second week of the term, the B Ed students attended the same psychology lecture as the postgraduates; the latter were a group from various universities who were taking a one-year education course leading to a certificate qualifying them as teachers.

Irene was concentrating on the lecture and taking copious notes, unaware of the tall, blond postgraduate who could not take his eyes off her. He had seen her somewhere before but could not remember where or when their pathways had crossed; perhaps it had been in a previous life. As the son of Reverend John White, Philip was a strong believer in God and the idea of rebirth, whether it had been a brief encounter in this life or during a previous existence her presence now was certainly affecting his concentration on something as mundane as psychology.

After what seemed like an eternity, the two-hour lecture came to an end; he watched her pick up her bag and leave the room; she walked to her car not noticing that she was being followed. He had heard someone call her Irene and he now knew that she drove a red mini and lived off campus; she was not a postgraduate student so she must be one of the B Ed group.

He returned to his room in the hall of residence, made a cup of coffee and then settled down to the psychology assignment but his mind was not on the subject; he lacked concentration; she was an enigma; where had he seen her before?

Back at Fordingham, Wills greeted Irene with the words, 'Hello, m'duck, had a good day?'

She instinctively knew there was a problem. 'Well, m'duck,' she replied, 'sounds like my day's been better than yours, what do you want?'

'There's a greenhouse sale on Saturday.'

'Yes, it's been on the calendar since the beginning of the year.'

'Barry's gone home ill and...'

'I know, Geoff resigned last week, you're short staffed on Saturday and Forest are playing at home!'

He laughed, 'You know your old dad so well!'

'Yes, I'll do Saturday afternoon.'

'You're an angel, m'duck.'

'I know, I'll get my wings in heaven.'

For Irene, that meant a busy Saturday; she had to help Charlotte in the morning prepare the cottages, and then she would be spending the entire afternoon in the greenhouses with Mark selling produce.

Irene began her psychology assignment that evening. Philip, on the other hand, had found his lack of concentration prevented him from getting beyond the first paragraph; he needed to find out more about this mystery woman and solve the enigma. He went into the college bar and saw Brian, one of the resident B Ed students he had already met; after ordering an orange juice, he joined him; they chatted about the delights of psychology and the human mind before Philip steered the conversation towards Irene.

'Who's that B Ed student with the dark hair, drives a red mini, Irene somebody or other?'

'You mean, Irene Stephenson.'

'Irene Stephenson?'

'Yes, she lives at Fordingham Hall. Her father's the estate manager.'

'Where's Fordingham?'

'The other side of Buxton. Why?'

'I'm sure I've seen her somewhere before but I can't imagine where. Has she ever lived anywhere else?'

'I don't know. She's always been aloof. She's never taken any interest in college life. Just comes in for lectures, tutorials and the library.'

'A woman of mystery?'

'I've heard rumours. She helps run her father's property business. She's tied up working on the estate. She had a boyfriend who was killed in a car crash. She stayed in Fordingham to visit his grave. Her father bribed her to stay at home. Don't know if any of it's true.'

'Where have all these rumours come from?'

'Don't know. Think people have made them up for amusement. She's been asked to several college dances but always refuses.'

'Is she a...you know?'

'What?'

'You know. One of them?'

'Oh a...'

'Yeh, a...'

'A lesbian. I don't think so, but what a waste.'

Instead of satisfying Philip's curiosity Brian's comments had increased it. He would take a trip out to Fordingham at the weekend.

Time & Tide

On Saturday afternoon Philip set out in his old Ford Anglia car in search of Fordingham. He found it eventually, after a detour which brought him into the village on the main road; the first buildings he saw were the junior school and the church. It reminded him of his own home at Battersley in Shropshire; a quaint little village full of 'ye olde worlde charm.'

He parked his car outside the church; this place of worship had attracted him like a magnet and he thought it would probably be the focal point of village activity; he made a note of the services and decided to return and worship there on Sundays. He walked along the main road and noticed several posters and arrows directing people to a 'Produce Sale' at the Hall; this was his lucky day!

As he was passing the grocer's he remembered that the coffee jar was almost empty; he went inside and was served by a young lady.

'I've seen signs to a "Produce Sale" at the Hall,' he said, 'could you tell me how far it is to the Hall?'

'Sure,' she replied, 'Turn left, walk t' the junction. Turn left onto Buxton Road. The 'all is on the right. It's about a five-minute walk. Me 'usband is doing the sale today.'

Philip's mouth gaped open in total astonishment; this woman was pregnant and looked no older than Irene; Was this woman Irene's stepmother?

'Is anythin' wrong?' Jane asked.

'No, no, thank you very much.' Philip answered and hastily left. He walked up the road, clutching his jar of coffee in a paper bag; he found the drive and walked along it following the signs; he passed the orchard and Orchard Cottage and found the greenhouses.

There she was; his hunt was over, he had found her in her home environment.

'Hi, Irene!'

'Hello!'

'This looks like a nice place to live.'

'Yes.'

'How long have you lived here?'

'Almost twelve years.' She was being polite, but who was this man and why was he asking personal questions?

'Is your father around?'

'No, it's his weekend off. Mr Adams is in the next greenhouse if it's estate business.'

'You don't recognise me, do you?'

'Should I?'

'Wednesday, psychology?'

'Psychology?' She repeated the word; it had already been a long day; the morning spent with her mother had not been an easy one; she had only had time for a sandwich and quick drink before rushing out to help Mark with the afternoon sales. There were two hours left before closing time and a fair amount of produce still to sell; she did not have time for riddles or guessing games.

'Yes. Gifted children.'

'I know what Wednesday's lecture was about but I fail to see its relevance at this precise moment.' The tone of her voice was a clear indication of her displeasure.

Gifted children was the last thing on her mind; she had far too much to do; he sensed her irritability and wondered if using the sale as an excuse to find out where she lived had been such a good idea after all.

'That's where we met,' he said.

'I don't remember speaking to you. I don't even know your name.'

There were people picking up plants and an elderly woman with a basket of cooking apples.

'Excuse me,' she said as she turned to the woman with the apples; she weighed them.

'That'll be 50p please.'

'Fifty pence,' said the old dear, 'that's ten shillings.'

Irene smiled, 'That's correct,' she said as she gave her her change from a £1 note.

'I don't know what the world's coming to. When I was young a family could live for a week on less than ten bob. It's all to do with that Common Market.'

She left the greenhouse and Irene served three more customers who were waiting patiently to buy plants. Philip wandered round and decided that a spider plant would look nice on the window sill in his room. He picked one up and returned to the entrance; by this time there were no customers and he could continue with the conversation.

'I couldn't take my eyes off you. I'm sure we've met somewhere before.'

'I don't think so. The spider plant's 10p.'

'My name's Philip White. I'm on the PGCE course.'

'Oh a postgraduate here for some "PG Tips".'

They both laughed, even though Philip was beginning to find the joke more of an embarrassment than amusing.

'Yes.'

'What's your degree?'

'Theology.'

'I did scripture knowledge to 'A' level then specialised in English and history. How did you find me?'

'I asked.'

'I'm flattered,' she said giving him his forty pence change, 'but I've got work to do.'

'Perhaps you'd like to have coffee with me in the Student's Union next week?'

'I don't think so. Thank you but I've got too much to do. College is a means to an end for me, not one long party.'

He could feel the ice between them; it was not melting but he was not going to give up.

'I'll see you around then. Bye.'

'Bye.'

He took a last look at her, appropriately dressed in black trousers, green polo-neck jumper and beige anorak; she had on a small amount of red lipstick but wore no other make-up; her shoulder length black hair was tied back but she still looked gorgeous. He knew he had made an impression on her; she now knew who he was. He found his way back to college by the direct route as opposed to the scenic one.

The next morning at 9.30 am, he was sitting on the back pew in Fordingham Church; the bells were ringing calling people to the Family Service and Holy Communion.

He waited and hoped; again he had picked the right time; she walked through the door with two other adults. She was carrying her own prayer book and a shopping bag; he watched her say something to the other couple who he thought must be her parents and then she went to the front pew and joined a group of children; she was the Sunday School teacher. During the second hymn he watched her take the small group of children into the vestry.

When the service ended he waited for her to leave; she was wearing a bottle green midi-coat and her hair hung loosely around her shoulders; she was dressed for Sunday, so different from the apparel she wore yesterday. She had good dress sense, but she was one of those people who always looked good; if she wore a sack she would still be attractive.

'Hello! We meet again,' he said.

'Yes.' She was surprised to see him

'So you take a Sunday School class. Is there no end to your talents?'

'I'd make a lousy nurse. I can't stand the sight of blood.' She did not really know why she said that; it was just one of those redundant statements that one makes in useless chat; Wills was calling her.

'I have to go. We're going to my grandmother's for lunch. 'Bye.'

'Bye.' He watched her leave with the couple who he now knew were her parents; he had learned so much about her; he was in love with her and would do anything for her. In the Old Testament Jacob had served seven years for Rachel, but they had seemed like a few days because of the love he had for her; he was Jacob and she was going to be his Rachel.

The Stephenson family went to Whistbury for Sunday lunch with Elizabeth; such occasions were fewer these days but still enjoyable for all concerned. After lunch they would all go over the road and place fresh flowers on John's grave. Irene noticed that the garden was still immaculate, just like her grandfather had kept it; Elizabeth continued to employ a gardener but the inside of the house had not been redecorated since 1958.

Charlotte tried to persuade her mother to get the interior done, but Elizabeth was reluctant: she wanted things left just as they had been when John was alive. After a tremendous argument Charlotte convinced Elizabeth that John would have had the decorators in years ago, and the house would deteriorate if she did not do something soon. In the end Charlotte promised to spend time at Whistbury doing some of it herself; Irene knew that meant that SHE would be left doing more cooking and cleaning at home! Even more of her time would be spent on domestic chores. The redecoration took place in November, to be ready for the annual party.

In addition to the extra work for Irene it seemed that every time she went to college she managed to meet Philip. On each occasion there was only time for a few words because she was always in a hurry. She had not realised that Philip was familiar with her timetable and made sure that their paths crossed as frequently as possible. By December, there had been several brief encounters in college and after Church on Sundays. Irene found herself thinking more and more about this blond-haired youth; there was something about him that fascinated her, but she did not know what it was.

Finally, in the last week of term she decided to take up the invitation he had first made in October and joined him for coffee in the Student's Union. He told her about his family and the hectic Christmas schedule they had as a vicar's family; his mother was a teacher and had a part-time job in a secondary school; his younger sister attended a boarding school in Whitby. She listened but said very little about her own life.

They parted, promising to meet up in the New Year; he would be doing his twelve-week teaching practice and she promised to give him what help she could.

The festive season followed its usual format in the Stephenson household. There was one exciting event which made the nativity scene more realistic on the estate; Jane gave birth to her second child on Boxing Day, another son and brother for Thomas: he was named Stephen after St Stephen, which the family thought was appropriate for a child born on 26th December.

Throughout the holiday period Irene found herself thinking about Philip; he kept returning, like a boomerang in her mind; she tried hard to forget about him but he would continue to bounce back. On New Year's Day, as the family celebrated her twenty-second birthday she found herself counting the days until the new term started and she would see him again.

When she drove to college on that first day of term in January, 1972, she wondered if she would see Philip. Had she been like a boomerang in his mind during the Christmas period? Perhaps he had been too occupied with his father's parish affairs to even think about her.

Her first question was answered when she reached the car park; he was standing by the wall waiting for her. She parked her car, opened the door and stepped out, as she locked it he moved towards her.

'Hello. Happy New Year!'

She replied, 'Hello, and a Happy New Year to you. Have you had a good Christmas?'

'Same as usual. Have you?'

'Same as usual!' She laughed and then added, 'there was just one thing which made it different. Jane had a son on Boxing Day. Somehow, it made the nativity seem more real. Apart from that it was Christmas at Fordingham, New Year at Whistbury, as usual.'

'I've missed you,' he said, 'I've been counting the days.'

'You have? So have I.'

He put his arm around her shoulder and together they walked into the college.

'Where're you going?' he asked.

'English lecture.'

'I'll walk over to the English block with you. I've got to sort things out for my teaching practice. Following the syllabus laid down by the head of department is easy. It's that first bit about aims I find difficult in the work schemes. Surely, the aim of every lesson is to convey certain material to the pupils!'

'Which school are you going to?'

'Fordingham Grammar.'

She stopped walking, turned and looked at him in total amazement.

'You lucky thing. A grammar school. I got secondary moderns. Fordingham Grammar's my old school. You'll find it a piece of cake.'

She had certainly cheered him up; they arranged to meet in the afternoon before parting at the entrance to the English block. When Irene went home she was walking on air, her head in the clouds; Wills noticed her dreamy state and suspected that he was going to lose his little girl to this fellow student who attended church in Fordingham.

The long cold January seemed to pass more quickly than usual; they saw each other most days and their relationship developed. In February they had their first proper date; it seemed appropriate that it should be to the College Film Society showing, 'Romeo and Juliet' and afterwards they enjoyed a fish and chip supper. They felt as if they had known each other all their lives.

Wills, aware of his daughter's involvement with Philip, decided that he should accept the inevitable; it was time to invite Philip to the family home. After the church service, when Irene and Philip were having a chat, he went up to them and said, 'Why don't you ask Philip to join us for lunch?'

'Really, Dad?'

'Sure.'

She looked at Philip, 'Well, would you like to join us?'

'I'd be delighted. Thank you, Mr Stephenson.'

The only person who was not pleased was Charlotte; she thought it inconsiderate of her husband to offer an invitation without consulting her. Wills gave her a staring look which she knew meant that she was to be a gracious hostess; she must accept his decision and make Philip a welcome visitor to their home.

After that first occasion he became a regular Sunday visitor; he and Irene were spending more and more time together: she was his Rachel, he was her Jacob and he was going to marry her. Philip always got his own way, throughout his childhood he had always managed to manipulate his parents round to his way of thinking; they had wanted to send him to boarding school but he had, by gentle and cunning persuasion, managed to talk his mother out of the idea; he promised that he would excel at the local grammar school and she would be proud of him, he would rebel if sent away: the plan had worked. Now, like then he planned his moves carefully; he told her about himself and his family; she told him of her early life at Silkington, her brother, their move to Fordingham and her family but she carefully avoided mentioning Danny. He did not mention any previous girlfriends because she was his first – and going to be his last; he assumed that it was the same for her.

He wanted to do things properly and as Jacob asked Laban for his daughter's hand in marriage, he asked Wills for his permission to marry Irene. Wills was rather surprised and asked if he had already proposed to Irene; he felt sure that if Irene had any inkling of his plans she would have told her father.

'No, sir,' he replied, 'I wanted to ask your permission first and then I thought I'd ask Irene to come home with me for Easter. I plan to propose on Easter Sunday.'

Wills was impressed, which was what Philip wanted.

'You have my blessing, Philip, but I suggest you don't mention it to her mother before Easter. Irene has always been special to me. We have a close father-daughter relationship. I've dreaded the day she leaves me. Look after her. Welcome to the family, son!'

Term ended a week before Easter but on Maundy Thursday Philip returned to Fordingham and a happy Irene was waiting with a packed suitcase. Wills tried to hide his sadness as he kissed her on the cheek and told her to enjoy herself.

Battersley was a small, attractive village, similar in many ways to Fordingham; they drove along the main street with the village pub, two shops and several quaint cottages before they reached Saint Bartholomew's Church and The Old Rectory.

It was late afternoon when they drove through the wrought iron gates and along a short drive to a parking area in front of the main entrance.

Irene's first impression was of a rambling old stone house with small latticed windows; she could see the Reverend John White in the porch way waiting to greet them. He was a tall man with grey hair neatly combed back; his face was round with small features, the lines on his brow and his rugged complexion indicated a lifetime of troubles. He was wearing his clerical attire and smiled as he welcomed her to his home; he seemed to radiate warmth and comfort; it was as if he had a deep contentment with life, a contentment which comes with an unquestioning belief and faith in God. She was sure that it was faith which had brought him through his own trials and that his parishioners would find him to be a tower of strength, when their lives were in torment and their faith put to the test.

They went through the front door into a large hall with an impressive central staircase leading to a balcony on the first floor. The hall had beautifully polished floorboards with eye-catching Persian rugs; they reminded her of her grandmother's home, but this house was considerably larger. The white-painted walls were decorated with pictures and portraits; there were two corridors and several doorways leading from the hall. The aroma of freshly baked bread wafted along the left-hand corridor; John led her along it to the kitchen where Esther White and her daughter, Ruth, were preparing dinner.

'Here's Irene,' he said, 'this is my wife, Esther, and daughter, Ruth.'

Irene could see that both Ruth and Philip looked very much like their mother; Esther was a tall, thin, middle-aged woman with natural blonde hair, it looked as if she had been to the hairdressers for a shampoo and set before Easter. Ruth was a tall, slim young girl of sixteen with shoulder-length blonde hair.

Esther stood at the kitchen sink preparing vegetables; she turned towards Irene and said,

'Hello, nice to see you at last. Would you like a cup of tea or coffee?'

Before she could reply Philip had joined them in the kitchen and said, 'Yes please, mum. Two coffees.'

'Ruth, be a dear and make us all a drink.'

John said, 'Not for me, thanks. I'm going back to my study. I've still got to put the finishing touches to Sunday's sermon.'

'Daddy, dear, I'm sure it will be up to your usual standard and the congregation will hang on to every word,' Ruth said as she finished preparing the apple pie; she walked over to the sink, washed her hands and made four cups of coffee.

Meanwhile, Esther was having a chat with her son and the woman she rather suspected would be his fiancée before the weekend was over. First impressions were important and her first impression of Irene was favourable; her son had never shown any interest in girls before and she was pleased with his choice. In her opinion, and after twenty years of teaching, she felt she was a good judge of character. Irene was a good-looking, intelligent, polite, young woman who would make her son an excellent wife.

Time & Tide

After the introduction and refreshment Philip showed her round the house before taking her to her room. There were eight bedrooms on the first floor, four had en-suite bathrooms and a further four rooms in the attic, which were used for storage. The ground floor had a dining room, drawing room, family room, study, cloaks and an extremely large room on the right-hand side of the main entrance which was used for village functions and had a separate entrance, it was known as the 'village' room. Irene thought the term 'old' was an appropriate description for this rectory; all the ceilings were low and there were many beams which added to the 'olde worlde' feel; all the walls were painted white and had pictures on them just like the hall. The building may have been there for two centuries and belonged to the church, but Esther had clearly given it a 'homely' feeling.

Her room overlooked the orchard and beyond that, she had a superb view of the Shropshire countryside. As well as the standard bedroom furniture, there was a writing desk and chair by the window; she opened the drawer and found envelopes and paper, with *The Old Rectory, Battersley, Shropshire*, neatly printed on it. She opened another door in the room and discovered her private bathroom; this was like a five-star luxury hotel room.

She had an hour to rest and change into suitable evening wear before dinner at 7.30. With nerves and apprehension, wearing her simple dark green, midi-length dress and black casual shoes, at 7.20 she ventured out of her room and noticed that both the door and floorboards creaked. She walked along the corridor to the balcony and down the stairs, comparing herself to Scarlet O'Hara in 'Gone with the Wind'. This made her feel like a film star, a woman with confidence and sophistication.

She was about to enter the dining room, where the table was set for the meal, when Philip appeared and escorted her into the family room. Her hosts were drinking a pre-dinner sherry.

'Dry, medium or sweet?' John asked.

'Oh, dry, please.'

She looked at the family; Esther was wearing a pale blue dress with a 'V' neckline and belt around the waist, which emphasised her slender figure; Ruth was attired in a more fashionable red gingham dress; both Philip and his father were wearing suits. She wondered if dressing for dinner and sherry was a regular occurrence or was this in her honour?

There was a grandfather clock in the room; as soon as it chimed 7.30 John led them across the hall into the dining room. Esther and Ruth went through to the kitchen and returned with the roast lamb and vegetable dishes, which they placed on the table; the family waited and John said, 'Let us thank the Lord for this food.'

They put their hands together, closed their eyes and stood in silence waiting for 'Grace'; Irene felt some embarrassment because this practice did not take place in her home before Sunday lunch; she wondered what Philip must think about her family's lack of thanksgiving for their food. However, she followed their lead and stood with her hands together, eyes closed and silently waited.

'Dear Lord, on this night let us remember your time of agony in the Garden of Gethsemane. Let us remember that last meal which you shared with your disciples. Let us remember the example that you gave them of sharing; your words to them on that last occasion...'

Irene was listening to this with irreverent thoughts; she could smell the delicious lamb and it was on the table in front of them. If John did not hurry up it would be cold!

'...Let us remember the sacrifice you made for us. And let us give thanks for this food which we are about to eat, remembering those who are not so fortunate as ourselves. Through Jesus Christ, our Lord. Amen.'

To which they all said, 'Amen.'

Irene breathed a sigh of relief as they sat down; at last, their meal could begin. After the pre-dinner sherry it seemed odd that the only beverage on offer was water. It was one of those occasions when etiquette and table manners were of paramount importance, with polite conversation.

John carved the roast, put each person's portion on a dinner plate and then passed the plate down the table. Irene received her portion first and Esther politely handed her the vegetable dishes. Ruth began pouring the water and eventually, when everyone had something in front of them, in unison they picked up cutlery and began to devour their Maunday Thursday, Passover meal.

The table was covered in a beautiful white cloth which made Irene terrified of spilling anything on it; each place setting had a tablemat decorated with a picture of a church on it. The dinner service was Worcester china and the silver cutlery sparkled; it had probably been cleaned for Easter. Complementing the tableware were two silver candlesticks, one at each end of the table but the white candles were not lit.

Conversation was made between mouthfuls of food. It seemed that John would be spending most of tomorrow in church leading prayers and meditation throughout

Time & Tide

the hours of Christ's agony on the cross. At 3.00 pm he would be reciting the last words Jesus made from the Cross and there would be the re-enactment of the tearing of the Temple curtain in two, as recorded in the Gospels. Also, throughout the day parishioners would be coming to the 'village' room for refreshments; on Good Friday, the tea urn would be on all day for people to come and have tea and traditional hot-cross buns after their participation in the church service.

After the first course was over the plates were collected and apple pie and custard brought in; Irene was told that apple pie was Ruth's speciality. After tasting it, she naturally complimented Ruth and said that it was the best she had ever tasted. When the meal was over, they adjourned to the family room for coffee and mints. Then she discovered that breakfast would be served at 9.00 am although John would be in church from seven o'clock onwards, and for that reason they all retired when the grandfather clock chimed nine; she could not remember the last time she had gone to bed before ten.

The next day she had an insight into the demands on the family of a vicar. Esther and Ruth were on hand all day as parishioners came to the village room; John spent most of the day in church and she could sense the morbid atmosphere: It was as if Christ were dying in 1972, this family were indeed dedicated Christians.

After breakfast, Philip took her for a walk through the village before showing her the rectory gardens and orchard; he knew the area was small in comparison to what she was used to. Lastly, that morning they went into the church to take part in the service; Philip read some of the biblical passages; this was his normal practice, along with church servers and wardens. In the afternoon, she helped the family serve tea and talked with the villagers. By the evening she realised how tiring this lifestyle was; there was always work on the estate but she had grown used to that. Dinner that evening was an easily prepared cold meal; the atmosphere was so different from the previous night, more like a 'wake' than a family meal.

On Saturday, there were preparations in the church for Easter Sunday; that great event in the Christian calendar marking the day when Christ rose from the dead. In the afternoon, Philip took Irene and Ruth into Shrewsbury; they visited the abbey. Looking round it Irene realised how little she had seen of the British Isles; apart from the holiday in Torquay after her grandfather's death she had not travelled beyond the Peak District and Nottinghamshire.

From the abbey they walked over the bridge to the town centre and wandered round the streets, window-shopping. When they reached a sweet shop Philip went in to buy wine gums; they were his vice: other people smoked, took drugs or drank heavily, he just ate wine gums; through lengthy essays, exams and strenuous times he would chew wine gums. Although she had already told him about Uncle Jim, Irene commented that her uncle had a chain of sweet shops; as they left the shop he suddenly stopped; now he knew where he had seen her before. In his years at Nottingham University he had been a frequent visitor to the sweet shop near the castle; the one with the sign,

'Stephenson's Tobacco & Confectionery'

Why had he not realised before?

'Your uncle owns the shop, Stephenson's Tobacconists, doesn't he?'

'Yes, remember I told you he's got seven at the last count. He's only just bought the last two.'

'That's where I've seen you before. In Nottingham, when I've been buying wine gums.'

'Well, I've been in his shops and I've served from time to time so you may have seen me there.'

For Philip, this was the answer to the ultimate question; the great puzzle was now solved.

Back at the rectory, things were brighter that evening; the church had been adorned with flowers, the altar cloth prepared and everything ready for the morning. They had chicken for dinner and a much easier conversation than on the previous nights.

The great day of Easter Sunday arrived; John took two Communion services before the family had eaten breakfast and then they all attended the ten o'clock service. After that, with everyone shouting a joyous, 'Happy Easter', they, and the parishioners went to the village room where coffee and sherry were being provided.

For Philip, the big moment in his carefully planned campaign was approaching; after Sunday lunch, he took Irene for a drive to Stokesay Castle, a place he had loved to visit as a child. This was a thirteenth century, picturesque building with a seventeenth century timber gatehouse; he hoped that she would find it as charming as he did. A fortified manor house with beautiful scenery surrounding it, in the Shropshire countryside; with her interest in history, he could not have found a better place. She was overwhelmed, even on an overcast, dreary day which that Easter Sunday was, her enthusiasm for every detail of the place was apparent. She was engrossed in the historical aspect and spent ages in the great hall looking at the central hearth, the fascinating roof beams and windows before approaching the oak staircase and upstairs. Outside, the separate tower building was another form of intrigue; they went up to the roof and looked across at what they could see of the surrounding countryside.

Everything was going to plan; she was like a child at Christmas; she had not been this happy for a long time. They left the tower and walked back across to the gatehouse; there, they turned and looked back, it was the moment he had been waiting for. He said, 'I love you. You know that, don't you?'

'Yes, I love you too.'

He took her left hand in his, went down on one knee, and said, 'Irene, will you do me the honour of becoming my wife?'

She was overwhelmed and knew that she was so lucky to find love for the second time; to be given a second chance of happiness. God had been punishing her for her sin in the hayloft, but now He must have forgiven her. Philip was a kind, considerate, caring, loving man who idolised and worshipped her; she was blind to the manipulative side of his character.

She looked down at him; he was doing things properly, even to the extent of getting down on one knee.

'Philip, I'd be honoured to be your wife.'

Whereupon, he took a diamond ring out of his right-hand jacket pocket and placed it on her finger. At 3.20 pm on Easter Sunday, 2nd April, 1972 in an idyllic setting, they agreed to become man and wife; they were going to spend the rest of their lives together. He stood up; they kissed and embraced each other, the rest of the world did not exist.

Then he said, 'I've loved you from the first moment I saw you in that psychology lecture. For me, you were like Rachel at the well. I want to be your Jacob.'

'Rachel. Mmm. Yes, I like that. I'll be Rachel. You can be Jacob.'

'I've a slight confession to make.'

'What, all ready? We've only been engaged two minutes.'

'I wanted to do things properly. As Jacob asked Laban for his daughter's hand in marriage, I asked your father for his permission during the last week of term.'

She was stunned. 'You asked Daddy?'

'Yes.'

'What did he say?'

'He didn't want to lose his daughter but he gave me his blessing and welcomed me into your family. At least, he can't cheat on me like Laban did. There's no elder sister in your case.'

'So, Daddy knows and he didn't say a word. Good old Dad. He'll probably even look surprised when I tell him.'

They walked back to the car and started to discuss their future together; they would have to find teaching posts in the same area and a house to live in; mid-August would be a nice time for the wedding.

Back at the rectory the champagne was already on ice; John could read his son like a book and showed no surprise when Irene showed him the ring; he was just pleased that his son had found someone whom John thought would be right for him: they were made for each other.

He said, 'Congratulations. Welcome to the family, Irene.'

They celebrated the occasion; John was only able to have a sip of champagne because he had another service to conduct. For Irene, this was an exciting time and one which she never thought she would experience. They discussed some plans that evening but realised that finishing their courses and finding teaching positions were their first priorities.

On the Monday, he took her back to Fordingham; Wills was waiting for them and knew what he had to say.

She shouted, 'Daddy, Daddy, we're engaged.'

'Congratulations! M'duck, I hope you'll be very happy together.'

Charlotte smiled, but was less welcoming; she was jealous of her daughter who seemed to have everything handed to her on a plate.

After Philip had left, Irene spent the evening in discussion with her parents. The next day there was one thing she must do; it was almost six years since that awful accident on the outskirts of Leeds: it was time to let go: time to say the final goodbye: time to move on with her life.

She went to the hayloft for the last time and looked round at what had been their special place. During the last few years she had visited it on occasions and for her, it was a shrine; as long as his things remained, he was there with her. She picked up the pair of scissors, ruler and string which he had used to make their rings; he had forgotten to put them back in his satchel when they left on that Friday afternoon. There were also three of his exercise books, cups, an empty lemonade bottle, a blanket and odds and ends which she had left as a reminder. She picked up the dusty exercise books and opened his English essay book, the first title was, 'My life ten years from now'; his handwriting was perfect, his aims and ambitions clearly stated. Tears streamed down her face as she collected the things together, put them in a bag and deposited them in the dustbin; when everything had been cleared she took one last look and said, 'Goodbye, darling.'

The news of her engagement was received with great jubilation on the estate and in the village; there was still the one person who had watched her grow up with Danny and knew about the hideaway, and who hid a private sadness.

She graduated in July and Philip received his certificate enabling him to teach; he obtained a post at the King George Grammar School in Birmingham and she found a job at the Harwood Comprehensive School, in Harwood, a suburb of Birmingham.

They decided to live in Harwood and bought a three-bedroomed terraced house for £3,500; Irene used the money her grandfather left her plus some savings for the deposit. They wanted everything in their marriage to be a joint operation, she paid the £900 deposit and Philip planned to pay the mortgage.

They spent a lot of time in June and July organising the house with the intention of moving in after their honeymoon. The deep blue carpets and curtains came with the property and it had been recently decorated by the previous owner. The downstairs rooms were all painted in magnolia and the bedrooms decorated in flowered wallpaper. Their vendor obviously had a preference for blue, the outside décor was also blue; it was a colour they decided they could live with for the time being. For furnishing, John and Esther bought their bedroom furniture and Wills and Charlotte the dining room suite as wedding presents; this left them with their front room, kitchen, guest room and study to furnish. Then there was the basic equipment, linen, crockery, cutlery, cooking utensils: the list seemed endless. Naturally, some of these items were bought for them as wedding presents but somehow the list did not seem to get shorter. They knew they were luckier than many other couples because they could afford to move into their own home straight away, but this was cold comfort when they were trudging round shops with a long shopping list!

The date set for the big day was Saturday, 19th August; they wanted a small wedding with just relatives present but there was still a lot of planning to do; Philip's father had arranged with the vicar to conduct the service in Fordingham Church and the White family were staying in one of Wills' cottages for the weekend; they arrived on the Friday evening. On the Saturday, there was so much excitement and tension; Irene could not believe it was actually happening. Wills hid his sadness and put on a brave façade; his daughter's happiness would be marred if she thought her father was not sharing it with her.

The wedding was scheduled for one o'clock; this enabled the family to travel on the day – apart from Elizabeth who had arrived on Thursday. She wished her husband was still around; it had been his dream to see Irene walk down the aisle. Charlotte was more concerned about her own appearance than that of her daughter; as the mother of the bride, she felt she had an important role to play and people were going to notice her. She had chosen a royal blue two-piece suit with matching accessories; while she was busy preparing herself for the event, it was Elizabeth who was helping Irene get ready.

Her long white satin dress had full sleeves, and a low cut top decorated with lace which matched the veil. Elizabeth gave her a gold cross and chain to wear round her neck, which had been a present from John to her on their wedding day on 7th August, 1926, just over forty-six years ago: she could remember it as if it were only yesterday.

'Oh, Gran, it's lovely. Thank you'.

'Your grandfather wanted to see your wedding day. He'll be with you in spirit. He'd want you to have this. You know when he gave it me, don't you?'

'Yes, Gran. I'll look after it.'

They were both wiping away the tears when Wills came in to look at his daughter. Her beautiful natural curls were arranged up on the top of her head with her veil resting on them; her make-up was perfect. In his eyes, she looked a million dollars.

Elizabeth and Charlotte left for the church at 12.40. For Wills, there were just ten more minutes to spend alone with his daughter before he took her to the altar and, in traditional manner, gave her to another man.

'You look radiant, darling.'

'Thanks, Dad.'

'You're happy about this, aren't you? Marriage is what you really want.'

'Yes, Dad. There's just one thing that would make today complete.'

'What's that?'

'If James were here. I often think about him, all alone in that churchyard.'

Wills swallowed hard. 'I know, m'duck, but it wasn't meant to be. What about Danny? You loved him, didn't you?'

'I've said "goodbye". He's a ghost I've laid to rest.'

Wills breathed a sigh of relief; he had never noticed her fingering the 'string-ring' that was still in her jewellery box.

'You know I'll always be here for you, don't you? If something goes wrong you can always come back to your dear old Dad.'

'Oh Dad. Don't make me cry. My mascara 'll run.'

He took hold of her left hand and said, 'We have a very special relationship. Marriage won't change that.'

'Oh Dad.'

'Come on, put your shoes on. The flowers are downstairs. The car'll be here any second.'

She put on the white sling-back shoes and stood up; he followed her down the stairs and into the kitchen, where she picked up her flowers and walked to the door. She could remember so clearly the first time she came through that door; so much had happened since then and now she was to go through it for the last time as a single girl, when she returned in a week's time, she would be married.

In the courtyard was her first surprise; there was no car waiting but Lord and Lady Fordingham with their son and daughters and one of the horses harnessed to the open-top carriage which had been in the Fordingham family since the last century.

Lord Fordingham said, 'We wish you every happiness, my dear. We would just like to make the journey to the church one that you'll remember.'

'How kind of you, Sir, and you've already given us a beautiful canteen of cutlery.'

He helped her into the carriage and Wills followed with a polite, 'M'Lord, Milady,' to the Fordingham's.

She looked at the man in the driving seat, so finely dressed for the occasion, 'Mark! It's you.'

'Yes. We've all be'n 'oping for fine weather. We want you t'ave a day t' remember.' No one knew Mark's real feelings that day as he watched the woman he loved marry another man.

They set off for the church; standing by the greenhouses and unseen by Irene was the bitter, jealous Jane. Once again Irene had managed to achieve more than she had: a degree, her own house, a good job, a professional man for a husband and a much brighter future. She was trapped in a marriage with two small children and no career prospects; for extra money she helped out in her father's shop. There was just no comparison in their lifestyles. Irene had had all the luck in life and she had none. Lord Fordingham had not provided her with a carriage to the church, but he had given Irene one and even asked her husband to drive it.

They went down the drive out into the road; many people were standing there watching and waving; it seemed that everyone knew about the carriage ride except Irene. When they reached the church she put her veil down over her face; she knew that Philip would be thinking of Rachel and Jacob. Jacob did not see his wife's face until after the service and then he discovered he had been given the wrong daughter and worked a further seven years for his Rachel; there was no Leah, but Irene was sure Philip loved her just as Jacob had loved Rachel.

They walked up the aisle to the usual accompaniment of 'Here Comes The Bride'; she stood next to Philip dressed in his new dark grey suit, and looked at her future father-in-law who was shortly to pronounce them 'man and wife'. The front pews on either side of the aisle were occupied with their families and standing next to Philip was an old friend from University, acting as his best man.

The service began with the hymn 'Love Divine', and then John addressed the congregation with the age-old rubric: 'Dearly beloved, we are gathered together here in the sight of God, and in the face of this congregation, to join together this man and this woman in holy matrimony; which is an honourable estate... Therefore if any man can show any just cause, why they may not lawfully be joined together, let him now speak, or else hereafter forever hold his peace.'

John then addressed the couple, 'I require and charge you both, as ye will answer at that dreadful day of judgement when the secrets of all hearts shall be disclosed, that if either of you know any impediment, why ye may not be lawfully joined together in matrimony, ye do now confess it...'

After the introduction there was the usual silence while time is given for objections to be made. Then the service continued. John looked at Philip and said, 'Philip, wilt thou have this woman to thy wedded wife, to live together after God's ordinance in the holy estate of matrimony? Wilt thou love her, comfort her, honour and keep her in sickness and health; and forsaking all other, keep thee only unto her, so long as ye both shall live?'

Philip answered, 'I will.'

John then turned to Irene,

'Irene Joy, wilt thou have this man... so long as ye both shall live.'

She answered, 'I will.'

'Who giveth this woman to be married to this man?'

Wills stepped forward; he was holding back the tears and forcing himself to smile as he gave her to the minister.

Philip took her right hand and gave his troth to her, 'I Philip take thee, Irene Joy, to my wedded wife, to have and to hold from this day forward, for better for worse, for richer for poorer, in sickness and in health, to love and to cherish, till death us do part, according to God's holy ordinance; and thereto I plight thee my troth.'

Then it was Irene's turn; as she said those words she tried to erase the memory of the last time she had uttered them. Suddenly she was aware, not of being in a hayloft, but of a ring being placed on her finger. John continued, 'Let us pray.'

Then John joined their right hands together again and said, 'Those whom God hath joined together let no man put asunder... I pronounce that they be man and wife together.'

She lifted her veil and they kissed; Jacob and Rachel, officially Mr and Mrs Philip White; she was a married woman and in love. The service continued; they signed the register and left the church. Outside they had the photographs and the throwing of confetti. Mark was still waiting with the horse and carriage, and the newlyweds travelled in style the short distance, to the Fordingham Arms.

The wedding breakfast awaited them in the function room on the first floor, above the bar where Charlotte played the piano.

The bride and groom, with the best man and both sets of parents, were seated at the top table. There were two longer tables on each side of it where the relatives were seated, looking across at each other. On Philip's side there were a couple of aunts and uncles, three cousins, Ruth and his maternal grandparents.

On Irene's side there was the gathering of the clan. Elizabeth was seated near the top, Irene was pleased to see that for once she had forsaken her black attire and was wearing a brown suit with beige accessories, a move in the right direction. With her were Mavis and Gerald with their son Nicholas, who was also starting at a new comprehensive school in September.

Jim and a very pale looking Julia were with Martin and opposite them were Ann and Hillary. Both Martin and Hillary felt that once again Irene had been dealt an ace card in life.

Martin felt trapped in his father's empire; the Bakewell shop was doing well but his father felt that it was time he found a girlfriend and got married before people thought he was 'queer'. Jim was particularly concerned about the fact that his male assistant had moved into the flat above the shop with him; he thought people would talk about them and question their relationship, even though the idea of his son being 'one of them' was unthinkable. Martin was tired of the constant hassle from his father when he had no desire to marry.

Hillary was also trapped in her father's empire. In an attempt to cure her of her casual, uncaring, irresponsible way of life and after much pestering from Ann he had bought her a shop. As she had become reliant on her money coming from Jim, and did not like the alternative of finding her own employment and home, she decided to conform and start working for a living. She had been forced to move to Chesterfield and begin a new life and now, like Martin, she was trapped in her father's empire. If only she could have found a nice boyfriend like her cousin, who had found two good men without any effort.

The glasses were charged and the toasts given; it was time for the second and big surprise for Irene. Where was the honeymoon going to be? He had booked them into a hotel but that was all she knew; they went to the cottage to change but he would not tell her.

Shortly after five o'clock they were waved off and two and a half hours later they reached their destination, Southport. It was somewhere Philip had visited on family holidays and he was sure she would like it; he had booked a suite in a hotel on Lord Street. After unpacking, they took an early evening stroll along the sea front; it was beautiful and romantic for a honeymoon couple. They found a small restaurant for their evening meal before going back to the hotel.

This was their first night together as man and wife; they were both nervous and apprehensive. He undressed in the bathroom while she slipped into her elegant nightdress and got into bed. He joined her.

'Good evening, Mrs White.'

'Good evening, Mr White.'

'May I kiss you, Rachel ?'

'I've waited so long for you to make love to me, my darling, Jacob.'

'Shall we?'

'It's legal now. I thought that's what we were waiting for. To do things properly. Tonight's the night, darling.'

She was arousing him: this was his first time and he wanted it to be good for her. He had heard gossip from his schoolmates and boasting from his friends at university, but he was a novice.

'Well, I've got some of these,' he said, producing condoms. 'We can't make any mistakes until we're ready for a family.'

'Darling, I told you; I've started taking the pill. Everything will be fine,' she said slowly and quietly as she stroked his penis.

He convinced himself that it was going to be good, as he started to make love to her. It was a wonderful experience for him; entering her was easier than he had expected; she lay back and looked so beautiful, clearly enjoying his love-making already, even if not absolutely wonderful, she knew it would get even better with practice.

As he tensed and ejaculated, her sensations reached their peak: she had yet to experience the height of physical and emotional ecstasy when she really climaxed but she was for now perfectly content and it had been good for both of them: the perfect end to a perfect wedding day. Her eyes were closed and he gently kissed her on the cheek.

'Oh, Dan...ny,' she whispered softly.

'Dandy,' he replied, 'fine and dandy, what a quaint expression.' He was bowled over by what he thought was a complimentary phrase for him. 'Dandy, I'll remember that.'

On hearing his voice, she was suddenly and sharply brought back to reality; she was in a hotel room in Southport, not in the hayloft. She looked up at him; he was not Danny. Feeling her become tense he withdrew quickly; he realised the expression on her face had changed. Thinking that his withdrawal had been too sharp and she had felt pain, he murmured, 'Darling, have I hurt you? I'm so sorry, I tried to be gentle.'

She could not reply at first; she just stared at him. There had been something about him that like a magnet had attracted her to him: now she knew what it was: the sudden realisation hit her in the pit of her stomach: he bore a resemblance to Danny, not just in his blond hair, but in his features and his charismatic personality, his kind, gentle, caring and loving nature. But he was not the real Danny, whom she was so in love with, and she did not love this stranger.

On her wedding night she realised she had made the biggest mistake of her life; a mistake which even her Daddy could not put right: she would have to live with it. She had made her solemn vows and would have to do her duty and be a good wife to a man she did not love. Yes, she would be a good wife. Little did she realise that although times had changed and her lot in life as a woman was far easier than her mother's was twenty years ago, she was saying exactly the same as Charlotte:

she would be a good wife!

'Darling, darling, are you all right? I'm sorry darling, have I hurt you?'

She could hear him talking but found it hard to reply. How do you tell your husband on your wedding night that you do not love him? It was impossible, but duty without love was the only answer. She forced a smile,

'No, darling, I'm fine. Dandy, in fact!'

The word, 'darling' almost choked her.

'It was good, wasn't it?'

'Yes,' she lied. Her life was just going to be one big lie from now on.

Philip promptly fell asleep and hardly stirred all night; but she hardly slept at all, but lay awake, her mind in a turmoil. The week was one of the longest she could remember; at the end of it they returned to Fordingham. Irene collected the rest of her belongings and she drove her own car back to Harwood. Wills sensed something was wrong but there was nothing he could do to help his little girl. It was late August when Irene arrived at her new home; she was to begin her new career. Her old life and all that had been familiar to her for years had gone; the chapter had closed and a new one was beginning. She arrived after her husband; he was watching for her so that he could, once again, do the right thing. He greeted her, whisked her off her feet and carried her over the threshold; the threshold of change...

Chapter 12
Harwood, 1972

MARRIAGE FOR IRENE was the beginning of a new chapter, in more ways than one. Living in a small terraced house and sharing her life with a man she did not love was an ordeal in itself. In addition, she had to come to terms with living in an urban environment and starting a career.

During that last week in August she felt isolated; she had experienced loss and loneliness before, but this was a new and different feeling. It was as if she had moved to another planet, and was an alien amongst a different species from those on her own planet.

There were thirty other houses in that street and enough people living in them to fill a village. She and Philip introduced themselves to their immediate neighbours but were not invited into their homes or in any way made to feel welcome; not one person in the street made any effort to communicate with them. She became aware of the coldness and distance of urban people; their homes were their castles and once inside them, the drawbridges were closed: life in villages was so different.

On the Tuesday of that week, they walked the hundred yards from their home in South Street to the High Street. There was one positive aspect of town living; they were within walking distance of every type of shop: a massive supermarket, pubs, restaurants, a fish-and-chip shop, a Chinese take-away, building societies and banks, chemists, shoe shops, hardware shops, butchers, greengrocers, antiques, fashion and electrical shops. The street was a hive of activity; people were everywhere but all these people seemed to be in a hurry. As they passed the bus stop Irene stopped to look at the timetable and noticed that they were only a ten-minute bus ride away from the city centre.

Philip said that at the end of each working week, on a Friday evening, they would treat themselves to a trip to the cinema and a fish-and-chip supper afterwards. It would be like their first date all over again; he thought it would keep the romance in their marriage. Remembering those Friday evenings, in the early sixties, when she and Danny went to the pictures in Buxton, she smiled and dutifully replied,

Time & Tide

'What a nice idea.'

After discovering the High Street they wandered round other roads and found what must have been the village church before Harwood expanded and became a part of the conurbation around Birmingham. They noted the service times and decided that they would worship there and become a part of that community. Surely, they would find more warmth in the church congregation than they had found amongst their neighbours.

Irene stopped suddenly and looked around her; all she could see, and all that existed for miles were houses and other buildings. Where were the fields? How do these people live without any form of nature around them? When do children see calves and lambs? She became quite overcome by claustrophobic feelings. For the first time she understood why Martin had enjoyed his holidays at Fordingham and why he envied her for living in the country.

At the end of that week they both went to their respective schools to prepare for the beginning of term. Irene's school was only a mile from their home but Philip's was on the other side of Birmingham, he had a six-mile drive each day.

Harwood Comprehensive, which covered the eleven-to-sixteen age range, had 1200 pupils on the roll. Unlike Philip, Irene would not have the luxury of teaching sixth formers. Each year had eight forms in it, identified simply by the letters of the alphabet, from 'A' to 'H'. Unlike Fordingham, there were no 'Alpha's' and 'Beta's'; there was the 'A' top set and 'H' remedial, apart from that, the other forms were mixed ability classes from year one.

She drove up the long driveway and parked in the staff car park near the administration block; she thought how big the school must seem to incoming first years. The English teaching area was situated on the top two floors of 'E/M' block, so called because it housed English and Maths; the other blocks had equally appropriate names. That's what the school was, a large number of cold, uninviting blocks of cubic proportions; there was neither a welcoming atmosphere nor a sense of history. The school had been purpose-built in the sixties and, although it was not yet ten years old, it already looked grubby and in need of repair. Irene surveyed it and compared it with Fordingham Grammar. This modern building would not withstand the elements and last for a hundred years; there were more windows than brickwork and you could still see where the caretaker had attempted to remove graffiti. There were pathways everywhere connecting the 'ice-cube' blocks, but what were once garden areas between the blocks were now well-trampled additional pathways. It looked as if the children were more interested in destroying the habitat than they were in using it for learning purposes.

She went into 'E/M' building, climbed the two flights of stairs to the English block and found her head of department in his office. The door was ajar, so he noticed her come in and called, 'Ah, Mrs White, Irene, come in. Welcome to Harwood and the English department.'

'Good morning, Mr Taylor. Thank you.'

'How's married life suiting you?'

'Very nicely, thank you,' she lied, as she smiled politely.

'Well, first of all, my name's David. There are eight of us in the department and two part-time staff. I like to think of us as a family in a happy home. You're our only probationer this year and we'll all do our best to help you. Some of our children can be a handful, but every school has its problem children. In today's society they're par for the course.'

She looked across the desk at this man; he was in his late twenties, with light-brown hair that surrounded the bald patch on the top of his head. His nose supported spectacles; these kept slipping off and he repeatedly pushed them back on. He was clean-shaven, and had thick-set lips with one gold filling in a front top tooth. She knew his English degree was from Cambridge; she thought that was an indication of his high intellectual ability. She assumed from the ring he wore that he was married and probably had a young family. There was so much that she had to learn about her colleagues, in addition to the school routine.

He went on, 'I'll be directly responsible for you during your first year and making the appropriate reports. You've been given a first year form. They are situated in 'L' block, as in L for languages.' He pointed out of the window to the building on the far side. 'This block is the fifth year one. Mrs Morgan's the first year tutor. She's sent some information across for you and will see you on Monday. I've got form lists and syllabuses for your classes here and the 'black book' which tells you all you need to know about the school.'

By this time, Irene was aware of a pile of literature and books in front of her.

'Is there anything you want to ask me?' David continued.

'Er, which is my teaching room?'

'You'll see from the timetable that you're in E3. It's next door. Come on, I'll show you.'

They went back into the corridor and to the room with 'E3' on the door; he, gentleman that he was, opened the door and stood aside for her to enter. She liked the room; it was large and had sixteen tables with chairs all neatly placed in rows facing the blackboard. There were windows on two sides of the room that let the light pour in; store cupboards were under the windows and display boards decorated the remaining wall.

'I like to see displays on the wall and use of the space in the room. It makes it look more attractive and inviting,' David said, 'but all in good time.'

They discussed the syllabus and what he expected from her before she left, taking all her materials in a large box, and wondering if she would ever be ready for the start of term.

Back at home, she was ploughing through the black book when Philip returned from a similar induction session with the head of Humanities at his school. Having enjoyed their first Friday evening trip to the cinema to see 'Young Winston', the rest of the weekend was spent in the endless task of preparation.

On Monday 4th September, they both set off for their respective staff meetings. That evening they were shattered and the term had not even started! Irene thought back to her childhood days, when she had yearned to be a grown-up because adults had so much more freedom and fun than children did. Now she had her freedom, but with it came responsibility and discipline. She was trapped in a hostile environment and a marriage. Her two comforts from what she now realised had been an idyllic past were the big teddy bear Daddy had given her on her fifth birthday and the string-ring. The teddy bear sat on a chair in the corner of the bedroom, the ring remained in her jewellery box.

The next morning they kissed goodbye and wished each other good luck before leaving for their first day in teaching. Irene arrived at the school, parked her car and went to the assembly hall where the first year pupils were gathering. Isobel Morgan had put form lists on the wall, and each form tutor had been given a card to hold with the appropriate letter of the alphabet on it.

Irene had the pleasure of '1C's company for the year.

What she did not know was that if she stayed it would more than likely be for five years! Such was the system. She stood at the side of the hall between '1B' and '1D'; a group of children assembled in front of her. When everyone had arrived Isobel went on to the stage and addressed the throng.

After her welcoming speech, like the Pied Piper Isobel led all of them across to the Language block. Irene thought that this matriarch, small in stature, with grey short tidy hair and a long, thin face, had probably been teaching before she was born. She was wearing a knee length brown skirt with a white blouse and cardigan; her shoes were flat, sensible walking shoes: she had the appearance of an old schoolmarm.

Once in the room with her form, Irene followed the instructions given to her. She distributed notebooks, gave out the class and homework timetables and told them about the school routine.

After break she launched into her first lesson with her second year class, 2D. All her classes were mixed ability; only experienced teachers were given the top and bottom classes. She understood that this was in the interests of both educating the children and, in the case of the bottom classes, protecting the sanity of the staff: that sounded reasonable.

She also discovered that her teaching room was next to David's; this was a deliberate plan on his part so that he could give her as much support as possible. She did not know that the post had become vacant due to her predecessor's nervous breakdown in his first year; David did not want the same thing to happen to her.

At the end of the first day she was exhausted despite only having taught two classes; there had been so many other things to find out about. She had her form responsibility and there were break duties, lunch duties, meetings, clubs, library, drama and the staff cover system to be aware of in the event of staff absence; her diary seemed to be overloaded with dates for so many things.

She had met her other colleagues in the English department; they had all greeted her with warmth and offered her any help she might need. Their real concern was that if she went on sick leave after Christmas, just like her predecessor, they would be the ones left covering her classes! However, she naively thought they were genuinely nice people and was beginning to have second thoughts about the hostility of town people.

At home that evening she and Philip discussed their respective days; clearly his had been easier than hers. He had not been given any form responsibilities and his only teaching that day had been to intellectual fifth and sixth formers preparing for examinations.

By Friday it seemed as if she had worked a whole month, rather than just a week, but David told her that she had made a good start; then he invited her to a department soirée which he was giving at his home. Such occasions were a regular occurrence; he felt that they fostered a good working atmosphere amongst his staff and spouses were invited; his first one for the year was on Saturday 23rd September.

When that Saturday arrived they had been working for three weeks and settled into a new routine. The church community had welcomed them and they had slowly accustomed themselves to the new environment. She had found out that David was thirty and a widower, his wife had died of leukaemia three years before; he had always been devoted to the job, but, after her death, it had become his whole life.

David lived in a semi-detached house with garage, garden and patio, situated on the outskirts of Kidderminster. She and Philip arrived just before 7.30p.m. Irene introduced her husband to David and he led them into the lounge where three of her colleagues were already seated and drinking sherry.

Karen Williams and Jane Meadows had both been teaching for four years; they lived in bed-sits in the same house, had similar interests and spent a lot of time together. Karen, who was in her late twenties, was the more domineering of the two; her positive and forthright manner was an asset in the classroom but could be overpowering elsewhere, as Philip found out that night. She was a blonde girl who believed that blondes were put on this earth for fun and to attract men; on discovering that Philip had strong religious beliefs, taught theology and was a vicar's son, she instantly developed a strong interest in religion and sat chatting to him all evening.

Jane was a more demure character: thoughtful and considerate, she considered other people's feelings before her own. David had found her to be a great comfort after his wife died; she had been like an anchor through one of life's storms for him, and he had found strength from her compassion. He had developed a kind of special affection for her; it was a kind of loving but different from the real thing he had shared with his wife.

However, Irene had now arrived on the scene and he was inevitably seeing a lot of her. Jane's nature was such that she had not noticed the special concern he was showing for Irene. She herself was concerned about Irene and gave her what advice and help she could with ideas, lessons and troublesome children: Jane was too nice for her own good.

Tom Carter was an older man, a confirmed bachelor and head of fifth year pupils, which was why the English rooms were also used for the fifth form registration periods. He was set in his ways and outside work his energies were devoted to gardening and train-spotting.

The rest of the department were married and had arrived with their respective partners. There was Joan Kelsey with hubby Frank; they were a middle-aged couple with three children, she had returned to teaching after taking time off to bring up the children. Then Bob Stephenson arrived with his wife Angela. Each time someone mentioned his name Irene thought about her father and uncle; she had not really got used to her new name and when she heard people referring to him she would habitually turn but she was no longer a Stephenson and must break the habit. Bob was in his thirties, but already going grey; Angela was a secretary in a junior school. Finally, Christine Hammond with John, an elderly couple; Christine was very friendly with Isobel Morgan; they had started teaching at the same time and were both looking forward to retirement in a few years. Irene would look at them and wonder: what would she be like in thirty years time?

David's parents lived in Nairobi; he had spent three weeks of the holiday there and produced a superb slide show as a result of it. Irene learned that his soirées always had some form of entertainment; they had had 'Monopoly' evenings, Victorian parlour games, film shows, beetle drives, and all sorts of things which enabled a group of working colleagues to relax and meet each other in more social circumstances. Each evening was a surprise, they did not know what he had planned until they arrived; she now knew why he was a popular head of department.

The slide show was illuminating. He had pictures of animals in their natural environment, the Bush, which he had taken on safari and, in contrast, slides of the modern Nairobi. After the show there was a buffet supper and then people started to utter their thanks and leave. As usual, Jane would be the last; she would help with the washing up: dear Jane!

For Philip, the evening had been a revelation; it was the first time he had seen any of Irene's colleagues. He vowed to give the voluptuous Karen, with her beads, bangles and 'hippie' image, a wide berth in the future, but liked the idea of such evenings and wondered why the Humanities head of department at his school did not do anything like it.

After that weekend their routine continued. He did everything he could to make their marriage perfect: sometimes he bought her chocolates or flowers. No one could ever doubt his love for her. From the outside an onlooker would see a picture of happiness, but the angle of vision can make such a difference to the picture. Irene was being a dutiful wife with the emphasis on duty; she had made her vows and intended enduring her lot in life but she was unhappy. Only Philip and her father could see that she had created a faúade; her father could make an intelligent guess: he had seen how Philip resembled Danny from the outset.

Philip had noticed her fingering what looked like a piece of string when she thought she was alone but did not know why. He only knew that he was working hard at his marriage, he loved her, he worshipped her but since their wedding night she had changed; there was a distance between them. He had always managed to get what he wanted in life, he had learned how to twist his mother round his little finger when he was still an infant; he had been 'Mummy's' boy and used it to his advantage.

Esther had always supported her son. She had talked John out of sending him to boarding school and had supported his application to Nottingham University when his father wanted him to go to Durham. He had wanted Irene and chased after her; she had married him, just as he had planned. Now he wanted her completely to himself, the present situation was unsatisfactory. There was to be no distance between them; somehow he must use his manipulating powers to completely control her.

They both had preparation and marking to do in the evenings and her marking load was always greater than his. They visited both sets of parents as often as possible and managed to stay with Wills and Charlotte for a couple of days at half-term. In November they spent even more time at school as they each prepared for end of term activities. They supported each other: she joined him at his school's carol service and he accompanied her to the concert at her school.

When they arrived home on the last day of term they were both shattered and wanted to hibernate for the holiday, but that was not a practical solution. For Christmas they stayed with his family and for New Year, as was customary for her, they joined her family at Whistbury.

The scene was familiar as Irene looked around; the only change throughout the years was in the people there. Elizabeth was the only person still living in Almond Blossom Avenue who had been there at the Coronation in

1953; she had new neighbours who were enjoying her traditional hospitality. Several of John's friends had died but the house was still full of people.

As usual, Charlotte was seated on the piano stool and after the welcoming in of the New Year, at eight minutes past twelve, she began playing 'Happy Birthday'.

Wills watched with some concern for Irene's happiness as Philip kissed her and said, 'Happy Birthday, darling. I love you so much. 1973 is going to be a great year for us.'

They returned to Harwood on Tuesday, 2nd January, intent on completing their probationary years. Philip continued working hard at being a loving husband and bought her small gifts as tokens of his love. She had quite a collection of scarves, pieces of jewellery, books and ornaments, which all told of how much he loved her; many a wife would be envious. He could still sense a distance between them and he knew it had something to do with THAT piece of string in her jewellery box.

One Saturday when they were preparing to visit his parents, he saw her open the box and take out the silver chain he had just bought for her. He asked, 'Why do you keep string in there?'

She was surprised he had noticed it.

'Oh, it's nothing really. You remember Dad talking about the Stanton family, who were killed in a car accident?'

'Yes.'

'Well, Daniel and I spent a lot of time together on the estate. We were the same age. One day when we were playing he made me this ring. It was the sort of thing children do. It means nothing. I don't know why I keep it.'

Her voice was beginning to quiver; she knew that Philip was unconvinced and she would have to be more careful in the future. Philip remembered a comment that Brian had made in the college bar about her: there was a rumour that she had stayed in Fordingham to visit her boyfriend's grave, and he was determined to find out more.

The next time they visited Charlotte and Wills, he managed to speak to his father-in-law about it. Wills answered the questions without realising the significance of his replies. He knew that Danny and Irene had been close friends and planned on going to university together; he was aware of the similarity between his son-in-law and Danny, but then people tend to fall for stereotypes and Irene had told him on her wedding day that Danny was a ghost she had lain to rest.

From Wills, Philip discovered that she had met Danny at junior school and their relationship developed after they passed the eleven-plus exam. They were inseparable throughout the secondary school years; it had been assumed that they would go to university and marry. He also learned of their Friday evening visits to the pictures in Buxton. Why had she never mentioned their relationship to him? He answered his own question: she was still in love with Daniel, in love with a ghost. She probably thought more about THAT piece of string than she did about the band of gold and the diamond solitaire on her finger. Like a Victorian husband he saw her as his property, she belonged to him and no one else, certainly not a ghost.

Before he had the opportunity to discuss the matter further or put one of his manipulative schemes into operation there was more sadness for the Stephenson family. There had been concern for Julia, Uncle Jim's wife, after Irene's wedding; other people had noticed how pale she looked. She had not been feeling well for some time but had a dislike of doctors, and hoped that it was all part of going through the 'change of life': sadly that was not the case. In February the family had to come to terms with the fact that she had cancer and was dying; she had ignored the lump on her breast in the faint hope that it would disappear and suffered in silence for too long. The cancer was spreading quickly: she was given only weeks to live. On 25th March, in hospital with Jim and Martin at her bedside, frail and almost unrecognisable, looking more like eighty-one than fifty-one, she took her last breath and died.

Jim thought about all he had achieved and suddenly it did not seem important. He cursed his father for that one conversation in the barn, 'Don't let the grass grow under your feet'. He could still hear those words; he had spent his life acting on them and building his empire. His one indiscretion had almost cost him his marriage but he learned from the mistake. When Julia returned to him he knew that he did not want to lose her again; his empire building had been to impress her. Now it was too late, he had wasted so much time in his life not letting the grass grow when he could have been spending it with Julia.

The funeral at the crematorium in Nottingham was attended by all the family including Ann and Hillary. The bleak day was made even more dismal by the grey clouds and persistent rain. The mourners included many friends and business associates, all arrayed in traditional black, which added to the sombreness of the occasion; only the numerous flowers brightened the day. Philip was determined to accompany and support his wife; it was a golden opportunity for him to show her how much he cared and that she needed him; from that point he could begin to manipulate her. For Irene the death and the funeral just opened up old wounds and she was glad of her husband's support.

At the beginning of April he came home with holiday brochures and put the first stage of his plan into operation. 'Darling, I've been thinking about our first anniversary. I thought we should do something special, like going abroad. I've always wanted to go to Israel.'

'Israel?' she exclaimed. 'I've never even been to the Continent, never mind the Middle East.'

'I've never been abroad either. Times are changing. More people are travelling further than Blackpool now. Look at your head of department David, he spent last summer in Kenya.'

'Mmm. You're right as always, darling. It's a great idea.' By agreeing with him and doing what he wanted she hoped she would continue to hide the fact that she did not love him. In fact she was playing right into his hands. 'What about passports, injections?'

'We need ten-year passports and the travel agent will tell us which jabs we need. I think it's polio, typhoid and tetanus.'

'Ugh. But it'll be worth it.'

They looked through brochures and eventually decided on a week touring the Holy Land and a second week at the coastal resort of Netanya. It was something to look forward to and something to plan for; it would also be a celebration after they had completed their first year of teaching.

They passed their probationary years and were given Scale 2 posts to begin in September. On 10th August with packed suitcases and passports they set off for Heathrow, embarking on the holiday of a lifetime. After a night in a hotel they boarded a plane for Tel Aviv; it seemed unbelievable but that evening they were enjoying dinner in a hotel in Jerusalem, less than eight hours after leaving Heathrow airport.

That week they were Jacob and Rachel; it was like a second honeymoon or an oasis in the desert of their marriage. They visited the sites in Jerusalem and on the road to Bethlehem they stopped at Rachel's tomb; on another day trip they ventured south and experienced floating in the Dead Sea; on the way north to Nazareth they sat at Jacob's Well in Samaria. They celebrated their anniversary on 19th August in Netanya and enjoyed the rest of the week there.

For the whole fortnight Philip did not have to share his wife with a ghost; it was time for his next move, the second part in his carefully calculated plan. He had persuaded her to come to Israel, somewhere he particularly wanted to visit, and now he was going to suggest starting a family. He chose his moment carefully; they were sitting on the balcony of their hotel room in the early evening, looking at the sea and the sunset. It was a magic moment when the rest of the world did not seem to exist; they were both relaxed and only aware of each other.

'Rachel, darling, are you happy?'

'Oh yes, it's wonderful here. I'm so glad we came, Jacob.' She put her hand across the table towards him and he took hold of it.

'I've been thinking,' he said, 'we've both settled into our schools now. We have a nice home, why don't we start trying for our first child? It's the next step and who knows how long it'll take?'

She was speechless and certainly not ready to become a mother. She did not love him, could she love his child?

'Rachel?'

Quickly she replied, 'Why not? If it's a boy we'll call it Jacob and if it's a girl...'

'Rachel!' he answered.

He was delighted; everything was going so well. Soon she would be occupied with pregnancy and motherhood and then she would forget Daniel; his fight with a ghost would be over. The final part of his plan was to persuade her to stay at home and then she would be HIS, all HIS property; totally dependent on him and everything would be perfect again.

Irene was thinking along different lines; she would go along with his idea and let him think they were trying for a baby, but continue taking the pill. She did not know that she was doing exactly the same as her mother had done in the sixties. Wills had never found out that Charlotte was taking the pill; he had just assumed that they were not to be blessed with any more children.

The holiday over, they returned home and prepared for the onslaught of the new term. Once again they were established in the old routine. Britain's economic crisis did not have a great deal of effect on them, sometimes they would leave the cars at home to save on petrol but schools remained open throughout the oil crisis. They enjoyed the day's holiday in November when Princess Anne married and like most people watched the service on television.

However, there was to be more tragedy in the Stephenson family. Uncle Jim had become depressed as a result of Julia's death and the state of the economy. He celebrated his fifty-second birthday on 29th November; Philip and Irene saw him at the beginning of December and she noticed that his hair was grey; the dark hair, a family trait, had completely gone; he had aged quickly and lost interest in the business. Ann was left to cope with the daily routine of keeping his empire afloat. She had tried to contact Bill many times during the last fifteen years. Her letters were unanswered and if she phoned he would recognise her voice and immediately replace the receiver. Now she had a good reason to speak with Bill; she was still married to him and wanted a divorce; Julia was dead and she was sure that Jim would marry her after a period of mourning. The only way to make contact was to go back to Silkington and confront him; this thought had been on her mind all year but before she managed to find the time there was another change in the family.

Jim decided that he wanted to see more of Martin; on the first Sunday in December he drove to Bakewell with the intention of surprising his son. Jim, like most people, had a conscience and at this time in his life, he was riddled with guilt. His conscience was telling him that he should have been more concerned with his family and less concerned with business. In an effort to make peace with himself he needed to pay more attention to his son and daughter.

He arrived at the shop and let himself in, expecting Martin to be upstairs in the flat watching television and relaxing. He seldom went out: it was probably his fault for neglecting him. Martin had become withdrawn in his teenage years but Jim was going to put that right by spending more time with him; this surprise visit was going to be the first of many.

He looked round and smiled at the tidy shelves, all fully stocked and ready for opening on Monday. He went through the shop and up the stairs to the flat; it seemed quiet, maybe Martin was asleep; he crept into the lounge but there was no sign of life. At first he thought he was out but where was his assistant who lodged with him? Someone should be in. Jim called, 'Martin, it's Dad. Where are you? Are you in?' He heard a shuffling sound from the master bedroom; he moved over to the bedroom door, knocked and said, 'Are you having an afternoon nap? Can I come in?'

Without waiting for a reply and expecting his son to be pleased to see him he opened the door and received the biggest shock of his life. Discovering that he had an illegitimate daughter fifteen years ago was only a mild shock in comparison.

Jim stood in the open doorway, his mouth fell open in utter disbelief; his son was in bed with his male lodger.

'Dad, what're you doing here?'

'What am I doing here?' Jim shouted back in anger. 'What's HE doing here? Get out of my son's bed, you QUEER, you PERVERT.' Jim was moving towards the bed with the intention of dragging this other man from it.

'Dad! Stop it!' Martin screamed. 'We love each other.'

'You can't, you can't love him. It's not natural.'

'Dad, I'm…I'm...gay.' At last, Martin had told his father his great secret. It had been a burden and he was pleased that he no longer had to keep it to himself. He expected Jim to be angry at first but was sure that after he had had time to get used to the idea he would accept it.

'No son of mine is a QUEER. You're a disgrace to the family. I'm disowning you.' Jim turned and walked out of the room, down the stairs and out through the shop. He did not look back; he would NEVER come back; he had given him the shop on his twenty-first birthday, but he would have nothing else. There would be no further contact between them; Jim still had a daughter and her mother to look after; they would be his family from now on.

He went to Derby before going home and paid a surprise visit on Ann, who was in her lounge working on the books for the Matlock Bath shop; she never seemed to stop working these days.

'Ann. How are you? I don't know what I'd have done without you these last months.'

A surprised Ann looked up at her visitor. 'I'm battling on but the paper work is endless.'

'I'm sorry I've neglected you and Hillary in the past but that's all going to change now. We'll have a holiday after Christmas.'

'A holiday? You and me?'

'Yes.'

'You must be feeling better.'

'Oh I am. I've got things in perspective now.'

He stayed for sometime looking through the figures with her. She had certainly kept his businesses in good order; he had a lot to thank her for.

During the next fortnight Martin phoned him frequently but he refused to speak to him: he had no son. Then on Christmas Eve he received a distraught phone call from the lodger, who had been to see his parents on the Sunday and had returned on Monday morning to find Martin in the bath with his wrists slashed. Jim was stunned, his whole body froze as he imagined the gruesome scene: Martin's pale, naked body, the reddened, now cold, water and the ghastly wounds in his arms. Even worse was the agony and mental torture which his son must have felt: the unhappiness and loneliness and the final physical pain in those last desperate moments.

Martin had been unable to cope with his father's rejection. The note left in the bedroom was in an envelope and addressed simply, *'To Dad'*.

When Jim arrived, he opened it and read:

'My dearest Dad,

I am so sorry that you cannot accept me for what I am. I have always loved you and tried to please you. I've followed you into the business and have made a success of this shop for you. I knew when I was a young boy that I preferred male company to that of female but I did not want to disappoint you. I cannot live, knowing that you hate me. I have decided to join dear mother. I will always love you and I hope that in time you will forgive me. One day we will meet again. Until then,

Your loving son,

Martin'

Jim stared at the letter, the last words were staring him in the face, *'your loving son'*. The sudden realisation of what had happened broke over him like a tidal wave. His heart stopped, he felt dizzy and had to sit down. His body shook as he sobbed relentlessly. This was all his fault; he was responsible for his own son's death. If only he had accepted him as he was – a homosexual. He was vaguely aware of the undertaker's arrival and knew he had to make the arrangements at a time when families should be united and celebrating. Another voice spoke, 'Mr Stephenson, I'm so sorry. You must hate me. I presume you won't want me to stay working here.'

Jim looked up at this tall, handsome man, who had loved his son. He had probably made Martin happier than he, his father, had ever done.

'You're wrong. I do want you to stay here. His death was my fault, not yours. It was too much of a shock for me: I'm sorry I took him from you. I'm sure you made him happy. What's your name, anyway?'

'Tim, sir, Tim Jones.'

'Tim.' Jim paused, 'You must be heartbroken.'

'Yes, sir.'

Both men were desperately trying to control their emotions and keep a stiff upper lip.

'Tim, I want us to be friends.'

He made himself look Tim in the eye, and offered his hand. After only a moment's hesitation Tim reached out and took it. As they touched, the animosity drained away from Jim, and he found himself sighing with deep relief. The two of them made the funeral arrangements for New Year's Eve. The family wanted to cancel Christmas but that was an impossible task and so they were forced to carry on with the festive season albeit through a dark cloud. Irene kept reminiscing over those childhood days when she had idolised her cousin; they were long since gone but were still clear in her mind. She spent Christmas with Philip's family and then they went to Fordingham. She, Philip, Wills and Charlotte attended their second family funeral that year and it was again at the crematorium. They said their goodbyes to Martin– such a sad death of a young man who was only twenty-seven.

Elizabeth's New Year tradition went ahead; 1974 arrived. Wills watched as Philip kissed Irene; this year after two funerals all he could say was, 'Darling, things can only get better!'

He was thinking that she would be announcing her pregnancy soon.

Their life and work continued; the months passed by but there was no sign of a new arrival.

Time & Tide

Meanwhile Jim's feelings of guilt continued; he had befriended Tim for his son's sake as much as his own. He still had Hillary and Ann and was determined to look after them; he employed extra part-time staff to give them more freedom and he had a new philosophy. Instead of 'Don't let the grass grow under your feet', it was, 'Live for today'. They were in a position to spend time together as a family unit which was something they had never done before.

In the spring of 1974 he took Ann back to Silkington to see Bill; Ann's dreams were starting to come true. Jim had asked her to marry him: she needed a divorce.

He waited in the car while she went up to the front door; she could clearly remember her last hasty departure down that garden path and the door slamming behind them. Her last attempt at phoning had been three years ago; she had to find the courage to face him and ask for a divorce. They had been living apart for over fifteen years and the new divorce laws meant they could be divorced easily on grounds of either adultery or desertion.

She nervously knocked on the door. A young woman answered.

'Yes,'

'Er... I wanted to see Bill,' Ann uttered, not knowing who this woman was. 'He's my husband.'

'Bill? Bill who?'

'Bill Edison. Who are you, please?'

'Mary Lassiter. I live here with my husband, Jack.' Then Mary remembered about the previous owner of the house, which they bought last year. 'We've only been here for a short time. The previous owner died. I believe he's buried in the churchyard here.' Ann was stunned.

Mary continued, 'I'm so sorry, my dear, if it was your husband. I thought there were no relatives. His estate was sorted out by solicitors and I think the revenue went to various charities. Would you like to come in?'

'Er... No, thank you. I've someone waiting in the car. I'm sorry to have troubled you.' Ann turned and went back to the car; she was white and shaking.

'Well?' asked Jim.

She remained silent.

'Well?' he repeated.

'He's dead.' She paused and then with a quivering voice and tears streaming down her face, 'He was only fifty-two years old.' She paused. 'Let's go to the churchyard.'

They walked the short distance down the lane to the church and looked for the new gravestones. Jim paused by an unmarked grave. 'My nephew's here.'

Ann stopped and said, 'Of course, James, poor James.'

They stood silently for a moment as they both remembered that awful day back in 1956; then they continued until they found the stone.

William John Edison
1920–1972
Rest in Peace

Ann stood in disbelief; she was a widow and had been for sometime: How had he died? Had anyone attended the funeral? As questions flashed through her mind she noticed the name on the next stone, Frederick Thompson. She was sure that was the Fred who had been born in the house next to the church, married Betty and lived next to Wills and Charlotte. She knew she was right when a much older looking Betty arrived with flowers.

'Betty? It is Betty, isn't it?'

Betty looked surprised until she realised where this stranger was standing. 'Yes. It's Betty. Yer've finally come back to 'im, 'ave yer? Left it a bit late.'

'How did he die?'

"Eart attack. 'E changed after yer left. 'E drank a lot and kept himself apart from rest of village. It was as if 'e blamed 'imself for what yer did.'

Ann could feel the hostility; there was no point in trying to explain about her attempts at contacting him. She had been judged by the community and found guilty in her absence of the worst possible crime in their eyes, adultery, and she must accept that.

'Thank you, Betty. I'm sorry to see you've lost Fred. He was a good man.'

'The best, he were the best,' she replied, 'but I were a good wife. I kept me vows and did me duty.'

'Yes, Betty. It's nice to see you again.' She turned to Jim, 'Let's go'.

They returned to the car and decided to go to Chesterfield and tell Hillary about Bill, and that they were going to get married.

As soon as Hillary saw the expression on her mother's face she knew there was bad news coming. On hearing that Bill was dead, her world shattered; she could remember looking back and shouting, 'Daddy, Daddy,' as he slammed the door and ignored her. Throughout her childhood she had prayed that one day he would come back into her life; all her tantrums and wild ways had been in the hope that Ann would contact him and he would come and collect her. Those early days of childhood had been idyllic; he had been her father then, she adored him, he would always be her father: Jim was a substitute. The additional news that Jim was going to marry her mother was the final blow. She had to accept that Bill was gone and her mother and natural father were going to marry. However, she would remain an Edison; she would not change her name to Stephenson and she would never forget Bill.

The wedding took place on 20th July, 1974; it was a quiet affair at the registry office in Nottingham. Wills, Charlotte, Philip, Irene and Hillary were the only witnesses. Afterwards, they had a meal in a restaurant before Jim and Ann set off on the long-promised holiday. They said it was not really a honeymoon and asked Hillary to join them, but she declined. They flew to Malta and spent a fortnight on what proved to be for them a paradise island.

After the wedding there was one week left of the summer term. For Irene, it was time to say farewell to Joan Kelsey; her husband had been promoted, which meant moving to Devon. There was the end-of-term staff party where Joan and the rest of those leaving were given a good send off, and the grand farewell at David's home which Irene and Philip went to, but where he felt out of place. She seemed to be happier with David's English department than she was with him.

That summer they spent a lot of time with their families. Ruth was excited because she was going up to Durham University. Irene wondered what had happened to her friend, Christine; they had kept in touch until Christine's marriage and then somehow as their paths had gone in different directions they had lost contact: people come and people go; that's life!

As Philip had decided that they should always celebrate it abroad, their anniversary was spent in Portugal. Unfortunately, it was not as good as their holiday in Israel. They were not Jacob and Rachel in a world of their own and the distance between them was growing. Holidays together were not the solution; the only answer Philip could see was starting a family but it seemed that like Rachel, Irene was barren. For the first time in his life, it looked as if his manipulation was not going to work; he had no idea that she was deceiving him; she had never stopped taking the pill.

They began their third year of teaching in September. As the year progressed they spent less and less time together; Philip disliked going home and found reasons to stay at work; sometimes, he would not return until after ten when Irene was in bed and she chose not to question his whereabouts. When they were together, he would often lose his temper and start shouting at her about anything and everything, but their arguments always seemed to end with him blaming her for not being pregnant. His last words were usually, 'If you had a baby there would be no need for any of this'.

She thought about their college days together; he had been so different then, so loving and caring. He blamed her for their unhappy situation and she also blamed herself. He was probably having an affair and that would be her fault too, but the less she saw of him the better; she would rather remain in blissful ignorance than face up to the truth.

The next summer holiday came round; he had no plans for their anniversary, there seemed to be little point. One morning at the beginning of August he left the house early; he returned quietly in the afternoon and went upstairs to the bedroom. Her jewellery box was open and she had Danny's ring in her hand. He was extremely angry and shouted, 'That piece of grubby string means more to you than I do. I'm sick and tired of living with a ghost. There's three of us in this marriage and I'm tired of being the gooseberry.' Suddenly, a thought flashed through his mind. It was their wedding night again. 'You were with him on our wedding night, weren't you? It wasn't 'dandy' you uttered but 'Danny'. My God! My God! Even on our wedding night you were thinking about HIM.'

His voice was so loud that she feared the whole street would hear; she was frightened and tears were trickling down her face.

'You slept with him didn't you? When did he give you that ring? Answer me, woman, ANSWER ME, you WHORE.'

'Y-e-s,' she uttered.

'Yes, to what, yes you slept with him? Yes, you were thinking about him on our wedding night? Well?'

'Stop shouting at me,' she whimpered.

'I'm waiting. I should have realised you weren't a virgin but I was so inexperienced then. I trusted you. More fool me.'

'Yes, we made love. He gave me this ring afterwards. He made one for himself. We made our vows to each other, to stay together until death parted us.' Her voice was quivering.

'When, WHEN did all this happen?'

'Three days before he died. I...I...never saw him again. It was the Friday afternoon before Whit Monday. The Stantons were going to Leeds for the weekend. They never came back.'

'You never really loved me, did you?'

'I thought I did. I've tried. I've really tried. I never meant to hurt you.'

'When did you make that discovery? Or did you decide to go for second best?'

'On...on our wedding night.'

The truth was slowly dawning on Philip. In anger, he grabbed her right wrist, she hastily put the string ring in her other hand and tried to keep it away from him.

But he reached up, took hold of her other hand, brought it down on to the dressing table. He unclenched her fist and took the string; she desperately tried to get it back but he held it out of her reach.

'I'm going to lay this ghost to rest once and for all,' he screamed.

Still holding her right wrist with his left hand, he went into the bathroom, dragging her along with him. He put the grubby piece of string down the toilet and flushed it away.

She was crying and screaming, 'No, no, please, no.'

But it was too late; her precious possession and tangible reminder of Danny was gone.

'I haven't finished with you yet.' He dragged her back into the bedroom and threw her down on the bed. He then lay on top of her and as she struggled to escape he ripped off her skirt and pants, unzipped his trousers and forced her to have sex with him. She was trying to fight him off but he was too strong for her.

'No, no, no,' she kept repeating until her voice was just a mild whimper.

'This is your duty,' he screamed at her, 'you're my wife. Daniel's gone. You're mine. You'll never forget this.' He was a man in torment and totally out of control.

All she could feel was the intense pain; he was inside her and hurting her. The more she fought the more it hurt; her instinct told her to fight but she was weakening, her strength was slipping away. She felt that if he continued he would kill her.

Suddenly, as if he had realised what he was doing, he stopped. He stood up and looked down at her, this semi-naked woman with a tear-stained face and red marks on her wrists where he had held her so tightly.

'This mess is all your fault. If only you'd got pregnant, like I planned,' he said as he finished dressing. Then he walked out; all she heard was the door slam. She wanted to shout after him but her throat was dry after the screaming and whimpering; she was exhausted and unable to speak. She wondered what he meant by 'a mess' but did feel that it was probably all her fault. She lay there, weak and in agony, for some time. Eventually, she regained enough strength to move from the bed, but her whole body ached and she felt dirty and abused. For the first time in her life she knew what real fear was. What would she do when he returned? What would he do? Would he return? She ran a hot bath and washed herself all over; then she did it all again. Each time she tried to wipe away the hurt: if only it were that simple. Then she put the clothes she had been wearing in a bag and disposed of them, but she could not end the pain and tears so easily.

Next morning her bruised body still ached: What should she do? He must be having an affair; she could handle that but what if he NEVER came back? She would have to tell Daddy. Daddy always knew what to do. She hugged her teddy bear; she no longer had the ring but she still had the teddy bear for comfort.

He returned mid-morning with the same words that he had uttered the day before.

'This is all your fault.'

'What is? Tell me.'

'I've been having an affair.'

'I guessed that, but it doesn't matter.'

'It doesn't matter,' he shouted. 'Oh yes it does when she's a sixth former. And pregnant.'

'Oh, my God.' Irene put her head into her hands. At that moment the phone rang. It was a distraught Esther, who hoped that Philip had arrived, because his father was being rushed to hospital. He had had a heart attack shortly after Philip and Sarah had left that morning.

'Just look what you've done. If you hadn't been so distant none of this would have happened. Sarah was a comfort to me when you were so cold. I've been forced to resign to avoid a scandal at school. Sarah can't take her 'A' levels. I took her to see Mum and Dad last night. Dad has sorted something out for us but look what it's done to him. If he dies, I'LL NEVER FORGIVE YOU. If only you'd done as I wanted, been a decent wife and loved me, ME. Was it too much to ask?'

'Oh Philip…'

'You're going to divorce me on grounds of adultery. You can have the house. I'll be back to collect my belongings. Get a solicitor. You'll soon be hearing from mine. If Dad dies, I'll NEVER FORGIVE YOU. Goodbye.'

The door slammed. She sat in silence for a while, thinking. There was only one thing to do; she picked up the phone, dialled and was so relieved to hear his voice.

'Oh Daddy,' she sobbed. She gave him a garbled version of events, he understood the main thing; Philip had left her.

'I'm coming to collect you.'

That evening she was back with her parents at Fordingham. She told her parents that they had drifted apart and as a result he had turned for comfort to a sixth former; the girl was pregnant and they had both been forced to leave. She tried to keep Danny out of it but her father said, 'He wasn't Danny, was he?'

'No.'

'When did you realise?'

'Early on in the marriage, but I tried, Daddy, I really tried.'

'I know, me duck. Philip knew there was something wrong. He asked me about the Stantons sometime ago. How he made the connection between you and Danny, I don't know. But remember, he chased you. He came to the produce sale and to the church. He was determined to marry you. He was the manipulator, not you. It was unfortunate that he was so like Danny.'

She mentioned neither the hayloft nor the ring and she remained silent about him raping her. Her father would be really upset if he knew just how Philip had hurt her: she wanted to spare him that.

'He wants me to divorce him on grounds of adultery. I have to get a solicitor. Oh, Daddy, it's all such a mess. His father's had a heart attack. What if he dies?'

'We'll pray that he doesn't, but if he does it won't be your fault. I'll go and see the solicitor tomorrow. Why don't you think about coming back here? There's nothing to keep you in Harwood now.'

That August was so different from the previous three when they had married and celebrated their anniversaries.

Wills sorted things out for her with his solicitor, who had become a friend after acting for him when he first invested in property. Divorce proceedings were started.

Wills kept trying to persuade her to sell up but she refused. She had become an established member of the staff at Harwood Comprehensive and wanted to stay; there were times when she thought it would be easier to build an igloo in the Sahara than teach, but there are bad days in any job.

Unfortunately, John White did not survive his heart attack and left a sad community behind in Battersley, along with the widowed Esther and fatherless Philip and Ruth. Their lifestyles changed; Ruth continued her degree course at Durham University but Esther was forced to leave the rectory. She chose to join Philip and Sarah in their new home in Wales; John had found a cottage for Philip in a small Welsh village where he and Sarah could live together without questions being asked. It was fortunate that John had so many friends and acquaintances throughout the country; many of them travelled to Battersley for his funeral. Irene felt guilty about his death but decided it would be better not to attend. Wills kept trying to reassure his daughter that the heart attack would probably have occurred anyway and she should not reproach herself: it was cold comfort. Esther had to find a new job and Philip's career was ruined; he would have to find some other job to support him and his new family.

Idly, passing the time away until September in Fordingham, Irene noted that her mother was still keeping her diaries; she had seven brightly-coloured files full of events in addition to her early notebooks. Picking up one, she started reading.

'*1970*

BRITAIN

Ann Nightingale is the first female disc jockey on Radio One; women are being admitted, for the first time, into Lloyds Insurance Company in London. (Not before time!)

It's the beginning of a revolution in air travel, a Pan American 'jumbo' jet has arrived from the United States at Heathrow airport...

February: Prince Charles takes his seat in the House of Lords...

March: the New English Bible is published...

June: general election, Harold Wilson lost, the new Conservative prime minister is Edward Heath, with a majority of thirty-one seats. The most serious problem facing the new government is the state of industrial relations. Strikes have become the 'in-thing' after the 'feel-good' factor of the sixties. Everyone wants to make more money. The unions have grown in strength and power during the Labour Government and discovered that a good way of achieving their demands is the withdrawal of labour, which has a snowball effect on the rest of society.

July: the Ford Motor Company builds its millionth Cortina for export...The Reverend Ian Paisley voices strong objections to the Roman Catholic Mass being celebrated in Canterbury Cathedral for the first time in 400 years... 22nd July, Mr Henry Holloway is the first man to have an atom-powered heart pacemaker installed, another great achievement for the field of medical science... The first public Hindu temple is open in London...

Time & Tide

The famous Beatles pop group of the sixties are splitting up, causing much heartache amongst young people...

November: it's the first Gay Liberation Front march through London.

SPORT

Brazil win the World Cup! They beat Italy 4–1 in Mexico...

Chelsea beat Leeds 2–1 to win the FA Cup...

Edinburgh hosts the Commonwealth Games.

THE ARTS

The Young Vic Theatre Company is starting in London... Television, "Coronation Street" reaches its 1000th episode... On the BBC, "Monty Python's Flying Circus" is a new comedy programme with zany humour and is popular viewing... Germaine Greer is challenging the masculine world with her controversial book about feminism, "The Female Eunuch".

ABROAD

Munich: the first nerve transplant operation is performed...

March: in Washington, the Nuclear Non-Proliferation Treaty comes into effect...

Following the successful moon landing in 1969, the Americans are continuing to send rockets to the moon in the hope of further discoveries... April, Apollo 13 sets off for the moon but fails to land after an explosion on board; the three astronauts struggle to survive as they return to earth and in the end land safely in the Pacific... Russia, cosmonauts land safely in Soyuz 9 after a record seventeen days in space...

RACIAL PROBLEMS continue... May: six black people die in racist riots in Georgia, USA...

May: Czechoslovakia signs a twenty-on-year peace treaty with the USSR...

June: Tonga gains independence from Britain...

July: The Aswan High Dam on the River Nile in Egypt is finally completed. It has been built to keep the river level constant throughout the year and control flooding; also for the provision of hydroelectricity and irrigation water. As part of this massive project the Abu Simbel burial memorial was raised ninety feet up a cliff to avoid submersion. Lake Nasser has formed behind the Dam.

September: Jordan, three airliners have been blown up by Arab Guerrillas... Egypt's President Nasser dies: his successor is Anwar Sadat...

October: Cambodia is declared a Republic... Fiji gains independence from Britain...

Seoul, Korea, 790 couples from all over the world, members of the controversial Unification Church are married by their leader, Sun Myung Moon in a mass ceremony...

November: Charles de Gaulle dies in France. The people are in mourning for the man who led the 'Free French' opposition to the Nazis in World War Two. He was also the president who granted Algeria its independence in 1962. He introduced the "Fifth Republic", a new constitution in France; he increased the country's international standing and brought about reconciliation with Germany BUT he blocked Britain's entry into the Common Market in 1967!

1971

BRITAIN

January: We're having a postal strike, the first ever... 16th February, "D-day" has arrived; it's goodbye to £/s/d and hello to decimal currency. No longer will twelve pence make a shilling or twenty shillings make a pound. The cash registers will become museum pieces as new tills take over. It is now 100 New Pence = £1 and not 240 pennies. There is a new currency of 1p, 2p, 5p and 10p pieces – ½d, 1d, 3d, 6d (tanner!), 1/- (bob!), 2/- (florin), 2/6 (half-a-crown) will all be obsolete soon as we come to terms with paying 25p instead of 5/- !

The first divorces are granted under the new Divorce Act as a result of the Reform Bill of 1969...

The Immigration Bill is published, ending the right of Commonwealth workers to settle in Britain...The Daily Sketch, Britain's oldest tabloid newspaper, closes down... British Rail approves a plan to develop a high speed Advanced Passenger Train...

The government announces that in 1973 Purchase Tax will be replaced by Value Added Tax (VAT) so that Britain will be in line with Europe... The government also announces plans to extend the motorway network by 1000 miles by the end of the seventies.

25th April, THE CENSUS indicates that there are 2½ million more people living in Britain than in 1961.

Mrs Thatcher, the Education Minister earns herself the title "Thatcher the milk snatcher", because she is abolishing the supply of free milk to the seven to eleven age group.

ABROAD

A coup in Uganda puts the dictator, Idi Amin into power... America, following the moon landing in 1969, and the disastrous flight of Apollo 13, successfully lands

Time & Tide

Apollo 14 and later Apollo 15 on the surface of the moon; David Scott and James Irwin are the first astronauts to drive on the moon in a battery-controlled Lunar Roving Vehicle, spending two hours covering a wide area and transmitting clear colour pictures back to Earth... Three Russian cosmonauts die in the capsule of Soyuz 11 on a return trip from space.

1972

BRITAIN

January: Edward Heath signs the Treaty of Brussels, ending ten years of negotiation and puts Britain in the Common Market. Norway, Denmark and Ireland are joining at the same time; full membership will begin on 1st January, 1973 when the original six countries will become ten. 25th January, Bloody Sunday in Ulster. A civil rights march in Londonderry begins peacefully but ends in a massacre after demonstrators try to break down a roadblock; thirteen people are dead and a further seventeen injured...

February: Electricity workers are on strike... the miners are taking industrial action as well.

April: Five of the Oxford University men-only colleges announce that they were going to admit women for the first time... London Zoo announces the death of Chi-Chi, the great panda. (Even pandas are not immortal!)

May: The West Midlands orbital route is open; that should ease congestion when travelling through the Midlands.

July: a National Dock strike!

November: Edward Heath imposes a wage and price freeze in an effort to stop all industrial action...

The Queen and Prince Philip celebrate their silver wedding anniversary.

ABROAD

America: The space probe Pioneer 10 is launched on a twenty-one month voyage to Jupiter...

Apollo 16 lands on the moon and astronauts John Young and Charles Duke spend eleven days exploring the moon's surface; they've brought moon rock back to Earth for analysis... President Nixon has a summit meeting in China; this is a breakthrough in Sino-American relations... The Strategic Arms Limitation Treaty, to be known as SALT, is signed in Washington; this agreement prevents both Russia and America from producing more intercontinental ballistic missiles for five years... In the presidential elections Richard Nixon is re-elected in a landslide victory...

June: After several incidents of hi-jacking aeroplanes pilots from over thirty countries have decided that it's time to take positive action; they are staging a strike and bringing European airports to a virtual standstill.

THE ARTS & MUSIC

"Grease" opens in a theatre in New York... Oscar winning films are "Cabaret" and "The Godfather"...

London: Andrew Lloyd Webber and Tim Rice produce a new controversial musical, "Jesus Christ Superstar"...

The pop scene begins the year with The New Seekers at the top of the charts with "I'd like to teach the World to sing".

Cilla Black, Gilbert O'Sullivan, Elvis Presley, Tom Jones, Johnny Cash, Elton John, David Cassidy, Donny Osmond and Gary Glitter all have hits this year. Prominent groups are Slade, The Rolling Stones, 10cc.

The compact disc (CD) is developed by the Philips Company and will have an impact on the music world... On our television screens new programmes are "Emmerdale Farm", a lunchtime series about a farming community in Yorkshire, a quiz, "Mastermind", and a comedy, "Love thy Neighbour".

SPORT

Red Rum wins the Grand National at Aintree... 20th Olympic Games are in Munich; the Black September Arab terrorists storm the Israeli building in the Olympic village and kill two athletes, others manage to escape; the terrorists are holding nine hostages and demanding the release of 200 hundred Palestinians in Israel's jails and a safe passage out of Germany. The hostages are shot by the terrorists when German police attempt to prevent them from leaving the country; a tragedy which will always be remembered instead of the Games.

OBITUARIES

28th May, the Duke of Windsor dies in his home in Paris. He will be remembered as the uncrowned King who abdicated in 1936 to live with Mrs Wallis Simpson, an American divorcée, the woman he loved. His body lies in state in St. George's Chapel, Windsor. After the funeral he is buried in Frogmore.

28th August, Prince William of Gloucester dies in an air crash.

1973

BRITAIN

The Equal Opportunities Commission is the new official body for equal rights for all British people "regardless of gender or colour..."

Time & Tide

Strikes! Strikes and more strikes! That's all that seems to be happening at the moment...train drivers, dockers, mine-workers, Ford car workers...it's difficult to know who's actually working! Our economy is not looking good; petrol-rationing books are being prepared because, in addition to problems here, there's a worldwide shortage of crude oil. The oil producing countries have decided to use their own asset to their own advantage by restricting the supply for export and putting the price up. This means dearer petrol, less petrol and speed restrictions. The oil crisis and continual industrial action has prompted Edward Heath to put the country on a three-day working week.

14th November: Princess Anne marries Captain Mark Phillips at Westminster Abbey. This occasion brightens Britain's gloom, if only for a day. The usual well-wishers are lining London's streets, waving and cheering as the couple make their way to Buckingham Palace after the ceremony. All schools are closed and millions of people watch the service on television.

1974

Morale is low as we begin 1974. The good years of the sixties have almost been forgotten; the three-day week continues. The prime minister asks the question, "Who rules the country, an elected government or the unions?" It's clear there's a battle between them. In an effort to gain power, Mr. Heath calls for a general election...

March: Labour wins the general election with 301 seats but no overall majority; Mr Wilson is reinstated at No.10... Princess Anne's the victim of an attempted kidnapping when she and her husband are returning to Buckingham Palace; a car swerves in front of them bringing them to a halt; Ian Ball, the would-be-kidnapper, shoots the Princess's detective and then attempts to pull her out of the car; his plan fails when the police and members of the public manage to restrain him, but not before several people have been wounded.

September: Great administrative changes are taking place, new authorities and counties are emerging; the map of Britain is changing; these changes involve the loss of the smallest county of Rutland as this area becomes swallowed up in Leicestershire and Lincolnshire and also, the loss of the Yorkshire Ridings as Humberside arrives...

October: the second general election of the year; Parliament, which the Queen opened on 12th March, has lasted for only 199 days, the shortest one since 1886. Labour are the victors again, but with a majority of only three...

It has been a good year for the great train robber, Ronald Biggs: after his escape

186

from prison he's turned up in Brazil, where he's been given security and immunity from the British police, because he's the father of a Brazilian child.

1975

BRITAIN

Donald Coggan is the new Archbishop of Canterbury... Burmah Oil collapses... The idea of a Channel Tunnel is abandoned by the British Government...

11th February, Margaret Thatcher is the new Conservative leader, after Edward Heath resigns... A London policeman, Stephen Tibble, is shot whilst helping detectives chase IRA suspects...

Ex-Minister John Profumo, who resigned from the government during the scandal in the sixties, is awarded the CBE for his charity work...

NORTHERN IRELAND

In revenge for Bloody Sunday in 1972, when several Northern Irish people were shot by soldiers, the IRA is claiming responsibility for several bombing incidents. Northern Ireland's problems are spilling over on to the mainland... car bombs in London... 5th October, 1974, bombs explode in two public houses in Guildford... 21st November, 1974, bombs planted in two Birmingham pubs cause the deaths of twenty-one people and injure a further 182... As a result of these incidents the IRA are outlawed in the UK... In the weeks leading up to Christmas there are other explosions in London, including one in Oxford Street.

THE EARLY SEVENTIES

There's a noticeable change in fashion. Where minis, Mods and Rockers were the mark of the sixties, the seventies have flares, platform soles and punk.

One-piece swimsuits are back in fashion, rather than bikinis, along with cheesecloth smock dresses, corduroy trousers and long skirts; there's a new elegance in clothes resembling the Edwardian era, and a new trend which no individual would have even dreamed of in earlier years: at Twickenham, during a rugby international match a fan streaks across the pitch.

Streaking is the term given to appearing in a public place completely naked; after the initial episode there have been reports of other streakers at various events; there's even a record in the music charts called "The Streaker".

MUSIC

Eric Clapton relaunches his career after a troubled period of drug dependency and Paul McCartney is found guilty of growing marijuana plants. The Osmond family is the most consistent pop act in both chart performance and sales; a new group, Queen, releases its début album and have a No.1 hit, "Bohemian Rhapsody".

A group known as Abba rises to fame in the 1974 Eurovision Song Contest with the song "Waterloo".

Elton John releases his tribute to Marilyn Monroe, "Candle in the Wind".

TELEVISION & FILM

Sooty is celebrating his twenty-first birthday.

The Goons are enjoying fame on the radio... 26th May, 1973, "That's Life" is now on the air... December, 1973, "Some Mother's Do Have 'Em" is an overnight success. In 1974, "Colditz" and "The Wombles" are very popular. The cinemas are losing some of their popularity and being replaced by bingo halls, but for those who remain faithful to the cinema world, "The Sting", "Murder on the Orient Express" and "Jaws" are on general release.

SPORT

The 1973 FA Cup winners are Second Division, Sunderland who beat Leeds United 1-0; it's the first time a Second Division team have won in forty-two years...

Red Rum wins the Grand National at Aintree in 1973 and 1974... 1973, top tennis players are boycotting Wimbledon as a protest against the poor contracts offered to them by the Lawn Tennis Federation... 1975, Arthur Ashe becomes the first black man to win the men's singles championship at Wimbledon.

ABROAD

1973

January: Lyndon B Johnson, the former US president, dies of a heart attack...

April: the Afghan monarchy is abolished in a military coup and the new Afghan Republic is created; this puts an end to fifty-four years of monarchy rule...

May: NASA launches Skylab, the world's first space-based scientific research laboratory, into orbit from Cape Kennedy...

June: Greece becomes a republic... Tragedy hits the Paris air show when the Soviet Supersonic plane crashes... The West German Chancellor, Willy Brandt, makes a historic visit to Israel. The Soviet leader, Leonid Brezhnev, makes a nine-day state visit to the United States in an attempt to improve East–West relations...

July: President Amin expels American Peace Corps workers from Uganda...The Bahamas gain independence from Britain... The French test the H-bomb in the Pacific...

September: President Salvador Allende of Chile is killed by rebels... Juan Peron is elected president of Argentina.

October: Egypt and Syria attack Israel in the Yom Kippur War...
NASA's Pioneer 10 flies past Jupiter and sends photographs back to Earth...
1974
Solzhenitsyn, the Russian author is expelled from the Soviet Union...The United States and Egypt are resuming diplomatic relations after seven years.
March: the US spacecraft, Mariner, photographs the planet Mercury and sends the pictures fifty-seven million miles back to Earth.
April: the French president Monsieur Pompidou dies... Golda Meir resigns as Israel's Premier; the new Premier is Yitzhak Rabin...
May: the West German Chancellor Herr Brandt resigns over a spy scandal; he's replaced by Herr Helmut Schmidt...The new French president is Valery Giscard d'Estaing... Israel signs a truce with Syria...
July: President Peron of Argentina dies... In Cyprus President Makarios is ousted in a military coup.
WATERGATE
After two years this scandal appears to be coming to an end. 8th August, President Nixon resigns from office. He made the decision after revelations about his role in the break-in and attempted bugging at the Democratic Party's National Headquarters, The Watergate Building in Washington DC on 17th June, 1972. In March, the Grand Jury indicted seven of President Nixon's former aides on charges of conspiracy and obstructing justice. After demands for his impeachment, President Nixon admits that he withheld information and made misleading statements regarding the affair. Vice-President Gerald Ford is sworn in as America's new president.
Christmas Day: A cyclone wrecks the city of Darwin in Northern Australia and kills forty-nine people. What a day to choose!
1975
March: Ethiopia, the monarchy is abolished... The country is also making headline news as the world is made aware of its sad plight, it is stricken with drought and famine; newspapers all over the world have reproduced a photograph showing a poor elderly woman begging for food...
May: the Japanese, Junko Tabei becomes the first woman to climb Everest... Stuttgart, the trial of the revolutionary left-wing West German Rote Armee Faktion (Red Army Faction,) more commonly known as the Baader-Meinhof group after Andreas Baader and Ulrike Meinhof, the two leaders, begins. It is responsible for several terrorist attacks and assassinations in Germany and has helped other

terrorist groups around the world.

June: the Suez Canal is reopened by President Sadat as a gesture of peace; it was closed after the 1967 Six-Day War...

July: the Terracotta Army is unearthed in China... History is made when the Soviet and US astronauts shake hands in Space 140 miles above the Atlantic Ocean...

Papua New Guinea gains independence from Australia...

Spain, General Franco's death leads to the return of a monarchy.

THE WAR IN VIETNAM

Is it really over? In 1972, when the North Vietnamese forces made inroads on three fronts in South Vietnam, it was thought that the end was in sight. Towns and cities of South Vietnam were wiped out as the northern forces headed for Saigon in April. The American forces are being ferried out in helicopters, the last one left at 8.00 am on 30th April; President Duong van Minh surrenders to the new regime in Saigon, known as the National Liberation Front (the "Viet Cong"). They're entering into negotiations with the Hanoi Government about the reunification of the country.'

While Irene was flicking through the pages, picking up various pieces of information from her mother's journals, she wondered why Charlotte was so jealous of her. She had so much, her journals which had become a hobby, her musical skills which she enjoyed, the properties, a nice home, a loving husband, who worshipped her and could never harm or rape her. After Irene's recent encounters, the latter was something she felt her mother should certainly appreciate.

She returned to Harwood at the end of August to begin the new term in September; when she crossed the threshold of what had been their marital home she was– and felt– totally alone. Her life was changing yet again; after three years of marriage she was a single person and must no longer think of herself as a married woman.

She had reached another turning point in her life...

Chapter 13
Harwood, September, 1975

THE HOUSE seemed strangely different: Philip had removed all his personal possessions; he had never existed. She walked in and out of the rooms, up and down the stairs trying to accustom herself to her new environment. Even the pile of mail was all for her; Philip now had his redirected.

She had the weekend to sort herself out before school on Monday; the new term started the day after. Her first priority was to stock up the larder. She went to the supermarket, collected a trolley and started her customary walk up and down the aisles; at the end of the first aisle she realised that she was buying groceries for two; old habits die hard, but this was one she just had to break. She retraced her steps back to the entrance, replacing goods on the shelves, and began again; this time she made a conscious effort to buy for one, small tins not large ones and smaller amounts of perishables.

She began thinking about her future. On Sunday, she should go to church, but what will people say? How should she answer questions? The congregation knew that Philip was a vicar's son. She would be the one they would blame for the breakdown; on Monday she would have to face her colleagues and the usual conversations about how they had spent their holidays. She did not want to discuss the awful experience; the more she thought about it, the worse it seemed. Thinking things through alone is difficult when you are used to discussing things with a partner. She knew that at all costs she must keep Danny out of it; no one must know the real cause of the break up.

It seems that when life is not rosy and the bad patches arrive, one remembers more vividly the previous agonising events; they are escalated out of all proportion until it is impossible to see any light at the end of the long dark tunnel. Irene's solitude forced her to remember all the previous trying times in her life. She was only twenty-five years old and God was punishing her; she was still paying for that last hour spent with Danny. If she had been able to accept and love Philip properly things would have been different. She should have stopped taking the pill; but it was too late now; the damage had been done and the happier times had been forgotten.

On Saturday, after much deliberating, she decided to phone David. She would tell him first about the break up of her marriage and perhaps that would ease the situation with her colleagues.

'David? Hi, it's Irene. Have you had a good holiday?'

'Oh, fantastic. Kenya is wonderful at this time of year. It's winter there but it's so warm. The pace of life is much slower and carefree. The sunsets are gorgeous. The days seem longer; time passes by more slowly. It's like paradise, sitting under palm trees, taking tea in the afternoon. It's a different world. Anyway, enough of my ramblings. What about your holiday? Did Philip surprise you with an exotic holiday again? Was it the Pyramids or Madeira this year?'

Irene was almost in tears; she knew that was the kind of question her colleagues would be asking. Her voice was shaky. 'Neither. We didn't go anywhere together.' She paused. 'We're getting a divorce.'

'Oh, my God. I'd never have thought that. You seemed good together. I'm so sorry. What went wrong or shouldn't I ask?'

'Yes, no. Oh, it was awful. I don't think I can face anybody.'

'Oh dear. What do you want me to do? Shall I come over?'

She thought for a minute and decided that it would be a good idea. She could then talk to him face to face before Monday.

'That would be nice.'

'I'll be there in about an hour. Put the kettle on.'

'OK, bye.'

'Bye for now.'

David arrived just after four; she did not know what to say, but needed to practise before Monday or she would burst into tears. He was standing on the doorstep; she just stared at him.

'Well, aren't you going to ask me in? I'm sure the tea's going cold.'

'Er...yes... Um...come in.'

He followed her in and they went into the lounge.

'How're you coping?'

'I'm not. I've never been on my own before. It seems strange. I lived with my parents until I married. I don't know how to live alone. I don't know what to say to people. I don't know how I'm even going to walk into school, never mind teach.

People will ask questions like you did. I can't answer them. They'll be talking about their wonderful summer.'

He could see that she was close to tears.

'Have you been to the doctor?'

'No. I'm not ill. I'm getting a divorce.'

'If you're not ready to come back to work you'll need a doctor's note and right now you don't look in a fit state to teach.'

'I hadn't thought about a doctor. If I put off coming back next week, will it be any easier later on?'

'Have divorce proceedings started?'

'Yes.'

'When will it all be over?'

'Probably early next year.'

'Well you won't want to sit here twiddling your thumbs till then, will you?'

'No.'

'Well, it seems you have two options. You can either come back on Monday or go to the doctor.'

'I don't like the idea of going to the doctor's.'

'Then you have to return next week,' he said softly. 'Why did you phone me?'

'I thought I could practise talking to you first and then it might be easier next week and I thought that if you knew you could help me tell the others and fend off questions.'

'Yes. I'll do all I can, but you have to do something first.'

'What?'

'Pour the tea.'

She laughed.

'That's more like it and it wasn't too difficult was it?'

She poured the tea and offered him biscuits. Suddenly, things were not so bad.

'Well,' he continued, 'are you going to tell me about it?'

She told him the same story she had told her father. They had drifted apart; he had wanted children and she had not; he had had an affair with a sixth former; she was pregnant; he had been forced to resign; his father had died after a heart attack, which she felt had been brought on by the whole mess; he and the girl had gone to live in Wales; his career was ruined; his mother's life had changed and he and his sister, Ruth, were now fatherless. She left out their final encounter and how he had forced her to have sex with him; that scenario, as far, as she was concerned, should remain between them. After she'd finished he said, 'Well, that wasn't so bad was it?'

'No. I guess not. But I really don't want to discuss it with everyone else. They'll ask questions about his affair. Why it happened and, well, you know what gossips are like.'

'Yes. I'll tell you what: when we start chatting about the holidays, just say that you spent it quietly with your family, which is true, and that Philip is well, which is also true. I'll steer the conversation away from you with the department staff. Leave the divorce situation until a later date when everything's settled. After a couple of days no one mentions the summer.

It always seems a lifetime ago. You mustn't blame yourself. Philip knew what he was doing. Sleeping with a sixth former had to be instant dismissal. If you play with fire you get burnt. He played with fire.'

If he knew the whole story he wouldn't be so keen to blame Philip, she thought to herself, but then he was right about Philip knowing what he was doing and the possible consequences.

'Yes, you're right, but I didn't realise how hard it would be on my own. Dad wanted me to leave work, sell up and go back to Fordingham. It was my decision to come back. I want to carry on teaching. But it seems so strange in this house on my own. No one to talk to. No one to make decisions with. And then there's the financial side. There's only one income instead of two.

There are so many complications to divorce. When I go out, everywhere I look there are couples and I'm frightened of bumping into people I know because I don't know what to say.'

'That's easy. Tell them you're getting a divorce by mutual consent. The marriage's over. There's nothing to discuss.'

'Is it really that easy?'

'It is if you want it to be. What are you doing about eating tonight?'

'I haven't thought.'

'Why don't we have a take-away? There's a Chinese on the high street.'

That was Saturday night taken care of. They went out to get the Chinese meal together; they enjoyed it with a bottle of wine and chatted about life alone after death or divorce. It does not matter which it is, they are both painful experiences and only time helps you come to terms with them.

By the time David left she was feeling much happier; she had also decided that it was time to part company with God. All her life, she had had a strong faith but suddenly she felt nothing; if God was there he had tested her faith for long enough; whatever storms he had thrown at her she had remained faithful, but not any more: from now on she was an atheist! Let God torment someone else for a change!

On Sunday, she stayed at home; let the other suckers go to church! In the afternoon she went out for a drive because she knew she had to get used to doing things on her own: this was her first battle. After driving round and round the streets, and eventually ending up in the park, sitting alone feeding the ducks and watching the world at large getting on with life, she returned feeling triumphant. Tomorrow, with David's help she would cope with seeing her colleagues.

David kept his word; they assembled for the meeting. He rushed them through the preamble of holiday chat before introducing the newcomer, who was replacing Joan, Alice Evans, a probationary teacher. The meeting continued with the official business and David gave out the invitation to his first soirée of the year. The routine had begun and tomorrow the children would be arriving in their new uniforms, equipped with new pens and pencils. After the long holiday they would be keen and eager to start work; this enthusiasm usually lasted at least until the third week of term.

Tuesday came: Irene boldly went to work. Her form group were now fourth year (4C); she knew them all well and they, unknowingly, helped her through the first week. By Friday, she knew she had made the right decision to return.

As the term progressed, she gradually told people that she was getting a divorce. David was a tower of strength for her; people noticed that he was giving her a lot of time and attention and less to Jane who had given him so much help. Jane did not mind; even when he stopped asking her over to Sunday lunch and invited Irene instead she said, 'David's such a nice person. He'd help anyone in their hour of need.'

Jane herself tried to help Irene by suggesting trips out together. Sometimes it was just for a drink or the theatre or cinema; they both enjoyed these outings.

By the time Christmas arrived Irene had readjusted to her new way of life and could hardly remember what it was like to be married. She spent Christmas at Fordingham with her parents; after spending the last three with Philip's family she thoroughly enjoyed being with her own relatives again. There was some sadness as they remembered Martin's tragic death two years earlier on Christmas Eve and his funeral on New Year's Eve. However, Irene was getting used to associating holidays and special days with tragedy. But she caught herself thinking, how could he be so selfish as to commit suicide at Christmas time and one week before her birthday?

The New Year came as did her twenty-sixth birthday. She celebrated knowing that in three weeks she would receive the official decree that would end her marriage. She returned to Harwood for the start of the new term. As the school year progressed so did her relationship with David; he had liked Irene from the first time he met her at the interview and had been disappointed to hear that she was getting married. David had been delighted when she turned to him for assistance when it was over.

By the beginning of the summer term they were spending a lot of time together. They were just good friends as far as Irene was concerned, but she was the only one who believed that. Her colleagues felt sorry for Jane, but she was pleased that two of her friends were so happy together and wished them well. She was one of those rare people in life, who only knew kindness, a person who gave but did not take, the type who should wear a halo.

In June, David suggested that as Irene had missed out on a foreign holiday last summer, she might like to accompany him to Kenya. His father lived in a large house and she could have one of the guest suites. She was surprised and flattered; it was a nice idea; after seeing Kenya in his slide shows she could now see the real thing. The only person who was disappointed was Wills; he had expected his daughter to spend the summer at Fordingham.

So, term ended and four days later she and David were on a flight to Nairobi.

By the time they landed at Nairobi Airport, Irene thought it had been the longest night of her life. The plane was a scheduled flight from Heathrow via Frankfurt and, usually, Entebbe before Nairobi.

They had waited for three hours on the runway in Frankfurt before the German passengers boarded and then, when they were airborne for the second time, the long awaited dinner was served. The crew began serving from the back of the plane, which meant the new arrivals were served first and the starving Britons were eating dinner at midnight. That was followed by orders to go to sleep as blankets were issued and the lights went out. Sleep? Were they joking? There were three seats in each row on either side of the aisle and she was in the middle one, seat B. A stranger sat in the window seat and David occupied the seat nearest the aisle; at least he had some flexibility with leg space. The seats were designed for midgets. You needed a shoehorn to cram yourself into the allotted space and sleeping in such an uncomfortable position with the constant engine noise was an impossible task for the average person. Seasoned travellers might have accustomed themselves to the situation, but she was not a seasoned traveller. Suddenly, the blinds were opened to reveal the bright, imposing dawn. Irene was not prepared for this, but David was used to such nights and reassured her that their uncomfortable night would soon be forgotten once she experienced Kenya.

Only four and a half hours after eating the long-awaited dinner, they were attempting to digest a continental breakfast; the coffee was the most welcome part of the meal, it helped to quench her thirst, ease her dry throat and more importantly, wake her up. After breakfast, there was a queue for the toilets as everyone attempted to improve the way they felt and looked.

The troubles in Uganda meant that the plane landed early: it had avoided both Entebbe airport and Ugandan air space. So now they were sitting in the plane on the runway and could see the airport building in the distance, but they had to wait until the appointed time to disembark. Three hours in Frankfurt and now a further wait; David kept trying to reassure her, but she wanted to be at her best when she met his parents, and after such an ordeal that was impossible. Naturally, as a man, he could not understand why she was so fraught.

After what seemed like an eternity, they taxied nearer to the building and were allowed to leave the aircraft. Then there was the queue through immigration, the long wait for luggage and customs before they were officially in Nairobi. It was 10.25 am when David introduced her to his father, as they walked across the road to his car.

Andrew Taylor was a grey-haired and tanned Nairobi businessman in his early sixties.

'Pleased to meet you, at last. We've heard so much about you,' he said.

They drove to Newbury House, making polite conversation along the route. Irene was amazed when she saw the palatial building. Andrew and his wife, Margaret, had come to Nairobi in the fifties with their three children to invest in a coffee business; it had clearly been successful.

The white-painted house, set in acres of gardens and with its own swimming pool, made Irene wonder why David chose to teach in a comprehensive school and live in a semi in Kidderminster.

Inside, Margaret gushed towards her with outstretched arms, 'Welcome, my dear, welcome.' She was clearly putting on an air of superiority. She had aspired to a status well above her middle-class station in England and was enjoying the role of Lady of the Manor; she was mistress in a house with large rooms, expensive furniture, terraces, bedrooms with balconies and private bathrooms, and a staff of six African natives to do everything for her.

'You must be exhausted after that awful, tiring journey. I told David to bring you first class, but he said it was a waste of money. Silly boy!'

David smiled, 'Mother, dear, less chatter and let me take Irene to her room.' He had a way of handling his mother and her newfound pompous attitude towards things. Money had changed her, but not David or his father.

'Yes, dear,' she replied, clapping her hands to summon a servant to take the luggage up to the bedrooms. Irene could not believe she was still in the seventies. Slavery had been abolished at home, but not here.

After settling in and enjoying a shower and change of clothes, out of her practical beige travelling suit into a light summer dress, she joined David and they went downstairs for lunch on the front patio. Andrew had returned to the office in Nairobi and would not be back until the evening. Lunch was a selection of salads with meats, cheese and bread, nicely set up in a conservatory area leading onto a patio. They selected their food, went outside and sat at a table already prepared with cutlery and drinks. The big decision was whether to have the parasol up or down, in the end they decided to leave it down. Irene was enjoying the view; the steps from the patio led down to a barbecue area and beyond were immaculate gardens and trees, all surrounded by a high wall.

After lunch, it was siesta time until after three; then David took her for a stroll around the gardens before early evening and sunset. Sunset meant it was time for a sundowner drink before they dressed for dinner: it was all so decadent.

She learned a lot about his family that night. It was strange that, although their relationship had developed during the year, she knew very little about them. Somehow, he had always steered the conversations away from them. His younger brother, Richard, lived on the plantation and managed it whilst Andrew dealt with the administrative side in the office in Nairobi; she would see both tomorrow. They had all lived on the plantation until ten years ago, when Richard had married and Andrew bought their present home from a family who were returning to England. They renamed it Newbury House because they were originally from Newbury; Andrew and Margaret moved, leaving Richard and his bride, Josephine, to live on the plantation. Irene already knew about his sister, Stephanie; she was married to a doctor and lived in Cornwall.

She was also given an education about coffee; how the berries were picked and the beans taken out of them and dried before being put in sacks and sent all over the world, to sit in packets and jars on supermarket shelves. After dinner, she was able to grind some beans from the Taylor Plantation for their coffee; she would never drink another cup of coffee with so little thought again.

The first week was spent in Nairobi, where she met Richard and Josephine and had a tour of the plantation. Shopping with Margaret was an experience she would never forget; they took one of the six African natives with them, just to carry the parcels! Margaret wore beautiful brightly-coloured kaftans; she looked so cool and comfortable in them, and after Irene had tried one on, she knew why so many people wore them. Margaret took her shopping specifically to buy an array of kaftans; they went to an exclusive store and all heads turned as Margaret walked in; she was obviously a valued customer. They were served by the senior assistant, who had her juniors bringing garments from all parts of the store, and modelling them just for her to look at; she wondered if she had acquired celebrity status overnight. After fifteen minutes of her private fashion show, she decided on a mauve and white one, but Margaret had other ideas.

'My dear, you simply can't take just one. You must have at least half a dozen.'

'But...'

'No buts. I insist; you shall have this one, and that one...' she pointed to two red and orange multi-coloured ones. 'They will brighten up dull days when you're back in England.' Margaret continued selecting the ones that she liked, in her usual overpowering manner, and ordered them to be charged to her account, leaving the overwhelmed Irene speechless. They left the store, with their African boy walking behind them, carrying her purchases.

Wherever they went in Nairobi, it was obvious that Margaret was well-known as people rushed to greet and serve her. She was impressed with Nairobi; it was an attractive city with pleasant white-painted buildings, modern in appearance with tree-lined avenues which gave a gentle breeze keeping shoppers nice and cool. There were mosques, a university, schools, offices, hotels, and indicative of modern architecture was the Kenyatta building with a tall round tower as its centrepiece and named after Jomo Kenyatta, the first president of independent Kenya. It seemed strange that only miles out of Nairobi a different world existed; the real Third World where people lived in small villages in an array of huts without any modern conveniences.

Time & Tide

She and David spent the second and third weeks on the coast at Paradise Beach, south of Mombasa. He drove the 300 mile journey down the A109, but it was more like a cart track and extremely dusty. She had already learned that each time they ventured out of Nairobi she returned covered in a red dust. This was an exciting journey, a journey with a difference; it took them through one of the national parks where wild life roamed freely; they saw monkeys, gazelles and elephants, which were impressive, not the sort of thing you would see on the motorway at home. It was late when they reached the bungalow, she did not appreciate the view until the next day.

He woke her up on the first morning with a cup of coffee and then drew back the curtains enabling her to see a breath-taking view of the blue ocean, clear blue sky and white sand right on the doorstep. She put on her dressing gown and joined him on the terrace.

'This is beautiful. I've never seen anything like it. Why on earth do you teach in an urban comprehensive and live in Kidderminster?'

'Why not?'

'Well, the lifestyle you enjoy here is SO much better. Surely, you could teach here or work with your father?'

'You can have too much of a good thing. Do you think I would enjoy this as much if it weren't a holiday?'

'Your father and brother do.'

'True. But working the plantation is not my idea of fun. Neither was it Stephanie's. She's happy in Cornwall.

'I remember the early days, the struggling, Mum working in a shop in Nairobi because there was no money. Dad working all hours. More than once they thought about going back to England.'

'But it's different now.'

'Oh yes. Mum and Dad wouldn't swap it for all the tea in China'' He paused. 'That's a joke in the coffee business!'

'Oh yes.'

They both laughed.

'It's only in the last few years that they've been able to enjoy the lavish lifestyle. It's changed Mum but Dad knows that if the weather conditions aren't favourable and they have a bad harvest everything could change. He has good contracts at the moment but in business anything can happen.'

'I suppose so.'

'Enough. We've got two weeks to enjoy this and then it's back to the grindstone. BUT in a few months I'll be back!'

She went back to her bedroom, showered and dressed; when she returned to the terrace, the table was laid ready for breakfast with fruit juice, rolls, jam and marmalade and, of course, coffee.

'I have to admit I own this place,' he said. 'Four years ago, Dad decided that the company profits should be split five ways: himself, Mum, me, Richard and Stephanie. He and Richard have an annual salary, as well, but this way he feels that we all benefit. You can't take money out of Kenya; it's bad for the economy. So I have a bank account here which I live on during the holidays. I bought this for us all to use with my first income from the company. The land rover's Stephanie's. I use her vehicle, she uses my holiday bungalow. We've never been out here at the same time. The rest of the family take breaks here as well.'

'It really is paradise,' she said, looking out at the Indian Ocean.

'Don't forget your Palodrine tablets,' he said, 'a dose of malaria and it won't seem like paradise.' He watched her swallow the tablets, a necessary precaution to avoid the illness so easily contracted from mosquito bites. Then he continued, 'Later, we'll take a stroll along the beach and enjoy morning coffee at one of the hotels.'

They went inside. The lounge was the main and central room. On each side a door led off to a double bedroom and at the far end of the lounge there were three doors. The centre one led into a small well-equipped kitchen and the other two into single bedrooms. Between each double and single bedroom there was a shared shower room. It was all very well planned. There were nine other bungalows in the complex but David's was the nearest to the beach. The others had less of a view and more gardens between them and the beach. The land was privately owned and leased to the bungalow owners, who paid an annual site fee.

They ambled along the mile stretch of white sand without seeing another person and enjoyed morning coffee at the Paradise Beach Hotel.

'We'll eat here this evening. It's even better when you're enjoying a good steak and the lights are on. You can hear the gentle waves of the ocean in the distance. It's very romantic,' he said.

Like any other man and woman they had progressed from just holding hands and she was becoming sexually attracted to him. He had wanted to make love to her for some time but everything would have to be perfect. His instinct told him that the time would be right after dinner that night. They were single people, but for both it would be the second time around.

They spent the rest of the day on the beach. In the evening wearing one of her kaftans and already having a nice tan she felt happier than she had been for a long time. They drove round to the hotel where they enjoyed their meal on the terrace, under the coloured lights. The background music, the red wine and the warmth of the night air created the best romantic atmosphere that David could have hoped for. They drove back to the bungalow.

His instincts were right: they were in the lounge, the lights were off and the curtains open. They could see the moon in the clear sky and hear the water gently lapping in the distance.

He moved towards her. They kissed. There were no words spoken as he led her into his bedroom. She slipped out of her kaftan, he quickly removed his clothes and they fell onto the bed and made love. It was the perfect end to the perfect day.

Afterwards, he said, 'Any regrets?'

Her reply, '*Je ne regrette rien!*'

For the rest of the fortnight, Irene kept thinking she was dreaming. Every day there was sunshine. They spent a lot of time on the beach. The natives would come by on bicycles selling shells and jewellery made from shells. It was certainly a different lifestyle from anything she had experienced before.

On the last afternoon, as they were having tea on the terrace, he said, 'Have you enjoyed yourself?'

'Do you have to ask? It's been like a dream – my own paradise.'

'Do you still think about Philip?'

'What a question. He crosses my mind occasionally. You can't just wipe out three years of marriage.' She paused and then continued, 'You've never mentioned your wife.'

'Loretta?'

'Was that her name? Surely, you still think about her? Her death must have been hard to cope with.'

'Yes. We met at Cambridge. She was from Birmingham which is why I moved to the area. I still love her and I always will.' After thinking carefully about his next words, he continued, 'We've both been married before. Neither of us can forget that. I'd like us to try and make a go of it together. They say it's better the second time around. You know what I'm asking, don't you?'

She nodded. If she were honest with herself, she had known for most of the year but it was something she had tried to put to the back of her mind. She was getting over one relationship and not really ready for another. He thought her first love was Philip, he was wrong about that but she saw no reason to tell him. Danny's presence had ruined her first marriage and, anyway, the last link had gone now. There was no need to mention her childhood sweetheart; it would serve no purpose. Why complicate things?

'Irene, will you marry me?'

'I... I don't know. I need time to think. It's only been a year for me.'

'I know. When will you give me an answer?'

'On the first Sunday of term.'

'That means you'll come to lunch, I presume?'

'Yes.'

The holiday was over. They drove back to Nairobi, said goodbye to his family, and endured another night on the plane back to England where harsh reality awaited them.

The autumn term began and the nights were drawing in.

She had Sunday lunch with David, as she had promised. The last months of the year passed by. She went to Fordingham for Christmas but on 3rd January, she was back in Birmingham. In the presence of her parents and Andrew and Margaret, who had flown in from Kenya, once again she was saying, 'I take thee...for richer for poorer, in sickness and in health...until death do us part.' The registrar said, 'I pronounce you man and wife.' She was Mrs David Taylor.

It was New Year, new term, new name, new status!

There was no going back now, only forward...

Chapter 14
Harwood, January, 1977

THEY RETURNED to school on the Thursday of that week for the start of the spring term. The news of their marriage was greeted with surprise. In the department there was sympathy for Jane, who had been such a good friend to David in the past. Initially, Irene experienced a coldness from her colleagues but after Jane expressed her best wishes for the bride and groom's future the coolness died down. Jane, once again, had shown that she was an incredible person who was incapable of any malice. For that, Irene was grateful; she was the first person they invited to join them for a meal.

Before Christmas, they had both put their properties on the market; they were looking for somewhere to live without being haunted by memories from the past. During the week they spent their time at her home, because it was more convenient for work, and at weekends they went to his place. It was not a particularly good arrangement; they seemed to be permanently living out of suitcases or discovering that something they needed was at the other house.

They found what they considered to be the ideal home for them in a different part of Harwood, although it was a little further away from the school. The property was a large renovated Victorian house consisting of a large hallway with a cloakroom tucked away under the stairs; two reception rooms and a dining room, a compact kitchen and utility room. On the first floor were three large bedrooms and a bathroom and on the second floor a mini-flat. The two rooms had been made into a double bedroom with en-suite shower room and a lounge with a fitted kitchenette.

At the side of the house was a double garage and at the rear, a lawn surrounded by flower borders, beyond which lay a small orchard. The mini-flat would be convenient for Margaret and Andrew if they wished to spend a period of time in England; it would also be suitable for new colleagues who were unable to find accommodation. The asking price was £28,000.

At the end of January she sold her home for £10,000, which even after the mortgage had been paid off left her with a handsome profit. It made her wonder just how much her father's properties were worth; house prices were rising: they were the best investment. Her father and uncle had made a wise decision when they spent their inheritance money.

From mid-February until Easter they stored her things in his garage and lived in his house which was not an enjoyable experience for Irene. It was definitely important to have their own home; David's house was sold for £17,000. After expenses were deducted they had about £24,000 from the sale of the two properties. David put in the rest of the money from a savings account; he still had money from an insurance policy he received on Loretta's death.

In April, they moved into their dream home. The summer was an exciting time organising everything; the furniture was moved several times before they were completely satisfied. They kept much of what they already had but some items were not required or they decided that they did not fit into their new abode and bought replacements.

Wills collected the spare pieces for his cottages. Maintenance was a growing expense and he was pleased with the surplus pieces.

By the summer everything seemed to be in its right place and they were looking forward to spending a month in Kenya. David had missed his visits there: since he bought the Mombasa bungalow he had been using it for most of his holidays. Even a week at half term was long enough: four days looking out at the Indian Ocean were a wonderfully relaxing time. The Taylor Plantation Company bought his tickets in Kenya which used up some of his Kenyan currency. From where he was sitting, it was like a free holiday and he was certainly going to enjoy this one.

At the end of July, Irene was sitting on a plane heading for Nairobi, but this time it was more comfortable. She had persuaded him to book first class! He agreed but not until she promised not to let such a lifestyle change her. He did not want her to become like his mother!

The first week was spent in Nairobi and then there were three glorious weeks in the bungalow. When they left, they knew it would only be two months before their return. They would spend October half term there, but not Christmas; Irene was adamant: if he went then, he went alone. She wanted to spend Christmas at Fordingham and, by family tradition, she had to spend New Year and her birthday at Whistbury. She had missed her father during the three Christmases spent with Philip's family and did not want to be anywhere else at Christmas again.

Marriage is a compromise and they were both good at that. She was happy to spend long weekends in Cornwall with Stephanie and most holidays with his family and he, in return, conceded over Christmas and New Year.

Good fortune was with Irene that year. Isobel Morgan and Christine Hammond retired and were amongst the staff who left in the summer. They left vacancies in the English and Language Departments to be filled by new teachers; but Isobel's year tutor's post was an internal appointment. Irene applied and was given the position. She was sad when her fifth year form left school and hoped that some of them would keep in touch. They had congratulated them on their marriage and bought a piece of Wedgwood pottery which Irene would always treasure. Her promotion gave her a Scale 4 salary which put her at the same level as David. The only difference was, he had reached the top increment and she was just beginning. The autumn term was a hectic one. She had her year team and 220 children to care for. Tom Carter, the second year tutor, was still using the English teaching rooms for his pupils and so she was given the maths rooms on the first two floors of E/M block. She also had an office on that floor and seemed to spend a lot of time going up and down the stairs.

Christine's replacement in the English department was Mrs. Susan Pickering. It was her first teaching year and her husband had a post in a local junior school. They spent the first term in Irene and David's little flat while they found a house. They moved just before Christmas into a terraced property similar to the one Irene had sold.

David continued to hold his soirées and Irene, also, had evenings when she entertained her year staff. They had new neighbours who were very sociable, unlike the people in South Street. It seemed that they were always entertaining people, being entertained or visiting the family.

Their married life was good. They had a maturity which comes from experience of previous relationships; it was like a foundation for them to build on. They both knew the importance of tolerance, trust, respect and compromise within a marriage. They were in love; it was a growing and developing love. He was seven and a half years older and she found that the age difference between them added something to the relationship. The second time around was certainly working for them despite the country's statistics to the contrary. They were a shining example of married life and the envy of many who knew them.

In 1978, they spent Easter, the May half-term week and a month in the summer in Kenya. In September of that year Wills and Charlotte celebrated their thirtieth wedding anniversary. As a present, Irene and David took them to Kenya in July and gave them a fortnight's holiday. Charlotte, like Margaret, enjoyed travelling first class and the decadent lifestyle which Newbury House offered. She was naturally jealous, but the years had taught her to keep such thoughts to herself. She had been delighted when Irene's first marriage had broken up because her daughter had failed at something which she had managed to make a success of, but Wills' attitude to the situation and his reply to any comments she made had been like a warning to her. She would never win where Irene was concerned so she must make the best of it or possibly lose what she already had. Wills was a man of property; she could not afford to lose him. Like a good wine, Charlotte had matured with age.

After three days in Nairobi, David drove down to Mombasa and they spent the rest of the holiday there.

For Wills and Charlotte, it was the holiday of a lifetime. To see the poverty of a Third World country was an education in itself and made Charlotte grateful for what she had. Wills was delighted when he saw animals in their natural environment. As a man who loved nature, animals and the outdoor life he would never forget watching elephants, zebras, lions and other animals roaming in the African Bush. Charlotte enjoyed being waited on and taken out for dinner each evening; it was a way of life she would never grow tired of. Unfortunately, all good things come to an end. They all went back to Nairobi and spent a night there before Wills and Charlotte returned home; then David and Irene returned to Paradise Beach for the rest of their holiday.

Late in August they came back to England. Margaret and Andrew spent some time with them and other people stayed in their mini-flat. The seventies were drawing to a close and a new decade was approaching. There was only one thing missing in her life, when they celebrated New Year's Eve in 1979, and that was a baby. She blamed herself for taking the pill and avoiding pregnancy in the first place.

The bells were ringing and the clock had chimed twelve. It was a new decade and she was thirty. As David kissed her and wished her, 'Happy Birthday', she hoped that soon she would have some good news for him.

Charlotte was thinking about the seventies: they were gone forever, but in her own way, she had immortalised them.

1976

BRITAIN

The Queen opens the £45 million National Exhibition Centre at Birmingham...
The Labour Party's George Thomas is chosen to succeed Selwyn Lloyd as Speaker

in the House of Commons... The Race Relations Bill is published, making it an offence to incite racial hatred... The post office announces the end of Sunday collections and Saturday afternoon opening... Harold Wilson retires and is to be succeeded by James Callaghan as prime minister... Princess Margaret and Lord Snowdon announce their separation after fifteen years of marriage... Jeremy Thorpe resigns as leader of the Liberal Party after he's alleged to have had a homosexual relationship with Norman Scott...

June: it's the end of the Cod War between Britain and Iceland.

July: Donald Nielson, the "Black Panther" is found guilty of murdering Lesley Whittle and given five life sentences.

August: the disgraced MP John Stonehouse, who disappeared dramatically in 1974 and resurfaced in Australia before being brought back to Britain, is found guilty of fraud and theft and imprisoned for seven years.

September: the first women cadets are admitted to Dartmouth Naval College... British Rail introduces its high speed 125 train capable of travelling at 125mph.

The National Theatre on the South Bank is officially open... The four-millionth Austin mini rolls off the production line... David Steele is to be the new Leader of the Liberal Party.

IRISH REPUBLICAN ARMY (IRA)

January: They murder five of the Social Democratic and Labour Party (SDLP) men in two shootings in County Armagh and then kill a further ten Protestant workmen in an ambush. The first SAS troops are sent to Northern Ireland...

February: An explosion at Oxford Circus...

March: A bomb explodes on an empty train as it leaves Cannon Street Station...

21st July, the British Ambassador, Mr. Christopher Ewart-Biggs and a secretary, Judith Cooke, are killed when a landmine blows up the ambassador's car in Dublin...

There's a sign of hope for peace; the Peace People's Movement is formed and marches are taking place in Londonderry and Trafalgar Square.

ABROAD

Civil war continues in Angola and Beirut... The apartheid is still apparent in South Africa; there's the worst outbreak of violence between the black population and the police since 1910...

June: "RAID ON ENTEBBE AIRPORT", six Palestinians hijack an Air France Airbus in Greece with over 250 passengers on board. The hijackers order the pilot to fly to Entebbe. They keep over 100 hostages who are either Israeli citizens or Jews... 4th July, three Israeli transport planes land at the airfield; in less than an hour, 200 commandos overpower the Ugandan guards, kill seven terrorists, snatch the hostages and fly them back to Israel.

4th July, America celebrates 200 years of independence; The Queen makes a State visit...

The spaceship Viking lands on Mars and sends the first photographs of the red planet's surface back to Earth... The Seychelles gain independence after 162 years of British rule.

SPORT

The Olympic Games are taking place in Montreal... John Curry is becomes the world champion in men's figure skating... Southampton wins the FA Cup beating Manchester United 1–0... At Wimbledon, Bjorn Borg is the first Swede to win the singles title and at the age of twenty is the youngest champion for forty-five years.

LITERATURE AND TELEVISION

Jeffrey Archer, who resigned as an MP because of bankruptcy, resurfaces as an author with "Not a Penny More, Not a Penny Less"... On the television, it's a sad goodbye to "Dixon of Dock Green", the popular police series.

1977

BRITAIN

The average house price in London and the South East is £16,700... New, smaller, pound notes are being introduced ... Freddie Laker launches his Skytrain... Roy Jenkins resigns from the Cabinet and Parliament to become the first British president of the EEC Commission in Brussels... Anti-hunting saboteurs dig up the grave of the legendary Lake District huntsman, John Peel... A vote of "no confidence" by the Conservative Party in the government gives rise to a Lib-Lab pact in order to help Mr Callaghan keep office; this also gives the Liberal Democrats a greater say in government affairs... British Aerospace is formed to run Britain's nationalised aviation history...There's a strike of undertakers... The State Opening of Parliament is blacked out by industrial action... The firemen are on strike for a thirty percent wage increase.

1977, THE QUEEN'S SILVER JUBILEE YEAR

7th June: The service of thanksgiving takes place in St Paul's Cathedral. The crowds throng the Mall as the Queen passes by in the Gold State Coach, which was last used on Coronation Day. After the service there's a walk-about amongst the people; it seems as if Her Majesty is attempting to create a new image... this year *she's visiting many of the Commonwealth States as well as touring England and visiting Northern Ireland.*

But perhaps the most important event of the year for her Majesty is the birth of her first grandchild. Master Peter Phillips born to the Princess Anne and Captain Mark Phillips on 15th November.

ABROAD

January: Moscow, several people are killed in a bomb explosion on the underground... America: Jimmy Carter is sworn in as the thirty-ninth president; and Gary Gilmore is the first person to be executed for ten years, as the death penalty is reinstated, his final words are "Let's do it," before walking out to the firing squad at Utah State Prison... Cairo, forty-four people are killed as a result of students and workers rioting over price rises; President Sadat imposes a curfew...

November: The Baader-Meinhof terrorists, Andreas Baader, Gudrun Ensslin and Jan-Carl Raspe have been jailed for life plus fifteen years; in Munich, Ingrid Schubert, a founder of this terrorist gang, commits suicide.

In the Seychelles, President James Mancham is ousted in a coup while attending the Commonwealth Conference in London... At that conference, the Commonwealth leaders issue a warning to South African white people, they must change the way the country is run, or face more bloodshed...The Vietnam exodus begins; refugees are fleeing from the new communist regime in South Vietnam; the boat-people are prepared to risk hardship and possible death as they attempt to find another country to take them in.

SPORT

The Grand National race at Aintree: Red Rum romps home, victorious for the THIRD time... The horse is a superstar!

June: £15,000 worth of damage at Wembley Stadium is caused by fans digging up the pitch after Scotland beat England 2–1... Is it the age of the soccer hooligan? ...It's the summer of Kerry Packer's cricket circus...and for Geoff Boycott, it's a great summer: he scores the 100th century of his career!

OBITUARY 1977

16th August, Elvis Presley, the King of Rock 'n' Roll, dies at the age of forty-two; the music world is in mourning.

RHODESIA

31st August, 1977, Ian Smith wins the general election. 24th November sees the beginning of change after all the fighting and bloodshed. Ian Smith announces plans for a constitutional conference to prepare for black majority rule which will end almost ninety years of white rule... 15th February, 1978, the plan for black power's produced. ...March, absolute white rule ends as the first three black government ministers are sworn into office... 24th April, Abel Muzorewa, is elected as the first black prime minister... 1st June, Rhodesia's renamed Zimbabwe-Rhodesia and later, the prime minister announces that it would be known as just Zimbabwe... 21st December, 1979, after fourteen years of independence, Zimbabwe becomes a British Colony again; at Lancaster House in London, Mr Mugabe and Mr Nkomo join Bishop Muzorewa in signing a peace treaty... Lord Soames, the last British governor and the new one arrives back in Salisbury with British troops and declares an amnesty for the black guerrillas... The new decade is to begin with the long awaited peace for Zimbabwe.

SOUTH AFRICA

The struggle for equality goes on. Steve Biko's one of a number of black leaders arrested under the 1977 security legislation. He dies in custody, causing an international uproar; a post-mortem reveals brain damage and severe bruising. He's been denounced by the South African authorities as a violent revolutionary but the journalist, Donald Woods describes him as "the greatest man he has ever had the privilege of knowing". 15,000 people attend his funeral... 2nd December, 1977, twelve weeks after his death, a magistrate rules that the police were not responsible for the death. The lawyer representing the Biko family argues that one or more of the officers who had interrogated him should be charged with murder, but after the trial he said that two white doctors had joined a conspiracy of silence with the police... Donald Woods is banned from working for his newspaper after he attacks the government over the death... January, 1978: he escapes from South Africa and seeks asylum in Britain where he plans to write a book on the Steve Biko story, in the hope that it will help remove the apartheid from South Africa... July, Nelson Mandela, the ANC leader imprisoned in the sixties, celebrates his sixtieth birthday... September, Prime Minister Vorster resigns and is replaced by Pieter Willem Botha, the Defence Minister, who promises to apply a positive policy towards improving relations between South Africa's different racial groups.

THE MIDDLE EAST

There's optimism for a solution to the Middle East crisis as peace talks begin... April, 1977, Anwar Sadat of Egypt goes to Washington for talks with President Carter about peace... The prime minister of Israel, Yitzhak Rabin resigns over a money scandal, he's replaced by Menachim Begin... July, President Sadat orders his troops to observe an immediate cease-fire with Libya... November, President Sadat is the first Arab leader to visit Israel; he addresses the Knesset, the Israeli Parliament and states that he wants a permanent peace arrangement. "No more war, no more bloodshed" is the slogan agreed by the two presidents... December, Sadat severs ties with Syria, Libya, Algeria and South Yemen because they're opposed to his moves for peace... 1978, Sadat and Carter call for a Palestinian role in the Middle East peace process... June, Israel withdraw their troops from the south of Lebanon... September, at Camp David Summit the first peace treaty's signed between Begin and Sadat...

Israel gives up the Sinai which they had held since the Six-Day War in 1967 and Egypt agrees to move towards opening normal diplomatic relations with Israel... The first moves are made, a triumph for both men, and for President Carter who has acted as a go-between... The move also won the Nobel Peace Prize for Sadat and Begin jointly.

1978

BRITAIN

January: severe gales and in Scotland heavy snowfalls! Anna Ford is ITN's FIRST woman newscaster...

1st May is the first official May Day Holiday...

26th July, the FIRST test-tube baby, Louise Brown, is born at Oldham District General Hospital, Greater Manchester; she was born using a technique of fertilising an egg with the father's sperm in a test-tube; Patrick Steptoe has spent twelve years perfecting this method in a laboratory... The popularity of Freddie Laker's Skytrain offering cheap flights to America is causing chaos at Gatwick Airport.

6th August, Pope Paul VI dies from a heart attack at the age of eighty after being the Pontiff for twenty-five years... 26th August, the cardinals elect sixty-five year old Cardinal Albino Luciani, the Patriarch of Venice as the 263rd Pope, Pope John Paul I... Thirty-three days later, he dies from a heart attack! 16th October, Cardinal Karol Wojtyla, the Archbishop of Cracow is elected and takes the title John Paul II. 1978 will be remembered in the Catholic Church, as the year of three popes in three months.

ABROAD

The Solomon Islands gain Independence from British rule... August, China and Japan sign a ten-year peace and friendship treaty...

November: A mass suicide in Guyana of the 913 members of a religious cult who followed the Reverend Jim Jones and lived in an agricultural commune known as Jonestown; they died by drinking a soft drink laced with cyanide.... the United States of America and Vietnam have signed a twenty-five year Peace Treaty...

December: Russia signs a friendship pact with Afghanistan... The United States ceases to have diplomatic relations with China...

SPORT

In football, Argentina wins the World Cup... Bjorn Borg becomes the first man since Fred Perry to win the Men's Singles' Championships three times at Wimbledon... The Commonwealth Games are taking place in Edmonton and were opened by the Queen on her state visit to Canada.

MASS MEDIA

The BBC celebrates twenty-five years of television news...

After "Rocky", "Star Wars", "Annie Hall" in 1977, the cinema enthusiasts of 1978 are watching "The Deer Hunter" and "Julia".

On the television screen there's a new American series, "Dallas".

On stage, after a successful start to the Rice-Lloyd Webber partnership with their production of "Jesus Christ Superstar", they produce another musical, "Evita"; the No. 1 hit record, "Don't Cry For Me Argentina" comes from this... Other hits this year are "Rivers of Babylon" and "Summer Nights".

1979

BRITAIN

January: Britain experiences a Winter of Discontent.

The strikes, prevalent throughout the seventies, are creating havoc... The lorry drivers are on strike... there are "one-day" rail strikes... 22nd January, a twenty-four hour public employees' strike affects schools and hospitals... Gravediggers in Liverpool are on strike, preventing the burial of bodies...

The country's morale is low...

28th March, 10.19 pm For the first time in fifty years the government falls. The Tories carried a "no confidence" vote by a majority of one and Mrs Thatcher demands Parliament's immediate dissolution.

3rd May, the general election.

4th May, the Tories are in power again... Mrs Thatcher is Britain's first woman prime minister. She's promising that the country will see a complete transformation of its economic and industrial climate.

May: the ex-Liberal leader Jeremy Thorpe is accused of conspiring to murder Norman Scott. After three days of deliberating the jury have given a "not guilty" verdict which ends the thirty-one day trial...

Neil Kinnock, who has no previous government experience, is the Shadow Education Spokesman... London, plans are announced to revitalise the dockland area... The government announces that the postal service is to split from the telephone service.

August: the IRA is claiming responsibility for the bomb which exploded on Lord Mountbatten's boat killing him, his grandson and a friend and injuring other members of the family.

"THE YORKSHIRE RIPPER" is the name given to a serial killer by the police; he has murdered twelve women so far; the police are launching a £1 million publicity campaign because no woman is safe until he is caught.

November: four men are found guilty of newspaper boy Carl Bridgewater's murder.

ABROAD

Uganda: the dictator President Amin is forced to flee when invasion from neighbouring Tanzania destroys the southern towns and reaches Kampala; his reign of terror is over... 13th April, thousands of Ugandans line the route from Entebbe Airport to the capital; they are rejoicing as Yusuf Lule returns from exile to become president again...

Canada, Mr Trudeau loses the general election to the Progressive Conservative leader, Mr Joe Clark...

Vienna, 18th June, President Carter and Mr Brezhnev sign SALT Treaty II...

Lisbon, Maria Pintassiligo is Portugal's first woman prime minister...

East Germany, two families cross to the West in a hot air balloon made from curtains and sheets...

St Vincent and Grenada gain independence from Britain... Mother Teresa wins the Nobel Peace Prize for her work with the poor and homeless in India.

SPORT

Trevor Francis is the first £1 million footballer; he leaves Birmingham City to join Nottingham Forest... Oslo, Sebastian Coe creates a new record when he runs a mile in 3 min 48.95 secs.

MEDIA & MUSIC

"Fawlty Towers" and "To The Manor Born" are two of the successful television programmes...

"Kramer v. Kramer" is a box-office success... Cliff Richard celebrates twenty-one years in show business.

THE SEVENTIES

Time & Tide

At the end of the sixties, the great achievement was Neil Armstrong's "small step for man but giant leap for mankind." The race to the moon was over. Ten years on, the two super powers, America and Russia, are still battling for greater achievements with their space programmes. The States are probing beyond the moon to the planets of Jupiter, Saturn and Uranus. In Russia, two cosmonauts are claiming a record-breaking 175 days in space.

The world of fashion has changed in the seventies. After the mini in the sixties, it's midi, maxi, hotpants or anything goes in the seventies. From the hippies with long hair, baubles and beads, the trend has moved to punk rockers with brightly dyed hair and chains of safety pins.

Another change in the British way of life is the tendency to holiday abroad. Two weeks in sunny Spain, on a package holiday, singing "Y Viva Espana" is a more popular option than two weeks in a boarding house in an English coastal resort. We are also becoming obsessed with fitness; there's a growing passion for working out in the gym, or jogging.

The idea of high-rise living, so popular in the sixties, is dying out. The so-called ideal solution to a housing problem of building upwards rather than out of towns, in reality for those who live in them is an impracticable solution. Families feel that they are living in isolated boxes with no garden or recreation space. Frequently, lifts do not work, the blocks are targets for vandalism and there's no community life. The tenants, in many cases, are people who have been moved by the Council from terraced houses; when the houses were demolished, so was the community spirit. The general opinion seems to be to leave the tower blocks in Manhattan or use them as offices but certainly not as housing accommodation in Britain.

Probably the greatest advances in the seventies are in the field of technology. The invention of the microchip has led to computers becoming a part of every day life. A silicon chip contains thousands of electronic components and circuits and is so minute that it can pass through the eye of a needle. Suddenly, all records and information are being put onto disk and being stored in a computer. Life will never be the same again!

The seeds of change were sown in the fifties and grew in the sixties. The seventies mark the beginning of the harvest; a harvest of union power and industrial unrest resulting in strike action, high unemployment, nuclear power, streaking, legalised abortion, soccer hooligans, vandalism, terrorists and equality for all, beginning with the new comprehensive education system.

And so we progress forward, into the eighties...'

Chapter 15
Harwood, 1980

DAVID AND IRENE returned to Harwood. It may well have been a new decade, but for them it was the same old routine. They celebrated their third wedding anniversary with a theatre visit to see 'Salad Days' and completed the evening enjoying a meal at a Chinese restaurant. For Irene, it was like a double celebration; this time she had managed to stay married for three years!

The spring term began on Monday, 7th January; from then onwards work seemed to occupy a large amount of their time. Her group were third year and at a most difficult stage of their adolescence; they seemed to cause endless discipline problems. Some developed a poor attitude to work and were put on daily report; this meant that she had to see them daily to issue a report slip and check the previous day's record for adverse comments from staff. Others enjoyed truancy, which added to her workload. Sometimes she wondered why she had applied for the post in the first place; it was a thankless task and the financial remuneration was inadequate for the amount of work it involved. David's post as head of English was very much a case of an annual routine which he had become accustomed to over the years: his lot was a much easier one than hers, in her opinion.

The holidays in Kenya became more and more important to her; there were times when only the thought of escaping to their home on Paradise Beach enabled her to keep her sanity through all the chaos.

Andrew and Margaret now spent about six weeks in England each year. They would spend a couple of weeks in Cornwall and the rest of the time with David and Irene in the flat which served as a base for them in the Midlands area. Andrew celebrated his sixty-fifth birthday in 1981 and went into semi-retirement. Richard spent all his time at the office in Nairobi and Andrew only popped in a couple of times a week. They employed an overseer to work on the plantation with Josephine, although Josephine found looking after their three children more than a handful.

During term time they would visit Irene's family; she enjoyed the trips back to Fordingham which reminded her of the idyllic childhood she had enjoyed so much

Time & Tide

before 1966. Sadly, she noticed that her father was ageing. Like her uncle, his hair was showing signs of greyness, but he was approaching fifty-five. Charlotte, on the other hand, although she was the same age had remained fair, with no signs of grey or ageing.

However, life's disasters had changed Uncle Jim. There was not a day went by when he did not regret the amount of time he had spent building his empire. He could have spent more time with his wife and son; he should have got his priorities right. Julia and Martin had been the most important people in his life: but they were both dead: nothing could change that. He was not going to make the same mistake with Ann and Hillary; he put managers into all of the shops and resolved to stop his empire-building and 'Live for the Moment'. It is said that it takes tragedy and loss to make one realise what one once had; for Jim that was certainly true. He bought a large Victorian house with a granny flat in Bakewell, so that the three of them could live together instead of in flats in different places. Hillary lived in the flat and had her independence and a generous allowance; he made sure that neither Ann nor Hillary would ever work behind a shop counter again.

The Chesterfield shop remained in Hillary's name and the Derby one in Ann's; after all, they had been presents. The Bakewell shop with the rest of Martin's estate was returned to Jim; he transferred it to Tim, who he now thought of as a son, but it was on the usual condition that the Stephenson name remained. The other four shops he changed to joint partnership between himself, Ann and Hillary.

On Sunday, 29th November, 1981, Jim celebrated his sixtieth birthday with a party; he invited friends and relations to 'the party of the decade'. It began on the Friday evening and continued throughout the weekend. On the Sunday, when the shops were all closed, his managers and staff were invited to join in. During the forty-eight-hour period he calculated that over 250 people had visited his home. Irene , David, Wills and Charlotte went on the Sunday and wished they had spent the whole weekend there. The continuous flow of drink, never-ending supply of food and music created an unforgettable atmosphere.

Hillary certainly enjoyed the whole weekend. Partying was her scene and now she was in a position to enjoy it. She also saw the party as the ideal time to tell Jim that he had something else to celebrate; he was going to be a grandfather; she was four months pregnant. That was like the icing on the cake; he proudly told his guests, who added more congratulations. The atmosphere was such that no one asked the question which was uppermost in their thoughts: who was the father?

Jim did not ask immediately, assuming it was the man he had frequently seen leaving her flat. Only when the party was over did he ask, along with the question of when was she going to get married. He was planning a large wedding and reception for his only daughter.

Then she dropped the bombshell: she would not be getting married and intended bringing the child up herself. Yes, as a single mother, which was perfectly acceptable in the 1980s. Jim questioned her further until eventually she told him the last thing he wanted to hear; the father was a married man. He was silent.

'Well, why the silence? Wasn't I the product of your adultery?'

'That was different.'

'How?'

'It just was. My marriage was going through a bad patch and...'

'And what?'

'How can you make up excuses for your behaviour after the lives you've ruined. Julia's, Martin's. Bill's, Mum's and mine.'

'I've tried to make it up to you.'

'I had a good childhood with a man I thought was my father. I was dragged away from it. I still remember looking back and crying as Daddy threw us out of the house in Silkington. What can you do about that? NOTHING! You did the damage and nothing, NOTHING, can make it right!'

He was defeated: she was right; it was a case of history repeating itself. He was married when he had an affair with her mother; society was such in those days that Ann had felt obliged to marry for the sake of her child. At least in the eighties things were different.

'I'll make sure that neither you nor the child want for anything. After all you're making me a grandfather.'

'Is that all you think about, money. What about love?'

'I've always loved you and I'll love my grandchild.'

'LOVE? You don't know the meaning of the word.'

Having got the last word in, she left him sitting bewildered in the chair, and returned to her flat.

Irene received her cousin's news with mixed feelings; it seemed that everyone around her was pregnant. Stephanie had announced that she was expecting her first child. Robert and Josephine already had three children and now her cousin, who was not even married, was pregnant. The one thing she wanted to complete their marriage was a baby. Each month she hoped and then the hope turned to despair.

Time & Tide

On 3rd March, 1982, Stephanie gave birth to a daughter; David was an uncle yet again and she was an aunt. Hillary had a son on 1st May, a beautiful May Day baby; she named him William Martin Edison, much to Jim's annoyance; she still refused to change her own name and her son would have her surname; he was to be known as Bill after the man she would never forget as her father.

As the family rejoiced over the new arrivals Irene kept her sadness to herself. Even news of the Falklands conflict could not dampen the family spirit. On Monday, 10th May David was forty; Irene wanted to give him a party but he preferred dinner for two at their favourite Chinese restaurant in town. He said they would celebrate in Kenya, in three weeks time at the late spring holiday, with a beach barbecue for his parents, brother and any of the friends who were spending time at their holiday homes on Paradise Beach. It would be a squash having nine of them at the bungalow at once, but good fun. So, they looked forward to that.

As half term approached she felt at last that she might be pregnant but decided to keep quiet until the doctor confirmed it. On the Thursday David had a head of department's meeting after school. It was one of those occasions when they took both cars to work and returned home separately. At the end of the day she went into his room and said, 'Bye. See you later.'

'Bye. I'll be home as soon as I can.'

She left: he assumed she was going straight home to pack. They were leaving after school on the Friday. She went to the doctor's surgery, with crossed fingers and was over the moon when she heard the words: 'Congratulations, Mrs Taylor, you're six weeks pregnant. Your baby's due in the middle of January.'

At long last she was pregnant!

An excited Irene began packing and waiting for David to come home. This just had to be the best day of her life; then she remembered Danny and the hayloft on that Friday afternoon, sixteen years ago: it was the second best day!

She waited and waited; he must have taken Jane home, Irene told herself. Jane had taken her car to the garage at lunchtime for a six-monthly service, before going on a touring holiday the following week.

She looked at the clock again, 6.55 pm; the minutes were slipping by. Surely, he was not still at school. She phoned Jane, who was surprised to hear her voice. Sue Pickering had given her a lift home and the HoD's meeting was still in progress at 4.30. David was there when they left. Jane tried reassuring her, he was a workaholic, he would still be working and had lost track of the time. While they were talking there was a knock at the door.

'Oh, he's here now. He must've forgotten his key. Thanks, Jane. Bye.'

She put the phone down and rushed to open the door, saying, 'Darling, where've you...' She stopped abruptly when she saw two police officers: no David. Her instinct told her what had happened but it was not possible: it could not be: not again.

'Mrs Taylor?' the policeman asked.

'Yes,' she replied, her voice shaking and her eyes filling with tears. Happiness seldom comes from tragedy but it is usually marred by it. Irene had a feeling that the happiness she had felt for the last three hours was about to be shattered.

'May we come in?' his female colleague asked. She led them into the lounge and they all sat down.

'Is your husband Mr David Taylor?' the woman continued.

'Yes,' Irene replied faintly.

'Does he drive a car, registration DPR 326W?'

'Yes,' she whispered.

'I'm afraid we have some bad news for you. There's been an accident. The man we believe to be your husband died on the way to hospital.'

Irene was speechless. She stared blankly into space. Not a car accident. Again.

'Is there anyone we can call for you? We need you to officially identify the body.'

She could hear the policewoman talking to her but she was unable to answer. All she wanted to do was argue with God; the God who had cruelly taken away so many people from her. She had ignored him for some time and life had been good, but now He was back and making her suffer; that cruel God was back in her life and there was nothing she could do about it.

The policewoman repeated, 'Is there anyone we can call? We need you to identify the body.'

'How did it happen?'

'It seems like a child ran out in front of him. He tried to swerve, lost control of the car and it smashed into a lamp post.'

'A lamp post?'

'Yes.'

'Not a tree.'

'Pardon?'

'Oh nothing. He was a good driver. He lost control?'

'Yes.'

'What, what about the child?'

'He didn't hit her. Is there anyone we can call?'

'Jane. Yes, Jane. Dear Jane.'

The policeman called her while his colleague sat with Irene. Irene had forgotten that Jane was without transport until she arrived in a taxi; Jane would not let such a small thing prevent her from helping a friend in need. They all went to the hospital mortuary. It was David lying there; she had hoped that it would be a mistake; someone had stolen his car or there would be another simple explanation. They would return home and he would be waiting for her, but that only happens in films: this was real life! She stared down at his still, inert body; she wanted to shake him and shout, 'Wake up'; she knew it would achieve nothing. He was dead. The child who ran into the road was alive. He was dead.

You can't put the clock back and change the course of events. She agreed that it was indeed David and the police took them back to her home. Once again, Irene's world had crumbled; she was feeling, empty, lost and alone.

'Have you eaten?' Jane asked.

'No.'

'I'll make you a sandwich. You need to make a list of people who need to be told. There's the funeral arrangements to think about.'

Irene was in floods of tears.

'There, there,' said the comforting Jane as she put her arm around her. 'I'll miss him, too.'

'Of course you will. How silly of me not to realise.'

Irene sobbed. 'Daddy,' she shouted suddenly, 'Daddy'll know what to do.'

It was late, after ten, but she still phoned him and was relieved to hear his voice.

'Oh, Daddy,' she wailed, 'I'm pregnant. David's dead.'

'What?' Wills asked, thinking he had not heard properly.

'Oh, Daddy. David's been killed in a car accident. He's dead.' As soon as she had uttered the last words she realised how silly and unnecessary they were. If he had been killed he must be dead!

'Dead?' asked an unbelieving Wills.

'Yes, dead.'

'What else did you say?'

'I'm pregnant. He's dead and he didn't know he was going to be a father. Oh Daddy, what am I going to do?'

'I'll be right there? Is anyone with you?'

'Jane.'

Jane, having heard the second piece of news was looking even more aghast. Congratulations were in order, but they were also inappropriate.

'OK. I'll be there in about three hours. I'll go and see Mark and then I'll be able to stay and help you.'

'Oh Daddy.'

'Let me talk to your friend.'

She passed the phone over to Jane.

'Hello. Jane, is it?'

'Yes.'

'Can you stay with her?'

'Oh yes. I came prepared.' That was dear Jane, always prepared and helpful. The ideal companion in a crisis.

'Thanks. I'll be there in about three hours.'

He put the phone down and walked out of the office. Charlotte had heard snatches of the conversation. She looked at him.

'The good news is you're going to be a grandmother.'

He did not realise that his daughter's pregnancy would not give Charlotte the same joy it gave him. He continued, 'The bad news is Irene's a widow.'

'What?' she exclaimed in disbelief.

'David's been killed in a car accident and Irene's pregnant.' He said slowly. 'Pack me some clothes. I'm going to stay with her for a few days. This time she'll be coming home for good. I'm not letting her struggle as a single parent to bring up our grandchild. I'm going to see Mark.'

He walked out of the door, went through the orchard and gardens to Mark's cottage. For once, Charlotte felt sorry for her daughter and agreed with her husband: she must return to Fordingham.

Mark answered the door in his dressing gown.

'I'm sorry to get you out of bed.'

'Wha' is it?'

Wills swallowed hard. 'David's been killed in a car accident and Irene's just found out that she's pregnant. I'm going to stay for a few days...'

'Right, sure. I'll keep things going. Tell Irene...tell Irene I'm sorry. I'll be thinking about 'er.'

He closed the door, deep in thought, the woman he loved was suffering; he wanted to help alleviate her pain, but what could he do?

Irene ran out to greet her father like she used to do when she was a child.

'Oh Daddy, what am I going to do?' she sobbed.

'Daddy's here now.'

Wills took control; there was nothing they could do that night. He suggested that they got some sleep and started to do things in the morning. He took Jane to work on the Friday morning and promised to collect her later and take her to pick up her car. She gave both pieces of news to their colleagues but this was one pregnancy they could not celebrate.

Wills cancelled the seats on the plane to Nairobi, made all the necessary phone calls and the funeral arrangements. During the next few days he gently persuaded her to sell the house, resign, and return to Fordingham.

It was a conversation they had had before; then, she had wanted to continue with her career, it had been important to her, but not now. This time, things were different; she agreed that bringing up her child alone, and as a widow, would not be easy. Besides, staying in Harwood without David would be difficult; there were so many memories at home and at work. Back at Fordingham, she would have to tolerate her mother, but she would have her father's support.

Margaret and Andrew came straight over from Nairobi; Richard and Stephanie came later, just for the funeral which was at St Michael's Church, Kidderminster. It was the church where Loretta had worshipped and was buried; he had bought a double grave when she died and it had always been his intention to join her. Irene was happy with that arrangement; she and David had had a wonderful life together, for which she would always be grateful, but she was his second wife. First loves, as she well knew were important; it was as if she had borrowed him temporarily and now he was to return to Loretta.

The head closed the school for the afternoon enabling colleagues, if they wished, to attend the service and say their last farewells. The only people who remained in school were pupils taking GCEs and staff not going to the funeral.

The church was packed; he had so many friends at Kidderminster and in Harwood. Many of their neighbours were there as well as about sixty colleagues, some pupils, ex-colleagues and ex-pupils. Irene followed the coffin into church with Margaret and Andrew; behind them were Stephanie and Richard and then Wills and Charlotte.

The service began with the hymn "Abide With Me", then the vicar read from the prayer book and spoke about this man who had lost his life in a tragedy. He spoke about the David he had known as a loving husband and caring teacher, a man to whom God had given a second chance of happiness with Irene. Most of the service drifted over Irene; suddenly, they were following the coffin to the prepared grave; the stone with Loretta's name on had been removed and the bearers were lowering David to join her. Loretta, the woman he met twenty years ago at university; they had married expecting to spend a lifetime together but it had come to a premature end and now they were reunited. The stone would be returned with his name on it, it was all over for Irene who was left to carry on with her life and bring up his child.

She returned to work for the last weeks of the term. The house went on the market and was sold in late July for twice as much as they paid for it. When everything was added up, bank accounts, insurances and the house, she was a wealthy widow worth over £100,000, plus a bungalow in Mombasa and a share in the Taylor Plantation. She intended signing over the latter two to her child.

Wills kept travelling between Fordingham and Harwood to help clear things up. He got on well with Margaret and Andrew and all of them were extremely concerned about the child she was carrying; they were planning for his or her future and were adamant that he or she would want for nothing. But as Irene pointed out, neither grandparents could ever give their grandchild one thing, the main thing, the father. He or she would not have a father and no amount of money could change that.

The school gave her a good send-off at the end of the term. She promised to keep in touch and she would always remain friends with Jane. She had arrived in Harwood in 1972 and invested £900 in her first home. On 28th August, she returned to the home she had left as a young bride ten years and two husbands ago. Her career was over. She was a pregnant and rich widow. In ten years, her circumstances had certainly changed.

It was time to go home and move on...

Chapter 16
Fordingham, September, 1982

FOR YEARS September had meant going back to school; it seemed strange that she no longer had a job. Margaret and Andrew had asked her to spend some time with them in Nairobi before the baby was born, but for the time being she had no desire to visit either Nairobi or Mombasa.

She was now back at Fordingham: everything was different, but it was the same. The harvest was almost over, there would be the harvest thanksgiving service in church and the Harvest Supper at the Village Institute in the next month. There was a produce sale on Saturday; Wills had already asked for her help with that. In November, there would be the traditional village bonfire and then the Remembrance Service.

The Women's Institute were still having coffee mornings. Katy's mum, now in her early sixties, was still an active member of the WI; the tall, blonde Katy Langton who had befriended her on her first day at school and then had disappeared from her life when she went to boarding school, had married an Army officer and was now spending a lot of time abroad; she had a successful marriage (or at least one that had lasted) and a settled home life: she seemed to have succeeded where Irene had failed.

There were social events at the Village Institute throughout the winter months up to Christmas and into the next year. The village life cycle would continue as it had done for decades. Irene knew that, but things were different; it was as if she had woken up from a ten-year sleep and missed out on so much.

Lord and Lady Fordingham were grandparents: Thomas, Lucille and Susan were all married and had five children between them. There were new people in the stable flats and new staff; only one member of staff remained from the sixties and that was Mark, now forty with more white than ginger hair and a beard: he looked so different from the seventeen-year-old boy she first met in the sixties. He was still married to Jane – their marriage had lasted sixteen years. Irene thought back to their childhood days: Katy, Jane and herself. Jane, like Katy, had managed to make a success of her marriage; Thomas was fifteen and a reminder of what Mark once looked like. He was a fifth year pupil at the Fordingham Comprehensive School; his brother, Stephen, would be going there next year.

The arrival of the comprehensive was one of the changes in the seventies. The grammar school, like so many, had lost its fight under the Labour Government and been turned into the local comprehensive. The inverted snobbery no longer existed; everyone went to the much larger school which housed over a thousand pupils and three new buildings had been erected in the surrounding fields to accommodate them. The secondary modern schools had been demolished and houses now occupied those sites.

Jane was still the same; she bore Irene a grudge and had a chip on her shoulder over failing the eleven plus examination. It was clear to her that her husband had a certain amount of affection for Irene; she had never forgotten the day he drove her, in the open carriage, to her wedding. Mark talked about Irene's misfortunes openly with his wife; at least while she was away in Harwood she was out of sight and out of mind, and that suited Jane. Now she had returned; Jane saw her as a threat to her marriage. One evening, when they were sitting watching television and their sons were upstairs, Mark commented, 'Irene's six months gone. The baby'll be 'ere in the New Year and David didn't even know she were pregnant. It's awful, bringing up a child as a widow.'

'Oh, change the record. All you ever talk about is Irene. I don't know why you didn't marry 'er.'

'She was Danny's girl from the first time 'e saw 'er. That's why.'

'You mean you would've married 'er?' Jane shouted at him.

'She's clever, pretty, caring and YES, I would've married 'er but she wouldn't 'ave 'ad me. I'm only a gardener. Danny was going to be a doctor.'

'You bastard,' she shouted again.

'You're jealous, you've always been jealous of 'er, 'aven't you?' The truth suddenly dawned on Mark.

Jane looked down; she had not wanted her husband to know that.

'You, You've everything, 'ome, 'usband, children and you're jealous, jealous of a pregnant woman who's lost 'er 'usband. We should 'elp 'er.'

'A pregnant widow. For all 'er brains, 'er looks, 'er fancy education, she can't keep 'er men!'

For the first time, Mark raised his hand to her and she feared he was going to strike her. He managed to stop himself, but neither of them would ever forget the conversation. Jane saw it as a warning; Irene was a rival for her husband; if she were not careful, Mark would leave her and become husband number three.

Life on the estate had moved on and there were changes in the village as well: people had died or moved away. New properties had been built and she saw new faces when she ventured out beyond the gates. There was a new headmaster: Mr Blake had moved on. His replacement was Brian Madeley, a married man with two youngsters; his name sounded familiar, because he was the Brian who had been at college with her, and the person who had told Philip where she lived: it certainly was a small world. There was a new vicar: the Reverend Alistair Duncan, who saw it as his clerical duty to show help and spiritual guidance to this young widow. The butcher's was now a fish and chip shop; the two pubs were still there and Charlotte still worked as a barmaid and pianist. Wills still had his five properties and regular people who booked their holiday for the next year before they went home; he was established and this made life a lot easier.

Moving back meant that Irene saw more of her family. Hillary had taken well to motherhood and told Irene that it was the best thing that had happened to her. Jim and Ann were doting grandparents; the new arrival had somehow managed to pull them together as a family and they were closer than they had ever been. As Jim played at being a grandfather his shops were flourishing without him.

She also saw more of Elizabeth, who seemed to be ageing, but after all she was seventy-four and had been a widow for twenty-two years. Irene had that in common with her grandmother, and found her conversations and advice on coping with widowhood valuable. Her cousin, Nicholas, was twenty-two and pursuing a career in accountancy. She saw more of him and Mavis and Gerald; Nicholas had grown up but she had only seen him twice since her wedding to Philip.

By the time Christmas arrived, she was eight months pregnant. Charlotte had decorated the spare room, which had been beautifully transformed into a nursery; it was well-equipped, as family and friends had bestowed on her gifts for the new arrival. Elizabeth was particularly excited as she was to become a great-grandmother.

After New Year's Eve, the days seemed to drag by until 15th January. Then, in Fordingham Hospital, at 4.30 am her child was born. As Irene held her baby in her arms, with her parents at her bedside, she knew David was looking down on them and giving his blessing to their son, James David.

Three days later Wills, the proud grandfather, collected Irene and James from the hospital. The first thing Irene noticed was the new black Metro.

'I thought you weren't changing the car this year.'

'I didn't know I had to have your approval, m'duck!'

'Oh, Daddy,' she laughed as she got into the back of the car with her son sleeping in her arms.

They arrived home and Wills handed the car keys to his daughter.

'You're wrong you know – I haven't changed our car. This one's yours. I know you've grown attached to your little red mini; it's still in the barn. You can decide what you want to do with it. Sell it for scrap and keep the number plates would be my suggestion. This new Metro's for giving us a grandson.'

'Oh Daddy, you're wonderful.' She kissed him fondly on the cheek.

The new arrival meant a stream of visitors arriving at Orchard Cottage.

The bleak winter was certainly a lot brighter that year and the spring seemed to come more quickly. As a family Wills, Charlotte and Irene were closer than they had ever been. Even Charlotte was enjoying having a baby in the house. Maybe she felt guilty over her lack of maternal instinct with Irene and James. Now, she was happy helping her daughter with their grandson and playing the hostess to the numerous visitors. Wills also had a new lease of life; he would spend hours in the nursery chatting to James, telling him how they would play cricket and football together. James was the best educated baby when it came to the subject of Nottingham Forest football team.

One of the first visitors was her ex-colleague, Jane Meadows, who came at the end of January and stayed for the weekend. They discussed David and how he was missed at work; his replacement did not have the same caring attitude, that charisma which had made David so successful as head of department. Jane clearly adored James, which pleased Irene and led her to ask, on behalf of herself and David, if she would be one of his godparents.

'I know it's what David would've wanted,' Irene said as they were both choking back the tears.

'Oh, I'd be delighted – no, I'd be honoured!'

So, it was agreed and the baptism service was arranged for Easter Sunday afternoon; the godfather was to be David's brother, Richard. Wills and Charlotte made all the arrangements and sent out the invitations.

Margaret and Andrew arrived in March and were staying for a month in one of

Wills' cottages. There was great excitement as Mark took photographs of both sets of grandparents with James and Irene. Richard came over for a few days to officially take on his role as godfather.

James did not have a father but he was certainly not starved of affection from the remaining relatives. The Stephensons and the Taylors were united in their love and concern for the latest arrival.

On that Sunday afternoon, clad in their best clothes and Easter bonnets, they were all assembled round the font in Fordingham Church. This was the church where Irene had been confirmed and married; it was also the church where she had attended Danny's funeral service but all of that was behind her: this was a happy occasion. The day of Christ's resurrection was traditionally held as a time for new life and a new beginning; they had given and received Easter eggs, the symbol of new life, that morning.

Now, as the Reverend Duncan took James from her, Irene looked round at the family: Hillary with her son, almost a year old and Stephanie with her one-year-old daughter. The next generation were well represented and, for the adults, there was overwhelming joy. Elizabeth's dream of becoming a great-grandmother had been fulfilled; she knew John would be looking down on them and giving James his blessing, just as Irene was aware of David's presence. Wills and Charlotte, Margaret and Andrew, and other family members along with friends were there. By her side, with her brother-in-law, was her great friend Jane ready to make her promise to look after James.

'Dost thou, in the name of this Child, renounce the devil and all his works, the vain pomp and glory of this world, with all covetous desires of the same, and the carnal desires of the flesh, so that thou wilt not follow, nor be led by them?'

Jane and Richard replied, 'I renounce them all.'

Reverend Duncan continued and both godparents made their responses and then the vicar made the sign of the cross on James's forehead. At the end of the service Irene took her son from the vicar; the christening was over, and he was now a member of the Church.

That evening, when everyone had left, Irene sat quietly in the nursery with her son. She told herself that he would grow up to be as well-respected as his father was. She would tell him all about his father; they would spend time together at the bungalow in Mombasa, just like she and David had done.

She was planning his life out for him: private education, Cambridge University, after his degree, all avenues would be open to him. Perhaps he would live in Kenya and help run the plantation with Richard. Or work with computers, this new invention which seemed to be taking over the world. Maybe he would become a computer wizard. By then, it would be the new millennium and he would no longer be her little boy. She vowed to enjoy every minute of his childhood with him; time was precious.

For the next ten days Margaret and Andrew enjoyed spending time with their grandson. They planned to return to Kenya on Thursday 14th April, and Irene had agreed to visit them in the autumn; they would only have to wait six months to see him again.

On the Thursday morning, Irene went into the nursery as usual and looked into the cot. James seemed unusually still, she felt his body; he was rigid and not breathing. She screamed, Wills came rushing in and looked into the cot, he knew what a dead child looked like, but he could not believe it. Neither of them could utter the word; if they did not mention it, it would not be true; they would blink and suddenly James would come to life. The doctor came and pronounced 'cot death' as the reason for James's demise.

He had lived on this earth for ninety days; the joy he had brought to the family was over and now it was time for sorrow again. The news spread quickly and condolences came pouring in. For Wills, it was a second blow, first his son and now his grandson. Irene found some solace in her belief that he was with his father; David had taken him to that better place. Margaret and Andrew changed their plans and stayed for another fortnight; even the vicar found it hard to console the family as they planned for the funeral.

Seventeen days after his baptism the family were once again in the church; it was full as so many of the villagers wanted to pay their last respects. All eyes were fixed on the tiny coffin, covered with tulips and daffodils. The Reverend Duncan conducted the service; he spoke of the sorrow of the death of an infant and the loss to the family, but God moves in a mysterious way and there should be some celebration over the fact that little James was now in Heaven. Such thoughts were poor consolation to Wills although Irene firmly believed that James was with his father. After the service, the tiny coffin was carried out to a prepared grave; the family followed with flowing tears. Irene stood at the graveside and watched her son lowered into his final resting place. She turned and walked away: it was all over.

They returned to the cottage, another funeral, another loss. In less than a year

Irene had lost her husband and her son; they were in that 'better' place along with so many people she had once loved. The glorious spring turned into a bleak summer for Wills and Irene; there was comfort and help from many people who could only imagine the grief and were grateful that it had not happened to them. Charlotte, if she felt pain, hid it well. Her diary entries simply said, '*James died today*' and for the funeral, '*We lain our grandson to rest, He is with God.*' There was no indication of any feeling, grief or emotion. For Charlotte, life would go on; she looked back at some of her comments in 1980 and 1981.

1980
BRITAIN
The first national steel strike since 1926...
March: Robert Runcie is enthroned as the Archbishop of Canterbury...
May: London is the focus of the world's news; the SAS storm the Iranian Embassy in Knightsbridge to free hostages taken six days earlier by gunmen demanding the release of political prisoners in Iran...
30th June, the sixpenny piece, worth 2½p in decimal currency, ceases to be legal tender nine years after decimalisation...
October: the Housing Act comes into force allowing council tenants to buy their own homes. (That won't affect us!) Mr Callaghan resigns as the Labour Party Leader; he's succeeded by Michael Foot... The Queen has an audience with the Pope on the first State visit to the Vatican by a British monarch.
ABROAD
Mr Mugabe, exiled during the troubled years is elected prime minister of the new independent Zimbabwe....The Netherlands, Queen Juliana abdicates on her seventy-first birthday, her daughter Princess Beatrix succeeds her...Poland, there's the birth of the Solidarity Trade Union after industrial unrest.... Argentina's increasing its links with the Falkland Islands...
According to Britain's Disasters Emergency Committee, over ten million people are threatened by the world's worst ever famine in Uganda, Somalia, Ethiopia and the Sudan; two years of drought and warfare have led to widespread crop failure and an efflux of refugees.
SPORT
Moscow is hosting the twenty-second Olympic Games; Daley Thompson wins the first ever British Gold Medal for decathlon; Steve Ovett and Sebastian Coe also

bring gold medals home to Britain...Wimbledon, Bjorn Borg wins the Men's Singles Championships for the FIFTH consecutive year and, by beating John McEnroe in a four-hour five-set duel, Borg has won himself a place in sporting history – much to the dismay of his opponent!

TELEVISION

"Who shot JR??" That's the question everyone seems to be asking. The American TV show, "Dallas", concludes the series with the shooting of the ruthless JR Ewing, leaving viewers in suspense: will he live or die? Who, of the many possible candidates, actually shot him?

OBITUARY

The saddest death of this year must be the assassination of John Lennon . On 8th December, outside his home in New York, Mark Chapman, a man Lennon had given his autograph to earlier that day, shoots him five times at point blank range. It's been reported that he had been stalking Lennon for three days prior to the shooting.

1981

BRITAIN

January: Tremendous relief! The "Yorkshire Ripper" is arrested. Peter Sutcliffe, a long distance lorry driver from Bradford, confesses to the killings, but is pleading guilty to manslaughter on the grounds of diminished responsibility. The jury at the Old Bailey dismiss any possibility of mental illness and find him guilty of murder – he is sentenced to life imprisonment... Mrs Thatcher is stepping up her "privatisation" drive... The "gang of four", Shirley Williams, Roy Jenkins, David Owen and William Rodgers leave the Labour Party to form a council for Social Democracy...

April: in Brixton hundreds of youths are involved in fighting with the police, who are unable to maintain order; the youths are going wild and committing arson, looting and vandalism. The unrest is spreading to other cities and many places are experiencing the worst outbreaks of civil unrest this century: Liverpool, Wolverhampton, Birmingham, Reading, Luton, Chester, Hull and Preston are among those affected. After the rioting there's devastation; the areas resemble bombsites during the war...

30th June, blanks are fired at the Queen during the Trooping of the Colour. Marcus Sargeant, an unemployed youth from Folkestone, is charged under the Treason Act of 1842 of wilfully discharging a gun with the intent of harming her Majesty...

September: garages are beginning to sell petrol by the litre as opposed to the gallon... The Church of England's General Synod vote overwhelmingly to admit women to Holy Orders as Deacons...The "gang of four" who formed the Council for Social Democracy are forming the Social Democratic Party (SDP) and an alliance with the Liberal Party...

December: television licences are now £46 for colour and £15 for black and white sets... Arthur Scargill is elected as president of the National Union of Miners.

THE ROYAL WEDDING

For many years there's been speculation over who Prince Charles will marry: that's come to an end... Buckingham Palace announces his engagement to the Lady Diana Spencer, a shy young nursery teacher who has been headline news for some time... the nation is suffering from wedding fever as countless souvenirs arrive on the market.

The Wedding Day, 29th July, is a Public Holiday. Over 2600 people are invited to St Paul's Cathedral for the ceremony. The crowds from all over the world are swarming the streets, a further 700 million are expected to be watching on the television. The first view of the bride is when she leaves Clarence House with her proud father, Earl Spencer. She's wearing an ivory silk wedding dress with puffed sleeves designed by David and Elizabeth Emanuel, and a veil supported by the Spencer family tiara. Prince Charles is attired in his naval uniform and instead of a best man he has two "supporters", Prince Andrew and Prince Edward. The world hears the couple make their vows to each other and when the service is over they return to Buckingham Palace for the wedding breakfast. They make the traditional balcony appearance where an unprecedented event takes place: Prince Charles kisses his new twenty-year-old bride in full public view. They're honeymooning at Broadlands, the home of the late Earl Mountbatten of Burma, in Romsey in Hampshire and then cruising in the Mediterranean on the Royal Yacht.

ABROAD

New York: Mark Chapman pleads insanity to the charge of murdering John Lennon but he's jailed for life for the assassination... President Reagan is inaugurated as the fortieth president of the United States of America: he is the first republican in the White House for twenty-six years...

March: President Reagan is wounded in an assassination attempt; he quips to Nancy, "Honey, I forgot to duck"

May: the Pope is shot in Vatican City whilst blessing the crowds; after a five-

hour operation, his life is saved and he is expected to make a full recovery...

October: President Sadat of Egypt is assassinated while attending a military parade; his killers are Islamic fundamentalist gunmen who are opposed to the peace treaty he made with Israel; Hosni Mubarak becomes the new president... France, the socialist Francois Mitterrand is the elected president and he is to abolish the use of the guillotine... Greece has joined the EEC...'

Charlotte closed the file: why Greece joining the EEC should bring her back to reality was a mystery. The reality was that they had lost their grandson but it was Wills who felt really cheated. Lord and Lady Fordingham still had their five grandchildren and each time they visited them Wills felt his own loss. Jim tried to comfort him in big brotherly fashion but all he succeeded in doing was to add to the agony.

Irene had had a nice headstone made for her son; she also suggested that they place a stone on her brother's grave at Silkington knowing that she and her father thought about him frequently: she thought it might help him come to terms with the loss. Then there was one more thing to do.

The Mombasa bungalow and her share in the Taylor Plantation needed sorting out. In October she made one last trip with her parents to Kenya. Margaret and Andrew were happy for her to continue visiting, keeping the bungalow and taking a share in the company, but she was not, it was something that needed winding up. Kenya would not be the same without David, it was something they had shared and she would not enjoy it alone.

She promised to stay in touch with the family and Wills assured them that they would always be welcome at Fordingham. She removed their personal items from the bungalow and signed it and her share in the company over to Margaret and Andrew. It was a closed chapter.

All that was left were memories of happy times...

Chapter 17
Fordingham, January, 1984

ON HER BIRTHDAY, Wills kissed her on the cheek and said, 'Happy Birthday, m'duck! Don't leave your old Dad. Stay at Fordingham.'

'OK.'

'You mean it?'

'Yes.'

His eyes lit up, 'God bless you, Irene.'

She had toyed with the possibility of taking another teaching post in a different area. A fresh start was quite appealing but deep down she knew there was no escape from the past. New people, innocent comments would serve as a reminder of what she had lost; she needed her father just as much as he needed her and at Fordingham, they could continue to support each other. She had made one decision but she was only thirty-four and had the rest of her life ahead of her. What was she going to do? How was she going to spend her time? What did she want to do with her life? These were questions which she pondered over. Time was a precious commodity and she wanted to do something useful and worthwhile. The fact that she had promised to stay at home gave Wills a new lease of life; he had got his little girl back and the future was beginning to look brighter.

Mark was one of the people she saw daily and Jane often saw them together, chatting and laughing. He would always love her, and he wanted to show some concern for her; she had endured so much and experienced more than her fair share of tragedy. It gave him pleasure to make her laugh, in some small way he was helping her come to terms with her loss.

For Jane, who was obsessed with jealousy, Irene's presence meant trouble; the green-eyed monster was the cause of the arguments between her and her husband in the evenings. She would interrogate him over the conversations that had taken place between himself and Irene. Jane was slowly pushing him away from her and into Irene's arms, if only she had the intelligence to work out what her jealousy was doing to them as a family.

Time & Tide

Brian Madeley often thought back to college days, remembering the young, aloof Irene who kept her distance from those she saw as immature students. He recalled the conversation he had had with Philip about this woman of mystery. His life had been comparatively straightforward; after college, he had married and held two teaching posts before returning to Fordingham as headmaster with a wife, Marion and two children. He, like Mark, wanted to help ease Irene's pain and help her to find happiness. Marion had the same response as Jane Adams; she quickly grew tired of hearing about the tragic Irene and their conversations soon turned into arguments, with Marion stating clearly that she was sick and tired of hearing about 'that woman'.

Irene was oblivious of all the concern and had no idea that she was becoming a home-wrecker. In fact, that was the last thing she wanted to do; all she was looking for was a purpose in life, something to occupy her time and make her feel useful, a 'raison d'etre'.

In April, on the anniversary of her son's death, when she was placing a special bouquet of flowers on the immaculate grave, the answer came to her. She would do two things: first, she would look for supply teaching locally and second, she would become a charity worker. She had all the time in the world and she could give it freely to help those in need.

The man who would be able to advise her about charity work was the vicar, Alistair Duncan. She went across the recreation ground, passed the swings she had spent so much time on as a child and into the vicarage. She had often wondered why the recreation ground had been placed between the church and the vicarage: It seemed odd when the school was next to the church! Alistair reminded her of her late father-in-law; his faith was his staying power and had seen him through life's 'ups and downs'. He was ten years older than Irene and a confirmed bachelor who had dedicated his life to God. In religious thinking he was a traditionalist; only men were called into God's service; Jesus had chosen twelve men for disciples from all walks of life. Women had a different role in life, they were to be subservient wives, as St Paul had stated in his Letter to the Ephesians.

Alistair was putting the finishing touches to his Sunday sermons, as he usually did on Saturday afternoons, when he heard the doorbell ring. It was on those occasions that he wished he could close the vicarage; he hated being disturbed when he was working but when he saw Irene standing on the doorstep all thoughts of sermons vanished from his mind.

'Ah, hello, vicar, I hope I'm not disturbing you.'

'No, of course not. My door's always open. Come in.'

They went into the lounge and he invited her to sit down. He had frequently told her that she would always be welcome at the vicarage; she had taken him at his word. As he sat opposite her listening to her talking about the great decision she had made regarding the rest of her life and how she thought he could help her, he found himself thinking about her beauty as a woman and how much he would like to sleep with her. He quickly dismissed such irreverent thoughts: he was like a doctor in a position of trust.

'Well, what do you think? Where do I start?'

'Um...um.'

'Vicar?'

'Um...call me Alistair.'

Once again, Irene had done was she was best at; she had captured a man's heart with her charm, beauty and effervescent personality. This time, it was not an ordinary man but the vicar and a confirmed bachelor, a true man of God.

'Well, Alistair?'

He heard her speaking and gathered his thoughts together very quickly.

'To want to spend your life in the service of others is an admirable trait. You've suffered so much and yet you still want to give. You're a remarkable woman.'

'But surely all my suffering was part of God's plan. Isn't it through suffering one becomes a better person?'

'That is certainly one theory, Irene.'

'Well, how do I start?'

'Have you got a particular cause in mind? Do you think you should sort out supply teaching days first?'

'Children, animals, the elderly and the blind have always been the causes closest to my heart. Supply teaching can be slotted in afterwards.'

'So, cancer, heart disease and other illnesses, research, leprosy, Red Cross, don't interest you?'

'Well, not as much as the others.'

'In that case, you could start with the Dr Barnardo's shop in Buxton. They're always looking for volunteers to man the shop. Then there's the elderly in the village.'

'What about them?'

Time & Tide

'Some need visiting regularly. The housebound like being visited, they need their shopping doing and library books changed. The blind people like people to visit and read to them.'

'I could certainly do that.'

She left the vicarage with a new purpose in her life.

Wills was pleased to see some of her old sparkle back.

Her next move was to go to the new Fordingham Comprehensive School and offer her services as a supply teacher. She was welcomed with open arms and found herself spending the summer days back in the classrooms she knew so well from childhood; they were about all that was left of the old grammar school. The 'Alpha, Beta, and Gamma' classes had been replaced with 'U, V, W, X, Y, Z': it just did not have the same ring to it. The house system had gone and been replaced with year tutors as opposed to housemasters; it resembled Harwood far more than the old grammar school she had once known. The only remaining member of staff from her childhood days was Mrs Bennet, their form teacher; she was head of the English Department now and looking forward to retirement in a couple of years time.

Those two years in the mid-eighties passed quickly.

Irene's time was spent teaching, helping out on the estate just as she had always done, working in the Dr Barnardo's shop and with Alistair in the local community. They had started a youth club together; she helped him with all the church functions and visiting in the parish.

Her presence continued to cause problems in the Adams household. Thomas left home on his nineteenth birthday; he had found himself a job as a groom in stables with live-in accommodation and jumped at the opportunity of escaping from what he saw as a war-zone. After almost twenty years of marriage Jane decided it was time to make a stand; she packed her bags and took her younger son with her. She left Mark a note stating that she was leaving him and staying with her sister, it was an ultimatum and Mark was to make a choice: Irene or herself. She expected Mark to come running after her but she was wrong, when he found the note he felt a great sense of relief. He had married her in 1966 because she was pregnant although he had never been sure that the child was his and now he was free and so was Irene. Perhaps, if he got a divorce she would marry him; she would never marry the vicar because he was a confirmed bachelor. At last he stood a chance of having the woman he loved, the adorable Irene for himself. Life was looking up; Jane had given him what he wanted.

It was Wills who told Irene that Jane had left and Mark was alone; she wanted to help him because he had been a good friend to her through the years. She wanted to repay his kindness in her own way and that was to spend time with him. She started going to the cottage in the evenings just to chat or watch television, casting aside her own sad memories of the times she had spent in that cottage with Danny. Her genuine concern was for the deserted Mark, she encouraged him to participate in village events. Sometimes, she would ask him to join her in one of the 'locals' for a drink or she would suggest that they went for a walk together.

Unknown to her, he totally misunderstood her actions; he knew she spent a lot of time with Alistair, but that was just charity work. He had started divorce proceedings and when the 'absolute' came through he planned to ask her to marry him.

After two years of working alongside Alistair she had become more than just another parishioner. His soul was given to God but his body he wanted to give to Irene. At first, as a man with no previous experience of relationships with women he found that he was out of his depth. He did not know how to tell her about his feelings for her. She was a woman with two marriages behind her and if rumour was to be believed, evidence of a third relationship lay in the churchyard. There could also have been other boyfriends. She was experienced but he was a novice.

She always seemed to be at his side at village functions; she had assumed the mantle of the vicar's wife without realising it. It had been three years since her son died and each time she saw Hillary with Bill, there was a reminder of her loss. She was desperately trying to get her life in order and one way of doing that was to give and help other people; she was still friends with Jane Meadows, whom she admired for her capacity to think of others before herself: she wanted to be like Jane.

Alistair and Mark saw the good in Irene and were both fighting for her time and affection. Mark enjoyed the hours they spent chatting and Alistair found parochial duties much more pleasant with her by his side. Unfortunately, situations do not remain constant and circumstances force change; what Irene saw as an idyllic situation was slowly becoming torture for the two men. Mark was waiting for his 'decree absolute' and Alistair was just waiting for the right moment.

That moment came after the Harvest Supper in 1986; the supper took place in the institute but most of the crockery was kept at the vicarage. She helped as she usually did by taking boxes back to the more secure storeroom at the vicarage and as she was leaving he said, 'Don't go.'

'What?'

'Don't go.'

'Dad'll wonder where I am.'

'How old are you now?'

'I'd rather not say.' She laughed.

He took hold of her arm and pulled her towards him, 'I've never loved a woman before but I love you.' His voice was shaky and he was terrified of making a mistake which would sever the relationship.

'Now, come on. We're just good friends.' As she looked at him, she knew she was deceiving herself.

There was a pause; then she moved closer to him and gently kissed him on the lips. There's a first time for everything: for a celibate vicar, this was a first!

'Just good friends?' he said. 'I think we both want more than that. I was hoping... ' he paused, 'I'm not very good at this. I've had no practice; my life's been dedicated to the Church. I was hoping we could be more than friends. We were meant to be together. We're good together. I want God to bless our relationship. Irene, will you marry me?'

She was silent. This was the least romantic proposal she had ever had; she knew he was a good man, who would look after her. 'You're right. We're good together, but marriage? Let me think about it.'

She gave him her answer on Christmas Day.

On Saturday, 25th April, 1987, she was in her bedroom, dressed in a dark-green suit with her hair neatly pinned up under a matching green hat; her make-up made her look younger than thirty-seven. Elizabeth, wearing a grey suit which highlighted her silver hair was in the room with her.

'Let me put this on,' she said, taking the cross and chain she had given to Irene almost fifteen years earlier.

'Oh Gran, here we are again. This whole thing has a feeling of deja vu about it. What do you think Grandpa would say?'

'He'll be happy for you, just as I am.'

At that point the grey-haired Wills walked into the room.

'Oh, Dad. I'm doing the right thing, aren't I?'

'He's a good man, he'll look after you, m'duck.'

'I always choose good men. I just don't seem to be able to keep them. You and mum'll have been married for forty years next year. I've been married twice and together they don't even add up to ten!'

'It hasn't always been a bed of roses,' he thought back to her attempted suicide, 'but times were different in the fifties, if divorce had been easier maybe we wouldn't have survived. Who knows? I'll be sixty next month and I'm just glad I'm still alive and able to walk you down the aisle.'

'Oh Dad!'

'Come on, your mother's downstairs in her new suit. Remember to say how nice she looks.'

They went down the stairs and set off for the church in Wills' car; there was no carriage this time, no grand arrival of the bride.

Waiting in the church were Mavis and Gerald, but not Nicholas, who was now married and living abroad. Mavis and Gerald were the type of relative one only met at weddings and funerals! Her good friend Jane Meadows had come and, like Andrew and Margaret, had told her that David would want her to marry again. Her former in-laws were not present but their blessing meant a lot to Irene. Then there was Uncle Jim, Ann, Hillary, Bill and also Tim Jones; Hillary and Tim had been seeing a lot of each other and Jim kept hoping that Tim would announce his heterosexual feelings for Hillary because he would make a good father for Bill. Hillary had pleased him by finally changing their names to Stephenson, if only she would settle down with a husband! The rest of the church was packed with villagers who wanted to witness the marriage of a much-loved vicar. There was only one sad person in Fordingham that day, Mark. Mark, who was running the estate in Wills' absence. Mark, who had once again had his dreams shattered because his divorce had come too late.

The Reverend Ian Black, a friend of Alistair's, was waiting at the church to conduct the ceremony. After those immortal words, 'I pronounce you man and wife', they left for a reception. All the village had been invited for a celebration drink and buffet at the Village Institute. Later, the newly weds left for a short honeymoon in Scotland. When they returned she moved into the vicarage and began her new life as the vicar's wife. In many ways, things were the same. She still did supply teaching, her charity work and supported her husband at village events but there was one big difference.

She was now Mrs Alistair Duncan....

Chapter 18

THE WEDDING reminded Charlotte of her own wedding day in 1948; it had been
the best that money could buy but far from lavish; ration coupons had severely
handicapped the 'dream wedding' John had always planned for his daughter. She
had been so pleased to be getting married. Her first boyfriend had been a soldier
killed at the end of the war and she thought she was going to be left on the shelf, left
to become an old spinster. She had been delighted when Wills first came to speak
to her while she was playing the piano in The Star at Whistbury. When he proposed,
love was not part of the equation for her; she was just delighted to be married. Only
after several years of marriage did she realise how much she loved him. After looking
at her wedding album, she turned to her journals.

'1982,

BRITAIN

*January: Mark Thatcher is missing in the Sahara desert on the Paris–Dakar rally,
Mrs Thatcher is naturally very concerned – even shedding tears in front of television
cameras – and the Algerian Government are launching a massive search to find the
son of the British Premier (I'll bet they're wishing he'd never been born!) The UK
unemployment figure's topped three million... The Laker Skytrain which offered cheap
flights to New York has collapsed, leaving 6,000 passengers stranded...*

*Mercury is the first UK firm to receive a licence to operate a telephone service
in competition with British Telecom.*

*March: the London Barbican Centre is open and the Government's given the go-
ahead for satellite television... Cambridge, the first test-tube twins are born.*

May: Pope John Paul II visits Britain; it's the first visit of a pope for 450 years.

*June: the 20p coin is now in circulation... 21st June, the nation, along with the
Royal Family, is celebrating the birth of Prince William... An intruder manages to
get into the Queen's bedroom at Buckingham Palace; the Queen awoke to find him
sitting at the bottom of her bed.(There are red faces amongst the security staff!)*

Time & Tide

October: the inland telegram service ends... Mrs Thatcher tells the Conservative Conference that the National Health Service is in safe hands under Conservative power (How reassuring!) The flagship of Henry VIII fleet, the Mary Rose, is raised from the seabed off Southsea in Hampshire.

December: more than 20,000 women are clasping hands and encircling the air base at Greenham Common in a protest over the planned siting of ninety-six US Cruise missiles.

THE FALKLANDS CONFLICT

2nd April, Argentina's forces invade these islands and overwhelm our forces... 5th April, the Royal Navy Task Force sets sail for the Falklands, they leave in true British style with patriotic flag waving and military music. Aircraft carriers HMS Hermes and HMS Invincible leave Portsmouth crammed full of sailors and jump jets. Other ships leave from Plymouth and join with naval forces from Gibraltar... It will take three weeks for the gigantic naval force to sail the 8000 miles...

25th April, British Forces recapture South Georgia and place a 200-mile total exclusion zone round the Falklands...

2nd May, the Argentinian ship, the General Belgrano, is sunk just for being in the area – she hadn't fired a single shot!

4th May, an Argentinian missile sinks the British destroyer HMS Sheffield...

29th May, our troops land at East Falkland and storm ashore at San Carlos. They advance forward and take Darwin and Goose Green; Lt-Col Herbert "H" Jones is killed along with sixteen paratroopers as he leads his 450 men into Goose Green... The islanders, who have been held prisoner in the recreation hall, rejoice when the troops release them... The forces go on to free Port Stanley and then the Argentinians surrender.

14th June, the Falklands are occupied by the British again; a jubilant Mrs Thatcher tells the cheering House of Commons that victory has been won by a military operation that was "boldly planned, bravely executed and brilliantly accomplished".

ABROAD

Poland, basic food prices have soared, in some cases there is a fivefold increase; there are riots in the Baltic shipyards at Gdansk.

April: President Sadat's five assassins are executed... 17th April, the Queen signs an act transferring sovereignty of the 1867 Canadian constitution from Britain to Canada.

June: in London the Israeli ambassador Shlomo Argov is shot and wounded... In

Lebanon, Israeli jets bomb guerrilla targets in retaliation for the shooting and then Israel launches a major invasion on Lebanon by land, sea and air.

United States of America: Barney Clark is the first recipient of an artificial heart.

TELEVISION AND FILM

January: three new stations are on the air: Central, TV South and TV South West... November: Channel 4 arrives...The film which is capturing the hearts of children is "ET" and the phrase from it, "phone home" is popular... Another box office success is "Gandhi", depicting the life of the charismatic Mahatma whose efforts paved the way to India's independence from the "Raj".

SPORT

It is a World Cup year in football; Italy beat Germany 3–1... In cricket, Ian Botham scores 208, his highest test score, against India... The FA Cup is won by Spurs who beat QPR in a replay match 1–0.

CONCLUSION

The phrase "chips with everything" has taken on a new meaning; the "micro-chip" has become increasingly important. First, there was the home computer and then as people realised the potential use of the "chip" other items were created: electronic games, toys, video recorders, watches, personal stereos, laser beams. Our world today is very different from the one in the fifties; we're in danger of being taken over by a "chip"!

1983

BRITAIN

January: breakfast television begins... It is now compulsory to wear seat belts in the front seats of cars... Danish trawlers are banned from fishing in British waters... An innocent man, Stephen Waldorf, is shot by police in London, because they believed him to be an escaped prisoner, David Martin.

February: the Thames Flood Barrier is raised for the first time; London is no longer in danger of being flooded when high tides from the North Sea occur, just when winter rains bring an excess of water trying to reach the open sea from the river...Yorkshire and South Wales miners are going on strike as a protest at planned pit closures.

April: Britain's £1 coin is in circulation...

May: the first wheel clamps are introduced in London to punish parkers who overstay their permitted time, or park in illegal places.

9th June, general election, the Tories are victorious again with a majority of 147 seats; Mrs T. begins her second term of office; "Thatcherism" is here to stay;

Privatisation's slowly creeping into the country... Michael Foot resigns as Labour Leader and is succeeded by Neil Kinnock... Bernard Weatherill is to be the new Speaker of The House of Commons.

July: MPs vote against the restoration of the death penalty.

October: the Conservative Party is facing a scandal as Cecil Parkinson, the Trade and Industry Secretary, admits to having an affair with his secretary, Sara Keays; he's resigning from his post and his replacement is Norman Tebbit...

Mrs Janet Walton from Liverpool is said to be overjoyed after giving birth to sextuplets – six girls... As Christmas approaches, the IRA is claiming responsibility for a terrorist car bomb explosion outside Harrods store in London.

ABROAD

Washington, the Senate approves a bill to make Martin Luther King's birthday a National Holiday... The United States claims another first in the history of space travel – 24th June, Sally Ride becomes the first woman to return from a space mission in the Challenger space shuttle.

SPORT

In Ireland the 1981 Derby winner, Shergar, is kidnapped and a ransom of £2 million is demanded... The trainer, Mrs Jenny Pitman is the first woman to train a Grand National winner as Corbiere is the first past the post...Manchester United win the FA Cup after a replay match against Brighton, 4–0... At Wimbledon, John McEnroe earns himself a reputation for throwing tantrums and arguing with umpires but he is the winner of the Men's Singles title.

FILM AND MUSIC

At the Oscars Richard Attenborough's "Gandhi" wins eight awards, the highest number ever for a British film...

August, Radio Caroline returns to the airwaves, three years after the previous ship sank in the North Sea...In music, the compact disc arrives on the market – each 4.75-inch disc has a playing time of just over an hour; it gives the music lover a higher standard of recording with no background noise, no wearing out or scratching but at a high price.

1984

BRITAIN

The ½p coin and the £1 note are being phased out... Harold Macmillan accepts an hereditary Earldom for his ninetieth birthday and is to be known as Lord Stockton... In London, the Metropolitan Police are allowing some of their officers to carry guns...

Bailiffs are clearing the main women's peace camp at Greenham Common...

March: a nation-wide miner's strike begins...

17th April, WPC Yvonne Fletcher is shot dead whilst on duty at an anti-Gaddafi protest outside the Libyan Embassy in London. Britain breaks off diplomatic relations with Colonel Gaddafi's Libya and Libyan diplomats are being deported...

Richard Branson takes over the collapsed Laker Skytrain and his first Virgin Atlantic flight to New York leaves Gatwick Airport – passenger tickets cost £99... A new divorce law which enables couples to end their marriages after only one year comes into operation... The magazine, "Titbits" closes after 104 years... The Education Secretary, Keith Joseph approves a new GCSE examination to replace the GCE 'O' level and CSE examinations... An eleven-day-old baby, Holly Roffey is the world's youngest heart transplant patient...

12th October, a bomb explodes at the Grand Hotel in Brighton; most of the cabinet members are staying there during the Conservative Party conference; it is a devastating attack against British politicians and intended to wipe out the Government. The IRA gloated, "Today we were unlucky, but remember we have only to be lucky once." The MP Sir Anthony Berry, and the wife of the government chief whip, John Wakeham, are dead. More than thirty seriously injured people are pulled from the rubble – including Norman Tebbit, the Trade and Industry Secretary and his wife who is paralysed. Mrs Thatcher had a lucky escape, as the bathroom she had been in minutes earlier was wrecked. She said, "Life must go on". Patrick Magee is charged with the murder of the five who died. He is given eight life sentences for the Brighton and other bombings.

15th September, the birth of Prince Henry to the Prince and Princess of Wales; he is to come to be known as Prince Harry...

The plight of famine-strickened Ethiopia hits the world headlines. Bob Geldof is moved by the heartbreaking pictures he sees on the television screen and asks some of his fellow pop stars to join him in the making of a record, "Do They Know It's Christmas", the celebrities call themselves Band Aid and are donating the proceeds from the record to help the starving in Ethiopia.

ABROAD

The Space Programme

February: the first untethered space walk takes place from the USA Shuttle Challenger...

Time & Tide

July: the Soviet Union claim another first in the history of space travel when cosmonaut Svetlana Savitskaya is the first woman to walk in space.

31st October, after Indian troops storm the Sikh's most holy shrine, The Golden Temple of Amritsar, Mrs Indira Gandhi is assassinated at her home; her son, Rajiv Gandhi, will succeed her. The incident has led to riots and deaths in India as the Hindu's begin to take revenge on the Sikhs.

SPORT

Jayne Torvill and Christopher Dean are awarded a gold medal for their ice-skating at the Winter Olympics in Sarajevo; all the judges give them maximum points for their performance... The Olympic Games are being held in Los Angeles; the Russians are boycotting them and in their absence America are winning a spectacularly large number of medals... The FA Cup is won by Everton, who beat Watford 2-0... At Wimbledon Martina Navratilova wins the women's singles title for the fifth time and the dynamic John McEnroe, despite his arguments with the umpires, wins the men's singles.

1985

BRITAIN

Sir Clive Sinclair finds the answer to our traffic problems; the electronics genius produces a battery and pedal-powered tricycle, "C5"; he's predicting that petrol-engine vehicles will be museum items by the turn of the century... Kim Cotton, already a mother of two children, is a "surrogate" mother; she is carrying a child for a woman who is unable to have children...

Protesters are being evicted from the cruise missile base at Molesworth in Cambridgeshire... Prescription charges are going up from £1.60 to £2... The government announces a computerised screening programme in a bid to cut cervical cancer deaths... The Al Fayed brothers gain control of the House of Fraser chain and Harrods store... A thirteen-year old genius, Ruth Lawrence, is awarded a first-class degree at Oxford... Bob Geldof organises a Live Aid concert – a large number of singers and groups assemble and perform in front of audiences at Wembley Stadium and the JFK Stadium in Philadelphia to raise money for the unfortunate in Ethiopia.

ABROAD

March: The Russian premier, Konstantin Chernenko dies after thirteen months as premier. He is buried in Red Square, Moscow and Mikhael Gorbachev's the new premier....

The climate is giving us cause for concern; scientists are warning of a greenhouse effect causing global warming. The weather is changing, Nice is experiencing an Arctic winter: instead of sunshine the beach is covered in snow, an unbelievable sight.

South Africa: racial tension continues... 21st March: the twenty-fifth anniversary of the Sharpeville massacre...there's rioting at the Langa township and the police shoot dead seventeen black people... Two positive moves are being made to end the apartheid problems: the government has ended the ban on mixed marriages and promises to restore citizenship to fifteen million black people living in "Homelands".

TELEVISION, FILM & MUSIC

Boy George, a man who wears women's make-up and clothes, is the latest idol... Others include Michael Jackson and the Jackson family and Madonna. Popular records are "The Power of Love", "I Know Him So Well" and "Dancing in the Street", which is a spin-off from the Live Aid concert. The compact disc, the "CD" is growing in popularity and gradually replacing the record...

"Out of Africa" is being shown on cinema screens... On the television screen, a new soap opera, "Eastenders", is gripping the nation and in competition with "Coronation Street".

Cilla Black is hosting a new programme, "Blind Date", where two complete strangers are sent on a "honeymoon" together.

SPORT

April: soccer hooliganism amongst fans in stadiums reaches epidemic proportions. In an attempt at finding a solution, the government plans to ban alcohol from problem football grounds in England and Wales...

May: there's a soccer rampage in Brussels. Liverpool fans run riot... The FA in London are banning English clubs from playing in Europe for the next season... In Switzerland UEFA are banning English clubs from playing in Europe indefinitely... 11th May, another football disaster: a stand at Bradford catches fire during the match with Lincoln; over forty fans are killed... Golf; the Ryder Cup comes back to Europe from the United States... Tennis, the German, Boris Becker, at seventeen becomes the youngest man to win the Wimbledon championship.

1986

BRITAIN

London, the world's first test-tube quintuplets are born... Canterbury, Mrs Thatcher and President Mitterrand sign an agreement to build the Channel Tunnel... The

Time & Tide

NSPCC states that child abuse is on the increase; there has been a ninety percent rise in twelve months... Statistics show that there's a general rise in crime, the figures for mugging, rape and murder are higher than in previous years... Mrs Simpson (the Duchess of Windsor) dies; after a funeral service at Windsor she is lain to rest beside her husband, the uncrowned Edward VIII, who abdicated in 1936... Divers find the wreck of the Titanic on the seabed... Bob Geldof introduces Sport Aid, his third attempt at helping to raise money for Ethiopia; it is a "Race Against Time".

THE ROYAL WEDDING

March: Buckingham Palace announces the engagement of Prince Andrew and Sarah Ferguson... Wedding fever's gripping the nation again... 23rd July, the big day! The ceremony's at Westminster Abbey... The Queen has conferred the titles of Duke and Duchess of York on the royal couple.

ABROAD

January: Gorbachev, the Russian Premier, proposes a fifteen year plan to eliminate all nuclear arms by the turn of the century... 28th January, a tragedy in America's space programme; the Challenger explodes just after take-off from Cape Canaveral; all seven astronauts are killed including Christa McAuliffe, a teacher who won the competition to be the first ordinary citizen in space. The problem is later blamed on a spell of unusually cold weather in Florida, which covers the test site in snow and ice: the cold shrinks some vital seals and flames escape to ignite the massive fuel tank.

April: the nuclear disaster which people feared would happen has occurred at Chernobyl Power Station in Russia. During an experimental operation while the reactor is under manual control, the operators make a false move and the whole reactor overheats and red-hot uranium spills out: there is widespread radioactive contamination, some of it reaching as far as Wales, so sheep may not be eaten!

The discovery of the AIDS virus is announced in Washington; after deaths due to contaminated blood used in transfusions in the USA it is announced that blood donors will be screened for AIDS; Britain pledges £1 million for research into this new killer virus after the World Health Organisation stated that AIDS has reached epidemic level.'

* * * * *

Charlotte closed her file and sat deep in contemplation. The wedding was not the only celebration for the Stephenson family that year. Wills and Charlotte were both sixty and they intended remembering 1987 as the year of parties. Wills hired the

Village Institute in May to celebrate his own birthday and again in September for Charlotte's. Both occasions were enjoyed by the community and family. They promised another 'do' in September, 1988 to celebrate their ruby wedding anniversary. However, before that event took place Wills received a fraught phone call from Ann stating that Jim had died within minutes of suffering a stroke; it was just after his sixty-sixth birthday. Wills was speechless, only three days earlier he had congratulated his brother and they had all enjoyed a family meal together, he had seemed so happy and well. Wills remembered how his brother had failed the medical and avoided conscription during the war. He had said he had a heart murmur, but he just could not be dead, not just before Christmas.

A year that had begun with such joy over an engagement, a forthcoming wedding and birthday celebrations ended sadly with another funeral. Alistair conducted the service at Fordingham Church. It was a bleak and cold December morning, the ground was covered with a blanket of snow when they assembled to say goodbye to James (Jim) Stephenson.

The tragedy of death lies in the fact that, despite its inevitability, it is the one thing nobody is ever really prepared for. Irene tried to gain comfort from Alistair's religious viewpoint; those left behind should rejoice in the fact that their loved one had been taken by God into a better place. She knew that she should be used to loss and funerals by now; her real problem this time was that she realised her own father's mortality.

Dear Daddy, he had always been there and she had come to rely on him. To her, he was immortal, but the fact that Uncle Jim had died in his sixties and her paternal grandparents had died at a young age, brought home to her the awful truth that one day she would lose her father, her one staying power. Brother, son, husbands, she had learned to live with their loss, but could she live without her father?

After the service, the family followed the coffin for the last journey to the crematorium. Julia and Martin had both been cremated and their ashes spread in the Garden of Remembrance. Jim had not stated his wishes but Wills felt that he would like the same as his wife and son. Neither Ann nor Hillary raised any objection to cremation; they watched with sadness and each said their silent farewell as the curtains closed and the coffin disappeared. Later just Ann, Hillary, Irene and Wills returned to watch the ashes gently fall on the garden. And then it was all over.

Christmas was particularly stressful for Irene; she was now the vicar's wife and had a prominent part to play throughout the festive season. She remembered the

Time & Tide

Christmases spent at Battersley and how much time, effort and energy Esther put into the smooth running of the church's celebrations. She had never shown signs of fatigue and always had a smile for the parishioners. Esther had been a good support for John and she intended supporting Alistair in the same way: she would smile and hide her grief.

December, like every other month of the year, came and went. She gave a sigh of relief when it was all over.

The next hurdle was the New Year festivities. They went to Whistbury, as usual, but Alistair returned early on New Year's Eve for the Night Watch service and early morning communion on New Year's Day.

She was thirty-eight when she returned with Wills and Charlotte on 1st January, 1988. Wills had bought her a new 'organiser' handbag; as she looked at it, she thought about all the things her father had bought her over the years but the one present she treasured most of all was the teddy bear from her fifth birthday. 'Teddy', looking well for his age, still sat on a chair in the bedroom, much to Alistair's amusement. Philip and David had both accepted 'Teddy' as part of the family and Alistair realised that it and Irene were inseparable. It was a case of, 'Love me, love my teddy bear'. After losing her string-ring she had no intention of losing good old teddy. Since Jim's death and the realisation of Wills' mortality, she had found herself hugging good old teddy most days; he was a comfort to her in her father's absence.

Death has a habit of drawing families together and that was the case for the Stephenson's. Hillary and Irene found themselves reminiscing about the fifties and their early days together at Silkington before they discovered they were related. They enjoyed pretending to be children again and wondered why they had been so keen on the idea of growing-up in the first place. Childhood now seemed like a land of magic that was inevitably ruined by adulthood!

Bill was doted over by all of the family; Hillary would complain that she did not want him spoiling. Yet, deep down, she was glad he had a few relatives; it was better than having no one at all. Tim was thought of as 'family'. The remaining members of the 'Stephenson clan', Wills, Charlotte, Irene, Ann, Tim, Hillary and Bill were like survivors from a disaster; they spent as much time together as possible wondering how long it would be before the next one was taken from them.

Elizabeth celebrated her eightieth birthday in June; it gave her great delight to announce that she was eighty years young. There was no party; the last big birthday party she had given was for John's sixtieth and he had only lived for a fortnight after that. She was not going to take any chances! She wanted to live to be a hundred and receive a telegram from the Queen or possibly King by then. Her great achievement was marked by a special dinner at a Nottingham hotel for family and a handful of friends.

However, in September Wills and Charlotte had another 'do' as promised and everyone celebrated their forty years together. On the Sunday during the church service they renewed their vows to each other. There was a tinge of sadness as Jim's presence was sadly missed. Alistair's comforting words were that life went on and Jim was present in spirit: he would want them to enjoy themselves. Ten years earlier they had celebrated with a holiday in Kenya, this time Irene gave them a present of the holiday of a lifetime – a trip to the Holy Land which was somewhere they had always wanted to visit. Irene certainly had vivid memories of her anniversary in Israel! She expected that her parents' holiday would be rather different from her own spent there.

During the last year of the decade Irene thought about her life philosophically. She was approaching forty and felt that as a vicar's wife she had found her true vocation in life. She was content with her lot, visiting parishioners, organising events and supporting her husband. Each time she walked through the churchyard and passed Danny's grave she would think of what might have been. She would have been a good doctor's wife, too! Her son's grave would cause her to ask the question, Why? Then, she would remember, it was really through his death that she found Alistair and probably, her true vocation and purpose in life.

While Irene was feeling content with life Wills was thinking about his future and retirement and Charlotte was obsessed with her hobby.

'1987

BRITAIN

January: Terry Waite, the Archbishop's envoy has disappeared in Beirut whilst negotiating for the release of foreign hostages...

6th March, The Herald of Free Enterprise car ferry leaves Zeebrugge with the bow doors still open and within minutes, water floods the lower car decks and causes the ferry to keel over and sink suddenly – we are mourning the sad deaths of more than 100 people... The Duchess of Windsor's jewellery is sold for £31 million... One of Mozart's notebooks is auctioned at Sotherby's, London for £2.3 million. (Truly amazing!)

June: Mrs Thatcher begins her third term of office, the first prime minister to be elected for a third consecutive term for more than a century... Princess Anne is given the title, Princess Royal...

19th August, a Michael Ryan has gone on the rampage in Hungerford shooting everyone in sight and then killing himself: he leaves fourteen people dead and fifteen wounded...

18th October, the HURRICANE comes! Many people thought that a storm was on the way. Reassurance came from the BBC weatherman Michael Fish that although there would be some "strong winds" there was nothing to worry about, but hours later seventeen are dead and people in the South of England wake up to find hundreds of trees blown down, roads blocked, houses wrecked and cars crushed in the storm of the century!

19th October, Black Monday! The bottom has fallen out of the stock market and fifty billion pounds are wiped off the value of stocks and shares...

11th November, An IRA bomb explodes killing eleven people and leaving many injured at a Remembrance Day parade in Enniskillen... Thirty people die in a fire at King's Cross Tube Station caused by a faulty escalator...

The government announces that a community charge (called the poll tax) will be introduced on 1st April, 1990 and free dental checks and eye tests are to be abolished.

ABROAD

In France, the former SS Officer Klaus Barbie known as "the butcher of Lyons", is found guilty of war crimes and sentenced to life imprisonment...

October: Fiji leaves the Commonwealth... Is there much of the Commonwealth left?

BRITAIN

3rd January, Mrs Thatcher has become the longest continuously serving prime minister of the century, having been in office for eight years and 244 days...

March: the new Social and Liberal Democratic Party is formed, David Steele and Robert McLennan are the interim leaders before a proper election... Prince Charles narrowly escapes death when he's caught in an avalanche whilst skiing in Switzerland; his friend Major Hugh Lindsay is killed...

April: the traditional British passport is to be replaced by a European one when people have theirs renewed.

July: there is an oilrig disaster in the North Sea killing 166 people; survivors describe the gas explosion on the Piper Alpha oilrig as being "like an atomic bomb going off"... Mercury Communications open the first non-British Telecom pay phones at London's Waterloo station...

8th August, the Duchess of York gives birth to Princess Beatrice Elizabeth Mary;

she's fourth in line to the throne... 22nd August, a historical day for the breweries! Pubs are now allowed to remain open all day.

December: Edwina Currie is causing a storm: she is stating that eggs are infected with salmonella which has led to a drop in egg sales and a nation of angry farmers demanding compensation. She fails to tell the public that salmonella always has occurred quite often in eggs – you just have to cook them properly! 12th December, thirty-six people die and more than 100 are injured when two trains collide at Clapham Junction station, London... 22nd December, a jet airliner is blown up by a terrorist bomb whilst flying over Scotland and crashes on the town of Lockerbie, killing 270 people... It is a Christmas of mourning for the nation...

Statistics reveal that people in the north of England are getting poorer while those in the south are becoming richer. House prices are still rising and we are becoming a more affluent society in general, but there are more people living alone or in single-parent families. Crime and homelessness are also on the increase. Mrs Thatcher announces a ten-year timetable for the renewal of Britain's inner cities and plans are unveiled showing the proposed redevelopment of the Canary Wharf docklands.

In education, the new Education Reform Bill brings the biggest shake-up in the education system for more than forty years. A National Curriculum and regular testing of pupils is being introduced; there is also provision for schools to opt-out of LEA control and receive funding directly from the Government. The Education Secretary, Kenneth Baker, states that the basics of English grammar should be taught; his ideas favour a more traditional approach to education as opposed to the progressive ideas which linger from the sixties.

ABROAD

1988 is a year for celebration in Australia; the first Europeans arrived in 1788. The main bicentenary celebrations are in Sydney on 26th January. Two million people watch the arrival of a replica of the "First Fleet" which brought the first convicts to the colony. The Prince and Princess of Wales are present for the occasion, as are 20,000 Aborigines, protesting against the celebrations and their poor living conditions. The Queen and Prince Philip make a state visit to Australia and the Queen opens the Expo '88 Exhibition in Brisbane, Queensland.

SPORT

The fifteenth Winter Olympics are being held at Calgary, in the province of Alberta in Canada; Eddie "The Eagle" Edwards is a well-known participant: He is a rank amateur, but although he has come last in most events he's acquired a dedicated following... The Football League celebrates its centenary year... In golf, Sandy Lyle is become the first Briton to win the Masters tournament in Augusta, Georgia... Steve Davis wins his fifth Embassy World Snooker Championship... The Olympic Games are taking place in Seoul, Korea... Soccer hooligans are now such a problem that the government proposes new legislation; all fans will need ID cards to watch matches in England and Wales.

LITERATURE & THE MEDIA

In literature, two works are in the headlines. Firstly, Peter Wright's "Spycatcher", his memoirs of MI5, banned in Britain, but freely available in America. This year, the ban has come to an end after the House of Lords decided that it was so freely available abroad that a ban in England seemed pointless. The other book, Salman Rushdie's "Satanic Verses" is published in September; it's considered by Moslems to be blasphemous because it speaks against Islam, the Prophet Mohammad and the Koran. The Ayatollah Khomeini has ordered Rushdie's execution, under Islamic law. His book is publicly burnt in Moslem communities, but despite the protests the publishers are continuing production.

In the media, Michael Grade is the successor of Jeremy Isaacs as head of Channel 4. The Home Secretary announces that there's to be a shake-up in television and radio to give viewers more choice: at least one new television and two satellite channels are coming.

1989

BRITAIN

9th January: a plane flying from London to Belfast has engine failure: the pilot attempts an emergency landing at the East Midlands airport but crashes on the M1 at Kegworth only seconds away from the runway; forty-four people are killed...

15th April, disaster strikes at the Hillsborough Stadium in Sheffield where Nottingham Forest and Liverpool fans are assembled to watch the FA Cup semi-final. Too many Liverpool fans pressing to get in from the street as the game starts, are directed into the same area, causing a crush; fixed steel fences, designed to prevent hooligans from getting on to the pitch, prevent fans from escaping and ninety-five die...

June: the House of Lords pass a bill privatising the water industry; it seems that there's little left from the nationalisation of the fifties...

July: we're experiencing the hottest summer since 1976, a drought is declared and this is causing problems of water shortage and restrictions on use...

October: the "Guildford Four" imprisoned for the pub bombing in 1975 are found innocent and freed after fourteen years in jail.

AIDS, unheard of in previous decades, is now an international problem... May, 1987, the British government backs an anti-AIDS campaign... It's reported that one person is dying of AIDS every day in Britain... This leads the government to launch a more explicit AIDS warning campaign... 24th January, 1988, London, 3000 people march for the rights of AIDS sufferers at the beginning of three-day conference, attended by delegates from 148 countries... This disease is a global threat to humanity and there is no known cure, so research into it is essential... It's estimated that, worldwide, five million people could be affected with the virus which is spread through infected blood and bodily fluids... The largest number of reported cases is in the United States, but it's thought that Africa is the country where the disease is most rapidly spreading...

SOUTH AFRICA

May, 1987, the ruling National Party begins its fortieth year in power... 1988, the protesting against apartheid continues... February: South Africa's archbishops, Desmond Tutu and Stephen Naidoo are arrested for defying the law and protesting outside Parliament... 8th June, around two million black workers go on strike for the day, after being requested to do so by the Congress of South African Trade Unions, as a protest against proposed legislation from the all-white government which would reinforce apartheid... The imprisoned South African leader, Nelson Mandela is being remembered by the world at large on his seventieth birthday... 11th June, celebrities are staging a day-long musical tribute at Wembley Stadium, watched by 80,000 fans in the stadium and by millions of television viewers in sixty countries around the world... July, there's a rally in Hyde Park demanding Nelson Mandela's release after twenty-four years of imprisonment... The film, "Cry Freedom", the story of the life and death in custody of the black activist Steve Biko, is banned in South Africa's cinemas... 1989, F W de Klerk succeeds P W Botha as leader of the National Party; the pressure's mounting for racial freedom... 13th September, Cape Town holds its largest anti-apartheid demonstration in thirty years and the "Free Nelson Mandela" campaign's gaining momentum.

ABROAD

April: the Polish Solidarity movement's legalised after an eight-year ban...

In China, there's an uprising amongst the students in Tiananmen Square over their dissatisfaction with the leadership, they want democratic reform with the needs of youth given consideration. The Chinese Government responds after more than a month of protests by sending soldiers into the square and ordering a massacre. More than 2,000 are killed in the sad ending of what had begun as a simple protest for human rights...

14th July, Bastille Day, a special day for celebration in France; it marks the bicentenary of the Revolution... September: the last Vietnamese troops leave Cambodia, marking the end of an eleven-year occupation...

23rd October, Hungary becomes a new Republic... November: at midnight on 9th/10th November the Berlin Wall comes down as quickly as it went up in 1961. For the first time in almost thirty years East and West Berlin are reunited. People flood into West Berlin, after a small section is physically dismantled – once it starts, thousands of students hack away at various sections of the wall: westerners go to collect pieces as mementoes! There is ecstasy in Prague after the Communist Party, in power since 1968, resigns...

December: America and Russia declare an end to the Cold War... With the changes in government in the Eastern Block countries, the removal of the Berlin Wall and the end of the Cold War, there's a new optimism for the coming decade.

THE MEDIA

February, 1989, Rupert Murdoch launches his £25 million Sky Television satellite network... Films on general release include "The Last Emperor", "Fatal Attraction", "Three Men and a Baby", "Who Framed Roger Rabbit?", the controversial "Last Temptation Of Christ" and "Rainman" with Dustin Hoffman which draws attention to autism... Television, the BBC brings us "Neighbours" from Australia and ITV says farewell to the long running soap opera, "Crossroads".

THE EIGHTIES

Another decade has come to an end: the decade of Thatcherism, the decade which has seen change in Russia with the election of Mikhael Gorbachev who brought "Glasnost" (openness) and "Perestroika" (reconstruction) into politics and an end to the Cold War. A decade where the nuclear accident at Chernobyl made man aware of the dangers to his environment. A decade with disasters as unthinkable as the sinking of the Titanic in 1912. A decade of progress forward and backward as the realisation dawns that there's so much of value in the discarded antiquities of former years. The bad old days of the fifties and sixties are now the "good old days" before hijacking, hooliganism and terrorism: the days of community spirit, a time when families stayed together and it was safe to walk the streets.

The sixties had been the decade that changed the world and the eighties have shown just how things had changed. Now, it's forward to the nineties...

The last decade of the century...'

Chapter 19
Fordingham, January, 1990

'I REALLY can't believe I'm forty. Even if my hair is slightly grey and I need glasses for reading.' Irene said, as they were having Sunday lunch with her parents. 'If you think time went quickly before, you're in for a shock,' Alistair replied. 'It seems like only yesterday, I turned forty and now...'

'I know, you're fifty this year!' Irene finished his sentence for him.

Wills was also aware of time passing; it would soon be time for him to retire. Irene had always assumed that when he had to leave the cottage and make way for the new manager her parents would move into No. 34 on the main road. It made sense: they would live in the largest of the cottages and continue letting the four smaller ones. However, her father had other ideas.

'Time goes quickly all right, I'll be retiring soon,' he said.

'Not for another couple of years,' Irene replied.

'Yes m'duck, but it'll fly by. In February we'll have been here thirty years.'

'Thirty years?' Alistair spoke in a tone which implied a questioning disbelief.

'That's right. We came on 29th February, 1960.' Irene said. 'I remember it well. This cottage seemed so large and I'd never seen orchards like these before. Everything was so impressive.'

'Well,' Wills began speaking again, 'Old Harry at Settler's Lodge on the Buxton Road is planning to sell up in the next couple of years. I thought we could buy it and move there.'

'What?' shrieked Charlotte, in the middle of serving her delicious bread and butter pudding.

'We could sell the properties and invest in the one place. It's got a few acres of land, stables and a barn which would convert into two flats. The house has four good bedrooms.'

'How long have you been thinking about this?' Charlotte asked.

'Oh, a while. Retirement's going to come and we can't stay here. I like the idea of a small-holding, a bit of garden, and with two flats we could continue letting accommodation to the regulars; those who've been coming for more than ten years.'

Irene was the first to break the silence which followed the surprise announcement. 'Sounds great, Dad! Go for it, m'duck!'

'Thanks m'duck!' he replied, whilst Charlotte was still getting used to the idea.

They finished the meal, each in their own thoughts. Irene was forty, Wills was planning for retirement, Charlotte was in a state of shock and Alistair had his own problems.

For Alistair the unthinkable was happening: women were being admitted to the priesthood in the Church of England. America already had its first female bishop, the Reverend Barbara Harris, who had been appointed in the United States of America's Anglican Church in September, 1988 and subsequently, in February, 1989 she was consecrated as a bishop at the Boston Episcopal Church. Alistair along with many of his fellow clergymen had been outraged by the whole thing. He was aware of the discussions at the Synod, but he hoped that the whole idea would be a seven-day wonder in this country. It would be dismissed; the Church would surely realise that the teaching of St Paul clearly stated that woman was created for man's needs. A woman's role was to be at the man's side, supporting him throughout his life, just as Irene supported him.

After lunch they strolled back to the vicarage. Once inside their home, Alistair said, 'What do you really think, darling?'

'About what?'

'Your father's retirement plans.'

'It's great. Whatever Mum thinks or says, they'll do it. He'll have been thinking about it for sometime. Just waiting for the right moment to mention it. They'll have a short discussion and he'll sway her to his way of thinking. She'll see herself as "the Lady of the Lodge". She's always liked being the wife of a man with property. She'll enjoy redecorating. I'll bet the cottages are on the market before the end of March.'

'Why March?'

'Best time. They'll be sold before the summer. He'll invest his money and make a private deal with Harry. He'll have the stables and barns converted before they move in.'

'Your mother'll go along with his plans, then?'

'Yes.'

The distance and coldness between Irene and Charlotte had continued to grow;

she still remembered how she had felt when Charlotte had not been at the bus stop on that one school day: a child never forgets a thing like that.

Alistair was thinking how lucky his father-in-law was to have a wife who was subservient to him. Irene supported her husband, but she had her own life too and he feared that she would disagree with him over the ordination of women priests: this was something he must keep to himself.

Irene was right. In the middle of March, a month before Easter, 'For Sale' signs went up on three of the cottages. He was keeping two of the smaller ones to accommodate the regulars through the season. The property market was good, they were sold in two months and his income from the three sales was almost £300,000. He thought of his initial investment of £5,000 and realised how shrewd he had been; his idea of cottages for tourists had, over twenty-five years paid handsome dividends.

A year later he was the owner of Settler's Lodge. There may well have been a war in the Gulf but that did not stop Wills' plans. Settler's Lodge dated back 200 years; a stone L-shaped building with a large heavy oak front door which opened into a massive hallway. The stairs were on the left-hand side and at the back was a large ingle-nook fireplace. Large oak doors on each side of the hall opened into large rooms: the left-hand side was a lounge and the right, a dining room: both had ingle-nook fireplaces.

At the far end of the dining room was an addition to the original property. The exterior had been carefully built to blend in with the rest of the stone but inside was a modern kitchen in dark oakwood to complement the wooden doors. This was Charlotte's dream kitchen. Upstairs were four bedrooms and a bathroom. For the whole year before Wills' retirement, Charlotte was in her element; she carefully planned the décor of each room and was looking forward to their first Christmas in this 'olde worlde' cottage. She could visualise 'chestnuts roasting by the open fire'; their first Christmas in the lodge was going to be one that they would remember.

Wills was more interested in the outside. He eventually got planning permission for the conversions; the barn and the stables became two cosy flats. Then there was the garden, orchard and fields; these he planned to deal with properly after his retirement. He was going to have a farm again just like in his childhood days. The name was changed; he could not live in Settler's Lodge; it had to be Stephenson's Lodge.

They moved into their new home on 15th May, 1992, three days before his sixty-fifth birthday. His retirement was good news for Mark: Lord Fordingham promoted him to estate manager and he moved into Orchard Cottage. Things were looking up for him. One of the changes on the estate over the years had been the increase in the number of horses. When Wills arrived there were only three, now there were eight and a full-time groom was needed. Mark's son, Thomas, was given the position; he moved back to Fordingham to live with his father. Mark had given him the largest bedroom; he preferred the second room because that was the one Irene had used.

On Wills' birthday, there was a traditional retirement party in the afternoon. All the staff were called into the drawing room of the Hall and Charlotte, Alistair and Irene were invited as well. Wills had given thirty-two years of good service and Lord and Lady Fordingham, now in their seventies, wanted to show their appreciation for such loyalty. After the champagne and a speech from Lord Fordingham, Wills was given an exceptional retirement present, an antique grandfather clock. Both Wills and Charlotte were speechless; she was the first to utter, 'Thank you, your Lordship. It's beautiful'.

She could already see it in the hall opposite the staircase and knew that it was the finishing touch to her new home.

The staff all applauded and Wills was fighting back the tears. He had been happy and lucky to be able to earn a living in a job he enjoyed. He had also been fortunate enough to be in employment through the changing times, times of a recession and high unemployment.

Wills was aware of people saying, 'Speech! Speech!'

He had already received some gifts from friends and staff. Irene and Alistair had given him an unusual gift, but one that he wanted, a hencoop and hens! He was going to have his own free range eggs.

The staff had bought him a new lawn mower and he had received smaller gifts of whisky, plants for his garden, books and cards from well-wishers.

Eventually, he found his voice and said, 'I, we, Charlotte, Irene, have all enjoyed living here and thank you, Your Lordship, Your Ladyship, everyone for everything through the years.'

It was a clumsy speech, he knew that, but nothing could have prepared him for the way he felt; there were so many memories and emotions.

As the proceedings came to an end, Wills shook everyone by the hand and said a last 'thank you' to Lord and Lady Fordingham. It was a sad man who collected his few remaining belongings from what had been his office and home for so long. Mark had already settled in and it felt as if he had never been there; it was like walking into a stranger's home, he looked around and realised it was time to move on. He had a new life ahead of him. That evening, he and Charlotte were going out for a meal to celebrate his birthday and tomorrow he would begin working his own small farm.

Irene and Alistair walked back through the village to the vicarage. She was aware of a distance between them; she had enough experience of marriage to know when something is wrong. That evening as they sat in their lounge, she said, 'What is it, darling?'

'What's what?'

'You've been distant and dreamy for sometime.'

'Really, it must be my age, my love. Today, has made me realise how near I am to sixty-five.'

'Oh, come on, you've got years to go yet!'

'Thirteen, to be precise, and they'll fly by.'

'Shall I start planning now?' she laughed, 'Anyway, you're dedicated to the service of God. I can't believe that you'll ever retire. You and I will grow old disgracefully together. We'll still be here when you're seventy and I'm sixty. We'll be walking over to the church together, holding hands and supporting each other. We'll be talking of the "good old days" when we were young. God and our memories will keep us together.'

'Yes, dear.' He replied; he left her with her idyllic thoughts. He could not bear to hurt her. She had already suffered so much.

The summer months passed by. Wills and Charlotte were happy in their new home. There were freshly-laid eggs for breakfast every morning; Wills was enjoying his new life, a life which gave him freedom and less responsibility. He bought some sheep and a couple of goats; he had a nice vegetable garden and fruit trees in the orchard. Each time he went outside to tend his sheep, pick fruit or vegetables he was in his element, a child again back on his father's farm before the war: that awful war which changed everything.

Irene would often visit them in the mornings and Wills' strong bond with her told him that something was wrong; he feared his daughter was heading for another disaster in her life. If he questioned her, she would give the impression that all was well because she did not want to spoil her father's second childhood with what seemed quite trivial. On the surface her marriage was fine; the parishioners had not noticed any change in Alistair. Only she knew that something was wrong; they were in an ocean, drifting further and further apart but they still loved each other. It did not make any sense but as long as Alistair remained silent or fobbed her off with excuses, if she suggested that he had problems he was not sharing with her, there was nothing she could do.

Christmas came and Charlotte was more excited than she had been since her childhood days. She decorated the house with holly, ivy and mistletoe and had a large tree in the hall. If there had been a prize for the best decorated house in the district, she would have won it. Irene decorated the vicarage and the church. The traditional village events took place, the school nativity play, the parties, the Christmas fete, the carol-singing and parishioners came to the vicarage with Yuletide greetings. Irene welcomed them as she always did but deep down she had a feeling that it was all a grand finale. They went to Stephenson's Lodge for Christmas dinner with Wills, Charlotte and Elizabeth. Then, on New Year's Eve, they celebrated the end of another year and looked forward to a new one.

January had arrived and Alistair was in torment. God had put him in an impossible position; he was experiencing a 'crisis of faith'. He could retire from the priesthood; but Alistair had dedicated his life to God and retiring was just as impossible as remaining and accepting women priests. Why do things have to change? Change causes chaos and disorder in an organised society. Things were happening too quickly. His bishop was a trendy man, Alistair was sure that he would never understand his feelings on the new developments. Why could women not be content with their lot in life? This was a question which was haunting Alistair. Why could they not be subservient like St Paul had said they should be? Women participating in a man's world was unthinkable. After much wrestling with his conscience Alistair knew that there was only one course of action open to him.

On a Saturday morning at the end of January Irene heard the alarm clock buzz as usual at 6.30. Alistair always switched it off, got up, went into his study for morning meditation and would return at 7.30 with a cup of tea for her. The alarm carried on ringing.

'Switch it off, darling,' she uttered, half asleep. There was no response, the alarm continued. Irene woke up quickly; she looked at her husband's side of the bed. It was empty. She assumed he was already downstairs and switched the alarm off herself before going back to sleep. The next time she woke it was 8.00 am and she had overslept. Why had Alistair not brought her her usual drink? Their routine was like clockwork; it had to be that way because of their numerous appointments and responsibilities.

She jumped out of bed, rushed onto the landing and shouted, 'Darling, where are you?'

There was no reply. She thought he must have gone over to the church or been called out by one of his congregation. She quickly washed, dressed, and went downstairs for a cup of coffee and a piece of toast.

Thanks to her husband she was half an hour late. It was so inconsiderate of him but unusual; there would be an explanation but she would have to wait until later for that because she was opening up the Barnardo's shop and unless she hurried she would be late.

She returned at lunchtime to an empty vicarage. She walked over to the church, but that was empty. Had he an appointment? She went back to the vicarage and into the study to look at his diary which was on the desk; on top of it lay an envelope with her name on it. She opened it:

'My darling Irene,

I am sorry to do this to you. You have already suffered so much. In the changing circumstances, I cannot remain a practising vicar. I shall not be returning. I will always love you and pray that God will give you the strength to carry on.

Your loving husband,

Alistair.'

Irene sank into the chair, the words dancing on the page in front of her eyes, '*I shall not be returning.*'

It could not be true; he would never leave her or the Church. What were the 'changing circumstances'? Where was he? Was he contemplating suicide? Why had he not talked to her?

She did not want to believe it and for the time being she need not; if she ignored the letter and the fact that her husband had left her then it would not be true. She dismissed it from her mind; it was all a big mistake. She went upstairs; all of his belongings were still there. If he were leaving he would have taken his clothes and his most treasured possession, his Bible; he would never leave that behind and so he must be returning. He would walk through the door soon with a bouquet of flowers for her and go into the study to put the finishing touches to his Sunday sermons. There was nothing to worry about, nothing to fear: all she had to do was wait.

The afternoon passed by and her illusion of his return with a bouquet of flowers was sadly fading. She began to panic as the true reality of the situation slowly dawned. Tomorrow was Sunday: The sermons were prepared, but who would deliver them? In a desperate bid for help she phoned Alistair's friend Ian, the man who had married them. He came, read the note and wanted to contact the bishop. Irene pleaded with him to wait until Monday hoping that her beloved husband would have returned by then. His feelings of compassion for her persuaded him to arrange cover for the services rather than do his duty and tell the bishop.

She sat by the phone on Sunday hoping he would call. Early on Monday morning the phone rang; she rushed to answer it. 'Alistair?' she shouted down the receiver.

There was a silence at the other end.

'Alistair?' she repeated. He had not returned. Ian's heart sank. He knew what he had to do but found it difficult to speak to Irene. All his training and years as a priest had not prepared him for this. He felt that he was betraying his friend but he must inform the bishop.

'No, Irene. I'm sorry. It's not Alistair. It's Ian. He hasn't returned then?'

'No.' Her voice whimpered.

'You know what I have to do, don't you?'

After a short silence, she uttered, 'Yes. Do it.' She replaced the receiver.

She thought she had made peace with God, but it seemed she was wrong: he was still punishing her. She wandered round the vicarage, aimlessly, in and out of the rooms. What was she going to do? Then she picked up the phone and dialled.

'Oh Daddy, Alistair's gone. What am I going to do?'

The words were familiar to Wills.

'All right, m'duck. Daddy's coming. Everything'll be all right.' He spoke calmly, having been expecting something to happen, but inwardly he was seething. How could his son-in-law do this to her? Wills was not a violent man, but if he ever met Alistair again, he would not be responsible for his actions.

Charlotte, on the other hand, was secretly pleased that her daughter had once again failed in a marriage. She had succeeded where Irene had not. She smiled to herself as she looked at her diaries.

'THE NINETIES

Mobile phones are slowly creeping into society: the need for being in constant communication is growing. Modern life's fast and speed in all things is essential. The world appears to be shrinking; it's now possible to travel round the world in eighty hours, not eighty days! The phrase "global village" has been coined as the vast world, once thought to be unreachable by the majority is now only unreachable for a minority: it's been reduced to a village. The negative side of such progress is becoming apparent. The effort of keeping up with the ever increasing pace, the worry of keeping a job or just surviving in the global village is taking its toll on people's mental health. Sport and therapy are becoming increasingly important: Marathon running, keeping fit, aerobic classes, regular visits to a health club or a counsellor are considered essential for survival in the new rat-race.

1990

BRITAIN

June: Dr. David Owen announces the death of the newly formed SDP because its membership is too small to function effectively...

Brian Keenan, the Irish hostage, captured in Beirut in 1986 is released; he claims that at least one British hostage, John McCarthy, is still alive...

22nd November, "Mrs T" resigns; after disagreeing with European Policy, the Conservatives unite in an attempt to oust her. Her replacement is John Major. Thatcherism comes to an end...

1st December, 11.15 am there's celebration in the Channel Tunnel; the tunnellers from both sides meet. For the first time since the Ice Age it's possible to walk from England to France: Britain's no longer an island, but a part of Europe.

ABROAD

In football, Germany beat Argentina in the World Cup... 2nd/3rd October, the reunification of Germany takes place at midnight...

November: the declaration of the end of the Cold War is signed in Paris...

December: Lech Walesa, the leader of the Polish Solidarity Union wins a landslide victory in the Presidential elections; he's proclaiming the beginning of the Third Polish Republic.

1991

BRITAIN

Anne-Marie Dawe is the RAF's first female flight navigator... Dr. George Carey is elected as the new Archbishop of Canterbury...

14th March, another miscarriage of justice comes to light: the Birmingham Six, imprisoned in 1975 for the Birmingham pub bombings are released after serving sixteen years of their original sentence...

April: a Winchester man is the first in England to be convicted and sentenced to jail for raping his wife...

June: five homosexual couples marry in Trafalgar Square at a Gay Rights demonstration... John Major introduces the Citizen's Charter in an effort to improve public services...

August: John McCarthy is released after being held as a British captive for five years and three months in Lebanon... Jackie Mann's released after two and a half years in captivity in Beirut...

November: There's great rejoicing: Tom Sutherland and the last British hostage Terry Waite are released...

1st December: shops across Britain are opening on a Sunday and defying the Sunday trading laws.

ABROAD

5th September, Moscow, The Congress of People's Deputies vote to wind up the USSR and replace it with a new Commonwealth... 21st December, the Soviet Union ends... 25th December, Mikhail Gorbachev resigns; as he gives his resignation speech the red flag is lowered over the Kremlin for the last time: it's farewell to the old Russia...

1992

BRITAIN

The magazine, Punch, closes after 150 years of publication... Following the previous year's heatwave, the nation's suffering its worst drought since 1745; water reserves are at their lowest level and dropping. Scientists are warning that it's an early sign of global warming...

April, general election: the Conservatives are victorious: John Major continues as prime minister. Neil Kinnock resigns as Labour leader and is replaced by John Smith. Betty Boothroyd is the first woman in six centuries to be the Speaker of the House of Commons...

September: the Royal Mint introduce a new, smaller 10p coin...

THE ROYAL FAMILY, Are they a monarchy in crisis?

23rd March, 1990, The Duchess of York gives birth to her second daughter, Princess Eugenie Victoria...

June, 1991, Prince William has an operation on his skull after being hit by a golf ball; the media are focusing on the fact that his mother stays with him but his father leaves to attend public duties... There are rumours that all is far from well in the marriages of the Waleses and the Yorks.

December, 1992, the Queen describes her year as "Annus Horribilis"... After much speculation, the Duke and Duchess of York separate and Princess Anne and Captain Mark Phillips divorce... In June, Andrew Morton publishes his book about Diana's life, telling of alleged marriage difficulties, her eating disorder and attempted suicide; the book causes a storm, such revelations from within the House of Windsor are unthinkable... When the spotlight moves from Diana, it focuses on Sarah, the Duchess of York; there's an outcry when photographs appear of her sunbathing, wearing only bikini briefs, whilst with her financial advisor on holiday in France... In November a fire causes considerable damage to part of Windsor Castle; further public condemnation comes when it seems as if the money for the restoration would be coming from public funds... The final devastating blow comes on 9th December, John Major announces in the House of Commons that the Prince and Princess of Wales are to separate, but it will not affect the Princess' constitutional right to become Queen. Public reaction questions this fact. How could she possibly sit by his side as Queen, if they are separated, as opposed to married? The only happy event in the royal calendar is the second marriage of Princess Anne to Commander Tim Laurence in a private ceremony at a church in Crathie, near Balmoral... 17th December, the Australian prime minister announces that in the future Australians would swear allegiance to Australia and not the Queen... Finally, two days before Christmas, The Sun newspaper publishes a leaked copy of Her Majesty's Christmas speech: It's definitely not a good year for the Queen!

ABROAD

SOUTH AFRICA

11th February, 1990, Nelson Mandela, imprisoned since 1964, is released. This marks the beginning of real hope for change and an end to apartheid... May: Mr Botha resigns from the National Party over government talks with the ANC... November: the government announces that all political prisoners are to be released... 1st February, 1991, President de Klerk states that the last apartheid laws are to be abolished... 18th March, 1992, President de Klerk's reforms for South Africa are approved in a referendum... At last, South Africa achieves the dream of the American, Martin Luther King that "black would walk with white": Apartheid is over!

AMERICA

August, 1992, a twelve-year-old Florida boy makes legal history by winning a divorce from his biological parents, who he accuses of neglecting him... Hurricane Andrew is sweeping through the south of Miami, wrecking hundreds of buildings

271

and leaving the area in a state of complete devastation... September, 1992, the US Space shuttle, Endeavour, is launched to make America the first country to put a married couple into space... November: Bill Clinton, the Arkansas Governor wins the presidential elections; the Democrats are back in power after twelve years of a Republican Government...

Yugoslavia ceases to be one nation after the Bosnian Serbs create their own Republic... 15th January, Croatia and Slovenia declare independence...

March: fighting begins in Sarajevo after Bosnia and Herzegovina declare independence...

April: Euro-Disney opens near Paris...

July: the French lorry drivers are blocking roads as a protest against the new driving licence system: thousands of holidaymakers are stranded on French roads... Chris Patten is to be Hong Kong's last Governor...

September: the European Parliament celebrates its fortieth anniversary...

4th October, a cargo plane crashes into a housing complex in Amsterdam only minutes after leaving Schipol airport.

SPORT

July, 1991, Nigel Mansell wins the British Grand Prix and claims his seventeenth Grand Prix victory, a record for an Englishman... Boxing is now a controversial sport: Michael Watson faces brain surgery after he collapses in the ring after a fight against Chris Ewbank...

1992, Olympic year: The Winter Olympics are being held at Albertville in France... The Olympic flame is in Barcelona and Linford Christie is Britain's hero; he is only the third Briton ever to win the 100 metres title, in 9.96 seconds. Sally Gunnell wins the first British track gold medal since 1964 in the 400 metres hurdles.

ARTS & THE MEDIA

30th July, 1991, a crowd of around 150,000 listen during torrential rain to Pavarotti's free thirtieth anniversary concert in Hyde Park. News pictures show Princess Diana smiling in her plastic mac.

November, 1992, London, Agatha Christie's mystery, "The Mousetrap", is celebrating its fortieth year.

Films on general release are "Ghost", "Terminator 2", "Silence of the Lambs", "The Godfather III", "Dances With Wolves", "Robin Hood, Prince of Thieves".

Television is now the ideal companion for the couch potato. Breakfast television began in the eighties, but all day television is now a reality. "Soaps" are a part of

*daily life for many: "Home and Away" and "A Country Practice" are two imported
from Australia and popular in the afternoons. Another imported soap, which is
strictly adult material, is "Cell Block H".*

*Quiz programmes are a further form of entertainment; a popular one on Channel
4 is "Countdown" in which Carol Vordermann plays with numbers, and contestants
vie to make anagrams from a random selection of letters. ITV has a winning formula
for morning viewers in a magazine type of programme, "This Morning" with
Richard and Judy: a programme which covers all types of issues and has popular
daily features: Richard and Judy are becoming the Morecambe and Wise of the
nineties bringing sunshine, laughter and smiles into so many homes.'*

* * * * *

Charlotte was still smiling as she looked across at her tearful daughter. 'Cheer up!
Your father will sort things out. He always has done.'

Irene sensed her mother's sarcasm, but she was past caring. It seemed as if she
was jinxed; all her relationships ended in some sort of disaster and she knew that
her mother found some kind of perverse satisfaction in that. She had been blessed
with the best of fathers and the worst of mothers, but you cannot choose your
relations and even if you could, Irene felt sure her choice would be a bad one.

That February was a blur to her. The gossip went round the village; Alistair had
left his wife and conclusions were drawn! He had another woman; that's what
happened last time Irene's husband left her! It was a sad irony that she was loved
by so many men yet she seemed destined to be alone. Once again, through
circumstances beyond her control, her life was changing...

Chapter 20
Stephenson's Lodge, June, 1993

IRENE WAS SITTING in the garden with her parents and wondering why she was once again living with them.

Twice she had left home to marry and twice she had returned. Wills was pleased with her return but felt considerable anguish over the circumstances which brought her back to him.

In February the bishop had visited her with incredible news; even in her dreams she could never have imagined anything like it. Alistair had written and tendered his resignation; the bishop told her that on 11th November last year, the Church of England had voted in favour of ordaining women priests, the final straw for Alistair. He had gone abroad and did not want his whereabouts to be known; as far as he was concerned this crisis of faith was the most devastating thing in his life but it was completely personal and something he could not share; he had not expected anyone to understand his predicament. The bishop had been kind to Irene and allowed her to remain in the vicarage until the end of March.

During that time Wills had helped her sell most of the furniture and his personal possessions. His instructions had come in a letter to the bishop; the proceeds were to go to the Leprosy Mission because he felt he had been forced out of the Church and become an outcast like the lepers. His final words had been given to Irene verbatim, 'Tell Irene, I'm sorry. She knows we must stay married, our vows are until death. She has no idea what the Church has done to me. I really had no alternative. The Church will regret the day it opened its doors to women. I shall suffer for the rest of my life but I know she will be all right. Wills will look after her. He always has done. My father-in-law is a good man. I wish him a long and happy retirement.'

As the villagers learned the truth they were more sympathetic towards Irene; their hostility grew towards Alistair the man they had once respected as a man of God, but a true priest does not leave his flock and go into a self-imposed exile any more than a shepherd would leave his sheep. By the end of March Irene had moved to

Stephenson's Lodge with her few personal possessions. Wills had made one of the bedrooms into a bed-sit and added an en-suite shower room for her; he knew she would need her own space away from Charlotte. In her own space, sitting in a chair, was her most treasured possession, her thirty-eight-year-old teddy bear!

The whole situation had left Irene devastated. Alistair had assumed that she would return to her family and carry on with her life. He was wrong; she had returned to her family but she felt alone again and this time she was not even sure of her status in life. She could not divorce him because she could not find him; she was alone yet married. The law stated that in the case of a disappearing partner, the remaining party must wait seven years before applying for an end to the marriage and being declared widowed on the assumption that if the partner had not returned in that time he or she was probably dead. Seven years of not knowing where Alistair was; he had not realised just how hurt she would be or how she would feel about being deserted. He had been too wrapped up in his own crisis of faith to really think about the effect his action would have on her.

The year came to an end and she hoped that he would come to his senses and return; Christmas would be the ideal time for that. Sadly, he did not and when Christmas was over for another year the family celebrated her forty-fourth birthday in the usual way at Whistbury. Irene found it hard to believe that she used to enjoy the New Year and her birthday celebrations. Now, they just served as a reminder of the long gone, happier days of her life.

She had been dreading January and the anniversary of his departure. It meant one year had passed, one year of being alone, waiting, worrying and hoping; not knowing whether he was sick or well, had shelter or food, was alive or dead. People told her not to worry but to get on and enjoy her own life; they did not understand either the hurt or the feelings she still had for Alistair. She did not know how she was going to continue with her life in an ignorance, which was far from blissful.

Another year came and went; she slowly settled into her new way of life. Her strong character, friends and loving father helped her come to terms with the fact that she just had to watch time pass by, wait patiently and smile. There was nothing else she could do. The year 2000 was approaching and plans were being made for the Millennium. The only thing Irene could see beyond the turn of the century was official widowhood and a future of more long bleak days ahead but she carried on with her life and kept smiling; a smile which carefully hid her true feelings.

Each time she saw Hillary with Bill it was a sad reminder of the son she had lost. Bill was in his teenage years and tall for his age; he was interested in the Stephenson empire created by his grandfather and had every intention of creating an even bigger one when he took hold of the reins.

Irene frequently visited her cousin, who now lived in the house in Bakewell whilst her mother lived in the flat. On one of these occasions they were talking about by-gone days and Hillary said, 'I used to envy you. We both did, Martin and I. You seemed to have everything on the estate. Neither of us were happy then.'

'Everything! Oh come on. I'd lost my brother. My mother was hostile towards me, bitter and jealous. Still is. I lost Danny. Me, have everything?'

'It seemed like it at the time. Martin never wanted Dad's empire, neither of us did. But Jim had such high hopes for us. Both of us, and we let him down.'

'No you didn't. He felt he'd failed you. Martin took his own life and you rebelled and got pregnant.'

'So much wasted time, so much misunderstanding. All those years when I hoped Bill would come and collect me.' Hillary sighed. 'I did everything I could in the hope that Jim would send me back to Silkington. If only I'd tried, we could have been a happy family, Mum, Jim and me.'

'He loved you, Hillary, you gave him happiness in his last years, particularly when you changed your name. It was important to him, and young Bill, he loved his grandson. You made his last years good. Don't forget that. Bill's beginning to look like him, and if he carries on the business, Uncle Jim will look down and smile. It'll all have been worthwhile. Don't be so hard on yourself.'

'He never even knew who Bill's father was, yet it didn't make any difference.'

'Does Bill know who his father is?'

'Oh yes, he's known for some time but we treat it as a secret between the three us.'

'Who? Hillary. I won't tell. Remember our childhood days? We shared all our secrets. He was married, wasn't he?'

'No. I just told Jim that so I wouldn't have to get married.'

'Hillary. Who is it? Do I know him?' Irene was getting excited. At last she was going to find out the great family secret.

'Oh yes, everybody knows him, even Martin knew him.'

'Martin?'

'Yes.'

'Hillary...come on…'

'Tim.'

'Tim who?'

'Tim, Tim Jones.'

'Tim?' She exclaimed in total disbelief. No one would ever have dreamed that Tim could be the father; he had been Martin's lover; how could he have fathered his sister's child?

'Yes.'

'Are you sure? He's gay.'

'I know. That's why we kept it quiet. If Dad had found out… Could you imagine it? I just wanted a baby. It wasn't difficult to get him into bed when I told him what I wanted. I promised I wouldn't hold him to any relationship once I got pregnant.'

Irene took hold of her cousin's hand, 'Dad would have been delighted. But I won't tell. The secret's safe with me. Tim. Well, well.'

Irene kept the secret, but each time she saw Bill, after that revelation, she noticed a resemblance between him and Tim and wondered why she had not thought of it before.

Back on the Fordingham estate the wheels were still turning smoothly in Mark's capable hands. Mark had everything he had ever dreamed of; well almost everything! He lived at Orchard Cottage with one of his sons and ran a country estate; he had come a long way since his first day as assistant gardener back in the fifties. He would always be grateful for the help and training he received from both Alan and Wills. Despite his divorce and the fact that he hardly ever saw his younger son, he felt he had been lucky in life's lottery. The new National Lottery run by Camelot encouraged people to buy tickets in the hope of becoming millionaires. Mark did not buy tickets; money could not buy happiness. In the new millennium he expected his happiness to be complete. At last, he would be able to marry Irene; she had slipped through his fingers before but once the seven years were over he planned to marry her.

They were very good friends and saw a lot of each other. Sometimes, they would go out together but Irene did not consider their meetings as proper dates. They would go for walks, out for a drink or a meal, visit shows. They seemed to have so much in common, far more than she had realised. They would talk about the old days; there were some things which they remembered from the 'swinging sixties' which everyone else around them, had long since forgotten. The one thing neither of them mentioned was the hayloft; she thought it should remain her secret which would go with her to her grave. She had no idea that he had watched them escape to their hideaway and he was certainly not going to tell her.

Another marriage was the last thing on Irene's mind, but Mark had other ideas. He was planning to propose to her on Christmas Eve, one week before the Millennium. He knew that she would be at Whistbury for the annual party and her fiftieth birthday. It was to be his Christmas present to her and he was sure she would say, 'Yes'. When she returned in the New Year she would officially become a widow; they could plan a spring wedding and she could return to Orchard Cottage, her happy childhood home. They would have a blissful marriage; the type that dreams are made of. As the century came to a close Mark was a very happy man!

Throughout the nineties Irene kept in touch with David's family and her good friend, Jane Meadows. Jane kept her up to date with the developments at Harwood; some of the children who were now on the school register had parents who were old boys and girls of the school. It seemed impossible, but it was twenty years since she had taught there; her one memento and a treasured possession along with Teddy was the piece of Wedgwood given to her by 5C. She realised just how happy she had been in those early teaching days; it was nice to hear about the children she had looked after for five years. Some were successful in their chosen careers, others were not so fortunate; some had married and were still happy in Harwood and their children were carrying on the family name on the school register.

Philip was also a memory from those days, one she would rather forget; a cold shiver ran down her spine each time she thought about him. Despite all the love he had given her, there was only one thing she remembered; that last time when he raped her. She was curious however to know what had happened to her ex in-laws; her presence had changed their lives, that was something she had learned to live with.

One day when she was tending her son's grave and Philip was far from her thoughts, a figure clothed in clerical attire walked towards her, his grey hair and stature made her think her prayers had been answered. The nightmare was over, Alistair had returned.

'Alistair?'

'No, Irene. I was sorry to hear about Alistair.'

She looked again. Was she hallucinating? It couldn't be her late father-in-law. John was dead.

'Don't you recognise me?' the voice continued.

Irene stared and then uttered, 'Philip? Philip?' She went cold.

He knelt down beside her. 'Yes. It's me. I heard through the church grapevine Alistair had moved to Fordingham and married the estate manager's daughter, Irene. It had to be you. I hoped he would make you happy.'

'Philip, I never expected to see you again.' She paused. 'You're a vicar!'

'Yes. Like Dad.'

'How's what's-her-name, Sarah?'

There was a loud silence between them. Philip looked down and then casting Irene a short glance he said, almost in a whisper, 'She's dead.'

'Oh Philip, I'm so sorry,' she heard herself saying and was more surprised because she actually meant it.

'She died in childbirth. There were complications. We'd only been married a month.'

'The child?'

'Sarah, she's just made me a grandfather.'

'Congratulations.'

Philip suddenly noticed the name on the headstone, *James David Taylor.*

'Why are you putting flowers on this grave? Not Danny's?'

There was another loud silence before Irene spoke, 'James was my son.'

'Oh no. I'm so sorry.' He put his hand on her shoulder. 'You've really suffered,' he continued, 'I'm so sorry.

'There hasn't been a day when I haven't thought about what I did to you. It was unforgivable. There's never any excuse for what I did to you.' He paused; he wanted her forgiveness even though he knew it was impossible, just as it was impossible to change the whole past. Then, after looking at the name on the headstone again, he continued, 'James Taylor? Has there been another marriage?'

'Remember David Taylor? My head of department? Lived in Kidderminster?'

'Oh yes.'

She looked up at him, 'He helped me pick up the pieces, after you left.'

'What happened?'

'He was killed in a car accident. He didn't know I was pregnant. James's death was a cot death.' She paused. 'He lived for ninety days before joining his father.'

'You've really suffered, haven't you?' he said, almost in a whisper.

'We both have. Yet we must carry on.' Irene spoke with strong determination.

This was something she had learned over the years. Whatever happened to you, you just picked up the pieces, smiled and carried on.

'I never stopped loving you. You know that, don't you.' Philip said. She did not reply.

It was time to leave the cemetery. Philip was on his way to the vicarage for a meeting with his colleague and Irene was going home. It had been a chance meeting. As they parted they both looked across to the other grave where Danny lay at rest.

Philip's parting words to her were, 'One day you'll be together again.'

Irene just smiled.

In 1997 plans were well on the way for the year 2000. The Millennium dome was being built after much debate at Greenwich in London; it was to be the home of exhibitions showing the inventions and changes in the twentieth century. At the turn of the century bells were to be rung in every church up and down the country; the church was counting the days, the count-down began on 5th April when there were 1,000 to go.

On 1st May, Labour won the general election and Tony Blair became the new prime minister; the New Labour Party was the government which would take Britain into the twenty-first century and it was the government which declared that the last day of 1999 was to be a Public Holiday. Such news was greeted well by the nation and for the Stephensons; it meant that the party at Whistbury would start even earlier!

Wills and Charlotte were looking forward to another celebration in September, 1998, their golden wedding anniversary. Wills had sold his remaining properties on the main road; his whole life now revolved round his family and his lodge. He was planning a special celebration for family and friends in the village and a holiday in Australia for himself, Charlotte and Irene. It seemed odd to Irene that she should accompany her parents on such an occasion; it would be like going on honeymoon with them, although that often happened now days. It was what Wills wanted and so Irene agreed. Tim, Hillary and Mark were all going to look after Stephenson's Lodge in their absence. Before the celebrations in 1998 could take place, something happened in 1997 which shook the world.

On Sunday 31st August, Wills went into Irene's room in the morning as usual with a cup of tea. He was always cheerful and would wake her with a smile which helped her to get through the day. She was convinced that her ability to cope and smile through adversity was inherited from her father. That Sunday was different; there was no smile but tears in his eyes. His words caused her to jump up in bed almost knocking the teacup out of his hand.

'She's dead. Princess Diana's dead.'

'What?' Irene shouted.

Wills switched on her television set. She watched in total disbelief as the story unfolded. The media had been chasing Diana since her divorce. It seemed that at last she had found happiness with Dodi Al Fayed. Rumours that they were to announce their engagement had led to the final chase. In an attempt to avoid waiting photographers outside the Ritz Hotel in Paris, Dodi and Diana had left by a back exit; the car crashed just after entering an underpass. Dodi and the driver were killed instantly; despite attempts to save the princess's life, she was declared dead at 3.00 am. The only survivor was a bodyguard who lay in an intensive care ward in the Paris hospital.

For the Stephenson family the news was devastating; it was like losing a member of their own family; they had no idea why they felt that way. They went to church only to discover that everyone in the village felt the same way, stunned, shocked and saddened. Prayers were said for the Royal Family as usual but with special mention for the young princes left motherless.

When they returned home the television set stayed on all day as it did in most homes; information on the sad homecoming was given. Tony Blair paid tribute to her before going to a church service with his family and described her as the People's Princess; this phrase, never used in her lifetime, was used repeatedly after that, along with the princess's own phrase of herself, the Queen of Hearts.

Irene, Wills and Charlotte watched as Prince Charles left for Paris; they were still watching when he arrived there accompanied by Diana's two sisters. They watched him go to the hospital, they saw the coffin leave, draped in the royal standard; they watched the plane leave Paris and the touchdown at RAF Northolt where it was met by the prime minister. The coffin was carried by eight pallbearers to a waiting hearse; Prince Charles flew back to Balmoral to be with his sons: it was a sad day in every home in the country.

In the days that followed it became clear that the princess's popularity was worldwide. There was a sea of emotion and a tidal wave of guilt as tributes poured in. Who was to blame? The media or the people for wanting the photographs? The people in their masses descended on the palaces leaving flowers and other tributes;

they queued for hours to write their messages of condolence in books at Kensington Palace. The Royal Family were a target for the people's anger; the Queen was criticised for remaining at Balmoral and not allowing a flag to fly at half-mast over Buckingham Palace until a week later. Her Majesty in response gave an unprecedented address to the nation. It was a long week of grief which led up to the funeral on Saturday, 6th September.

There were only two places to be on that day, either in London or at home with family and friends watching the television. The Stephenson clan were all at Stephenson's Lodge, comforting each other. The Stephenson shops were closed as were ninety-nine percent of shops in the country; town and city centres were deserted.

The ceremony was relayed across the world and watched by millions, regardless of the time of day or night; thousands of candles burned for her. The coffin left Kensington Palace on the gun carriage; the three princes with the Duke of Edinburgh and Earl Spencer walked behind it from Marlborough Gate to Westminster Abbey; they were followed by 500 people from charities the princess had worked for. The route was lined with people from all over the world who wanted to be in London to pay their last respects. It was a sad and unimaginable ending to what began as a fairy-tale wedding sixteen years earlier.

At Westminster Abbey the service lasted for an hour. It was a service as promised by the prime minister, for the people as well as her family. It was not a State Funeral but described as a unique funeral for a unique person. Elton John rewrote "Candle in the Wind" as a tribute; his professionalism as an artist meant that he was the only person with dry eyes as he sang "Goodbye, England's Rose".

It was followed by a tribute from Earl Spencer, after which there was a surge of applause, unheard of at any other funeral, such was the intense emotion of the occasion. People sitting outside the abbey had been the first to clap at the end of his heartfelt oration: this was heard through the open doors by people at the back of the congregation, and soon a tumult of sound filled the cathedral. After the service the coffin made its final journey to Althorp Hall, travelling slowly down the public roads and up the M1 motorway, giving the people a last chance to say goodbye. Flowers were strewn all along the route and people stood on bridges and at the side of the road. The final public picture was of the hearse entering the gates of Althorp to take the princess 'home'; the burial on the estate was a family affair.

For Irene, it made her think her own problems were trivial. She was still alive.

Diana had had a remarkable effect on people's lives but no one realised just how much until it was too late. The sadness and mourning continued alongside the count down to the Millennium. A depression seemed to overtake the nation; it was incredible to think that one person could have such an effect or make such a difference to people's lives.

Life for the Stephensons continued. 1998 came, as did their anniversary. They enjoyed their month down under and all too soon it was 1999. By late September there were only 100 days to go to the Millennium and for Irene a few more days of waiting for widowhood.

Charlotte was in a better position than most when it came to reminiscing.

'1993

BRITAIN

1st January, the European Commission creates a single market. The next major issue in Europe which will affect Britain is that of a single currency. The Governments are hoping it will be operative by the year 2000.

February: Jamie Bulger, a two-year old toddler is abducted from a Liverpool shopping centre, his mutilated body is found later on a railway embankment and the offenders are two ten-year old boys. The nation is horrified. There are demands for more discipline both in the school and the home. Questions are being asked about our present-day society and its moral values or lack of them; severe punishments for young offenders are being called for and the debate over capital punishment is being raised once again...

The government has outlined plans to privatise British Rail... Insurance companies place a wife's value at £349 a week... The Queen announces that she will pay taxes...

20th March, two bombs explode in Warrington, causing the deaths of four-year old Jonathan Ball and twelve-year old Tim Parry...

24th April, another IRA bomb explodes in London, killing one man...

Buckingham Palace opens to tourists in the summer: tickets are £8 each: the proceeds will help to pay for the restoration of Windsor Castle...

November: the nation is mourning the tragic deaths of eleven children and a teacher after their minibus crashed on the M40 near Warwick; they were returning from a concert at the Royal Albert Hall in London. The sad incident has led to mounting pressure for the government to make seat belts compulsory on school minibuses... At the trial for the killing of Jamie Bulger in February, the boys are

*found guilty of murder and ordered to be detained for "very, very, many years".
The judge has given permission for their names to be revealed: Child A and child
B are Jon Venables and Robert Thompson...*

*December: The Princess of Wales announces her decision to withdraw from
public life in 1994.*

ABROAD

*America, Bill Clinton is inaugurated as the forty-second president... New York,
a bomb explodes at the World Trade Centre, killing five people... The fifty-one-day
siege in Waco ends when FBI agents storm the building housing the Apocalyptic
leader, David Koresh and his ninety-five followers; fires are started and only eight
survive the self-inflicted inferno... Americans are following the Bobbitt case; John
Bobbitt is found not guilty of raping his wife Lorena, who cut off part of his penis
after he allegedly raped her; she's found not guilty of malicious wounding on the
grounds of insanity.*

*1st January, 1993, Czechoslovakia, after seventy-four years, ceases to exist and
over fifteen million people are now citizens of either Slovakia or Czechland... Paris,
Rudolf Nuryev, the star of the ballet world, dies of AIDS...*

*February: Ranulph Fiennes and Michael Stroud return from the first successful
unsupported crossing of the Antarctic.*

*May: Paris, toddlers are taken as hostages in their classroom by Eric Schmitt;
they're held for two days before police manage to kill Schmitt and rescue them...*

*September: Yasser Arafat of the Palestine Liberation Organisation and Yitshak
Rabin, Israel's Premier shake hands and sign a peace agreement for the Middle
East. President Clinton looks on as the event takes place on the Lawn of the White
House...*

*The Nobel Peace Prize is awarded jointly to Frederik de Klerk and Nelson
Mandela for their work to end apartheid peacefully.*

1994

BRITAIN

21st February, the age of consent for homosexuals is now down to eighteen.

*6th May, the Channel Tunnel is opened by President Mitterrand and the Queen...
12th May, the Labour leader John Smith dies after a heart attack; his successor is
Tony Blair...*

6th June, Commemoration day for the "D-day" landings, fifty years ago in 1944...

28th August, shops are open legally for the first time on a Sunday... 31st August, the IRA announce a cease-fire after twenty-five years of bloodshed; there's new hope for peace in Northern Ireland.

2nd September, Roy Castle dies after his brave fight against cancer; only weeks ago he completed his "Tour of Hope" in his gallant attempt at raising funds for research into cancer; his efforts have resulted in a research centre being set up in Liverpool...

19th November, The National Lottery's first draw.

ABROAD

February: twenty-nine Muslims are massacred at the Mosque in Hebron... April: in retaliation for the massacre, nine people are killed in Israel in a suicide car bomb attack on a school bus...

The first multi-racial elections taken place in South Africa: Nelson Mandela is the first black president of South Africa.

1995

BRITAIN

15th January, British troops end their daylight patrols in Belfast...

January & February: animal-rights protesters are protesting against the cruel conditions calves are kept in at Coventry Airport whilst waiting to be exported. Jill Phipps is killed when she falls under the wheels of a lorry carrying the animals... Mike Foale is the first British born astronaut to "space-walk"... Flt Lt Jo Salter is the first woman bomber pilot in 617, "The Dambusters", Squadron.

May & August: the nation celebrates VE and VJ Days; it's fifty years since the war ended first in Europe and then Japan.

November: Rosemary West, wife of Fred West, the notorious serial killer who was found hanged in his cell at Winson Green Prison in January, is convicted of murder.

December: Alison Hargreaves, who became the first woman to climb Everest alone and without oxygen in May, is killed on her descent from K2. She leaves a husband and two small children.

ABROAD

1st January, Sweden, Finland and Austria join the EU bringing its membership to fifteen... In Hawaii, astronomers find the most distant known galaxy at fifteen billion light years away from Earth... The trial of football hero, O J Simpson, begins in Los Angeles; he is accused of murdering his former wife and her friend, Ronald Goldman in June last year...

April: a car bomb explodes in Oklahoma City, killing 168 people.

8th May, it's the end of fourteen years of Socialist rule in France; President Mitterrand's lost the election to right-wing Jacques Chirac.

October: President Clinton visits Northern Ireland in an attempt to help the peace process... After a lengthy trial O J Simpson is acquitted... Canada, the people of Quebec vote to stay in Canada, and a Quebec disc jockey makes a hoax phone call to the Queen, pretending to be the prime minister of Canada.

4th November, The prime minister of Israel, Yitzhak Rabin is assassinated by a Jewish extremist after he has made such progress at creating peace in the Middle East.

SPORT

February, 1993, the football legend Bobby Moore dies of cancer... April: the Grand National is a national disaster! It's declared void after two false starts... The 1994 Winter Olympics are being held at Lillehammer... July, Brazil wins the football World Cup for the fourth time...1995, the footballer Eric Cantona is banned for the season and fined £20,000 after attacking a fan who insulted him with a flying kick... April: an outsider, Royal Athlete, wins the Grand National at odds of 40–1... At Wimbledon, Steffi Graff wins the women's singles title for the sixth time... October: the Grand National winner, Red Rum, the only horse to win the race three times, dies and is buried at Aintree.

THE MEDIA

1993: some films on general release are "The Piano", which won the Golden Palm at the Cannes Film Festival; "Jurassic Park" and "Schindler's List"

1994: there are indications of a revival in the British Film Industry; the film, "Four Weddings And A Funeral" with Hugh Grant is a huge success.

Two other films are "Mrs Doubtfire" and "Forrest Gump".

1995: "Nell", "Bridges of Madison County", "Babe" and "Apollo 13" are all on general release...

On the stage, "Riverdance" is an overnight success for the stars of Irish dancing after their performance at the Eurovision Song Contest... Cinema-going is on the increase but television is still a favourite leisure pursuit. "Soap" operas, drama, sport and quiz programmes are increasing in popularity. One very popular programme is the "Panorama" interview on 20th November, 1995 when Diana, Princess of Wales, speaks openly about her life and the Royal Family... Some programmes from the sixties have been revived and just as popular in the nineties,

Des O'Connor hosts "Take Your Pick", a remake of the Michael Miles programme and "Dr Finlay" returns to the screen.

As the nineties progress there seems to be nostalgia for the sixties. "Heartbeat" has viewers glued to their seats watching Nick and Kate Rowan in their police house in the sixties with each storyline having a background of music from that era. There is also a revival of the sixties' pop groups. The four remaining Stones and three BeeGees have re-established themselves along with the Monkees and The Beatles.

Some of the new musical groups are Blur, Oasis and Take That.

THE MID-NINETIES

"Surfing on the Internet" is as common as surfing on Bondi Beach; electronic mail and the worldwide web have invaded our lives like aliens from outer space. It's hardly possible to remember a time before the computer; it is such an integral part of the twentieth century now. Recycling is an extremely important aspect of daily life, particularly by the young, who are concerned about saving the planet and being "environmentally friendly". "Recycling centres" have emerged in vast quantities; people are encouraged to leave their newspapers, books, cans and bottles for recycling and to buy recycled products: concern for protecting the environment has never been so great. With the new pace of life, people are encouraged to believe that it is "good to talk" and not "bottle up" problems. In addition to talking, it seems that a good and "safe" sex life is essential for survival in the "rat-race". Gone are the days when sex was a chore for women, now it is something to be enjoyed; like so many things, it is no longer a male-dominated area.

However, a new, unsavoury aspect of modern life is developing: "road-rage"; pent-up anger and anxiety in traffic jams is beginning to take its toll on the public. In extreme cases, it's not a tirade of words but physical violence which explodes and results in injury or even death of innocent travellers.

1996

BRITAIN

9th February, it is the end of the IRA cease-fire as the first bomb explodes at the London Docklands... The oil tanker Sea Empress runs aground off the Welsh Coast, producing a forty-mile oil slick.

March: the environmentalists are objecting to the Newbury by-pass by sitting in trees to prevent them from being cut down... 13th March, the "Dunblane Massacre": sixteen schoolchildren and a teacher are shot dead by Thomas Hamilton while they *were preparing for a PE lesson in their school gymnasium; the assassin then turned the gun on himself; the nation is plunged into mourning and it's just before Mothering Sunday, which adds to the intense sadness and heightened emotion of the whole incredible situation. There is an outcry over the free use of handguns and a call for the law to ban such weapons... May: the Duke and Duchess of York divorce after ten years of marriage...*

June: an IRA bomb wrecks Manchester city centre...

August: the Prince and Princess of Wales divorce. The princess, like the Duchess of York, will no longer be known as HRH... British Forces are leaving Hong Kong in preparation for the hand over to China...

18th November, there is a fire in the Channel Tunnel: it starts in a lorry coming from the French side; when the train stopped for the lorry driver to escape into the service area the section of the tunnel burned out for several hundred yards: the tunnel will be closed for several months... 30th November, the Stone of Scone is placed on view in Edinburgh Castle after its return from London, where it has been held for six centuries...

December: the public are in a frenzy over Christmas shopping; some supermarkets are staying open for twenty-four hours on the day prior to Christmas.
ABROAD

January: the former French president, Monsieur Mitterrand dies; it turns out that he had a long-term mistress, AND another daughter: both appear at the graveside. President Chirac announces the end of nuclear testing in France...

February: Russia becomes a member of the Council of Europe...

April: only weeks after the Dunblane Massacre, at Port Arthur in Tasmania, a man shoots thirty-five people dead and injures a further seventeen...

July: Boris Yeltsin is re-elected as the president of Russia... China states that it is conducting its last nuclear test...

August: NASA announces that a meteorite may offer evidence of life on Mars... Belgium, the police are investigating an international paedophile ring...

September: NASA's Atlantis docks with the Russian spaceship Mir...

24th September, a comprehensive Nuclear Test Ban Treaty is signed by America, Britain, China, France and Russia...

October: in the Nevada desert RAF Squadron Leader Andy Green is the first man to take a jet-propelled car through the sound barrier...

November: Bill Clinton wins the American elections and is the president expected to take the United States into the twenty-first century.

SPORT

The 1996 Olympic games, the twenty-sixth, are being held in Atlanta, Georgia. The Olympic flame is lit by former boxing champion, Muhammad Ali; new world records are set in the 200 and 400 metres by the American athlete, Michael Johnson. Tragedy mars the event when a bomb explodes in the Centennial Olympic Park during a rock concert; two people die and 111 are injured... In football, Germany wins the Euro '96 final at London's Wembley Stadium... In Japan, Damon Hill proves to be following in his father's footsteps when he wins the Formula 1 drivers' championship.

1997

BRITAIN

February: Dolly the sheep is a celebrity; she's being presented to the world as a clone and her arrival has caused fear and panic that human cloning's a step closer... 21st February, Jim Robinson, Michael Hickey and Vincent Hickey, convicted in 1979 for the murder of Carl Bridgewater are freed after it was clear that they had been wrongly imprisoned...

1st May: general election; Labour win a landslide victory; forty-three-year-old Tony Blair is Britain's youngest prime minister since 1812. John Major resigns as leader of the Conservative Party and he is replaced by thirty-six-year-old William Hague, the youngest leader of the Party for 200 years.

1st July, Hong Kong is officially handed back to China; after a ceremonial handing over, the last governor, Chris Patten leaves in style with his family and Prince Charles on the Royal Yacht...

September: the people of Scotland's dream is now a reality under the new Labour Government; in a referendum, the people voted in favour of a Scottish Parliament; this is to be operative in Edinburgh by the year 2000.

LOUISE WOODWARD

February, 1997, the nineteen-year-old au pair finds herself in jail in Boston accused of murdering eight-month old Matthew Eappen by shaking him violently – which she vehemently denies... September & October: her trial is being televised and watched by millions on both sides of the Atlantic; she has considerable support from her friends and family in Elton, Cheshire; they are campaigning on her behalf and have tied yellow ribbons round posts, trees and every possible place in the village to show their support... She is found guilty of murder in the second degree despite defence medical evidence that shows that the injuries must have occurred some weeks ago. But it must have been her; there was only the baby's three-year-old brother – and the parents, of course – in the house. The Eappens made a great play on how VERY fond Matthew's brother was of him – but was this a smokescreen?? And we've only their word for it... In Massachusetts second degree murder means life imprisonment with no parole for at least fifteen years. She is being taken back to the Women's Prison where she has been held since February... On appeal the judge reduces her sentence to manslaughter and sentenced her to 279 days in prison, the number of days she had already served, but she must stay in America while the legal battle continues and the parents of Matthew exercise their right of appeal... 16th June, 1998, after further deliberation by a number of judges her sentence is upheld but she is free to return to England as a convicted child killer... The nightmare will remain with her as the Eappens continue exercising their right to take her to a civil court hearing in America for compensation.

ABROAD

February: Bill Gates is the richest man in history, having made his fortune by making his company, Microsoft, the monopoly supplier of the operating system for the personal computer...The Hale-Bopp comet can be seen clearly in the skies – but only when the moon is set... March: the Gdansk shipyard which had been the birthplace of the SOLIDARITY movement closes...

California, thirty-nine members of the Heaven's Gate cult commit a mass suicide...

May: NATO and Russia sign an agreement allowing NATO expansion in Eastern Europe...

June: Timothy McVeigh is given the death penalty for the Oklahoma City bombing when 168 people were killed... The Canadian Liberal Party is re-elected into office for the second time... The West Indian island of Montserrat is devastated by volcanic eruptions...

15th July, the Italian fashion designer, Gianni Versace, is assassinated outside his Miami Beach home... August: India is celebrating its fiftieth anniversary of independence...

5th September, only days after the death of Diana, India announces the passing of Mother Teresa. The world is in double mourning; two people from such different backgrounds but who shared a common concern for humanity have both been taken from us...

October: the Hubble space telescope discovers the universe's brightest star, which is ten million times more luminous than the sun...

PRESIDENT WJ CLINTON

July, 1997, President Clinton is at the centre of a sex scandal. Paula Jones accuses him of sexual harassment which he denies. Other reports are being filed against him of a similar nature by various women... 1998, Monica Lewinsky insists that she has had sexual relations with the president in the Oval Office of the White House on several occasions. He denies that intercourse took place but DNA evidence shows that something reprehensible did occur and forces an apology from him for his sins... Autumn 1998, his political career lies in the balance as there are demands for his impeachment.

1998

IRELAND continues to be headline news. The new Cabinet Minister for Northern Ireland, Mo Mowlam, seems to be near a solution with the Good Friday Peace Agreement. The end of the hostilities is in sight... August: a group calling themselves the REAL IRA plant a bomb in Omagh with devastating effect; twenty-eight are killed and 200 injured...Will there ever be REAL peace?

The world is suffering from the aftermath of Diana. A memorial fund has been set up and landmines are a major issue; her final trip to Bosnia had been to highlight the inhumanity of such weapons and to promote a campaign to ban them. As a tribute to her, many countries have banned them, but it is going to take a long time to find and destroy all the ones which are already in place...

January: NASA announce that seventy-seven-year old John Glenn, the first American to orbit the Earth in 1962, will join the crew on Discovery later in the year and become the oldest person to go into space...

March: Jonesbro in Arkansas is the setting for another massacre; two schoolboys open fire on their classroom mates: four girls and a teacher die... April: Linda McCartney, wife of Paul McCartney, often thought of as the fifth Beatle but well-known in her own right as a vegetarian meal supplier, loses her battle against cancer and dies whilst on holiday at the McCartney ranch in America...

July: as a result of the heat, fires in Florida are causing many people to lose their homes... There are also bush fires in Greece and Southern Italy as temperatures rise in unusual heatwaves believed to be brought about by global warming...

August: Cyprus is too hot for many of the holidaymakers; they prefer their fan-cooled rooms to the beach... In Central America temperatures soar above a hundred degrees daily for almost three weeks, whilst in China they are experiencing unprecedented floods... Hong Kong, one year after the ceremonial handover, celebrates the opening of a new airport which is larger than all four terminals at Heathrow... Dozens of people have been killed and hundreds injured in two bombing attacks on the US Embassies in Nairobi and Dar es Salaam. President Clinton is retaliating by ordering air strikes on suspected terrorist camps in Afghanistan and Sudan...

September: Russia's undergoing an economic crisis which has led to a fluctuating stock market and concern over another crash... A great discovery! There's water on the dark, sub-zero side of the moon; this has led to questions being asked about the possibility of living on the moon or using it as a station for inter-galaxy travel.

SPORT

1997: the Grand National horse race is abandoned as a result of an IRA bomb scare: it takes place two days later... Golf, twenty-one-year old Tiger Woods becomes both the youngest and the first black person to win the US Masters.

This summer is being dominated by the Soccer World Cup, the last one of the century and being held in France. Never has there been a World Cup like it; it seems as if Europe and most of the world are suffering from Football Fever. In Britain, there's been much controversy over Glenn Hoddle's decision to drop Paul Gascoigne from the squad before the matches even start. As the games progress so does the drama. Liverpool's Michael Owen is the youngest man to score a goal in a World Cup match. David Beckham's received the red card in the England v. Argentina match for a very half-hearted attempt at kicking an opponent and after extra time Argentina won a place in the quarter-finals on a penalty shoot-out. When Newcastle's David Batty missed the final penalty goal, England's dream of bringing the cup home was over. The teams battle on, the tension mounting towards the final between Brazil and France. After a disappointing game with Brazil not really in fighting form, France are victorious and win the cup with a score of 3–0.

THE MEDIA

30th March, 1997, Channel 5 arrives in a blaze of publicity by the Spice Girls; the Feisty Five, as they have become known, are an all girl group which took the world by storm in the mid-nineties until Ginger Spice, Geri, split from the group; the remaining four are continuing with a tour of America...

Elton John's tribute to Diana, "Candle in the Wind 1997", is the biggest selling single record of all time...

On the television screen the battle of the soap operas continue with "Coronation

Street" in the lead when Deirdre is sent to jail; it is headline news and the reality for some is so great that they're sending donations for the Free Deirdre campaign...

Digital television's slowly becoming a reality. The revolution, brought in by the computer age, means more channels and more choice for the viewer. Where one channel used the space provided on the analogue broadcasting system, ten channels can be transmitted on the digital system, but we all have to get a conversion box to make over the existing signals.

The big screen is growing in popularity. Cinema chains are expanding to meet the demand. Films released include "Evita", "The English Patient", "Titanic" and "The Full Monty".

Finally, in 1998, the famous comic, The Beano celebrates its sixtieth birthday!

CONCLUSION

As the twentieth century draws to a close there is a feeling of nostalgia for the "good old days", tinged with sadness over the bitter memories of the numerous tragic occasions. The 1990s have brought Britain a change of government; a United Europe so much closer; the longed for freedom from apartheid in South Africa; change and chaos in the Eastern Bloc countries and Russia; change in Hong Kong; technological and scientific breakthroughs; change in American Government and a scandal; a lack of reverence for the monarchy in Britain and the death of the much loved icon, Diana.

However, as the end of the century approaches, it is with renewed hope and confidence that nations are moving forward into the birth of the New Age. A time when there are hopes that there will be peace between all nations: a time when selfishness will give way to thinking of others: a time when materialism will yield to spiritualism: a time when massacres cease and communities learn to live harmoniously: a time when morality will take priority over immorality: a time when good will conquer over evil. There's hope for a Utopia, a hope that with the new century there will be the "Dawning of the Age of Aquarius".

* * * * * *

The Epilogue
Whistbury, 1st January, 2000

IRENE'S THOUGHTS were interrupted when Wills came into the room. He walked over to where she was sitting in the rocking chair and sat on the bed beside her.

'I thought you'd be here! Fifty, it's hard to believe, m'duck.' He too was remembering the New Year party when she was born.

Irene looked at him and round the room. 'It's not changed much over the years, has it?'

'No; Elizabeth likes things just as they were when John died.'

'Tell me, Dad, who decided to call me Irene?'

'Your mother. She thought it meant "peace". Peace was the thing everyone talked about in those days. The war was still on people's minds. I added Joy, because I wanted you to be happy. For us, you were new life, new hope for the future.'

'That's a sad irony, Daddy. But you meant well. You've been the best father anyone could have. At every disaster in my life, you've been there for me. I couldn't have survived without you. I'll always love you. You know that, don't you?' There were tears in her eyes as she put her hand out to hold her father's arm.

'That's what daddies are for. My life changed the day you were born. Having you made my life worthwhile.'

His voice was beginning to tremble. He too, was close to tears, as he rose to his feet and gently kissed her on the forehead. 'Happy birthday, darling. The party's almost over for another year. Your mother's playing her party piece. You're coming down?'

'Yes, Daddy, in a minute.'

As he left, she could hear Charlotte playing and the remaining guests singing, 'Oh Danny Boy, the pipes, the pipes are calling…'

She laughed to herself at the sad irony of her naming. 'Peace' and 'Joy'. She had experienced only one hour of real joy in her whole life, when time and the rest of the world had ceased to exist; the one hour she could never forget and was still paying for; that one hour of ecstasy in the hayloft.

She followed her father downstairs and walked into the front room, in time to join the others in singing, 'In sunshine or in shadow, oh Danny Boy, I love...you...so.'

She went over to the piano and held her father's hand, as they sang the last verse together.

After the last words had been sung, out of habit after so many years, people started to leave. Elizabeth was still seated in her chair between the television and the window. Everyone went over to her, to wish her a 'Happy New Year' and thank her for yet another party. Elizabeth was just thankful for seeing this particular New Year; soon, she would be joining her beloved John.

When the guests had left, Irene was alone with her parents and Elizabeth. The twentieth century was over, gone forever; there was no going back, only forwards until the day when she could once again frolic in the hayloft with Danny. Princess Diana was already with her Dodi, but she must go on with her life and accept what the future held in store for her. She had been flattered by Mark's proposal, now she had her answer for him; he was to have his dreams fulfilled.

In her heart she knew that one day, she would see Danny again, but until then she must continue living her life, smiling and taking each day as it came. For, just as night follows day, 'Time and Tide wait for no man'.

****

THE END

Author's Acknowledgements

THE WRITING of this book has entailed a large amount of research and a lot of support. I would like to thank all those who have in a number of ways helped me: my cousin, Angela Hamill and my friend, Joan Dempsey; they did not tire of my constant questions and progress reports, without their encouragement I would never have reached the last chapter! And finally, my editor, Michael Russell, who has guided and encouraged me from the start, and has done his best to ease my initial efforts onto the printed page.

****

Bibliography

For historical facts I have used various newspapers and the following texts as reference books.

Pictorial History of the Twentieth Century, 1997 Edition, published by Chancellor Press, Reed International Books Ltd.

People's 20th Century, Volume 2, 1996 Edition, published by B.B.C. Worldwide Ltd.

The Country Life Book of Britain in the Seventies, 1980 Edition, Edited by Ronald Allison, Published by Country Life Books, Reed International Books Ltd.

Illustrated Dictionary of Essential Knowledge, 1995 Edition; *Hitting the Headlines*, 1995 Edition; *Do You Remember?* 1993 Edition. All three published by The Reader's Digest Association Limited.

Her Majesty The Queen, by Hugh Montgomery-Massingberd, 1995 Edition, published by Collins Willow, of Harper-Collins Publishers.

The Hutchinson Encyclopaedia (8th Edition) Copyright Helicon Publishing Limited 1988.

The author expresses her thanks to the above publishing companies for granting permission for the use of their books for reference purposes.

The following works were also referred to:
Chronicle of the Twentieth Century, 1995 Edition
The Golden Years series, 1996 Editions
The Book of Knowledge encyclopaedias, published in the 1950's by The Waverley Book Company Ltd.
The Year Books 1962-1967, published by The Grolier Society 1960's.
The Fifties, by Peter Lewis

*